"I know something of love," he said. "A comely lass like you doubtless has the young men running in circles around her with their tongues trailing in the heather. Surely you know what I speak of."

She gazed at him, open-mouthed. In truth, she did not. She knew many young men, but never cared for any so deeply that she'd allow them to lay a hand on her.

He understood her silence. "Well, then, you'll need some learning," Alasdair whispered. He leaned into her neck, brushing his lips against her skin.

She trembled all over, sure she'd crumble into pieces at any moment. The touch of his lips burned like a flame and she longed to be consumed by it. It wasn't right, it wasn't decent, she thought. Then passion rose up in her like a mighty wave and swept away all thoughts of modesty and prudence . . .

PRAISE FOR MEGAN DAVIDSON'S
ROAD TO THE ISLE:

". . . a sweeping epic that whisks us to a time of high drama and deep passion. Ms. Davidson is a writer of great promise."
—*Romantic Times*

"ROAD TO THE ISLE takes the audience on a breathtaking journey through the Scottish Highlands . . . Ms. Davidson captures her reader in the tangled web of adventure and swiftly sweeps us toward the conclusion . . . a fast moving, passionate story."
—*Rendezvous*

DANGEROUS GAMES   (0-7860-0270-0, $4.99)
by Amanda Scott

When Nicholas Barrington, eldest son of the Earl of Ulcombe, first met Melissa Seacort, the desperation he sensed beneath her well-bred beauty haunted him. He didn't realize how desperate Melissa really was . . . until he found her again at a Newmarket gambling club—being auctioned off by her father to the highest bidder. So, Nick bought himself a wife. With a villain hot on their heels, and a fortune and their lives at stake, they would gamble everything on the most dangerous game of all: love.

A TOUCH OF PARADISE   (0-7860-0271-9, $4.99)
by Alexa Smart

As a confidence man and scam runner in 1880s America, Malcolm Northrup has amassed a fortune. Now, posing as the eminent Sir John Abbot—scholar, and possible discoverer of the lost continent of Atlantis—he's taking his act on the road with a lecture tour, seeking funds for a scientific experiment he has no intention of making. But scholar Halia Davenport is determined to accompany Malcolm on his "expedition" . . . even if she must kidnap him!

THE SONG WITHIN

Megan Davidson

Zebra Books
Kensington Publishing Corp.

http://www.zebrabooks.com

ZEBRA BOOKS are published by

Kensington Publishing Corp.
850 Third Avenue
New York, NY 10022

Zebra and the Z logo Reg. U.S. Pat. & TM Off.

First Printing: January, 1998
10   9   8   7   6   5   4   3   2   1

Printed in the United States of America

Chapter 1

My love is the song of my life.
The strings of my heart is he,
My fingers on the trembling harp,
The lark outside my window,
The song within my soul.

1724

At fifteen, Una knew every bird of the air and water that might be found in Glenfinnan or anywhere else within the vast lands of the great Clan Donald. Eagles sometimes circled her parents' little flock of sheep like shadows on the sky, drifting between the ancient stubs of the mountain peaks. Now and then stray seamews would come crying over the valley, as if they had been banished from their home in the sea. Kestrels circling in small groups were a sure sign that some creature had died.

One spring evening Una saw a swarm of birds wheeling over Corrie na Chreaig. It looked as if tiny bits of the mountain itself had come to life and hovered over its head. She felt a sudden pang of fear in her throat though she knew the birds were harmless.

Una watched them as she walked toward the fields where her father had been plowing all day. She carried a wooden cup filled with milk mixed with whisky and kept glancing up and down, up at the black flecks in the gently graying sky, and down at the drink, willing it not to spill over. When she saw her father, stooped under the weight of his footplow, she forgot the cloud of birds for a moment and hurried to bring him the whisky. He smiled when he saw her.

"Thank you, little calf," he said, taking the cup from her and putting it to his lips. As he drank, Una could see he had noticed the birds, too. His blue eyes flickered and grew wider with each swallow of the dram. Her father gave her back the cup empty, still gazing up at the sky. "Are all the sheep in the fold?"

"They are, Papa." Her family had less than a score of sheep, but there were many lambs, and more coming every week.

"It may be a new lamb they're after," said her father, squinting at the birds. He slid the plow off his shoulder and leaned into it, as if he hadn't the strength to support himself alone. "I'd best have a look." He stayed where he was, though, reminding Una of the mountains themselves, rooted to the earth, and she felt sorry for him.

"I'll go," she said, touching his wrist. The feel of the coarse hair on his skin reminded her of being a child, feeling safe in the circle of his arms.

"Well, then." He smiled and patted her hand. "Go on with you, *a'nighean.*"

As Una walked up the hillside through the heather, she

glanced down now and again at her father. At first he stood, immobile except for the fluttering of his hair in the wind, but gradually he began to ease himself over the heath toward the plume of blue smoke that rose from the house. Una strode on, making up for her father's wearied pace. The birds were closer now. She could hear the screams of hawks and the cackling of crows as she neared the crest of the hill and the hollow just beyond it.

The mists were already descending on the glen, melting the peaks of the highest crags into a gray blur. The birds were very close. She could see their cruel beaks, their jewel eyes. The wind slipped past her, bringing a bad smell along with it. Her throat grew tight as she reached the crest and looked down on the corrie.

She glimpsed them. A flash of white and red. Quickly she turned her face away and forced herself to concentrate on the birds. There were a hundred at least, hoodie crows and kites. Most sat patiently on the rocks skirting the corrie, preening, waiting. Some minutes passed before she could bear to take a long look at what she had feared she'd seen: a swordblade red with gore. Finally she noticed a hand, a blood-stained sleeve, a blue bonnet, an entire body. Four bodies. Una waited, expecting some terrible thing to happen to her, but, except for the birds, the corrie was as still and peaceful as death itself. Part of her tugged and shoved at her legs, begging her to run from the corrie. Why did she wish to stay? Was it because so many of the birds were biding their time? Could they tell there was a living man among the dead?

Una walked forward on stiff legs. She glanced at the closest body, looked at another, and touched a third with her toe. The three of them were sprawled around a fourth who lay nearly in the center of the corrie. The three were outlaws; she could tell this quickly, easily, by looking at their flat blue bonnets that lacked any badge or emblem to link them to a clan. They were the bonnets of "broken men" without ties to any family or district, men who had banded together out of desperation.

The fourth man had dark red hair and scarlet lashes fringing his closed eyes. He looked neither young nor old. His torn clothes were still beautiful, so much finer than those of the others: a black kidskin jacket, a white linen blouse, and a badger-skin sporran, ripped open along one seam. A few coins and a silver snuffbox gleamed inside the ruined pouch. Everything he wore was spotted with blood, and the sleeves of his jacket were more red than black. Anyone who dressed so fine should expect robbers, and yet what a pity this hero should be lying dead among the thieves he had overcome.

Tasting the blood of the dead could restore them to life. That was what one of the chattering *chailleagean* of the district had told her once. It was a brainless thing to do, something that the priests would not approve of. Still . . . she laid a trembling forefinger on the man's bloody cheek. How would the blood taste? Should she swallow it or spit it out? The old wife had told her none of that.

The man's leg twitched. She felt and heard it move more clearly than she had seen it. Her hand froze on his face. She held her breath. Were the fairies playing tricks on her? A moment later the leg moved again, and this time she saw it bend at the knee.

"Dia!" she cried, stumbling backward.

The man's eyes sprang open. Round and gray, they stared straight through her. "Am I dead, then?" he asked.

The panic grasped her again, and now she felt it lift her to her feet and carry her out of the corrie, screaming "The dead have come to life!" into her ears. She heard the birds screeching and fluttering as she ran past, but she did not see them.

* * *

It was twilight and the corrie was filling up with mist by the time Una and her father reached the men. She was relieved to see only a few birds remained, braving the darkness, and most of those rose screaming when she blundered toward the rocks with her father's pony at her heels. She saw the red man at once, his face hidden in the crook of one arm, his other extended as though he were reaching out for help.

"This one, Papa," she said, pointing to the red man. She felt very calm now. Some of the bodies were beginning to fade under the cover of mist, and the wind from the mountains had blown away the worst of the smell. The red man himself might no longer be alive—he looked so gray against the stones, a man of mist and shadows.

Her father walked over to the man and prodded him with his hands. "Take the pony back to the house," he said at last. "Tell your mother I'll soon be home."

"And the red man?" When her father stood up, walked over to the closest corpse, and came away with a dirk in his hands, she understood. Una could not remember being so angry with her father before. "You'll not," she sputtered. "You cannot." You're talking as a child, she scolded herself, but she could think of nothing wiser to say. With the pony clumping behind her, she took a few steps toward the red man until she was only an arm's length from him.

"Go on now," said her father, an edge in his voice. "This is not for you to see. Ah, 'tis a pity I have no pistol."

Una could see the dirk very clearly, doubled-edged, with a point like a rat's snout. She felt a pain in her chest as if her own heart had been pierced. "I'll not go. I found him. How can I leave him?"

"As you wish." Her father sat back on his heels, laid the dirk across his knees, and brushed the man's hair away from his throat. Una tried to think of something to say or do that would save the dying man, but her mind was filled with mist.

The sound started very low and soft, and for a moment Una thought it was the rumbling of the pony's innards or the grinding of its teeth. No, the rumbling came from the throat of the red man. His eyes were open and he held his head well above the shelter of his arm as he stared at Una's father. "Have a care," said the red man. His head sank back onto his arms but the growling continued.

Una's father set aside the dirk and stroked the red man's face as though he were touching a newborn. "Who are you, master?" But the man's eyes drooped shut and the defiant noises ceased.

"See how brave he is?" Una said. "You'll not kill him?"

"This is a pretty mess," her father muttered, wiping his hands on his plaid as he stood up. "The pony won't do. The poor man would be jounced to pieces on its back."

Una flung her hand angrily against the pony's cheek, as though it were to blame for the red man's suffering. The little horse stumbled backward in alarm. "What can be done, Papa?"

He was silent, looking off into the mist that had almost filled the corrie. At the foot of the hillside, Loch Shiel caught the last bit of the light of day and spun it out in a long white line on its waters. Slowly her father bent over the red man and gathered him in his arms, cursing all the while, and Una was afraid they would both collapse at any moment. As her father walked off into the graying light, his legs brushed a wake through the bracken, and his plaid and that of the red man trailed together behind him.

Una thought of her father as she had seen him earlier that day with his plow, barely livelier than the mountains, and marveled at his speed. She and the pony had to trot to keep in sight of him, and as she jogged forward her bare foot came down on something so sharp she yelped. The pony shied, nearly pulling its lead from her hand. "Only a stone," she said to the horse, but as she peered into the bracken she found she was wrong. She had stepped on a small circlet of silver fastened to a man's blue bonnet, holding a sprig of juniper and the stub of a broken eagle's feather. She picked up the bonnet, squinting to examine the brooch, and then quickly crumpled up the cap and thrust it into the folds of her *arasaid*. It wouldn't be wise to show it to her father just yet.

"Will he be living?" Una crowded close to her mother and bent over to wipe a smudge of blood from the red man's face. Not a muscle on him moved, but the lace on his ruined shirtfront rose and fell in a steady rhythm.

"If the Almighty wishes it," said her mother. She led Una around to the man's head and had her sit on the edge of his couch of heather, plaids, and sheepskins. "And if he is strong enough."

At least now the man was off the corrie, away from the rocks and the chill of the mist and, worst of all, the patient birds. Her father had brought him into the "little room," rarely used by anyone but visitors. The room was small but cheery, with its own fire blazing in the center of the dirt floor. While it was not a room fit for a gentleman, it was the best her family could offer.

Una wanted to shake the man by his shoulders, rouse him so she might find out his name. Instead she let herself be guided by her mother, who showed her how to hold the man's head between her hands while stroking his brow with her fingertips. "He'll not harm himself if his head is kept down," she said.

Her mother brushed back the man's hair, patted it in place around his shoulders, and knelt down by the bed, sighing. "This is the worst part, now." Her mother had a mouth that turned down so often that Una could not tell by looking at her whether a matter was serious or no. As Una massaged the man's forehead, feeling the tension in his skin dissolve under her fingers, she listened to her father and sisters breathing loudly through their mouths as they slept in the other room. How could they sleep? How could all that was normal go on while the red man lay there suffering?

Una watched her mother pour clean water from a copper pitcher over the clothes on the man's chest, then trim away tiny bits of the cloth, woven through with blood, hair, and skin. Instead of stroking the red man's head now, Una used all her energy to hold it down as he struggled to raise it, rocking it back and forth in her grasp. Her mother continued with her cutting. Not once did the man scream out, but moaned deep in his throat. As she watched his face clench, relax, and clench again, a tear trickled from her eyes and splashed onto the man's forehead.

"You're suffering more than himself," said her mother with half a smile. She laid the dirk down on the floor, then lifted up the remnants of the fine shirt and jacket and let them fall onto the hide underneath the man. His skin gleamed white and red in the light of the tallow candles that lit the room.

The warrior's head fell back against Una's hands and she realized he had again sunk into his unnatural sleep. Knowing he was no longer feeling pain made her tears dry up and gave her the courage to look at his chest. A long purple gash ran from nipple to nipple in a jagged line. "Is that the worst?"

"If it is, it's bad enough," said her mother. She looked no more or less hopeful than she had been when she'd begun cutting the man's shirt. Una helped her dip some linen rags in a mixture of water, crowberry leaves, and gentian root, and with great care her mother positioned them on the man's chest. Una held his forehead as tightly as she dared but the man hardly moved.

Her mother unbuckled the man's plaid and removed part of it from his belly until he was nearly naked. Una had seen many naked men. On warm days the menfolk stripped to work in the fields and thought nothing of it. But seeing the red man bared gave her a curious, protective feeling, and she wished she could, without hurting him, peel back the blackened plaid that stuck to his left side.

"This will be very bad," said her mother. "Hold the man close."

Una put her hands to his temples but found she had no strength in her fingers at all. She stroked the man's hair and looked down at his long, candlelit legs covered with red down. The hair between his legs was just as red, but knotted in tight curls. Now that his face was cleaned of blood and she had had a good look at it, she knew he was not very old—five and twenty, perhaps. Mayhap he had a wife, or possibly he was still searching for one. How wonderful it would be to have such a fine, handsome husband.

Suddenly the man flung his head out of her hands. He lurched out of the bed. Una's mother clutched at his arm but she could not hold him. He staggered and fell in a heap, then stood up and fell again.

Una looked at him in horror. Her hands continued to caress the plaid where his head had been resting. Why was he on the floor when he should have been with her? "Mary mother of God!" cried Una's mother. "Get your father, child!" But Una could not move. From the next room she could hear the baby begin to cry. Her sisters shrieked. Her father cursed as he stumbled from one wall to another, thudding into furniture. It sounded as if the house were breaking in two. By the time her father finally entered the room, the red man had fallen back into his black sleep. Una began to weep, certain her champion was as good as gone.

She was wrong. The man refused to die. For two days Una's parents banned her from his side. "Best you had held his head tightly, as I told you," said her mother.

"Though you meant no harm," her father added.

Una tended the baby and endured the teasing of her sisters while she waited for her parents to change their minds. The house filled up with the musty smell of the herbs her mother used to treat the man's fevers and infections, a smell which even the tang of the peatsmoke could not cover. At night she listened through the wall that separated the two rooms, trying to catch the sound of the red man's breathing. She hid the bonnet in her bedclothes and, while her family slept, brought it out to look at it, smell it, and inspect the few hairs that clung to the wool and shone orange in the firelight.

On the third morning her mother relented. She had not slept for more than a few hours a night and her milk was not letting down easily. Una helped her mother care for the red man, cooling him with water when he was burning hot and piling blankets over him when he shook with chills. Late one night he became so cold Una feared he would die. She thought of chafing his arms and legs, as she had once done long ago when her mother was ill, but it was not possible; the man's limbs were covered with cuts and bruises, and she could not bear the thought of causing him any more pain.

As she searched in vain for more plaids to cover him, Una caught a glimpse of Rory Beag, the baby, nestled between his sleeping parents. An idea came to her. Slowly she unbuckled her belt, unwound the heavy *arasaid* from around her shoulders, and let it fall to the floor. Naked save for her linen shift, now it was she who was freezing. Without another thought she crawled under the plaids that covered the sick man, slowly, lest she disturb him. When she lay at last against his side she could feel his body sucking the warmth from her, turning her to ice, but she crept even closer to him, caressing his face. Sometimes he winced, and she would pause for a moment to think, *You are mine. It was I who saved you.*

She touched his shoulder, his neck, his hand—every part of him she could reach that was free of wounds. How soft his skin was, like the baby's. She fell asleep with tender thoughts for the red man spinning in her mind.

Una awoke in her own bedclothes beside the fire in the big room, where she always slept. Her little sisters, Morag Bhan and Morag Bheag, knelt over her, smiling like cats. "Are you going to have a baby with the sick man?" asked Morag Bhan, the elder and bolder of the girls.

Una pushed them both away and ran into the other room, bright with morning light from the skin-covered windows. Her mother was asleep in a chair and her father stood behind her, holding onto her shoulders as if to keep her from falling. "Una, the man's fevers and chills have broken," he said.

Una clasped the man's hand. It had a fine, normal warmth to it. She laid her hand behind his ear and felt the strong coursing of his blood. "He's well," she said, smiling at her father. She wanted to dance around the man's bed, shouting and laughing, but her father's sad face made the smile drop from her lips. While she waited for him to speak, she realized it was he who had carried her to her bed.

"He won't die now, I trust," he said. "Your mother and I spent half the night watching over him."

"He was so cold . . . " Una said, then stopped, not wanting to say why she had fallen asleep in the red man's bed.

Her father spoke no more about it, only waggled his head and gave her a glance of a smile. "Soon we'll know who he is."

"I know who he is. He's a grand gentleman, but . . . " Una stopped, trying to judge her father's mood. Was he at ease, or just exhausted from having stayed awake all night? She would take the risk. "But he's not of Clan Donald."

"How can you know that?"

The gentleness of his voice reassured her. She ran to fetch the bonnet from her bedclothes, then placed it in her father's hands. "You see?" Una pointed to the bull's head engraved on the silver badge that held a sprig of juniper and the broken feather. "The feather bespeaks a landed family, and the bull and juniper . . . "

"Tokens of Clan MacLeod," he finished for her. "Clan Donald's ancient rival. Why haven't you shown me this sooner?" He held the bonnet before her face, but she was silent. "You thought I would let him die," he said, nodding to himself, "because he's not of our people."

Una felt her hands clench at her sides. "You'd have killed him at the corrie."

"Aye, because I thought he was suffering and as good as dead. Believe me, my love, I'd do the same for anyone of Clan Donald, and expect him to do the same for me."

Una could not look at him. She crossed her arms over her chest to help her hold back the tears of shame she felt. If it hadn't been for her father, the red man would most certainly be dead. "What now, Papa?"

Her father fingered the man's red hair, and Una felt a twinge of jealousy ripple through her. There was no explaining it, but there it was. "We can find his people, and when he's well enough, send him home alive instead of wrapped head to foot in his plaid."

Una shivered. The red man would leave, return to his family. Her father was right, yet lately she had thought about the man as a part of her house, her family. And herself. A great pressure began to push at her forehead from the inside out, and she touched the skin around her eyes to be sure they weren't melting.

"Why are you weeping, my heart?" asked her father.

But she could not answer him.

Chapter 2

Una was soaking linen in a mixture of bilberry leaves and woundwort early one evening in the man's room when she heard a scream. She spun around so suddenly she tipped the poultice onto the floor. There before her stood Morag Bheag, her face frozen in horror. "What have you done to the man, little wretch?" Una snarled, seizing the frightened child by the wrist.

"I but touched his arm," Morag whimpered.

Una glanced at her red man. His face was clenched like a fist, and his bedclothes lay in hopeless tangles at his feet. But he was awake at last! "Out, out!" She gave the child a good clout on the shoulder and sent her racing from the room. "Master, did that creature hurt you?" she asked, crouching beside the bed, scarcely daring to breathe.

The man opened his beautiful gray eyes and stared at her silently for several moments. Then he tried to speak, but his voice was hoarse and the sounds that escaped his lips were not words. "Better you say nothing," she said, delighted that he had the strength to try, and called out to her mother, "The man! He's waked!"

"Whisky," he whispered.

She turned and smiled. That she'd heard clearly enough. O, the Almighty be praised! How thin he looked, but how handsome. His face glowed with astonishment, as though he were pleasantly surprised to find himself living.

Her mother entered, holding a wooden cup full of whisky. Had she heard the man, Una wondered, or had she simply decided he would have need of a stimulating drink? The man struggled to sit up, though it was plain he suffered. "Slowly!" Una said, raising his head a bit and holding the cup to his lips, but the stranger grabbed it away from her and drained it before she could stop him.

Una was about to rebuke him when the man addressed her. "You are Una," he said softly. "I . . . I heard your name more than once . . . when I was between waking and sleeping." He fell back on the bed, breathing hard.

Una slipped the empty cup from his hand. She remembered speaking to him when she thought him dead to the world, telling him her name and imploring him to tell her his. She'd thought if she could but name him, he'd be hers forever. "I *am* called Una," she said, touched by his tenderness. "And you?"

The man's eyelids fluttered. "He'll sleep again," said her mother. She sat down on a stool beside Una and began to drape his plaid over his bare body.

But Una would not give up so easily. She had to know what he was called, where he was from, what he was doing in Glenfinnan, so far from his own people. If she didn't know these things, she thought, how might she possibly fathom him? "Your name, if it please you," she implored the dazed man.

"Alasdair Ruadh," he said, "from north of Glen Beag, in Glenalt. I have to relieve myself. Help me rise."

Alasdair Ruadh. Red Alasdair. A fine name, that, a hero's name. She tried to slip her hands under his armpits to ease him to his feet, but her mother held her back. "The man's too ill to move," she murmured. "You'll harm him if you try."

The man growled and swore, and Una thought him wondrous fierce for one who, only days ago, had been holding Death by the hand. "For nine days you have been lying here," she explained, stroking the dun-colored sheepskin that lay under him. "Wet as you will. That is what the fleece is for."

The man seemed about to curse again, but as she stared into his granite-colored eyes, a change came over him, and his face took on a sweet innocence. "So beautiful," he whispered, reaching out to touch one of her long black curls. "Your eyes . . . as blue as frost in the morning. A Pictish princess, you are. You're certain I'm not in Paradise among the angels?"

Una sat back, stunned with the frankness of his sudden compliment, but her mother still had her wits about her. "Faith, Alasdair Ruadh, if you but knew her better you'd not make such a comparison so quickly, I'm thinking. She's aye willful, this one."

But the man had no reply; he'd fallen senseless again. She was his angel, Una thought. Willful or no, she'd protect him, this comely Alasdair from the north.

"Help me now, and we'll change the sheepskin," said her mother.

Later that evening, the man from Glenalt woke with a scream. Una rushed to his bedside, expecting Little Morag to be up to her pranks again, but the child was asleep. "You've been dreaming," Una guessed.

"I have," he confessed, looking around the room with a blank gaze.

"Dark dreams have roused me from sleep before," she

said, "and I have not been left for dead on a corrie after facing down three outlaws." The red man had good reason for dreaming his share of terror, she thought, though he did not wish to speak of it.

"For the love of God, will you bring me some food?" he begged her.

Una discussed the matter with her mother, and at last they agreed that the man might be able to stomach some brose. Una brought him a bowl of the porridge, thick with cream, honey, and whisky. "What have you there?" he muttered when she entered the room.

She knelt down beside him and held out a spoonful of the steaming gray paste, suddenly realizing how unappetizing it looked. "Take it. It will do you good."

Like her, the man had a will of his own. At first he turned his head away, but Una was persistent. After she had gotten a mouthful into him he needed no further persuasion but ate as fast as she could feed him. "I'll have more," he cried as she took back the empty bowl.

"Nay, you'll spew it up," she cautioned him, but he was not to be stopped. With a speed that astounded her he caught her by the wrist so hard she cried out and rapped his knuckles with the bowl. He released her hand, and the two of them glared at each other for a while until Una thought better of what she'd done. "Forgive me, master," she apologized, "but I don't want to see you sicker than you are."

"Please, lovely Una," he wheedled. "How long has it been since I've eaten?"

Nine days without food! For certain the man must be famished. She brought him more brose, and as she watched him eat, she remembered something the man would want to know. "My da has gone to Glenalt," she said, "to speak with your people. They'll be aye relieved to hear that you're not yet ready for a winding sheet."

Alasdair's eyes opened wide. "Glenalt? When will he return? When will my da be sending a man for me?"

Cold days and cold nights to the creature! He was not even able to stand on his feet and make water, but here he was, thinking of leaving. She didn't care to think of that just yet. "In good time, when you have your strength about you," Una said, rising abruptly. "My father will be back in a few days and he'll speak with you then." If only you might never go back, she added to herself.

"Tell me, Una, I didn't hurt your hand, did I now?" he said.

Una laughed. She could not stay angry with the man. "It's I should be asking you that, Alasdair."

Una was the first to see her father as he came up to the house over the fields one morning in the company of a short, bearded stranger. He was Mata, Alasdair's foster brother, and he had brought a pony for Alasdair and a fine plaid that smelled of lavender. Alasdair was not shoulder to shoulder with Death anymore, but he was as weak as Little Rory and could stagger a few steps only with two people supporting him.

Her family gathered around Alasdair's bedside, watching him and his foster brother as if they were strange new animals never before seen in Glenfinnan. "There were rumors he was dead," Mata told Una's mother.

"They were very nearly right," her mother agreed.

Una watched closely as Mata kissed Alasdair on the forehead and clasped the sick man's shoulders. Alasdair's entire body seemed drawn toward the stranger. "Mata!" he squealed, seizing his friend's arm.

"Alasdair, my dear companion! What a sorry state you're in! Can you ride come next week, do you think? I'll stay till then, if you like."

"It will take a fortnight at least before he's healed," blurted Una.

To her great relief, her mother agreed with her. "If you would have him open his wounds and bleed all the way to Glenalt so that he'd be ready to put in the ground after you got there, then by all means take him home in seven days. Earlier if you like."

Mata looked stunned. He blinked his great blue eyes and muttered "Och, och," to himself. Had he but seen Alasdair at the corrie, thought Una, he'd not be so surprised.

Her parents sent her outside to unload peat from a barrow while the four adults spoke together, but Una was undaunted. As long as she worked very slowly, she could make out their conversation as it slipped through the chinks in the stone walls. Mata was disappointed, but at last he agreed to leave and return in a fortnight, when Alasdair would be stronger. "You should be well enough to walk home by then," he chided the sick man.

"I ache even to think of walking," Una heard Alasdair say, and she did not know whether to sigh or smile. She'd have a fortnight with him, she told herself, which was better than losing him at once. He was hers and always would be, even after he left.

Mata stayed the night, which was just as well. Every other word he spoke was said in jest: a bottle of whisky became a man with a cork in his eye, and a wooden spoon became a pretty girl who scolded him whenever he tried to court her. Una liked him in spite of herself. His wild stories brought smiles to Alasdair's face and set the house ringing with his laughter.

But Mata had another side to him as well. His last story of the evening made Una shiver. It was about the shee, the fairy folk, who sometimes stole away the souls of healthy people in their sleep, mistaking them for dead. The shee

would take the living into their secret courtyards under-
ground, Mata said, "and that would be the last anyone
would see of the person." Later, after she was certain
everyone was quietly abed, Una crept to Alasdair's side to
assure herself that he had not been stolen by the fairies
during his death-like slumber. Thanks be to God, he was
still with her.

In the morning Una helped Mata prepare to leave, top-
ping off a whisky-skin for him and stuffing his saddlebags
full of food. "What if Alasdair's da insists on him returning
sooner?" she wondered aloud.

Mata gave her a broad wink. "Don't fret. I'll keep the
old man at bay."

What was he like, her darling's father? she wondered,
but the question went away as quickly as it had come. The
man must have been a fine gentleman; how else might he
have fathered her red man?

Mata rode off into a cold morning, but by noon the sun
had come out and warmed the entire glen. When Una
took the sheep out to graze she found harebells, primroses,
and violets growing among the green heather, though she
could not remember seeing them the day before. The
earth was soft under her feet and smelled like rosemary.

When she returned with the sheep in the late of the
afternoon, she found Alasdair outside the house sitting on
a plaid in a patch of fading sunlight, dressed in a long
muslin shirt Mata had brought him. He was smoking one
of her father's clay pipes. Bone weary though she was, she
trotted up to him and flopped down beside him on the
plaid. "Welcome back to the world of the living."

"Aye, if such you call it," said Alasdair, but he was smiling
as he spoke. "How could I stay inside on such a day?"

"Did my mother help you walk out?"

Alasdair smiled again. "I crept out by myself, hirpling
like a beggar and gripping onto the walls. Still, she deserves

the credit for that. Saved my life, she did, and for that I'm ever grateful. She must be very dear to you."

"Indeed she is! Just as your mother must be dear to you." A shadow passed over Alasdair's face, and Una knew she had somehow said the wrong thing. Perhaps his mother had been harsh with him. "And she is, isn't she?"

Alasdair smiled and nodded. "She was. She died when I was but six years old, you see. I was her treasure. It was a dark day when she left me." Alasdair sighed and took a puff from his pipe. He seemed so peaceful that Una decided she must sometime ask him more about this wonderful mother of his.

That evening Alasdair ate with Una and her family for the first time. It was a simple supper: trout fried in oatmeal, kale, oatcakes, and milk. He ate like a starving badger, but even so, Una was ashamed there was nothing better to offer him.

She dared not stare at him, though she wished to, but from time to time glanced up at him across the table, over the wooden trenchers and horn cups and bits of crockery, and whenever their eyes met he would smile at her. How could she go on living without him? she thought, and her heart sank to imagine the house empty of him.

Una did not sleep well that night and was up and beside Alasdair the moment he cried out. "Can a man have no privacy with his nightmares?" he asked.

"Not if they threaten to wake the house." He had nothing to say to that but lay back, his eyes closed. His face was damp and his hair had become tangled as he had tossed back and forth in his dreams. "Let me brush your hair." she said. "It's matted up like a horse's tail."

By the time she returned with her mother's brush, he was sitting up in the bed, his hair and face glowing in the light of two candles in sconces on the wall. She stood behind him, unraveling the worst knots with the brush, which was nothing but boar bristles set in a piece of antler, worn smooth by her mother's fingers.

"Your father told me it was you who found me at the corrie." Alasdair grimaced as Una picked away at a stubborn tangle.

"It was. Pray hold still. I'm sorry to . . . there! It's done." She continued brushing, but slower now and more carefully. Alasdair's hair shone brilliant bronze, and she smiled to herself at the silken feel of that hair between her fingers and the joy of tending to him.

"Then it was you who saved my life."

He spoke very slowly, and she thought he might have trouble believing the words himself. It must have been hard for him, feeling obliged to a girl. "My father saved your life when he carried you here, and my mother, too, with all her medicines."

"Aye, but your father said he would have left me had you not begged him to help," Alasdair insisted.

Una stopped brushing to admire her handiwork: Alasdair's hair fell in neat waves down his neck and glittered like a gold piece. It was well her father hadn't told Alasdair about the dirk.

"I don't know why you make so little of your compassion," he continued. "Still, I'm beholden. What would you like?"

What would she like? What she wanted she could never have, which he must have known.

Alasdair grinned and touched her cheek, as any man might touch the face of a friendly child. "Linens?" he said. "Holland cloth? Some chickens, perhaps, or bracelets? A lass like you should have so much silver on her arms that she clinks like bells when she walks."

"There's nothing I desire," she lied.

"What foolishness!" he said, snorting like a horse. "All women crave gifts. My Fiona is never satisfied, no matter what I bring her."

Una felt her entire world grow as cold and wet as a peatbog. "Fiona?"

Alasdair nodded. "Aye, my betrothed, my cousin. The two of us were pledged since she was but a child, and now that she's older, she's fit to wed. So, I shall wed her."

Una swallowed hard. She hoped that Alasdair could not see her face turn white, though she could feel the blood draining from it. "Is she bonny?"

Alasdair laughed, which made her feel like weeping. It would be painful enough if he saw her sorrow, but to jeer at her! She was glad to hear him continue in his soft, normal voice. "I think so, though not to my preference. My father and hers arranged the match, and if you must know, they pair lovers as cattlemen pair beasts—the red with the red, the tall with the tall. Faith, she looks as I would look were I female, only far more fetching."

An arranged marriage. One did not hear of those often, though they'd been common enough in the old days. Now it was love, Una thought, or the fruits of love, which brought couples together. "A handfasting?"

"Of sorts. They're a cautious lot, those two gaffers. Only Fiona wishes a priest beside us as well. That was what brought me to Glenfinnan, searching for a man of God among the men of Donald."

Una felt her gorge rise. "Do you love her?"

"Enough to wed her. Why are you so curious, Una? Haven't you suitors of your own?"

"None yet. Sometime next year, my mother says, will be soon enough." The next hundred years would be too soon. Could he tell what she was thinking? She made herself look down at the brush in her lap, concentrating on each bristle, trying to count them separately and empty her mind of thoughts, but as she was counting, the days that were left to her with Alasdair came into her mind and she counted them, too, slowly and painfully, afraid to move from one to the next. She had let her time with the red man slip past her. Only six days remained.

When she looked up again at Alasdair, she could feel the tears building in her eyes and was glad to see he was asleep. She waited some time before blowing out the candles, just staring at the man, then returned to her own bed and wept, not caring whether the two Morags heard her or not.

By and by she began thinking of other things: what the people in Glenalt were like, the fierce smell of the peat from the dying fire, the thin ray of moonlight that fell through a hole in the thatch. She thought of her parents and sat up to look at them. In the dim light she could see they breathed in unison as they slept together, and the sight of them filled her with peace.

She remembered the many times she had awakened late at night, a little girl afraid of raiding fairies, and heard the comforting noises of love coming from her parents' bed. She'd watched their shadows come together, separate, and weave into each other like the ancient shapechangers who could change form at will, from person to beast to monster. And yet there was nothing frightening about her parents' violent movements. It was tenderness, not terror, that caused them.

"Do you and Mammy love each other?" she'd once asked her father, after such a night.

"Aye, we do," he'd answered, smiling as he took her up onto his lap. "Ours is what they used to call a love match. Every child born to us is proof of our love."

Soon Alasdair and his new bride would have many proofs of their love, Una thought, and she herself would have nothing. Without Alasdair, that was what life held for her: a nothingness as vast and gray as the mist in the corrie.

Her red man grew a little stronger every day, and every day she watched him as he walked about the yard or played with the children or helped her mother stack peat. Every day he looked a bit broader and ruddier than the day before. He was getting well, she thought sadly, preparing himself for his journey north.

One blue spring morning she left the house early and drove the sheep up into the hills. The air smelled new and fresh; she could not get enough of it, but stood gulping it down for several minutes as she crested the little rise that overlooked her house. It struck her that she had not taken a long, hard look at it since Alasdair had come, and now it seemed different somehow. Like so many of her clansfolks' houses, it was built of unmortared stones, rounded at the corners to invite the wind to pass around it. No chimney, no windowsill, no shutter broke its sleekness. The thatch roof was old but still in good repair.

No, she realized, the house had not changed. It only seemed new and alive because Alasdair was living there.

"Hi! Hi! Halloo! Una!"

She turned to see Alasdair running toward her apace, his long hair flying out behind him like a red banner, his fine shirt billowing about him. "Alasdair!" She wanted to tell him to stop, to slow down lest he hurt himself, but *Dia!* he was fine to look at, galloping toward her like a sorrel stallion. The sheep milled in front of her, bleating nervously. "Alasdair!" she called again. He glanced up at her. Suddenly he fell, landing shoulder first in the heath, his legs flying in the air above him, just as a horse might fall.

She forgot about the sheep and was beside him before

he could pull himself up. He didn't look to be hurt, but his face was bright red with shame. "You aren't strong enough yet for such running," she said gently, trying to ease the sting of his damaged pride. "You're not hurt?"

Alasdair stood up with difficulty and frowned at her. At first she thought he was angry with her, but soon he was laughing at himself and walking back and forth before her to show that he hadn't undone any of her nursing. "Well, if the truth be said, my manly sensibilities took a bruising, what with having you see me fall arse over head like a fool at the fair."

What had he been doing? Trying to impress her? Witless man! "You'd risk hurting yourself again after nearly getting your health back?"

"Why, I thought you would have been pleased if I'd broken a leg or two," he said, a wry smile splitting his face.

"Why would you think that?"

"For then I'd not be leaving for another fortnight."

Had he meant it as a jest? No doubt, and yet his words were ever so true: she'd be glad if he'd injured himself, if it meant he'd not have to leave her. She stared at him in silence, not knowing what to say that he hadn't said already.

The smile melted from his face and she knew from the sad glow in his eyes that he was well aware of her suffering. "Una, you know I can't stay, as much as I'd like to please you."

He took her hand, but she tugged it free and half turned from him so he would not notice the hot tears pooling in her eyes. Why would Jehovah, in all his wisdom, send her a man dearer than any other, yet take him away again so hasty?

"I know something of love," he said as he reached out to take her arm and slowly turn her toward him. "Your eyes are so beautiful 'tis a sin to hide them behind tears. I'm not gone yet."

When he held out the tail of his plaid, she grabbed it eagerly and swiped it against her face, obliterating her tears. "Love?"

"Aye. Kissing and embracing," he explained. "A comely lass like you doubtless has the young men running in circles around her with their tongues trailing in the heather. Surely you know what I speak of."

She gazed at him, open-mouthed. In truth, she did not. She knew many young men, but never cared for any so deeply that she'd allow them to lay a hand on her.

He understood her silence. "Well then, you'll need some learning," Alasdair whispered. He leaned into her neck, brushing his lips against her skin.

She trembled all over, sure she'd crumble into pieces at any moment. The touch of his lips on her flesh burned like a flame, and she longed to be consumed by it. "We'll be seen." She glanced toward the house, but all she could see of it was the very top of the thatch and the perpetual plume of smoke.

"No, we'll not," Alasdair said, his mouth buried in her hair. " 'Tis as good a place as the next for stealing a kiss or two."

It wasn't right, it wasn't decent, she thought. Then passion rose up in her like a mighty wave and swept away all thoughts of modesty and prudence. Alasdair, her red man, wanted to hold her, not like a child, but like a woman. His mouth found her lips. All her senses leaped to attention as a disturbing pleasure seized her belly and ripped through her innards. What was happening to her? She hadn't any notion at all, save that she knew now she loved her red man.

His mouth prowled to her neck, her jaw, her ear. Surely she would die from his touch! When she felt his great, gentle hands clasp her breasts through her *arasaid,* she flinched but the once, then laid her own hands on his, pressing him harder against her, into her heart, she imagined. It was wise that she'd kept the other lads away from her, for she wanted no one but Alasdair to ever touch her this way, so intimately, so tenderly.

"That's enough of a lesson for one day," he said, lifting his head. He eased away from her, an odd, yearning expression on his face. "Much more of this and I'll lose my wits."

Devil take him! He was leaving her! He was done with her, and her but getting used to the sweetness of his touch. In a burst of love and anger, she clawed at him with both hands, striking his thigh and fumbling against his sporran. Suddenly something hard and searching rose into her hand.

"Enough!" cried Alasdair, breaking from her and stepping back so quickly his weakened legs buckled underneath him.

Una cried out, in part because she felt him toppling toward her, in part because she realized what her hand had grasped. She slipped and fell forward against his chest, and together they tumbled into the bracken. Struggling to her knees, she looked down at her darling, flat on his back in the heather, his face a picture of bewilderment. "Are you well, Alasdair? Are you alive?" she cried. He gave her a sly, sidelong glance and burst into laughter. "What? You'd jeer me?" she said. "Me, that's only trying to find out whether you live or not? Cruel creature!" She hit his shoulder with the flat of her hand, which only made him laugh all the more.

He sat up, still chuckling. "Well, we're a graceful pair, are we no? I should think you'd know very well how much life is in me, since you yourself had it in your hand." He tried to stand, but Una gripped his belt, unwilling to let him go.

"Another kiss!" she begged him. "I'll not touch you again, I swear."

"Indeed you won't, little wanton! Unhand me, hussy! What would your parents say if they saw you clinging to a man this way?"

"And what would they say had they seen you with your hands on my clothing?" she spat back at him.

He sighed, looked up at the hills, then back into her face. "Come, Una. Your flock will be in Glenalt before I will."

His words brought her back to her senses with a start. She turned toward the sheep, which were halfway up the hillside and spreading out over the heather like melted snow. Alasdair rose, then helped her to her feet. "Well, go after them. They're likely to . . . to run over a cliff or something."

She paused, uncertain where to go, whom to follow. She felt caught between love and duty, an aye uncomfortable position, to be sure. "And the two of us?" she asked, clutching his hands.

"You're a bold one," said Alasdair. "If you don't learn to curb your feelings, one day you'll find yourself with a child and no husband for it."

She had no reply for that. It was a fine thought indeed: Alasdair's child. Such a wean would remind her of him whenever she looked at it. The notion came and went, like a dream.

Alasdair pried her fingers from his. "Someday, Una, you will fall in love and marry, as I am going to do. Now tend to your beasts. I'm for home."

She watched him amble off toward her parents' house, none the worse for his two falls. Had he fallen in love, she wondered, as she had?

On the day Mata was to return, the rain did not stop once from morning to night. Una was sitting by the fire next to Alasdair, showing him how well she could carve a spoon from a steer's horn, when the neighing of a horse took her so much by surprise that she dropped both knife and spoon. At once Alasdair was on his feet, sprinting from the house, his plaid bundled under his arm. "Stay!" cried Una. She dashed after him into the darkness, closing her eyes against the sting of the raindrops.

Through the rain she could see Mata, leading a fine, large pony. Beside him rode a tall man on another good horse, and as Alasdair stumbled forward, the rider called out to him. "Alasdair! Not even half dead, I see!"

Who was this impertinent creature? Who would dare speak so coarsely to her red man? Una stepped forward, looked up into the face of the rider, and hid a gasp behind her hand. It was as if she were looking at an older, bearded Alasdair. Age had washed most of the red from this man's hair, but there was no mistaking the high forehead and the thick, full lips. His face was so proud and stark it might as well have been carved out of limestone.

"I'm sorry to have disappointed you, Calum Mor!" shouted Alasdair. He threw the plaid into the older man's hands, and the rider wrapped it about his shoulders. Una couldn't help but wonder—had the plaid been meant for Mata? Who was this forward creature?

"Inside, the both of you!" cried Alasdair, reaching for the horse's reins, but the rider kept his animal at a standstill.

"Are you giving commands now, *a'mhic?*" he said and laughed.

Una stiffened. An older Alasdair. Alasdair's father?

Then all four of them stood in the rain, as if there were no choice but to stay and be drenched, though the house was not fifty paces away and the peat fire glowed blue through the windows. What manner of father was this, that would risk harming his son, and him but just rescued from the lip of the grave? And yet she herself could move no more than Alasdair could. The stranger's hard face fixed her to the spot.

Just then the rider dismounted, flung his reins at Mata, and ran toward the house. "Come, Alasdair! Have you no brains?" he shouted. "Mata! Take the beasts!"

Una let Alasdair lead her to the doorway. She walked in a daze. This selfish creature had begotten her darling, her kind, gentle Alasdair? "Your da?"

"Aye. Calum Mor, he's called. Don't let him frighten you, Una. It's the way he is. In with you now, or it's you who'll need nursing."

At his beckoning, she squeezed past him into the house. The warmth of it shocked her. She'd thought the entire world had gone cold.

Chapter 3

Inside the black house his father was as commanding as he had been outside. Rory and Sorcha gave Calum a comfortable seat by the fire and offered him the best they had to eat and drink—broiled salmon, whisky, and cream. There was no salmon for themselves, Alasdair noted.

Alasdair sat on a sheepskin by the fire and watched Una as she went about her task filling and refilling Calum's cup, as her mother bade her. She glanced back and forth between the two men of Glenalt, unwilling, perhaps, to believe they were father and son. Did he only imagine a look of fear in her eyes? No, he had felt the same fear, when he was younger.

During the first six years of his life he had rarely seen his father. It was his mother who stood out clearly in his earliest memories, a slender woman with a quiet way about her. Of the seven children she had borne, Alasdair was the only one to survive more than a few days. A night rarely passed that she did not take him in her arms and sing to him as he fell asleep. *'Mo phreiseil lur,'* she called him. 'My precious gem.'

He remembered the last birth. He had hidden in the cattle stall next to the big room, listening to his mother's groans. He stayed there an entire day. The household had flocked around his mother, and no one seemed to miss him.

The baby was stillborn. When he saw his mother at last, hours later, the healers would have had him believe she was dead, though her skin looked as pink and soft as ever. When will she wake? he'd asked them. Never in this life, someone had answered, and another said, Be strong, for your father's sake. He had no idea what that meant. Wasn't his da the strongest man in the district?

Calum Mor was forever leading the huge cattle drives that had made him a wealthy man of sorts, but he appeared suddenly the day after his wife's death, and then Alasdair could not escape him. He seemed to take up the entire house, wailing and shouting, lurching about like a wounded stag. Once he lunged into Alasdair and smashed his son against a stone wall. Though he suffered a great gash in his head, Alasdair was too afeared to feel pain.

That had come later, at the burial. Six men carried his mother on a litter to the Field of Cairns, a lovely mountain meadow full of graves. The cairns, tall mounds of stones, reached into the heavens like upraised arms. It had not mattered so much to him that his mother was placed in a deep hole, nor that the hole had been filled with earth. Sheep, he knew, had survived burial under many feet of snow. The keening of his mother's kinsmen was more frightening, though it was only noise and could do no harm. But when his father and several others started to pile stones on the gravesite, Alasdair had panicked. How could his mother breathe under the weight of those great gray chunks of granite?

As he threw himself against the largest rock and tried to wrestle it off the grave, his nostrils filled with the sweet smell of a new-plowed field. It was hard to breathe. He wondered if he, too, would suffocate just by pushing against those dark stones. Two great hands had slipped under Alasdair's oxters and hoisted him high in the air. He gazed into his father's blue eyes. "You'll not interfere," whispered the man.

Alasdair had felt the sensation of flying backward, cold air on his neck. Something broke his fall and he landed in a stranger's arms. He whimpered at first, but when his wind came back to him he began to shriek and scream, not only for his mother, unable to breathe under the great cairn that had begun to form on her grave, but for himself, because he could breathe and she could not. The man who had caught him carried him from the gravesite, fairly running through the crowd of wailing clansfolk. He never saw the man's face. He never even thought to ask his name. And yet, looking back, he was certain the stranger had saved his life.

A pine branch on the fire snapped and burst apart in a spray of blue sparks. Alasdair raised his head. His father was speaking to him, and for an instant he felt the fear he had just been recollecting.

"Are you dreaming?" said his father. Even his voice had a massive quality to it, a wall of a voice. "It is true you were as ill as these good folk claim?"

Alasdair paused to collect his thoughts and arrange his words just so. "Faith, whatever they say, you may be sure they are telling the truth. They saved my life, and I'll vouch for their honesty." He looked up at Rory and Sorcha, who were nodding their heads, and wondered what they had said about him. If he were they, he would have been deeply offended at this rude man of Clan MacLeod who dared question their word.

"I never doubted their honesty, only their imaginations," muttered Calum Mor. *"Arrah!* After all, you were running through the rain like a hound after a hare."

"Well may you be surprised, sir," said Rory softly, as if he were afraid of interrupting his guest. "Three, even two weeks past, the young man could neither stand nor speak above a whisper, but now he's strong enough."

"Aye so, from the looks of him," Calum mumbled, scanning Alasdair up and down. "And it's you and your wife deserve the thanks for it. In the long ago, you'd as lief have killed him as cured him. Now the Sassenach soldiers and the Black Watch keep our peace for us."

Alasdair listened to his da with one ear as he spoke of making reparation to Rory and Sorcha—cattle, sheep, perhaps a horse, gifts for their kindness to Alasdair. He could not even offer presents without sounding haughty, Alasdair thought, as though just the right number of animals would balance his debt to these people. Alasdair remembered how he had pressed Una to accept a gift and wondered if he'd sounded as cold to her as his father sounded to him.

Alasdair glanced at her, standing in the shadows behind his father, but he could not see her face. "We cannot take gifts for doing God's will," said Rory, though Alasdair was sure his heart was not in his words. Calum objected. Back and forth the argument went, until at last a suitable payment was decided: three steers, a cow, and a calf. Alasdair would have laughed had he not been so weary. Fiona's father had promised twenty head of cattle and three horses as a dowry with far less squabbling.

And there it was. Perhaps his father was right, that he had no brain. What sort of man would forget his own bride? "Fiona," he said, so loudly everyone turned to look at him.

"You've taken your time recalling her," Calum said.

"The poor woman is well enough, though she wept and howled like the *ban sith* when you did not return."

"I'm glad she's fine," said Alasdair, staring into the fire to avoid looking at his father. It would be good to come home to Fiona. He hoped she had not suffered as much as Calum seemed to think.

"This is your wife, then?" asked Sorcha, in the same respectful tone of voice her husband had used.

Una, refilling Calum's cup, spilled whisky on the man's hand. Instantly the room fell silent, but Calum merely sucked his fingers clean. Alasdair winked at Una, and she backed into the shadows. "Not quite yet, but soon," his father said.

There was more talk, mostly about the coming wedding and such like, though it was clear the whisky was affecting Calum Mor: long pauses separated all his sentences. When he failed to answer at last, Alasdair rose and covered him with a plaid. "He'll sleep fine where he is," he said over Rory's and Sorcha's protests.

Una gently pried the full cup of whisky from the man's hand and offered it to Alasdair. "To drown your black dreams," she told him. Alasdair drained the cup and lay down on the familiar heather bed, but he could not fall asleep for some time. He was thinking of Fiona and his father, imagining the freedom he would have once he was married and a father himself. Perhaps then Calum Mor would be satisfied. Mata, curled up on a pallet of straw and plaids at the foot of the bed, chuckled in his sleep. The fire in the main room crackled. Ashes fell.

Alasdair awoke to the feel of strong fingers stroking his cheeks and the stubble of his chin.

"Are you awake, *mo mhic*?"

Alasdair kept his eyes closed but turned his face toward the warmth of the great hand. It smelled of whisky and wet wool. As he lay enjoying the touch of the hand, it withdrew, then returned to caress the top of his head. "Sleep well, my heart. God keep you, and a thousand thanks to Him for returning you." The hand disappeared. As Alasdair began to doze, it came to him that his father would never have said such a thing had he known his son was awake.

A whispering voice woke him later, how much later he could not tell at first. "Come, arise. I've something to show you."

"Mata?" Alasdair opened his eyes. The room was still dark except for the light of the stars through the windows. It was Una who stood before him, the starlight glittering in her eyes like fairy lanterns. "Let it wait until morning. I'm aye weary."

"It's very nearly daybreak," she insisted. "Come, we'll not be gone long."

After he had dressed she led him by the hand through the sleeping house, past Calum Mor and her parents, and over the two Morags stretched out near the doorway. Outside the air was delightful, like wine. The taste of it woke him completely, and he stared about at the hills, the stars, and the blue-black sky. "There's no mist. I've never seen such a clear night. Is that what you wanted to show me?"

For an answer she came up close beside him, dropping his hand and circling his waist with her arms. In the darkness he felt her head sink onto his chest and smelled the peatsmoke in her hair. Ah, she hadn't given up on him! He held her close, bending over her to kiss her cheek. They'd not had much of a first encounter, and he felt ashamed to think how clumsy he must have seemed to her. Perhaps, if they had another chance, he could teach her something without hurting her.

"Did you like our little bit of fondling, silly as it was?" he asked as he stroked her neck. He felt her hand on his hip and knew her answer. "Well, then." He smiled and kissed her again, on the mouth this time. He must be careful not to smile too much, or she would think he was laughing at her. In truth he was touched by her feelings for him and hoped he was wrong, that she did not actually love him. But she was only fifteen; what did she know of love?

"I acted unseemly, I think," she said.

"Eager, perhaps, and there's no sin in that. Would you like to walk together? Just for a bit? A private place. The corrie. You can lead me there."

"The corrie?" She stared at him, puzzled. "Why go there? It's an odd place for . . . for . . ."

"Loving? No, it's grand. You're thinking I'll not be able to face it because of my dreams, but they're gone now, I'm sure of it. I want to see the corrie, as I'll not soon have the chance again." It seemed fitting, somehow, that the place he first saw her should be the last place he was alone with her.

They walked barefoot through the damp bracken, pieces of leaves clinging to their legs. She broke their silence only once. "Why is your father so cruel to you?"

"Do you mean his jests or the haughty way he has about him?"

"Aye. Both."

Alasdair remembered the kind touch on his face during the night and longed to keep that memory in his mind. "Calum means no harm by the way he talks," Alasdair explained, "only he thinks he'll make me a stronger man with this show of his, and I've learned to accept it."

"As strong as he is?"

Alasdair snorted and shrugged. His father hid the truth of his loving touch under a bluffness that could not be approached. "A man is whatever he is, and there is no shame in that. Besides, there are many different kinds of strength, a thing my father has never considered."

"Surely your father is satisfied with you now. Anyone who could survive what you have is strong enough."

"Endurance does not impress him. It's a sort of hardness he's after," Alasdair said.

"Look you. Here it is." Una pointed to the east, where the sky had just begun to turn a lighter shade of blue. The rocks of the corrie rose bold-black against the sky. Alasdair walked among the rocks, remembering the unequal battle. He waited to feel the terror he had felt that day, but this corrie was not the same place as the corrie where he had almost died. There were no bodies, no broadswords, no blood, only rocks and heather. "It's smaller than I remembered," said Alasdair. "It's just a place."

He looked at Una, and though the stars had long faded, they still seemed to shine in her eyes. "Do you remember offering me a gift?" she asked.

"Aye, and I mean to give it to you." She looked surprised, and for a moment he forgot she had accepted his kisses earlier and wondered if he could have mistaken her intentions. But when he undid the folds of his plaid from his waist and wrapped them about her, pulling her close into him, he saw her face relax and felt the sweet pressure of her arm around his neck.

He half lifted her, bending at the knees and easing their captive bodies down side by side onto the heather. Wrapped in his plaid, they writhed together as Alasdair brought his mouth down toward her breast, drew back her camisole with his hand and finally tasted the hard berry of her nipple. Her nails dug into his scalp. Did men and women have the same feelings at a time like this, a need for having the life crushed out of them? He took her hand, guiding it onto his thigh. "Touch me, then."

It was so difficult to speak even those few words that the steady cadence of her voice shocked him. "Indeed I won't. You'll put the babe in the heather, not in me."

"A babe!" he gasped. "You'll get no baby from me. I'm not as careless as that."

"But that is your gift."

Dia! He had read her completely wrong! She was either more of a woman than he'd thought or more of a child. "You can't just make a babe so easily," he sputtered, drawing back from her so fast his plaid pulled away from his belt and fell down around Una. "Are you unsullied?"

She was silent a moment, then nodded. "I am."

"Then you'd be wise to know that a first mating never makes a baby." This was not so, he knew, but it might seem true to her. He held himself over her, half-naked, his body suddenly ice-cold at the touch of her hand on his flank.

"So they say, but I don't believe such a thing," Una replied. "Nor does my mother. That's how I was made, she says. She's been telling me about these things so I'll not be a child when I marry. Now is as likely a time as any, Alasdair Ruadh."

"And if there is no wean?"

"Then I'll still have had this time with you."

"You forget I'm bespoken."

She was not to be stopped. "Your betrothed is no doubt a kind and generous woman and hardly one to begrudge me a few minutes of what she'll have for a lifetime."

Alasdair flung himself backward onto his haunches, then stood upright. Una rose and stood in front of him. There was something commanding in the set of her mouth.

"I want no child by you," he growled. Should he slap her, the impudent thing, or merely walk away from her? She had no right to a child of his. And yet, if it had not been for her, he'd not ever have any child.

"I beg you, please!" Her hand shot out to grab his sleeve, but he jerked his arm free. "I'll never ask you for a thing more. I'll make no claim on you, I swear."

Alasdair took a step backward, then another as she followed him, circling him with that bold look still on her face. When he stopped suddenly, she brought herself up short, as a fox does when its prey makes a stand. Sweat burned his eyes, and he saw that her face was glistening, too.

Alasdair had lain with enough women to know that males were direct and females coy. The man approached and the woman withdrew, pretending she wanted none of it. Why do you do this? he'd asked one strumpet, who time and again had brought his passion to a peak, only to inch away from him and force him to pursue her. Hadn't he seen blackcocks and hens on the heath? she'd said. It was no different for a man and woman—a courting dance to make them each burn brighter.

Here was a courting dance, right enough, with Una the cock and he the hen. "You're crazy-mad! Having a wean will make it harder for you to find suitors."

"Then I'll not wed! It matters not to me what people think, and surely God, who is all-merciful and all-knowing and understands the pain I'm feeling, will forgive me." She paused a moment, panting. "If He doesn't, then I'm quit of Him, too. The Virgin will understand, and my parents."

Surely this was the maddest conversation two people ever had. "Why, Una? Why *my* child?"

"Because," she gasped, "because." The horizon cracked open behind her, spilling silver light onto the great loch below. "Because you're mine and you're leaving me. Because. Because you cannot leave me feeling as I am. Nothing, with nothing."

"Una." He lifted his hand, caught between wanting to strike her and longing to caress her. How wild she looked with her breasts gray in the half-light, her hair a blackbird's nest. *You've started something here, Alasdair, and woken a*

woman inside of a girl. It was a mistake that bore consequences a man couldn't run from.

When she took a step toward him, he grasped her shoulders. If he could search himself deeply, he would find out
what he felt for this brazen girl. Surely it was not love. It was
some sort of enchantment she had over him. He thought of
the water-horse, the fairy creature that captured unsus-
pecting people by taking the form of a beautiful steed
prancing in the reedy margins of a loch. Once a man
touched the monster, he was frozen to it, then dragged
underwater and devoured. Only a story for children, of
course, to keep them from venturing into the water.

He could not let go of her, nor did he wish to.

Una walked down the hillside in the blue light of the
early sun, limping, several feet behind Alasdair's broad
back and swinging hips. All around her the larks and lin-
nets were tuning their chanters, as a piper would say, and
now and then she broke through their songs with a loud
sniff. She hated them.

She had not known it would be painful. Her mother
had not spoken of that, and the cattle she had watched
struggling with each other in the pastures had never shown
any pain on their dull faces. The village girls who said they
knew something of men had talked of nothing but kissing
and gifts and their swains' attempts at poetry. She decided
they hadn't known so much after all.

Only Alasdair had understood, only he had been true.
"I might hurt you," he'd whispered, and though she knew
exactly what would happen to her, she wasn't expecting
pain to be a part of it. At first she had felt pressure and
had thought nothing of it. Then he'd entered her. She
was being torn apart, she'd been sure of it, sure that all
the blood was draining from her and that she would die

without even seeing the bonny wean she knew they would have. She had cried out to him as her body arched under his, but he was moving back and forth atop her like the tide of the sea, engulfing her, far beyond hearing her. Just when she was certain he would kill her he stopped, holding himself motionless above her and finally collapsing upon her. The taste of salt water stung her lips and she realized with a start she'd not known she'd been crying.

After a short while the terrible pressure inside her had subsided and she pushed her face against his neck to drink in the comforting smell of his skin. She wouldn't die after all. How could love have done this to her? She had to behold the reason. "Let me see you."

"Faith, there's little to see." Still, he'd been accommodating, rolling onto his back and lifting his shirt over his waist. She'd seen nothing she'd not seen before: a small, sleepy creature curled into itself, no longer the weapon that had torn her open.

"Your parents will wonder where we've been," he'd said, and sprung to his feet.

Once they began walking, he didn't speak a word to her. She should have felt joy or at least relief for having succeeded in her plans, but her mind seemed to ache as much as her body. What could he be thinking of now, marching ahead of her like a stone-horse, without once looking back? "Do you hate me?" she asked, dismayed at how weak her voice sounded against the noise of the birds.

He turned so abruptly she almost walked into him. "Did you speak?"

"Do you hate me?" she repeated, louder this time. A change had come over Alasdair. The overwhelming oneness she had felt with him at the corrie a short time ago was gone, and when she thought *You are mine* to herself now the words rang false. He looked very much his own man, a man who would soon be leaving her.

"Nay, 'tis myself I hate," he said. "I've never forced myself on a woman before, much less a girl. And then there is Fiona. I'll have to hope she'll still want me."

"You'll remember this thing was my suggestion, and no fault of yours," Una reminded him. It was incredible, the pride of the man. He could not admit it was she who had taken advantage of him, but perhaps that was hard for any man to admit. "The baby, should there be one, is your gift to me."

Alasdair glared at her, scorching her with his smoke-colored eyes. "A fine gift indeed. Your father will hardly think so, now there's a chance he must either find you a husband or provide for your child himself. A fine way to repay his hospitality! I could have shown restraint, but no, I couldn't. The truth is I was not man enough to respect you nor to keep my troth."

Suddenly the pain of their lovemaking was nothing compared to the pain of Alasdair's words. "And do you yet feel no respect for me?" she cried.

He looked away, a frown creasing his broad brow. " 'Tis better you ask me nothing about my feelings, because I've no skill at getting a grasp on them." He paused, gazing down into the glen where the smoke from the house slashed blue across the heather, his whole body as tense as a bowstring. He turned and gave her a hard look, up and down. His eyes were distant, and she shivered under their appraisal. "Sometimes, *m'ghraidh* . . . well, there's nothing for it. It's over and done with. You're not in pain, I take it."

She shook her head. The dull ache between her legs was nothing compared to the pain in her heart.

By the time they returned, the household was awake and lively. Una was sure no one noticed her or Alasdair until her mother touched her arm and took her aside. "Where

have the two of you been?'' she asked, a look of worry
darkening her face like a shadow.

"To the corrie.''

"That was your doing.''

"Not at all. It was his.''

Una felt her arm tremble in her mother's light grasp.
You should have let me know, thought Una. All those nights
she had been comforted listening to her parents nickering
to each other: they meant nothing now she knew her
mother must have hidden the truth of the pain. When she
had daughters of her own, she vowed, she would let them
know how things truly were for the woman.

Una busied herself by helping her mother serve breakfast to the three men of Clan MacLeod. Alasdair had
changed his clothes, and though he looked splendid in
tight-legged trews, tartan jacket, and brave new bonnet,
he seemed to have taken on a new personality as well. She
waited on him while he ate breakfast, hoping for one caring
word or the return of that sweet bond between them, but
all he said to her was, 'More milk, if you please,' and 'A
thousand thanks.' His polite words tore the skin away from
her, leaving her raw.

After the meal, Mata went to fetch the horses, and Alasdair made a formal, pretty-sounding speech to her parents
and herself. It was full of English words and gratitude, but
there was nothing of Alasdair in those words. Una wished
she had the courage to shake him, slap him, or find some
other way to bring him back to himself. Even his hate
would have been more welcome than dead niceties.

When Alasdair was finished, Calum Mor said very nearly
the same things in different words, and Una could see for
the first time that aye, they were clearly father and son.
There was a hardness about Alasdair she hadn't noticed
before. After Calum had spoken, many handclasps and
kisses were traded all around, but Una pressed herself

against the wall of the house, away from the two men, and when Alasdair looked at her she could not bear to meet his solemn gaze.

"Good luck to you, Una," he said.

She said nothing, only glanced up to see a look of sadness pass over his eyes. At once she knew it was Alasdair who had spoken to her, not his father's son. Her hand jerked toward him but he had turned away, a figure blurred in motion, first shaking her father's hand, then saying something to her mother, then turning to Mata and mounting the horse that stood ready for him.

She was so terrified at the thought of never seeing him again that she could not wave or call out to him, though he nodded at her before turning his horse's head. The family stood, shouting farewell to the three of them as they headed north up the hillside and out of the glen. Her father left, then the Morags, leaving only herself, her mother, and the baby to watch the men and horses become smaller and smaller. When they looked no larger than the wooden toys that fathers carved for their young children, Una felt her mother's hand stroking her cheek. "Come, dear," she murmured, "he's gone. Inside with you now. You can churn the butter for me."

Una nodded but continued to watch the little procession make its way up the slope, Calum Mor in front, Alasdair in the rear, and Mata in between, walking at the head of Alasdair's horse. By the time they reached the top of the hill, they had almost lost all color against the gray flatness of the sky, yet Una was certain it was Alasdair who stopped his horse, raised his bonnet, and waved it over his head. She waved back, and was still waving long after Alasdair had ridden on and vanished over the summit. She had held that head, she had brushed that fiery hair, and the memory of those simple things flooded her with solace.

M'ghraidh, he'd called her. My love.

Chapter 4

Una loved the end of summer. It had a savage beauty all its own, made more vivid by the knowledge that winter would soon put an end to heat and color for many months. The last of the heather was turning from pale purple to pale brown, and the streams, as tame as they would ever be, cut silver through the dying bracken.

As the season lay fading, something new was taking place within her. Her time did not come. She fell asleep during the daytime. No food pleased her. "What's fashing you?" asked her father, and like as not her mother would answer for her, "Can't you see the child is ill?"

Una kept her secret to herself, hoping that she would never have to tell her parents, that they would see for themselves one day and know. And as she wondered at her good fortune, a fortune she knew most people would neither understand nor wish for themselves, she loved the last of summer even more, because of its beginnings.

One morning Una awoke with the ray of light streaming

in from the hole in the thatch, feeling poorly. She hurried from the house just in time to reach the midden, and stood there for what seemed like hours, retching, her head spinning. But through her misery came a streak of joy when she remembered the times her mother had raced to the midden in the early morning.

Her mother remembered, too. When Una returned to the house, her mouth still bitter with the taste of bile, her mother was sitting in the cattle stall, milking the cow. Without missing a pull on the teats, she turned and looked full at Una. "What is this?"

"I've been ill." Her stomach felt as though it had been turned inside-out, but even that could not keep her from smiling a little. Her mother's face was kind and concerned. She would risk telling that face. "It's a baby."

Her mother stopped milking and wiped her hands with the hem of her petticoat. For a moment her eyes flitted away from Una, then back again without changing expression. "Alasdair's."

"It's fine, isn't it?" Well, it was fine to her, and though she didn't truly expect her mother to feel that way, it was pleasant to pretend she did.

"That's not the word I would choose, but what's done is done." She was silent for a short while, then rose, gently running her hand over the cow's red flank. She'd left the wooden milking-pail under the cow, something Una had never seen her do before. Finally her mother spoke again. *"A'ghraidh,* no one is dearer to my heart than you, and I wish you well. I needn't tell you what the priests would say, but this has happened to women before and will go on happening, no matter what priests say. *Arrah!* If only you had a husband."

"I need no husband," said Una. "Only the wean. We'll be no burden to you."

Her mother smiled sadly. "Ah, my heart, that doesn't

worry me. But you'll have to answer to your father. He and
I were hoping that perhaps you would find someone to
love, as we did."

"I have found him."

"Aye, but you can't have him, can you now?"

"I'll have the babe instead." She was glad that all her
mother's questions had such simple answers.

"Would you have me believe this child was not a product
of chance?"

"Chance? Nay, indeed, it took great planning."

Her mother stood, gazing past Una, her hand on her
temple, as if she suffered a headache or were thinking
very hard about something other than her daughter and
grandchild. "Come away inside, my darling. We'll see what
your father has to say about this." Her mother went inside
the house, and Una retrieved the abandoned milk pail.

Una knew her father was the quietest man on earth.
Nothing riled him, except cruelty to the helpless. He was
usually so mild-tempered that the people of the district
called him *Ruairaidh Mionn*—Gentle Rory. She suspected,
though, that not even he would remain unmoved by her
news.

After the other children had fallen asleep and the house
was silent except for the spattering of rain on the roof,
her mother offered him whisky, cup after cup. "I think
there's something you mean to tell me," he said.

"Una is with child," said her mother.

Her father paused, his cup halfway to his mouth. When
he looked at Una, she saw the same anger in his eyes she
had seen years earlier when Morag Bhan had toppled Little
Morag out of her cradle. "Whose?"

She was about to tell him when he waved his hand and
interrupted her. "From the very first I knew you had a
liking for the fellow." Her father finished his whisky before
he spoke again, and he said nothing Una had not expected.

"What a terrible way to repay a man for his hospitality! Well, now you must have a husband."

"I want no one save Alasdair." He didn't seem to listen to her, but said aloud the names of all the unmarried men he knew who had had trouble finding a wife—One-eyed James, Alan the Halt, Old Calum, Pocked Peter.

"I want no husband."

He snorted and shook his head. "There's no need for defiance from you, hoyden. A man's as good as found for you, so you needn't chafe against the harness. You'll have your child, but marriage is the price you'll pay for it. *Dia!* I'll not have people putting their hands over their mouths whenever they see me."

"Rory, you selfish creature!" her mother cried. "It's your own pride you're thinking of, not your poor daughter."

"I'll not argue over this."

The two of them continued to argue. Una watched them, scarcely venturing a word in her own behalf. When she went to bed, they were still discussing her, and though they spoke softly, she could hear the heat in their words. Later in the night she woke up with the moonlight streaming in upon her face. Before she rolled away from it, she caught a glimpse of her parents asleep, their faces turned toward each other, her father's arm flung across her mother's back. A truce had been called, it seemed.

As the weeks went by, the weather turned colder but Una paid it little mind. She wanted nothing more than to sit by the fire and try to imagine the babe that was growing within her. It would have Alasdair's blazing hair but her eyes and a calm disposition, like her father's, and perhaps her mother's quick mind. She would surround it with love, and it would grow to be a man or woman of substance.

When she was not thinking of her babe or her lost love, Una tried to persuade her father to put an end to his search for suitors, but she pleaded in vain. Rory was as determined as a tupping ram. He was forever gone, in the village of Inverloch two miles from the house or in the surrounding hills, looking for fish, as Una's mother said. The first such fish he'd brought into the house was Sean Padraig, fifty at least, a widower and well-off. He sought a wife only because he lacked a nursemaid for his youngest children. When he tried to touch her arm she spat in his face.

"A thousand devils!" shouted her father, and would have grabbed her and shaken her had her mother not intervened. Padraig excused himself and left in great haste, and Una burst into tears. There was nothing wrong with Sean Padraig. He was gentle and kind, but he wasn't Alasdair.

The next month she endured more would-be wooers, all of them decent and soft-spoken. Her father had at least seen to that. But all had some flaw: one stammered, another was half-blind, and some were simply old and worn out. Una fought against them, but it was sad warfare indeed. She slipped out the door as they came in. She huddled in a corner and refused to speak. When one persistent fellow who had survived the smallpox made so bold as to kiss her hand, she scratched his blotched face with her nails. The poor man apologized for his rashness and took his leave.

"What's to be done with you?" growled her father. "Why do you shun these fine men?"

"Let me be, I beg you." Una sat in her corner, trying not to weep. She was weary of attacking people she had no wish to harm.

"Rory, Una is in love. You can see that," said her mother. "Would you force her to wed?"

"There is such a thing as propriety. It's only a matter

of finding a man she'll have, and then she'll need no forcing."

"O Papa!" There was only the one. At the thought of him and her hopelessness, Una put her hands to her face and sobbed. It's the baby, she heard her mother say. The girl's not herself.

I am, thought Una. I am. I am.

On a mild day not long after the harvest, Una's parents woke her early while the sky was still dark. "The three of us are going to the *clachlan* of Craigorm," said her mother. Una was unprepared for this news. The clachlan lay miles away, on the northern side of Loch Shiel, and Una wanted no part of a long walk through the heath. She was slow and ungainly and needed to sleep in the afternoon.

"Let me stay with Little Rory," she pleaded. "His cough is worse than it was yesterday, and I'm not very well myself."

"You'll not be well again for several months," said her mother. "I'll take the child." Her tone of voice was so firm Una could not dare oppose it. "Your father has fished out Inverloch, but he's heard of a fine young man in Craigorm, the smith's son."

Una shook her head. She knew the creature: he'd burned his right hand so badly in his father's forge that his thumb and forefinger had fused together into an unusable stump. "The boy with the claw. I'll not have him."

"You must come with us, in any affair."

"Why is that?"

"To see Seanag, the midwife. She'll want to take a look at you."

Una remembered Seanag, a young woman with straw-colored hair and front teeth so large they spoiled her smile. Una had seen Seanag almost a year ago when her mother birthed Rory, the only son she'd had who'd lived more than a few months. Seanag had a son of her own whom she'd delivered by herself. Not a woman in the district would willingly do without clever Seanag at the childbed.

The journey to Seanag's home in Craigorm was not as dreary as Una had thought it would be. The sky was leaden but the rain held off, and the sun broke through the clouds occasionally for minutes at a time. She and her mother took turns riding the pony and her father trudged behind them, leading a half-grown lamb. He meant to sell it, Una supposed, or perhaps it was a gift for the blacksmith.

A haze of blue smoke and the salt-smell of the sea hung over the tiny village when they arrived early that afternoon. Everyone in the district, from the Sound of Slate in the west to Loch Lochy in the east, knew there was a good smith in Craigorm, an adequate but unreliable weaver, a fine midwife and several families that made a living fishing the loch.

There was an inn, too, a sorry-looking stone house, bigger than its neighbors but in worse repair. Una noticed that the thatch had holes in it, and missing stones in the walls had been replaced by cakes of peat. "Look at these wastrels," muttered her father as they approached the inn yard. He cocked his head toward a pack of young men who lounged under a tree by the side of the inn, a rowan tree whose branches were bowed under the weight of orange berries. Some of the men leaned against it, passing a whisky-skin back and forth. Another was perched high up on a branch, stretched out on his belly, an arm tucked under his chin, his legs and the other arm dangling free. He was big and rawboned, handsome in the same disturbing way a wild animal was handsome. He reminded Una of a lynx she had once seen watching her from a pine tree. The man smiled as she passed him, and she trembled. It struck her that she had never seen him or any of his cronies before.

She did recognize one older man, the weaver of Craig-orm, a lazy creature who spent more of his time at the inn than in his own cottage. This man nodded at her, then glanced up at the man in the tree. "This one refuses to take a husband!" the weaver shouted.

The lynx-man sat up. "But there are some things she does not refuse, from the looks of her."

Una felt her face begin to burn with shame. She tucked her chin into her neck and hurried on.

Beside her the horse came to such a sudden stop that her mother, riding sidewise on the saddle, leaned far forward, pressing the baby's back against the pommel. The child fell into a fit of coughing. "Sons of hell!" cried Una's father. He turned to face the young men, who still laughed and chattered among themselves. They were only twenty feet or so from the path, so close that Una could smell their common odor of sweat and whisky.

"Indeed?" said the fellow in the tree. He was much older than Una—twenty, perhaps. His hair fell in sandy waves beneath his bonnet, framing a sturdy face without expression. "Is it us you're addressing?" The other young men stopped talking and glared at Una and her parents. Inside her the baby kicked and struggled fiercely, and she worried for it.

"Walk on, walk on, Rory," said her mother as she soothed her whimpering child. "You're too much of a man to waste words with these idlers. Walk on and be done."

Her father hesitated, and Una realized what a bad way he was in. He wasn't a fighter by nature, but he would stand up for his family if he had to. "Where are you from?" her father shouted to the man in the tree.

"Glengarry."

"Well, go back there, then!"

Una thought he sounded serious enough, but the young

men screeched like crows, all but the fellow in the tree. To Una's relief her father turned and walked forward. From the corner of her eye she saw the man in the tree slip off the branch and drop to the ground amid a spray of red berries. His companions roared. The lynx-man raged and swore, first at one buck, then another, but all of them only grinned, helpless in the grasp of whisky.

When she and her parents were a fair distance down the path, Una looked back at the young strangers. "What men are they, Papa? What brings them here? Glengarry is miles away." She shuddered, watching the lynx-man finger the brace of pistols clipped to his belt.

Her father pointed to a distant field, brown and furrowed, but as Una watched more closely it seemed the furrows were moving. Then the wind brought her the sound of bellowing and the smell of dung. The field was alive with scores of shaggy cattle. "Drovers," said her father. "Craigorm is on the drove road from Glengarry. They're only a day or two here resting their herds, then it's on they go, toward Carlisle near the border. Why so late in the season only the devil knows."

Una knew about the droves, though she rarely saw them. Every summer, professional drovers contracted with cattlemen to lead huge herds of beasts south to feed the beef-hungry English. Some farmers could spare only a steer or two; a wealthy gentleman might have fifty or a hundred. All these men were at the mercy of the drovers, who sold the cattle at agreed-on prices and were paid some fraction of the profit. Sometimes, Una knew, there were troubles: a low price, a missing cow, a disagreement over commissions. All ended in a broken nose or worse. If she were a cattle-breeder, she would not have trusted the lynx-man as far as she could spit.

"The brazenness of those lumps!" Una's mother said. "Making a poor, unfortunate girl a butt of their jests!"

A butt of jests. That she was. The weaver had known about her. Probably so did all of Craigorm, and even most of the district of Clanranald. Perhaps she herself was the only one who had not been aware of her own ill-fame. When the child was born, she thought, no one would laugh at it.

Seanag's house was set well-off from the others in Craigorm, backed up against a hillside as though it was taking a stand against an enemy. As Una walked up the steep path with her mother, she had the feeling she might roll backward down the slope at any moment. Riding would have made the journey easier, but when her father had stopped to see the smith he insisted on resting and feeding the horse. Una wished she could rest and eat, too. Her mother led the lamb now, so weary that it followed her like a dog.

The midwife was outside, plucking weeds from her kale-yard. There were no cabbages and few turnips in the garden, but dozens of wild plants—fennel, silverweed, and foxglove—still flourished there. A little boy, scarcely two years old, sat by a puddle, sailing leaves in the muddy water.

As soon as Seanag saw Una and her mother she straightened up and her face broke into a homely smile. She kilted her skirts up to her knees and trotted over to meet them.

Una watched her mother and Seanag as they hugged each other, fussed over the baby, and exchanged compliments on their appearance, their children, their clothing. "Is this Una? Why, she's a young lady now, no child at all. How are you, lass?" Seanag reached up to pat Una's hair, and Una smiled at the gentleness of her touch. Then Seanag touched Una's thick waist, and she felt the child inside lean into the midwife's hand. "Ah," said Seanag. "This is a quick one. Inside with you now, and we'll have a proper look at you."

Una's mother tied the lamb to a foot-plow resting against the side of the house. Not a word was mentioned about the beast, and Una realized that it was a gift for the midwife.

On her way into the house, Una took a good look at the little boy, Seanag's son. He was a sweet-faced child, with eyes the color of charcoal and sandy hair with just a breath of red in it. As she passed by him, the child glanced up at her, gave her the briefest of smiles, and returned to his game. *The boy must favor his father,* Una thought, and idly wondered where Seanag's husband was.

The house was smaller than Una's own but delightfully dry and cozy. Seanag made tea from cloudberries, boggrass, and chamomile. Una would have liked to fall asleep, but Seanag, in her gentle way, would not let her. There was so much she wanted to know about Una. How far along was she? What phase was the moon in on the night she'd conceived? and much more. The sounds of the midwife's voice became a sort of music, lulling her into sleep. From the edge of wakefulness, she thought she heard the lamb bleating.

"Is someone outside?" asked Seanag, in her water-soft voice.

A shot destroyed the quiet. Una jumped.

"God save us! My son!" cried the midwife.

Pol scrambled inside and crawled under his bedclothes. From outside came the low mutter of male voices. "Come out here, strumpet!"

In the midst of all this, Una felt oddly calm. It was the calmness that came of understanding a mystery. She recognized the voice of the lynx-man she had seen at the inn. Completely alert now, she rose and walked to the door. "Una! Stay here!" cried her mother.

Una paused at the low doorway. She could see the legs and bellies of several men and a smoking pistol dangling from a hand.

"It's the drovers," Seanag said. "Stay here, Una. I'll see to this." Now that her child was safe, Seanag had regained her steady voice.

Una hesitated. Always do as your elders bid you, her mother had taught her, but she had to face the Lynx, to let him know she was unashamed. As she ducked under the doorway, she heard her mother's shocked voice calling her name.

She saw him clearly. A cloud of gunsmoke hovered over his head. At first she thought he had shot the lamb, but it was alive and unharmed, shivering on its belly at the foot of the plow. The lynx-man grinned, showing all his teeth, and swayed slightly. The pistol in his hand wavered, then dropped. He didn't seem to notice, but shifted his weight from foot to foot, as if he didn't trust his legs to keep his big body upright. Two of his companions from the inn stood behind him, mumbling to each other.

"Connach! Fearghas! Cailean! What brings you here like this?" It was Seanag. She stood in the doorway, holding a hoe across her chest like a pikestaff. "Go on with you! You've had a dram too many."

"Not at all," the Lynx said. He stepped forward and Una stepped back, almost to the wall, afraid he would topple on her if he came closer. How did Seanag come to know these three creatures?

One of the men held up two fingers, indicating the two quarts of whisky in the Lynx's belly. He walked up to the man and took his arm. "Come with us, Connach," he said softly. "Come back to the alehouse and have another dram."

"Get away with you!" Connach flung back his arm, sending his companion staggering backward and just maintaining his own balance. If he were not armed and didn't have the look of madness about him, Una would have laughed at him.

"Go on, go on," Seanag shouted at the two men. "He has no need for the likes of you. It's you that poured the whisky for him, I'll warrant."

The two men exchanged a few words, then turned abruptly and ambled off in the direction of the inn. Una didn't care for them, but she was sorry to see them go. They had meant to help. What had Seanag been thinking, to drive them away so quickly?

"You should be ashamed to show yourself to women in the state you're in," Seanag scolded the Lynx. "What do you want of us?"

"A kiss, to begin with." Connach took another step, and Una inched back until her shoulders touched the wall. "This little one seems to be somewhat free with her favors," he said, stumbling forward.

Una searched his fierce half-smile and hard eyes for feeling and found none. She did not know whether to stand or flee. "Seanag! What shall I do?"

"Away, *a'ghille!*"

Seanag thrust the hoe between Una and the man, but Connach reached out and wrenched the staff from her hands. "You could harm someone with that," he said, tossing the hoe behind him with one hand. With no effort at all he gave Seanag a shove that hurtled her into the doorpost and sent her sprawling onto her back before the doorway.

Una swallowed hard to fight the panic that rose to her throat, choking her. The man was indeed dangerous. "I'm with child." She could think of nothing else to say.

"Well, I'm knowing that," mumbled Connach. For a while he stood still in front of her, as if his body and his brain were arguing over what to do next. As she began to creep away from him along the wall, Connach followed her, and when she reached its end, there was Connach, so close she could smell the reek of his breath. "Come back with me to the inn," he said.

Una raised her head, defiant. "I'll go nowhere with you. The drink is doing your thinking for you." He caught her arm. His fingers sank into her flesh and she winced under their grasp. What might he do to the baby? "I'll strike you," she growled, remembering Alasdair at the corrie. "Have a care." He laughed. Then suddenly his lips were pressing down on hers and his free hand was clutching at her breast. Her hand shot out toward his left cheek as if it knew what it must do. She felt it clap down on the hard ridges of his ear.

"The devil roast you!" he cried out, staggering away from her. Blood trickled between his fingers. He gazed sideways at her, his eyes stretched open, steer-like and wild. As he lunged toward her, his eyes went white and he fell to the ground at her feet.

Una stood with her back still pressed against the wall, gazing in terror at Connach's gray face and the scarlet smudge that extended from his ear to his collar. He lay motionless on his side, his mouth gaping open. Even so, his body seemed to pulse with rage. She saw Seanag kneel beside the man and take his wrist in her hand. From inside came the wail of the baby and the sound of her mother's anxious voice shushing him. "Have I killed him?"

Seanag laughed. "When the time comes that a girl can kill a big man with the flat of her hand, I'm going into my house and never coming out. I think he would have fallen anyway, he was that drunk. My God! How his ear bleeds. He'll be feeling that for a while."

"I thought . . . I thought he'd hurt the baby."

Seanag smiled, but there was no joy in her eyes. "I know he gave you a fright, but this man couldn't have hurt you or your baby, not in the way I think you mean. He was too full of drink for that. Don't fear, Una, you did the right thing. Connach had no business pawing you as he did. Did he harm you?"

Una looked down at the red fingermarks on her wrist and shook her head. Her mother came through the door-way, the baby in her arms, coughing as he tried to nurse. "It's quiet now . . . *Dia!* What has happened here?"

Seanag briefly explained what had taken place between Una and the drover, then, with many an apology, asked Una and her mother if they would mind taking their leave. "I think it's best for you and him. We've finished speaking, anyway."

"Are you hurt, *a'ghraidh?*" Una's mother came up to her and patted her cheek. The touch alone made Una feel calmer. "You look like a bird in a cat's mouth."

Una shook her head. "The sooner we're away the better I'll be."

Her mother eyed the unconscious man. "Seanag, if you have any manner of trouble, remember that you'll not be a stranger in our house. You've always a refuge there, for yourself and the wean."

Seanag smiled and nodded. "Thank you, Sorcha, but I doubt I'll ever have to come to you in distress. Connach is a good man when the drink doesn't rule him. I'll be seeing him off with the droves come morning, I'm sure."

When her mother kissed Seanag farewell and began to leave, Una lagged behind. Why did her head ache and swim so? Even though she knew Connach could not hurt her now, she walked in a wide circle around his outspread legs. "You're safe staying with him?" she breathed, her mind full of doubts about leaving Seanag alone with the Lynx.

"Safe as with my own self," Seanag reassured her. She leaned over the man and lifted his head into her lap. "It's been thus for some years, now. Don't worry for me."

Una stood frozen, still fearing for the midwife and her

child, but her mother called to her and she hurried away. After a moment she stopped and looked back at Seanag, who was gently wiping blood from the man's face. She caresses him as I caressed Alasdair, thought Una, and suddenly she knew why Seanag had asked them to leave: she loved this wild man, and she wanted to be alone with him.

As summer smoldered into autumn, Una became so round and fat she thought she looked as if she had swallowed one of the big stones the young men threw to prove the might of their arms. She didn't care for her awkward shape and constant weariness, but there was no remedy for either, save to wait.

If only there were a remedy for Rory Beag, Una fretted. His breathing had become more and more labored since the journey to Craigorm, and sometimes she was afeared that the child would cough the heart clear out of his body. She wondered if the terror of that day at Seanag's house had damaged the baby's health and prayed that her own child was not affected.

As the weather grew colder, his sickness grew steadily worse, and Una's mother despaired of routing it. One morning she sent for Seanag. No one but Seanag would do. The woman was gifted in the healing arts, and Una respected her wisdom. Still, to ask Seanag's help was a task one didn't take lightly: sending for her was as good as admitting that the child stood at the mouth of death and only the greatest skill could bring him back.

That evening Una stood in the doorway, staring into the darkness, pulling her *curraichd* around her face to ward off the sting of the whirling snow. She'd thought she'd heard the neigh of her father's pony. O, let him hurry! It was the first snowfall of the winter, a snarling storm that seemed to have sprung out of the bosom of a clear, quiet day. If only Rory had fallen sick earlier, when the weather had been better, she'd not be standing in the cold, straining her ears for noises in the dark.

There it was again, the whicker of a horse, and now the clump of its hooves in the snow. Una raced into the house and came back carrying a torch of bog pine. It sputtered as the snow struck it but kept alight, casting a yellow glow over the frozen yard.

"Una! Una!"

It was her father's voice, but when the gray pony trotted up to the house Seanag was riding it, her child clinging to her chest. Una's father strode up beside the beast and reached out to help the midwife from its back. Una nearly wept when she saw him. Frozen tears had cut long tracks across his face and his eyes were rimmed with red. "Bring the torch closer!" he snapped.

Una stumbled forward, but Seanag was already on the ground, hurrying toward the house. "How is the child?" she cried above the shriek of the wind. "Better? Worse?"

"No better, alas!" Una shouted back.

Una felt her father's hands on her back, pushing her forward, and then all three were suddenly inside. The two Morags were pressed against the wall where she'd bade them wait, threatening to cut off their hair if they so much as squeaked. Una took Seanag's little boy from her arms and helped the woman remove the plaid that covered her from nose to ankle. A cloud of snow rose from the garment. "Mama has tried a dozen vapors and tonics."

Seanag breathed in deeply. "Aye, yarrow and comfrey and sow thistle and globeflower root."

Una gasped in amazement. "How did you know?"

"The smell," Seanag explained. "Does any of it help?"

Una shook her head. Seanag took her hand. "Come, Una. I'll need your help. Think good thoughts. Take me to the poor child. And Sorcha? Where is she?" Suddenly

the house was filled with the desperate barking cough of
Rory Beag. "Quickly."

Una led her into the second room that reeked of herbs
and bile. Her brother lay on a bed of otter skins, and across
the room, with her knees drawn up to her chest and her
hands pressed against her face, sat her mother. Una knelt
down beside her and stroked her back, but she didn't stir.
Una felt like sobbing; this wasn't her mother. "O Seanag,
can you do nothing for her?" she begged.

"First the child," the midwife instructed. Una held a
candle over the babe's cradle so Seanag could inspect him.
His face was pale blue, and his skin was stretched as tight
as a hide over the frame of a *bodhran*. Rhythmic spasms
shook his body.

"Is he in pain, do you think?"

"Nay, 'tis you and your parents who are suffering."

"Can you heal him?"

"One never knows until the last breath is drawn," Seanag said, lifting the babe into her arms. "He's so light! My
little dog weighs more than this."

"He hasn't been nursing, not for a day or two. And
Mama won't hold him anymore. She says . . . she says . . ."
Her tongue grew too large for her mouth and she could
say nothing more.

Una watched as Seanag brought Rory Beag over to where
her mother sat, her hands still covering her eyes. "Sorcha,
take your baby. Hold him, nurse him."

"Nay, I cannot bear it," her mother whimpered. "This
one will live, I was certain he would. And now what will
happen to him, poor thing? I'd go in his place if I could.
Ah, it's some great sin we've committed, or the Lord would
not have brought this down on us." Her hands dropped
to her lap and her head fell against her knees.

Her mother. Always so neat, so sensible, so self-possessed.

Now she was none of these things. Her hair stood out from her head like boar bristles and her hands shook as badly as the child's body. "Please, give him the breast, Mama," urged Una. If only she wasn't so frightened to let the child go.

Her mother only wept in reply. "Seanag!" Una beseeched the midwife.

Seanag slipped the *arasaid* off her thin shoulders and lifted up her camisole so that the child's lips could seek out her nipple, still hard and dark from her own son's nursing. Rory Beag coughed and sputtered, but at last he began to suck. Now he would not die desperately, poor thing, but with the peace and gentleness a child deserved. Una placed her hands on her great belly and promised her child she would love it above all else. As she watched Seanag suckling the baby, her own nipples began to ache.

Her mother lifted her head. "Is he gone?"

"Nay, Mama, Seanag is feeding him," whispered Una, and in spite of the great sorrow in her heart, she felt a smile creep over her lips. She knelt by the fire where Seanag sat, soaking in the warmth of the flames, the woman, and the child. "How much longer?"

"It's not his time yet, lass. See now, he's sleeping." She handed the baby to Una and left to fetch the rest of the family. Una cradled the child and kissed his forehead. He smelled so wonderful, like a plowed field after a spring rain. When her father and sisters entered the room they clustered around her and the baby. Even her mother was drawn into the comforting circle of their warmth. The Morags patted the baby's legs. Her father began singing.

> Child, see how the stars look down on thee,
> They guard thy sleeping and thy waking,
> From moon rising to day breaking . . .

When Una rested her head on his shoulder he stopped immediately. Her Papa! How much she loved him. How deep his pain must be.

She saw Seanag lean forward and touch her father's arm. "You must believe none of you are at fault for this. No matter what you would have done, nothing would have changed what is happening. It's God's wish, and how are we to understand that?"

Suddenly Una felt anger rise to her face like a hot flood of tears. What did God understand of parents and their love for their children? He had given up His own Son, after all. Una held the baby close and begged him to get better. *Don't let my little one come on the heels of your death,* she pleaded silently.

She didn't go to bed that night, nor did anyone else. The Morags were the first to fall asleep where they sat, then her parents, then Seanag, with her own child snoring blissfully in her lap. Una dozed, woke, dozed, and woke again throughout the night. It was nearly her time, she knew. Once she rose to make water and in the light of the dying fire saw something thick and pink lying in her hand.

When the first light of morning shone blue through the window skins, she awoke to find the others still asleep except for Seanag. The midwife sat next to her, holding Rory Beag and rubbing his back. Her nipple lay flaccid against his cheek. She looked up at Una and smiled weakly. "He's gone. We must undo all the knots in the house so his soul will have an easy passage."

"A thousand thanks," said Una. She felt a single tear course down her nose. She'd never see Rory Beag again, never hold him or hear him laughing. A hole opened up within her as she longed to deny what she knew was true. "Seanag, please don't leave. My mother will be no help to me now." She showed the midwife the pink stains on her hands.

"Any day, then. I won't leave you."

Una stroked the baby for a few minutes, then helped Seanag lay him gently on an otter skin inside his cradle, *God take this child,* thought Una, *and grant me a living one.*

Chapter 5

Una shivered. She felt Seanag's hands on her chest, pulling the plaid up to her chin. "Will you have a dram, dear?" asked the midwife.

Una tensed at the thought of strong drink. She'd not keep it down. "I'm too hot," she complained. "Where's Alasdair?"

Seanag held up her hands in a gesture of despair. "How many times have you asked me that?" she cried. "No one can leave the house to fetch him, as you well know. The snow is too deep."

"But Papa and Mama are out in it, out on Druimm Feidh, putting Little Rory in the ground. O, Seanag!" The pain built up inside her and just when she knew she could bear it no longer, Seanag worked a bit of cloth into her mouth and Una bit into it until the spasm passed. "Fetch Alasdair," she gasped. "This will kill me."

"Never fear, my heart," Seanag reassured her. "You're young and strong and made for bearing weans."

Una sighed. She felt old and weak and as helpless as a wean herself. Another contraction, stronger than the one before it, shuddered through her belly. It was living death. She threw herself against the bed. It was worse than death. "Fetch Alasdair!"

"Very well, I shall."

"Tapadh leat." Una lay back, panting. She knew Seanag wouldn't send for Alasdair. Even if she did, the babe would be born by the time he came, and likely he would choose not to come. It was no matter: the thought of seeing him was enough.

From the front room came the sounds of voices. Una forced herself to call out. "Mama, is it you? Come quickly!"

Her poor mother! What a depth of torment she must be in! At first she wouldn't let the child be buried, but sat with the corpse in her arms, singing to it one moment, keening over it the next. When Una's father had at last managed to take it away from her, she had followed him out in the snow and cold, sobbing, clutching at the plaid-covered bundle in his arms. If only her mother would show such love for the living!

Her father entered the room, the peat spade still in his hand. His frosted hair and shoulders glittered in the dim light. "Sorcha won't come," he said. His face was striped with the tracks of frozen tears. "She says she cannot bear it."

"But this is her daughter's first! Sorcha's first grandchild!"

"It can't be helped. She's in a bad way, Seanag."

"Then father must help daughter."

Una half-listened as Seanag gave directions to her da. He helped the midwife slip a large square of linen under Una's bottom, then rummaged about on the floor until he found the lambskin Seanag had brought with her. "For the baby, Una," said Seanag, holding up the skin. "Doesn't your father make a tolerable midwife?"

Nothing is tolerable, Una was about to say, when another bolt of pain sliced through her. "I shall die!" she cried, and she knew she would, had Seanag not been with her.

"I will be a rock for you," said the midwife, again taking Una's hand and squeezing it hard. "Come, you can give all your pain to me."

"I must move my bowels," said Una.

Seanag leaned forward. "Do so, then. It's the baby coming."

"Nay, it's unclean." She was whimpering, but there was no help for it. The pain was too great. The devil take that man Alasdair! It was he who had done this to her. The pain gripped her like a claw.

"Push!" Seanag cried. She raised Una so that she was amost sitting. Una pushed, and water gushed from between her legs, soaking the piece of linen. Again she pushed, and again and again. The pain all but subsided, and in its place came the greatest wave of weariness that she had ever felt, but she could not fall asleep, even if she had wished to.

"Seanag, isn't this the babe's head?" Her father pointed between Una's legs. The midwife gasped and raced to the foot of the bed.

Una pushed again. A sudden flash of pain made her cry out, but now there seemed to be a reason for it. Something was flowing out of her between her legs; she was giving birth to a part of herself.

"There it is!"

Una cried out and bore down again. A moment later, and only a moment, her father held a baby in his hands— a boy-child—dripping wet, splotched with blood and the white wax of birth. It wriggled and mewled like a kitten in its grandfather's grasp.

"Well, the three of you had no need for a midwife," Seanag muttered.

"The Lord be thanked! It's alive!" Una cried. Her father laid the baby on her belly, holding his blood-streaked hands just above its head. Suddenly she gasped in horror. "Seanag, what is wrong with it?"

The baby's head was covered with a saclike membrane, so thin that the face showed right through it. "A caul." Seanag hunched over the babe, ripped an opening in the sac, and slipped it over the child's head. "A token of good fortune. Save it. It means he's destined for a life greater than most men."

It was the strangest child Una had ever seen. Babies were pink or red, or sometimes almost blue. This babe had no coloring at all. His hair was pure white, like new snow, and his skin was not pale, but translucent. She hesitated before laying her hand on his back. "Look at it, Seanag. Is he well?"

Seanag held a candle up to the baby's face. He clenched his eyes shut and let out a thin wail. "There, there," Una crooned.

"It's a *gealtach*," whispered her father.

Seanag gripped Una by the shoulder and smiled gently down at her. "It's nothing. With all the many misfortunes that can befall a newborn, a lack of color isn't even worth a tear. The boy will be very pale, and he'll have pink eyes, too. 'Tis naught to worry about."

Una craned her neck forward to get a better view of the child. Small wonder it was crying, with the smell of death still in the house. It was a bad morning to be born. Death and life—how easily they fused together.

She felt exhausted, but also curiously alert and far from sleep. How could she rest when her new child, Alasdair's child, was lying in her arms? "It looks like a fairy calf."

Half human, half *shee,* a child with ice-colored skin and
ember-red eyes . . .

"What?" Seanag answered. "Would you have me believe
your lover was one of the silver folk? This is no goblin-
child!" Seanag picked up the baby and held him for a few
moments, cooing and crooning to him, then laid him down
on the bedclothes beside Una. "See? How lively he is! Your
gentleman would be proud to father a child such as this.
I'll wager he has the looks of his da about him, aye?"

While her father cut the baby's cord and Seanag delivered the afterbirth, Una held the child and ran her fingers
over his plump hands and perfect ears. He did look like
Alasdair at that: the same high cheekbones and wide-
flaring nostrils, the same long legs and stubby toes. He was
indeed full of life, and it filled her with pride to hold him
against her.

Seanag took the baby from her, cleaned him in a basin
of warm water, then handed him back to Una wrapped in
a piece of muslin. As Una cradled the child in one arm,
he gave such a sudden, sorrowful cry that she very nearly
dropped him. She looked at Seanag in alarm.

"Come, Una," her father chided her, "the poor wean's
starving! Your brother was aye hungry, too, when he was
born. Mayhap Little Rory's soul has entered this babe.
Such a thing is possible, isn't it, Seanag?"

Seanag nodded. "So I've heard. It's nice to believe it.
Here, Una. I'll help you feed the little creature."

Seanag showed Una how to nurse the babe, how to
support his head and fit the nipple well into his mouth.
As painful as it was to be suckled, it was wonderful, too,
like the pain of giving birth. The baby was part of her and
she a part of him, no matter what his appearance. *I am the
source of everything to you,* she wanted to say to him. As much
as she needed him, he needed her even more.

The child began wailing. "Let me hold him, Una." Seanag patted Una's arm, then picked up the child. "You have a good rest now."

Una reached out her hands. "Please don't take him from me." Seanag might as well have been taking away her heart. Perhaps she did need the child as much as he needed her.

"You will have him a lifetime. Try to sleep. I'll be back with the babe when you awake."

Seanag carried the baby out of the little room. Her father knelt down beside her and took her hand. "How weary you must be, *a'nighean!* Don't worry for the wean; Seanag is like his second mother."

Una sank back into the plaids of the bed. Against her will her eyes closed, and in the blackness she thought she could see Alasdair's face close to hers, gently smiling. Had she really consigned her beloved man to the devil? It was stange what a body would do when she was beside herself with pain.

A week passed, then a fortnight. The baby thrived and grew fat, and Una delighted in caring for him. Suckling him became a joy, and lying down with him in the crook of her arm, singing to him as he sighed and wriggled in his dreams, was akin to paradise.

Mata came one morning, bringing the six cattle Calum had promised and a seventh, to be traded for winter fodder. He also brought news from Glenalt: Alasdair had wed Fiona, and she had lost a child early on. Una was sad to hear it, but proudly showed Mata her fine son and bade him tell Alasdair that he was already a father. Mata swore that he would, though the look he gave the babe was hard to fathom. He stayed but the one day, and no amount of pleading could make him remain longer.

Seanag stayed on, though it was clear that the midwife

longed for Craigorm. Una knew it was not her cozy bothy she wished to see, but tall, manly Connach with his cat's eyes and dangerous ways. He'd promised to return with the first snow, Seanag had told her, which meant he was in Craigorm already, awaiting her. Una shivered whenever his name was spoken, and wished in the deepest valleys of her heart that she'd never see him more.

Still, she was glad of Seanag's company, and she kept praying every night and morning that her mother would come under the spell of the midwife's gentle magic and return to the ways of sanity. But such a change didn't seem likely; each day her mother slid an inch or two deeper into her own privy world. Every morning, if it were not too cold or snowy, Una would lead her mother to three small cairns in the burial field not far from the house where her brothers slept the long sleep. But the sight of the graves had little effect on this fragile woman who, but a month ago, had been as steadfast as a rock. She would stare blindly at the cairns, then turn and walk all around the field. If Una did not take her back to the house, she would start climbing a frozen hillside or march numbly in the direction of the great loch. It tore the soul from Una's body to see what her mother had become.

Inside the house, Sorcha was no better. She spoke little, ate little, and stopped attending to all the tasks she had once borne cheerfully. Una helped Seanag cook every meal. Occasionally she could entice her mother to hold the baby, and then Sorcha would weep as she stroked and fed him. Una wept, too, knowing that no child, no matter how endearing, would ever mend the rent in Sorcha's life that Rory's death had caused. Only in bed at night did she seem peaceful enough, asleep next to Una's father, who held her all night long and slept very little himself.

Three weeks after the child's birth, Seanag told Una she was leaving in the morning for Craigorm. There was no point in staying, she said. "You and the babe are in no danger. Pol misses his own bothy, and I have other women to attend to."

And a man, besides, thought Una, but she kept her neb shut on that account. "What of Mama? What are we to do? What will become of her?"

"I can't say. I can heal the flesh, and then not always, but never the heart. Time will heal her, but 'tis a slow and painful healing."

Una went to bed that night, cuddling her babe as she listened to her mother wandering through the house, trying to coax Rory Beag out of hiding. At last Una could bear it no longer, but rose and led the addled woman back to the warmth of her box bed and exhausted husband. She wept as she made her way back to bed, convinced that no power in the world was great enough to save her mother from the darkness of her own mind.

It was then that the name for her babe struck her. She had not decided on one yet, but knew she would need to before the spring came and the priests made their rounds to wed young lovers, baptize infants, and say prayers over the dead. No name had been noble enough for her child, not even his father's, but now a name spoke to her and seemed to choose itself. "Donald," she breathed aloud, stroking the baby's snowflake hair. "The world ruler." He would have a great destiny because of his caul, and perhaps the wisdom and strength to overcome evil and shape events for the better. As Una heard her mother rise a second time that night, she held Donald close and prayed her wishes for him would come to pass.

A light snow was beginning to fall when Seanag reached her bothy. A haze of blue smoke drifted over her head, and for a moment she paused in her tracks. "Cu! Cu!"

she called, and Pol, riding her back, echoed her, "Coooo! Coooo!" But no dog ran to greet them. The animal wouldn't come within arm's reach of Connach and would not abide in the house when the man was there.

She felt her heart hammering against her *arasaid,* both from fear and delight. Connach always brought her both. She entered the house and found everything as it should be: the cow in its stall, a good quantity of hay in the manger, the fire built up in the main room. Seanag breathed in the familiar smells of straw, manure, and smoke, the smells of refuge and peace.

But the house was empty.

It was all very strange. He had been there; where was he now? She set Pol down on a bed of plaids and offered him a stack of oatcakes Una had given her. "Arm," he said, clutching an oatcake in each hand.

"Does it hurt?"

He nodded and she knelt down beside him to examine his forearm. Some time ago the boy had pulled his father's hair out of sheer mischief and Connach had pinched him. His fingers had bitten deeply into the boy's skin, leaving blue marks. Now no marks remained, and the boy was not in pain, but O, how clearly he remembered it! "I'm sorry, my heart. You must learn to keep away from your da when the Black Dog is on him."

But it was not easy to tell Connach's grim moods ahead of time. One moment he could be full of sweetness, the next full of rage. She'd known from the beginning that drink fired his temper, and more than one night while her mother was still living the both of them had turned him out to sleep in the byre. But not long after her mother died, he'd come back from a drove and slapped her full in the face the moment she rushed out of the house to greet him. "What has become of you?" she'd asked, but he would not speak to her about it, and she wondered if she had incited his anger somehow. He begged her to forgive him. He'd never strike her again, he'd said, if she but gave him her hand.

She hadn't believed him, but try as she might she could not refuse Connach. He was the only man she'd ever loved. She'd had suitors enough before Connach came, but she had never lain down with a man until the lovely summer's afternoon she'd let beautiful Connach wrap her in the pasture, with the cattle gazing at them and the sweet smell of wild thyme rising up all about them. What was this magic the man had? He could reach down into the very depths of her and pull all the joy and feeling within her to the surface. She had given up her virtue for the love she bore him.

Pol pulled at her sleeve. "Sup-per!" he demanded.

Seanag shook herself from her memories. What good ever came from dreams of the past? She knelt down by the fire and filled a black kettle with water, then cut turnips and onions into the pot and added strips of smoked mutton, a double-handful of meal, a few sprigs of thyme, and a little rosemary. A fragrant steam soon rose from the kettle, coaxing the dog inside, his coat sparkling with snow.

When the soup was well-simmered she fed herself and Pol, then smoored the fire and got into bed with the child beside her. Together they watched the dog crunching on the leavings of the soup: a bone, onion skins, scrapings of meal, turnip ends. Of a sudden the animal lifted his head and growled.

"What is it, Cu?" Seanag gathered Pol into her arms and backed against the wall. Who knew what could come to the door at such a late hour? Kelpies, ghosts, silkies, even the shee could be about, or so the old wives said.

The dog bolted to the doorway, squeezed past the plaid and wickerwork that covered the opening, and was gone.

"Coooo!" cried Pol.

"Whisht, now!" Fear seized her, and she began to tremble. "Be still, love." The boy buried his head between her arm and breast. She heard a shout outside the door, but the wind changed it into a sound only half human. The plaid billowed and parted, the wicker barrier gave way, and into the house stumbled a creature made of snow. The features of its face were naught but black holes, its hands and feet shapeless lumps of ice.

Perhaps the villagers had been right when they spoke of goblins. Here was one in the house! "Get away, *uruisg!*" cried Seanag. She fumbled for her knife and clasped its deer-horn handle. "Begone!"

A low, rumbling sound rose from deep within the creature, and chunks of snow began falling from its body. The rumbling turned into gusts of laughter. Pol raised his head from the shelter of her chest. He looked at the thing and smiled shyly at it. "Da," he said.

God in heaven! It was her man! "Love? Don't frighten the child so!"

"Why, it's you that are terrified, woman!" roared the apparition. "Have you wet yourself? You should see the way you're speering at me!"

The creature pulled off the top of its head—a bonnet— and unwrapped its shoulders, which turned into a heavy sealskin cape. Bits of snow flew all about the room, and when they settled, Connach stood before her, his hair and whiskers encrusted with ice, but human at last.

She laughed at the sight of him, a monster suddenly a man, and he raised his arms and hovered over her, growling fiercely. She shrieked, though she was not afraid, and the three of them laughed together.

"And what of you, little tadpole? Still afeart o' your sire?" The boy stretched out his arms to show how brave he was, and Connach picked him up. He swung Pol around and around, high in the air, until the child screamed with glee. His face was as red as a rowan berry when Connach set him down at last. The man squatted by the fire and stripped the sodden plaid from about his waist and shoulders. Water trickled from his hair and shaggy brows. "Is there nothing to eat?"

"Connach," she murmured, as if by naming him somehow she might control him and ease all her doubts. "I told you not to come here again."

"What was that you said?"

Devil take the man! He never heard what he didn't wish to hear. "I told you, never come here again. Yet here you are."

"Aye, but I know better than to listen to you, love." He stared into the kettle and scraped at some meal with his fingers. "In your heart's core you're glad to see me, I trow."

He looked her full in the face and cupped her chin in his calloused hand. Though his touch was as cold as winter, she pushed her face into the hollow of his palm and clasped him by the wrist. How gentle he could be, when he wished. She should tell him to be gone. "Stay, then. I'll see that you're fed. Tell me, where have you been?"

"Well might I ask that of you," he countered.

"So you might. In truth, I was burying one child, delivering another." It would be best not to mention Una; Connach might not like the thought of Seanag caring for the only lass who'd ever clouted him.

"Here or elsewhere?"

"Elsewhere. Near Ardnamurchan." How near she would not tell him! She rose and set about boiling water for drammach as Pol wove himself about her legs. "Did you just return from the drove?"

Connach laughed, and Seanag realized how much she had missed that sweet sound. "I've been back two days. Haven't I been a good wife? I've even cooked for myself.

Just now I'm back from . . . don't look at me so! Not the alehouse! From dosing a sick calf. But here! Look what I have for you.''

He reached into his sporran and pulled out a small white roll of fabric, two yards of the most beautiful lace, from Belgium, he said, fully a forefinger wide. Seanag held the lace up to her eyes, her fingers soaking in the texture of it. ''O, Connach! What am I to do with such a fine thing?''

''It suits you,'' he said simply, and just then she was glad he'd thought her worthy of such beauty.

''Have you nothing for Pol?''

Connach glanced at the boy, then reached into the pouch a second time and pulled something out. The child sprang forward. Connach opened his hand to reveal a cunning metal horse no larger than an apple, standing on a green base with tiny red wheels. Pol grabbed the toy and clutched it to his chest, as though he thought it might trot away from him. ''Mind you don't break it,'' warned Connach.

''O, how lovely!'' gasped Seanag, kissing the child's head. ''What a good father!''

Connach pulled her toward him and kissed her hard on the mouth. ''I'd make a good husband, if you'd give me leave.''

She'd never wed him, and if she could but persuade herself she neither wanted nor needed him, she'd put him out in the snow come the morning. Or the next. Her ribs still ached from the blow he'd given her months ago, when he'd flung himself upon poor Una. That was no type of man to marry. ''Tell me of your journey.''

Nothing delighted Connach more than speaking of the fine buildings and markets he had seen on his droves down south to Perth, to Glaschu, even across the border into the English hill country. Seanag listened to him as she measured meal into the kettle and stirred it with the long spoon Connach had carved from a stag's antler. When she handed Connach a bowl full of drammach, the porridge slopped onto her fingers, and before she was aware of it he'd licked the food from her hand. She shivered at the feel of his tongue on her skin, somehow indecent and endearing and frightening all at once.

Connach managed to continue talking as he ate. Seanag listened but heard little. Her eyes and her heart were too full of the sight of the man. She longed to touch him, to stroke the fine hairs at the base of his throat, but she dared not. How could she touch him if she were to be·done with him?

She remembered when she'd first seen him, a lad scarcely seventeen but already taller than most men. Her widowed mother had trusted Connach with six cattle—a fortune for their little family—and Connach had returned with a good price, asking only a small fee. He had stayed on then to help with the cattle, a month, six months, a year. A few seasons later her mother was gone but Connach was still with her.

Connach looked up at her from his drammach. "You are so fetching. Even with a frown on your face, you look like a queen."

"Go on with you," she said, and inched away from him. She shouldn't have tried to remember him as he was, before he'd struck her. "Will you have some milk?"

He turned his head. "What did you say just now?"

Seanag repeated herself before she realized what was wrong. "Your ear! O, my love! You can't hear!"

Connach pulled his earlobe and smiled grimly. "Aye, the world has been a softer place for me, dear, since I've had this little gift from your friend Una." Suddenly he struck his fist against his open hand, and Seanag flinched. "The bitch! *A 'lunaisd! A'dhrab!* A short life to her!"

Seanag put her hands over her own ears to shut out the

sounds of his curses. "Don't disparage the child so! Faith, you frightened the wits out of her. Let the lass live in peace. Surely you have some hearing in that ear." He shook his head. "I can make poultices—nettles, sow-thistle . . ."

"To hell with all of it!" he shouted suddenly, and just as suddenly a heartbroken cry arose from the fireside.

Seanag rushed over to her son. "What is it, my calf? Have you burned yourself?"

Tears streamed down the boy's cheeks. In one hand he held the toy horse, three-legged now, and in the other the little platform it had stood upon, one black leg rising from the green base at an odd angle. Instantly she snatched the horse away from him, but too late. Connach had seen it. He rose and stood over the boy, his body shaking. "Do you ken the cost of that?"

"He's just a little lad," said Seanag, holding Pol against her breast. "He has no idea what he's done."

She cringed, expecting the sting of a blow or the cry of the child. All she heard was a gasp from Pol, and then her fingers shrank back in pain as Connach pryed the toy from them. She gazed at him without a word as he threw both pieces of metal into the fire. Pol clung to her tightly, watching the horse arch its neck and flex its legs in the heat. "That's put an end to it," Connach grumbled.

She refused to sleep next to him, but late in the night he woke her and crept under the plaid that covered her, naked and warm and bristling with love. I'll not have you, she said, even as he entered her, even as she ran her hands over his back, even as she drank in the wet sweetness of his kisses. The feel of him inside her was as natural as the feel of her tongue in her mouth. What a fool she was for thinking she had any power to deny him.

Chapter 6

There were no soft winters. Una had heard Mata say so once; yet, after the bonfires that marked the new year were dead, that winter seemed especially cold and lonely. It was all Una could do to see that the house was warm and the family fed. Her mother was no help: all she wished to do was wander in the fields when the weather would allow, walking wide circles in the snow. Whenever Una watched the cattle ripping their fodder to bits, she thought of her mother and the terrible hunger that was wearing away at her from the inside out.

Her mother never complained of thirst or hunger or cold. While Una and the Morags lay bundled in plaids around the fire, eating *brochan* and listening to their father tell tales of the famine he had lived through, her mother stood by the doorway, staring at the stone walls. Twice she had slipped outside into fierce squalls, only to be retrieved by Rory. He and Una slept in turns, one of them always awake and watching the restless woman.

No matter what work Una did about the house, churning butter in the morning or mending plaids by the light of the evening fire, she gripped fast to Donald. The baby rarely left her arms, except at night, and whenever she could she sat alone with him, stroking Alasdair's bonnet and showing it to the child. "This is your father's," she'd tell him, placing his tiny hands on the tattered wool. It was important that he knew he had a da.

Sometimes Una sat with her mother, too, holding her hand and spilling out the events of the day while her mother regarded her with vacant eyes. Once she laid her hand on Una's cheek. "Una, my jewel."

Una gasped. For days she'd been afraid her mother no longer recognized her. To know that she did was even more frightening. "I cherish you, Mama, with all my heart," she said.

"And I you. Only tell me, are you a dream, or are you lost, like your brother? Should I be searching for you, too?"

Una couldn't see for the tears that suddenly filled her eyes. *Where's my mother?* she wanted to say to the strange woman before her. She ran outside with Donald in her arms, ignoring the startled shouts of her sisters. The air was as cold as steel. "Papa! Papa!" she cried, as she blundered into something as hard as a wall that gripped her by the shoulders.

"Quiet, *a'nighean,* you'll wake the dead." Her father brushed a tear from her chin. "Why, you're weeping. It's your mother, isn't it?"

"O, Papa! Each day now is worse than the one before it. She asked if I were lost, like Rory Beag. What shall we do for her?" She flung herself onto his chest, into the warmth of his plaid. As a child, she had believed he could unravel any riddle and right any wrong. Now, though, she knew better. When she looked up into his face she saw that he himself was blinking back tears.

"I fear there's little we can do." Her father laid his hand gently on Donald's head. "You have a child, Una, and memories of a man you love. Even if the worst should happen, at least you will have that to sustain you."

What was her father telling her? To accept the worst without a struggle? Everything that went wrong had a cure, she was certain, if one could but find it. "Surely we can do something. Letting her be is but making her worse."

"Indeed," he said, "but what else may we do but go on as we have? I fear we are in for a hard time of it."

Una clutched him to her, longing for protection, but from what she couldn't say. She tried to picture her parents as they had been an eternity ago, locked in each others' arms, writhing in the struggles of love. It was a comfort just to know that she had come about because of the love between this man and woman. The same sort of love had caused Donald.

The baby rooted against the front of her *arasaid*. "You'd best attend to him," said her father.

"Aye," she answered, and returned to her sisters and the silent stranger by the fire.

"Una, it's your watch."

Una roused herself and sat up in bed. Her father stood before her, a black shadow in the moonlight. "I'm awake, Papa. Indeed, I've slept but little."

"Have you?" he said softly. "Then back to bed with you."

"Nay, Papa. I'm not tired, and you must be."

"Very well," muttered the dark shape, and as she wrapped herself in her bedclothes she listened to her father settling himself down in his bed next to her mother.

"God keep you safe," he whispered, and in a matter of moments the wonderful rumbling of his snores filled the whole house.

Una sat by the fire, which had burned down to a bed of ashes and embers, a little gray cat asleep. When a stick of pine caught fire suddenly and burst into long, red flames, she watched the blaze, enthralled. It put her in mind of the night she had brushed Alasdair's hair. She closed her eyes and saw him, stretched out in his sleep, his hair encircling his head like flames.

To her horror Una found herself waking up. Had she dozed for only moments . . . or for hours? She rose and crept to where her mother and father both lay sleeping, the woman with her back to the man, his arms around her shoulders. Una scolded herself; she must keep more alert. Donald snorted in his sleep and she went to him, singing under her breath.

> Child, where go the stars by day?
> Into the arms of their fathers and mothers . . .

The baby rolled onto his back, and in the light of the smoldering peats Una made out every feature of his face, softened by shadows and gilded with fireglow. Now more than ever he resembled his da. Did Alasdair know about the boy? Mata had promised to tell him, but perhaps he hadn't. This dark thought vexed her as she returned to the fire and stretched out beside it, only for a moment.

A shaft of moonlight streaming through the thatch roused her. No, too bright for the light from God's lantern. She sat upright so quickly that her head spun. The Morags were still asleep; her father was yawning and stretching in the golden light of morning. Beside him lay no one.

Una hurried to the midden. "Mama?" Her mother was nowhere to be seen. The snow bit into her bare feet and she raced inside, her heart tripping like the beat of a *bodhran*.

Her father was awake, staring at the empty space beside him in the bed. "Where's your mother?" He pulled apart the bedclothes, searching. She tried to speak but her tongue refused to work. "Where is she?" he roared. Donald awoke, wailing.

"I know not." She wanted to scream, but her voice came out in a baffled whisper. "She's not here?"

"God's curse on you!" shouted her father. She'd never seen him so wild-eyed before. "Take these two creatures with you and find her. Find her! Hasten!"

The Morags were awake but too frightened to move. When shoving and shouting failed to rouse them, Una left them sitting with the baby and went outside to search alone. "Mammy!" she called into the wind. "Mammy! I'm coming for you!" But her mother seemed to have disappeared, another sleeper carried off by the shee. All morning she scoured the hills and corries, the glens and frozen peat-bogs. Late in the afternoon, when the shadows were stretching purple over the snow, Una came back and found her father sitting with her mother before the fire, stroking her coal-black hair. Her face and fingers were the color of harebells. The Morags sat at her feet, each girl chafing a blue foot.

"Papa?"

"My love," he sobbed, "I found her on Loch Shiel. A demon must have lured her out onto the ice while she was looking for Rory. She froze to death, looking for her child." In that one morning he had aged ten years, like one of the enchanted heroes in Mata's stories. His eyes had sunk into hollows in his face and white hairs dotted the stubble on his cheeks.

But her mother looked lovely. Her eyes were closed, her mouth curved in a gentle smile, and her fingers curled like flower petals. "Mama," said Una, crouching over her. "Wake up now, Mama." She held her breath. There was no waking.

This could not be happening, she thought. Her mother could not be dead; her mother would never die, never forsake her family. Tears streamed from Una's eyes and dripped onto her wrists as she leaned forward and pinched her mother hard on the cheek. She slapped her gently, then again, harder, and again even harder, so that the woman's head wobbled. Her father caught her by the hand, but she twisted away from him and struck herself on the shoulder. Again and again she hit herself until she thought her bones would break. It was a good feeling.

Her father rose and wrapped his great arms about her. She could scarcely breathe. "Give it over, lass. You're not to blame."

All the strength that had powered her arms suddenly flowed to her throat and she gave a long, wild cry, the sound of her heart breaking, she was sure. "I am!" she sobbed. "If I'd been awake, I would have stopped her. She'd be alive."

"Today, perhaps, but what about tomorrow?" he murmured into her ear, his voice cracking with grief. "Some other night would have done her just as well. Nothing and no one could have kept her from looking for that child."

That night lasted years for Una, and when morning came at last she woke to find her father gone. Seeking a priest, the Morags told her. It was a cold, long wait she had with Donald and her sisters and her silent mother. Una wept and keened like a fairy wife, but her sisters might as well have been two rowan trees for all the sound they made.

No one spoke a word more until her father returned. With him was a short, fat man dressed in a black cassock. The priest's face was the color of salmon roe and he could barely speak for puffing and gasping, but he knelt down beside her mother and said whatever he had to say. When he was finished, Una held Donald up before him. "Give him your blessing," she whispered.

The priest crossed himself. He stretched out his hands toward Donald. "The church will look after it for you, have no fear. It's fortunate for you our mission is to care for the despised of the earth."

Una hesitated. What was the man saying?

"She wants your blessing," her father explained to the holy man. "Donald is part of our family. His mother would sooner part with her two hands than with this child."

The priest coughed and turned an even deeper shade of red, then sputtered a few words that sounded more like a curse than a benediction to Una's ears. The creature! The maggot! Take Donald away from her! She wouldn't let the beast within arm's reach of the boy. When he finally left, she threw a stick of kindling at the doorway to ensure he'd not return. What a terrible thing, that *uruisg* in priest's clothing saying the holy words over Mama. Were she living, she'd not have let him in the house.

Una trudged barefooted through clumps of snow dotted with blue myrtle flowers. It was a long, hard walk to the clachlan of Inverloch, even with the snows melting at last and the glen turning green. She was alone save for Donald, a plaid-wrapped package in her arms.

"The black tinker is at Inverloch," Morag Bhan had told her that morning, "and 'tis you he wants to see."

What did the tinker want of her? she thought as she made her way along the mountain path. If the truth be told, Una was a little afeared of the tinker, a big, dark man who spoke in strange tongues and was said to have once stolen a child from its mother. But staying about the house was like being at a wake alone, without even a corpse for company.

The weight of the babe asleep in her arms threw her off balance, and she had to walk slowly, like an old woman. If only she had not fallen asleep . . . well, it was foolish to dwell on "if." If every pot were gold, she told herself, there'd be no tinkers.

When Una reached Inverloch, she had no trouble finding the man who had asked to see her. Half the clansfolk in the district seemed to be clustered at the back of one house, surrounding the fellow's bright yellow cart and the gray gennet that pulled it. Una could make out only the top half of the tinker's swarthy face and the tips of the gennet's ears above the heads of the crowd. The tinker had already passed through Inverloch once that year on his way north, just as he passed through every year about that time. How strange it was that he'd be traveling south through the village now and not choosing a better, fresher market. And why? To see a girl who had no money and no prospects of it?

Una walked on, her feet chilled by the frost on the bare clay. Through the throng of bonnets and *tonnags* she could see the glint of the tinker's gold earring. Some people at the edge of the crowd noticed her and turned toward her.

"Ah, Una! A thousand sorrows! Your poor mother!"

"What can be done for you? Let me do your milking."

"Let me feed your cattle."

Una knew she must be careful not to accept their kind offers, or they would be sore peeved with her. Still, their sadness was real enough. *"Moran taing,"* she whispered to them. "Many thanks. I'll send for you."

As she walked through the throng, men, women, and children stared at Donald with curious eyes. One old woman made a great show of avoiding the babe. "The devil's in this one," she said. "He sucks the boy's blood and steals his colors."

"Pay the daft old girl no mind," said one man, tapping his forehead. Before Una had a chance to thank him, he took her by the elbow and guided her forward until she was at the front of the crowd. "Here, look at this."

"O!" Una had never before been so close to the tinker's cart. There was so much to admire, heaps of bewildering things displayed without thought among the plain and the commonplace. Here was a floral enameled clock next to a copper pot, and there a saddle, and there a lacquered box dotted with gold leaf, a bolt of rose-colored brocade, iron skillets and pans and ever so many other odd or ordinary bits and pieces that drew people's fancies. Many things she couldn't fathom at all and had no idea why anyone would want them. Indeed, the tinker sold but little. People would rather have him repair their old vessels than buy new ones from him.

The old gypsy himself was as peculiar as his wares. He was nearly as tall as Alasdair and twice as wide. His iron-gray beard fell in curls to his chest and his wavy hair hung from his ears to his shoulders under a bald pate that gleamed like an egg. He spoke without pause, his voice sometimes as sweet as the barley sugar he sold from the bag at his waist, sometimes as shrill as the pipes. His Gaelic had an elegant lilt to it, and when he was excited he used words that were not Gaelic at all. Seeing that the tinker's patter was never-ending, Una called out to him. "Master, a word with you."

The tinker spun around so abruptly that a pot he was holding almost struck Donald's head. *"Diavolo!* What's your wish, young mistress? This, perhaps?" He held a length of blue linen up to her face. *"Gott sei dank!* See how it becomes you?"

"No, thank you, master," said Una, happy to have the

man's attention but unsure of what to do with it. "I am Una, the daughter of Rory, the son of Anghas. My sister said you had business with me." The people beside her turned to stare at her, and she smiled at them, wishing they'd disappear.

"Una! Of course you're Una! *Madre de Dios!* A moment, my child." The tinker reached into the bag at his side and tossed a handful of sweets into the heather. At first the crowd drew back, then surged sideways as a horde of squealing children dived after the candy. "That will hold their whisht," said the tinker. "Look at you, *mon cher*. How fetching you are! And what a fine *nino blanco*." The tinker drew back the blanket that half-covered Donald's face. "Did you know in Persia they still sell children like this for a high price?"

The man wouldn't hurt her baby; it was just his way of talking. Still, she pulled the blanket firmly over Donald's face. "You'd have something to tell me?"

"Nay, I have something to give you." He winked at her as he rummaged in his pocket and pulled out a small kidskin bag. "For you, from a gentleman who thinks dearly of you. Go on now, *cara mia*. It's paid for."

He laid the bag in her hands. Holding the baby in her arms, Una tried to undo the drawstring of the pouch. She felt nothing, not even anticipation. She was numb. Her fingers trembled so badly she almost dropped the bag, and when she at last got control of it again she held it up to her face, breathing in deeply, searching for the scent of her red man. The tinker smiled, took the purse from her, and opened it. Nine silver bangles rolled into his hand.

"Alasdair," she whispered, touching one bright circlet. It almost hurt to know that he had not forgotten her.

The tinker nodded. From another pocket he produced a tenth bracelet, much smaller than the others, made of thick intertwining wires of gold and silver. "This is for the child. The others are for you. Nine, he said, because of the nine days he lay senseless at your house."

You should have bracelets so that you sound like bells when you walk. Hadn't he said that to her? And might the number nine have another meaning as well? She laid Donald, asleep now, across her shoulder. As she picked up several of the bangles, she pinched them until they left red marks on her fingers and pressed the baby's bracelet deep against her cheek.

"Don't, mistress." The tinker gently pulled her hand from her face.

She tried to say something, anything, to let him know how she prized the bracelets. The beauty of the designs, the silver itself, meant nothing. It was Alasdair's love that mattered. But all that came from her mouth were wordless gasps and sputters. "You needn't speak." His voice was soft and he no longer seemed as tall or imposing as he had at first.

The crowd began to drift back to the cart. Una, clutching all ten bracelets in one hand, turned away from the people before they could see the marks the metal had left on her skin. If she could have, she would have driven the bracelets through her flesh to feel the touch of Alasdair's hands. "This is from your *father,*" she said to Donald and slipped the bracelet onto the sleeping baby's wrist.

Chapter 7

Alasdair woke with a start. The dream again. The outlaws in the corrie, stabbing and slashing at him, red all around. Whenever they fell dead, they rose again, fiercer than before.

Fortune was with him that night, though; he didn't cry out. His screams of terror frightened Fiona, and many a night since their wedding he'd awakened in darkness to find his dear one staring at him. Calum Mor detested his dark dreams, too, but for a much different reason. A sign of weakness, he called them. What would he say if he knew about Una's child? Alasdair would never know the end of his disdain.

His gaze roamed around the great stone walls of his father's house. There was but the one room, vast and well-nigh empty except for the bodies of sleeping servants and the few bits of chairs, tables, and benches his father had bought, bartered for, or made over his long lifetime. His father's house! If he were but in his own house, alone with Fiona and his dreams, he'd find sleep easily enough.

Alasdair rolled onto his side to look at Fiona, sound asleep and beautiful beside him, one hand draped daintily over her still-slender belly. Just a week earlier she had told him she'd taken again. The thought of her carrying his child made him grow hard with desire, but the time was not yet right. Half hidden in the shadows, Calum Mor waged war against sleep as he sat half-naked on his bed, smoking his pipe, an empty whisky-skin beside him.

Alasdair glanced at Mata's bedclothes. The last thing he wanted was Mata leering at him and Fiona, making bawdy sounds and mocking their sighs. No, Mata was gone. Once that would have been a rare occurrence, for Mata liked his sleep, but the birth of Una's babe had changed the man. Now he set off by himself at odd times, spent many a night in the alehouse, and kept company with strangers. Tell no one about the child, he'd told Mata. No one but himself, Mata, and Fiona would know of it. Well, there was the tinker, of course, but no one with half a mind would believe anything that creature had to say. Mata must have had a hard time of it, keeping such big news to himself.

Fiona sighed in her sleep. Alasdair felt his *slat* jerk toward her, as though it were listening to her. Calum Mor still sat upright with his back to the wall, a puff of smoke rising now and then, like a sentinel, from his pipe. The old man had a dim view of privacy. "False modesty, I call it," he'd say. "You can be sure everyone in this house knows how weans come about."

His own house would be different, Alasdair thought. It was his, or would be when it was finished, and he could use it as he pleased. He'd chosen the site himself, quarried the stones for the walls and cut the timber for the rafters, but bad weather had delayed him, and now, over a year later, he had nothing for his labor but four unfinished walls and the framework of the roof. Ah, but when all was complete . . .

He could see it in his mind, small but beautiful. It would have two rooms, one for living and eating and sleeping, and another just for books. Alasdair reached out and ran his hand across a familiar leather binding. Fifty-three there were, all stacked up at the head of the bed: the books his mother had taught him to read, the books he had bought in Glaschu and across the border, the damaged books his chief had given him long ago. Alasdair knew all his books by feel, the worn corners of *Pilgrim's Progress,* the broken spine of *The Decameron* and the warped pages of Dante's *Paradisio* and *Inferno.* What a pity that Una's child would probably never see a book, let alone read one.

His father would have approved of that. "All the learning a man ever needs he can get from his people and his cattle," Calum was fond of saying. "All this reading and talk of university . . . it does nothing but ruin the eyes. A man's first duty is not to books but to his clan."

And to Calum Mor, thought Alasdair bitterly. He glanced at his father and saw that the old man's eyes were closed. His pipe lay across his belly, rising and falling as the man breathed.

"*A'ghraidh?*" Alasdair brushed his lips against Fiona's cheek. She sighed, drew toward him, frowned, stretched, and lay still again. He was about to kiss her once more, harder, when he heard a low voice address him.

"*M'mhic?*"

It was Calum. His face had gone from red to white and pearls of sweat clung to his forehead. Had he not known his father better, Alasdair would have thought the old man was ill. He raised his head, careful not to disturb Fiona. "Father, can you not sleep?"

Calum ignored him. "This Una nic Rory . . . it seems I heard she had a child, and her unwed."

Alasdair's head pounded with such force he thought it might split open any moment and spill his brains onto the floor before him. It was no use trying to keep one's affairs private from Calum Mor. He should have known that by now. "She may have indeed."

"And is it you that's the father?" Calum continued.

Alasdair sighed. Well, of course the old man knew everything. His gillies ranged high and low, and nothing was hidden from them. No sense in denying the truth. "Da, Una does have a child, and it is mine, I believe. Your grandchild."

"Is that so? My grandchild, you say? Are you so ashamed of it you'd keep it a secret from its own grandsire? What could be more important to any man than his grandchildren?"

"Well, it is fatherless, after all . . ." Alasdair tucked his chin against his chest. "I'm not proud to have sired a child of shame."

"O, not proud of it, are you?" Calum growled. "Shamed, are you? And what of me? What will the people say of me? 'There's Calum Mor, whose son was so grateful to a woman for saving his life that he put a babe in her belly and left her to care for it by herself."

His father's voice was hardly louder than breathing, but so intense that the words struck Alasdair like the back of a hand. Quickly he gathered his scattered wits. "Da, I'll not speak of it just now. Tomorrow, whenever you like, I'll tell you as much as I know, which is precious little. I promise you I'll provide for it somehow. Please . . . Fiona has forgiven me. Will you not do the same?"

To his amazement, Calum Mor spoke not another word. Alasdair could hear his da muttering to himself as he wrapped himself in his plaid and stretched out on his bed. Moments later, his even breathing confirmed that he was

sound asleep. How happy he must be, basking in dreams
of fat grandchildren and cowering sons, thought Alasdair.

But Alasdair could not sleep. He stayed awake for some
time, thinking of the child he had fathered but never seen.
Whom did the baby favor? Himself or Una? Mata had said
it was a son and healthy enough, but was it large and strong
or small-boned and fine? He longed to touch it and hold
it, to gaze into its eyes. Gray, like his own? Or blue as ice,
like its mother's?

Una. Forever in his mind, even now, and him a husband.
He knew he would never forget her.

In the morning, Alasdair woke early and went to work
hauling stones to finish the walls of his house. He was
sliding a heavy rock onto the stoneboat when the little
horse harnessed to the sledge gave a sudden whicker.
"Whisht, Coll!" Alasdair looked out over the field to the
south, following the gaze of the beast, but could see nothing save the great cones of the twin peaks, the Paps of
Glenalt. He squinted into the sunlight. Coll had been right
after all. Calum Mor was striding over the field toward
him. Alasdair ambled forward to greet him, but the old
man hastened past him without a word and began lifting
stones onto the stoneboat. "Calum, what's biting you?"
Alasdair laughed, but still the old man said nothing, only
grunted as he worked, his face growing redder and redder.

When his father came to a stop at last and collapsed on
the stoneboat, Alasdair joined him. He offered the old
man his whisky-skin and Calum drank deeply, still without
a word. It was odd how his father loved to bellow curses
and insults, but when he was most vexed he said nothing.
"You're thinking of the child."

Calum Mor lowered his head and passed the skin to
Alasdair. "Have a good dram. What I have to tell you will
sit better on whisky."

Alasdair took a swallow of the burning liquor, but his

body could not contain his fear. He felt his testicles draw
close to his groin, his hands grow numb. Had something
happened to Una or the baby, or was Calum just baiting
him, as was his custom? "If you have news, pray speak it
outright."

Calum licked his lips. "I have word from Glenfinnan."
He took another gulp of liquor. "The child is a *gealtach*.
He has no color in his hair or body, and his eyes are as
red as a demon's."

Alasdair tried to imagine such a creature, but could only
recall a sickly white pup his father had drowned years ago.
"Una would never bear me such a goblin. I don't believe
a word of it."

" 'Tis true," Calum said, his voice rising in pitch as his
emotions mounted ever higher. "And that's not the worst
of it. Now you must go to Glenfinnan."

"To see it?"

"To be rid of it."

Alasdair jumped backward on his seat as if his da had
punched him in the chest. Surely he wasn't hearing him
aright. Even Calum Mor wouldn't harm a wean, no matter
if it looked like the water-horse. "Kill it?"

"Throttling, drowning, smothering . . . as you like. But
be quick about it, before its mother grows too fond of it."

"I'll do no such thing," Alasdair said. His voice shuddered with the horror of the thought. "I don't care if its
skin is checked like tartan or if it has no eyes at all. I'll
not slay my own son."

"Alasdair." A deep sadness came to his father's eyes.
"Have you ever heard of Donald Ban Ard?"

"Indeed I have." Donald Ban was Calum Mor's grand
uncle, and a terrible creature he'd been. Very few people
of the district spoke of his dark deeds, for fear of raising
the dead man's spirit and preserving his memory. Even

Mata, who loved a good story more than life itself, rarely spoke of Tall White Donald.

"Then you'll remember how he was described?"

"Aye, a big man with the strength of two."

"And his hair?"

"As white as the snow on the Paps in winter," Alasdair recited from a childhood memory, and suddenly he knew what his father was saying. Donald Ban was a *gealtach*.

"Aye. *An Searg* they called him, for he was as pale as a corpse. It would have been best for all had my kinsmen killed the creature, but no. His parents did what they could for it. They raised it up and loved it like a normal child." Calum spat into the heather. "What little silver they had went to sending the fiend to university where it learned to take on the airs of a gentleman.

"But this Donald Ban was no ordinary being. By the age of five he could fire a flintlock. When he was ten he shot and killed his own foster brother, which was thought to be a mishap, but some said otherwise. By the time he had a beard he'd forced himself on two maidens, and each bore a babe so monstrous it wasn't allowed to live."

"Just idle stories." Alasdair wished to hear no more about his accursed ancestor.

"Aye? Mind this," his father said, stabbing the air with his forefinger. "His parents refused to have him enter the house one night, as he had a drab with him. In any affair, what does the fellow do but set fire to his own house and roast his poor old sire and dam. 'Twas the fire of hell burned in him, I trow, to do such a thing."

"I remember, now you speak of it. He was hanged, was he no?"

His father stared at him and sighed in digust. "You can't hang a demon, Alasdair, and demon he was. He took to thieving cattle from his own people. What lower crime can there be? It's said he killed ten men before he was finally brought down himself by four shots and four arrows.''

"Why tell me all this?" Alasdair looked away from his father's gleaming face. Suddenly he felt nothing but shame for the blood that coursed in his body.

"So you'll do what you must, *m'mhic.* You've no choice. When the babe is older and steeped in its mother's love, you'll not have the heart to destroy it.''

Alasdair closed his eyes to crush the tears building up inside him. Una was gentle and kind. Surely her child was the same. He couldn't give her a wean only to take it away. "It's asking a great deal to slay a wean for the sake of an old tale."

"God curse you!" Calum cried. The pony whinnied in fear, and Alasdair grasped the halter rope to keep the beast from shying. "It's no story at all. It's the truth," his da went on, undisturbed by the frightened horse. " 'Tis our history, as my father told me, as his father told him. The seed of this *gealteach* saps the strength of the clan and blights each generation. If you care for this woman Una, you'll do what you must.''

Alasdair grabbed his father's elbow. He wouldn't let himself believe he had fathered a devil. "Perhaps this child will be different. An outcast, aye, but not evil.''

"And you'd take that risk?" His father pulled his arm away, and Alasdair was left grasping at the air. "You've too soft a heart, your mother's heart. But do as you like. It's your affair and none of mine. How many people will *this* Donald Ban kill?''

Alasdair clenched his fist. Another such taunt and he'd strike the man, father or no. "You can't expect a man to murder his own son."

"I did," Calum Mor said softly. "I killed your brother,

born a year before you, as he and your mother lay sleeping side by side. He wasn't even an hour old. He was as white as Una's child. It was easily done by laying my hand across his face. When your mother awoke she thought the child had died in its sleep." The old man pinched the skin between his eyes. "I never told her otherwise. I've had no regrets."

"Da." Alasdair hung his head and stared at the ground, waiting for hatred to well up inside him against this monster, but the hatred never came. He felt only sorrow for his father, who never wanted anything but children. If his father had slain the little white creature, then perhaps there was good reason for it. "What a terrible task to be contemplating! At least let me see Una's child before I decide what must be done."

"Decide first, then go."

"As it is my child, let it be my decision."

Calum Mor looked at him thoughtfully, then nodded once, stood up, and walked off on stiff legs. Alasdair sat watching his father's back until it disappeared in the distance over a gorse-covered ridge. He felt as if part of him had detached itself and walked away from him. "What shall I do?" he sobbed aloud.

The pony nickered. Alasdair went to it and stroked its velvet muzzle. How could a horse, a dog, a rat be born perfect, and his own son be accursed? Dear Una! She had nothing save the babe. If Mata had told him aright, even her mother was gone. Alasdair still saw Sorcha in his mind, her gentle face with the turned-down lips so slow to smile. What hell on earth Una must be going through, to lose her mother and bear a monster.

Alasdair flung his arms upward in anger, and the halter-rope danced in front of him. He began slashing the air with the rope, a helpless, hopeless movement, he knew, but movement all the same. It was better than standing still and letting his rage burn him to ashes from the inside. As he whipped the rope out in front of him again, without a thought as to consequences, it sailed forward and struck the pony square in its face. The horse screamed. The sound of its pain seemed right and proper. He lashed it again and again, with a purpose. Red stripes appeared on its neck. The beast reared and plunged, but harnessed to the heavy stoneboat it could do nothing in its defense but shriek in a wild voice that Alasdair recognized as the sound of his own rage.

Suddenly the rope flew from his fingers as the horse jerked it upward, and his own screams mingled with those of the frantic animal. Alasdair fell to his knees. The coarse rope had torn the skin away and opened bleeding gashes in his flesh. Aye, that was what he felt like inside: stripped.

Tenderly, Una lifted the babe from his cradle. "Won't you hold him, Alasdair?"

"Thank you, no."

Una sighed. Here was she, sitting at the fire with the man she loved, sharing a meal with him, and she could not coax more than three words at a time from the creature. "And you, mistress?" Una held Donald out toward Alasdair's pretty, fire-haired wife, who was just beginning to get a belly on her. Una knew Alasdair would be curious about his son, so it had been no surprise to her when she'd spied him and Mata stalking down the hillside toward the house that morning. But Fiona? Perhaps the woman was more curious about Donald's mother than Donald himself.

Fiona hesitated. "Very well," she said at last.

Una laid Donald carefully in the woman's arms, but the

moment she drew away from him he burst into loud wails of anger, and no amount of motherly shushing from Fiona or Una could quiet him. "It's you he wants," said Alasdair's wife.

"It's his father he wants." Una glared at Alasdair, but the man didn't even look up from his bowl of drammach. "My hands," he said.

It was true—Alasdair's hands were painful to look at. The skin had been rubbed right off the fingers, and each palm was torn by ugly sores. Rope burns, was all he'd tell her. "I beg you, let me dress your wounds."

Alasdair shook his head and continued eating his porridge. The bowl shook in his grasp, and Una's heart ached at the sight. It wasn't the pain of his hands that made Alasdair so grim, she knew: it was another, deeper pain that he bore in his heart. She could tell he didn't care for the way Donald looked. He had already inspected the baby thoroughly when he'd come to the house, and though he'd said nothing and shown nothing on his face, Una had felt his disappointment.

She forced her thoughts back to the present. "Do you wish to see my mother's cairn?" Her father, sitting on his box bed, lost in his own thoughts, murmured to himself.

The red man nodded. "After a bit. Faith, I can't believe she's gone." His voice grew soft for a moment, and the look he gave her was kind and sympathetic.

Una sat back, moved by his concern. As she was wondering what to say next, Fiona spoke up, asking for a cup of whisky. Suddenly the woman was full of questions, prying ones that Una didn't wish to answer: Did Una have any prospects for marriage? Did the bracelets on Una's arm belong to her mother?

Alasdair shot Una a nervous glance.

"The bracelets are mine," Una said simply. Fiona was

young, only a few years older than Una herself, yet there was a certain strength about her, reflected in her smug look and bold tongue. Did Alasdair really love this prattling creature? "My da has given up catching a husband for me."

Her father raised his head. "It's a hopeless business, finding a match for that one," he said. "She's never had a fancy for any man." He nodded at Alasdair. "Save one."

Una sat up suddenly, and her bracelets shivered and jangled against each other down the length of her arm. Again she stretched the babe out toward his father. "Please take him, if only for a moment."

Alasdair set down his empty bowl and edged closer to her. "List to me, Una," he growled. "This morning, two miles from this house, a woman stops me and says, 'Are you Alasdair Ruadh of Glenalt?' and I say, 'Indeed I am, but how are you knowing that?'" Alasdair paused and drummed his fingers on his knees. "Says she, 'God's truth, sir, every soul in the glen knows you are the father of the white child. Some think you've been dealing with the shee to have sired such a one, but me, I think you are more to be pitied than blamed.'" He spat into the fire, and the coals sizzled.

"Glenfinnan has its share of cruel and foolish folk," Una whispered. "That's no reason to reject the poor child who grew from your own seed, after all."

"I have no proof of that," Alasdair said.

Una's heart filled with rage. She would have slapped Alasdair, but suddenly a strong hand grabbed her arm. "My wife is scarcely one season in the grave, and the two of you that she gave life to are warring in her house like Jacobites and Royalists," said her father. "I'll not have it! For Sorcha's sake, behave like decent folk, or her ghost will come here to put a stop to your ranting."

Alasdair cleared his throat. "This is poor payment for

your hospitality," he told her father. "I meant no dishonor
to Sorcha's memory." But when he was finished apologiz-
ing he was as quiet and glum as before.

Una rose, red-faced, and gave the child to Morag Bhan.
"Poor Mata, what can be keeping him? I'll bring him some
supper." Immediately she picked up a dish of sowens and
a bowl of crowdie cheese, but she had gotten no more
than a few paces from the house when she heard footsteps
and saw Fiona stumbling after her, holding a basket full
of oatcakes.

"I had to leave the house and the smell of cooking,"
Fiona said. "The babe resembles you, ye ken."

"Indeed? He's his father's child, I'm thinking."

If Fiona were offended, she showed no sign of it. "I'm
sorry for my husband's behavior. It's not like him."

"O, it is," said Una. "He has his moods."

"What do you mean to say?" Fiona snatched at Una's
sleeve, but Una spun away from her. "What would you
know of Alasdair's moods, slattern?"

Una stood up as straight as she could. Even so, she had
to crane her neck to look the red woman in the eye. "You'd
do well to recall that your husband spent a month in my
parents' house with me, and half that time he was between
the living and the dead. If I know him better than you,
that's no fault of mine."

"Trollop!" cried Fiona. She lifted her hands high in the
air and upended the basket. Oatcakes rained down on
Una, crumbling in her hair. Tears came to her eyes, but
she brushed them away with one hand and with the other
pushed the dish of sowens into Fiona's face. The reek of
fermented barley filled the air.

The woman howled in outrage. Una stared at the wretch,
surprised that she did not feel more triumphant.

Mata came running from the byre. Suddenly he stopped
and laughed. "What sort of brulzie is this?"

"This creature threw sowens in my face," Fiona cried.

"The young mistress called me a trollop." Una shook fragments of oatcakes from her hair. She must have looked a sight, if Fiona were any measure of her own appearance. The woman's cheeks and hair, even her eyelashes, were plastered with the sticky porridge. Una looked at Mata, whose cheeks were fit to burst from trying to withhold his laughter, and she laughed herself. Fiona scowled at them both.

"Mary Mother of God!" Mata unslung the whisky-skin from his shoulder and offered Una a dram. "How sorry I am to have missed the row! *Mo dhia!* Ladies are ruthless. Have a dram, wildcats."

Una drank deeply and coughed on the burning, honey-sweet liquor, then watched in surprise as Fiona tipped the skin far back and swallowed as much as any man could in a single gulp. After another sip or two, Mata led them both inside the byre and nestled them down on soft beds of straw, well apart from each other. "Have you warriors heard of what I did to Maccus and Murdo on Cuckoo's Day a few years back?"

"I've not," said Una and saw Fiona shake her head, no, she hadn't either. Even the presence of Fiona couldn't take away the charm of Mata and his stories. "Tell us."

Mata arranged himself carefully on a pile of sheaves, settling his plaid under his bottom just so. "Well, as you know, it's custom to play some sort of prank on that day. Alasdair and I were for sending someone on a fool's errand, only we could think of no one simple enough to be had by such a trick.

"We were on the edge of giving up the sport entirely when Maccus MacIain, a glum sort of man, made his way to us and inquired as to whether we had seen Dark Murdo MacChoill, whom, of course, we hadn't seen a hair of. But the words weren't cold from his lips when Aly and I had the same thought at the same time. 'Maccus, my friend,' says I, 'not a handful of minutes ago we saw Dark Murdo walking toward the ford at Altnabeinn.'

"Now when Maccus hears this he turns pale and groans to himself, for Altnabeinn is a roaring river at that time of year and all but impossible to cross. But Maccus hated Murdo, so he swallowed his fear and set off for Altnabeinn. No doubt he had some terrible affair to settle with Murdo, as he most times had.

"When Maccus was well out of sight, Alasdair and I worked out our plan together. Then he ran home and I rode out to find Murdo. He was at his house, mending his plough, when I went up to him and told him Maccus MacIain wished to settle accounts at the alehouse of Aberinnis. 'Does he now?' said Murdo, and inside he went to strap on his broadsword. So away I fled to Aberinnis and told the good folk there, if they should happen to encounter Murdo, send him to the house of my friend, Anghas Bhan. Then away I galloped to Altnabeinn, where I found poor Maccus halfway over the stream, holding his clothes over his head and nearly blue with cold.

"'Come away,' I told him. 'Murdo has turned back. I saw him enter Red Alasdair's house not hardly a moment ago.'"

Una squealed with merriment. "O, Mata! You scoundrel! I hope the man didn't believe a word of you!"

Mata grinned. "For certain he did, my calf. Aren't I above all a man to be trusted? At least, most days. Nay, Maccus was still eager for the hunt. He worked his way out of the water and set off for Alasdair's house. Then I, my jewels, raced to home after home, warning people where they might send Maccus and Murdo so that the two would never meet.

"As it fell out, the two creatures spent the entire day hunting the cuckoo, each one going exactly where the other was not, and it wasn't until they finally met up at the alehouse of Cearnabhan that they realized how thoroughly Alasdair and I had duped them. But by then they were too weary to even think of brawling, and instead bided at the alehouse to sample the publican's brandy. The last time I saw them they were walking toward Maccus's house, arm in arm like brothers, so the prank had some good in it."

"Did you tell us all this to entertain," Fiona asked, "or to instruct us in the ways of friendship?"

"Love, I never instruct anyone," Mata said. "It would kill the whole art of the story should anyone learn anything from it."

Childish laughter rose from the door of the byre. "Will you tell us another tale, Mata?"

It was the Morags. But Donald wasn't with them. Una jumped up and seized Morag Bhan by the front of her shirt. "Where is Donald? What are you doing without him? You had the care of him."

"It was dreary in the house," Morag whined. "Papa and Alasdair are with the baby."

Una ran to the house, but Donald and Alasdair were nowhere to be seen. Her father, poking at the remnants of the fire, looked up at her when she entered. Kneeling down beside him, she clasped his shoulders. "Where's Donald, Papa?"

He shook his head, bewildered. "I told Alasdair where Sorcha sleeps, and he decided to visit her cairn. The wean's with him, I'll wager."

Una put her hand up to her lip and felt something wet seep onto her fingers. A sick feeling swept over her, and she struggled to fight it off.

"Una, you've bitten yourself." It was Fiona. The girl had appeared without warning at Una's shoulder.

Una turned to face her rival. "Would Alasdair hurt Donald, do you think?"

Fiona shook her head. "You would know better than I."

As he walked by the banks of Lochan Oran, Alasdair peered into the child's face. It looked nothing like him. Was this what Donald Ban had looked like? Death would be a kindness to such a demon. But it acted like no demon, lying quietly in his arms, sucking its fingers. It was pleasantly warm and soft and smelled of milk. Which was the lie, then? What it seemed or what it did? Or both?

Alasdair stopped. A breeze blew over him, and he shivered. He'd had to hide from Mata in the reeds, and now both he and the wean were so damp their clothing clung to their bodies. He worried lest the baby cry, but it seemed content to lie against his chest and examine the scrap of tartan that covered it. On an impulse he ran his hand back to front over the child's scalp so that its hair stood up in one white flame in the center of its head. The baby chuckled at him and Alasdair groaned. "What am I to do with you?"

Alasdair strode slowly around Lochan Oran, which shone pewter gray in the dying sunlight. He would tell the others that he'd fallen into the water with the child and couldn't save it. They would all know the truth, of course, but only Una would be truly aggrieved. God in Heaven, he didn't want to hurt her, but how could he suffer the creature to live?

Alasdair climbed out on a rocky shelf beside the loch and waited. Perhaps if he waited long enough, with the water rippling beneath him and begging for the child, he could do it. After a bit he knelt on the rock and held the wean out over the water but immediately drew the child back to his chest. The babe gurgled. Did it think this was some game? It might have been at that, a game Alasdair could not help but lose.

Again he held out the child, to no purpose. It wasn't the fear of God that stayed his hand. The Almighty understood the taking of a life and had allowed many a man to kill many others. No, it was the water itself that made Alasdair hesitate. He could almost hear its smarmy voice: *"I'll not hurt you! I'm as soft as your cradle. You'll sleep well in me."*

Alasdair glanced at the babe. Had it cried or laughed, he might have been able to lay it down in the cruel water, but it only stared at him, fluttering its ash-colored eyelashes. He could not take the life of anything so trusting.

Alasdair took the baby back into his arms and wrapped it in his plaid. There, with just its nose and a few wisps of white hair showing amid the red and black checks, it might have been his beloved boy. *"A'mhic, a'mhic,* my son." They were hard words to say to the changeling child.

He laid his own rough cheek against its soft one, and it scratched him with its nails. No, not its nails. He took the bracelet from its wrist, turned it in his hand for a moment to admire the gold and silver gleam of it, then threw it far out into the loch. It sank with a gulping sound.

Her mother's cairn was among the smallest in the Field of the No Returning. Even so, it caught the pink glow of the dying sun and stood out like a beacon against the deepening sky. The Field was a beautiful place to sleep the long sleep, a green jewel of a meadow set against the velvet darkness of the mountains.

Una knelt at the foot of the cairn. She was aye weary of searching for Alasdair and her son, and her mind was empty of everything but fearful thoughts. If her mother were alive, she mused, she would tell Una what to do, how to wait and be patient and lift her spirits. But even she would not have known what to do with Alasdair.

If he had hurt her darling, she'd rip out the man's throat. O, her dear Alasdair! She couldn't prick his finger with a pin. But if he returned without Donald? She'd cut him into quarters and throw his three smalls to the dogs. She would feel like doing that.

She watched the sky as the evening star appeared, then the Great Dog. It was what her mother called the mouth of the evening, when the children stayed outside playing touch-and-begone in the blue twilight. She remembered her mother so clearly she half expected her to be waiting at home in the doorway with Rory Beag in her arms.

She heard the crackle of heather branches. A huge shadow lay beside her.

"The devil!" she gasped. Or was it Mata, still hunting for his master? Her heart held its breath. She rose to face the shadow.

Her red man.

Una's arms and legs tingled in fear. "What have you done to the baby?"

He jounced his hip, and a thin wail rose from a bundle in his plaid. "We've been for a stroll, we two. You needn't glower so."

"O, a'mhic," she cooed at Donald. She lifted him from Alasdair's plaid, inspected him carefully, and wrapped him in her shawl. When she set him down in the heather, he began to cry mightily, but Mary be praised! there was not a mark on him. She kissed him and hugged him in her happiness, and he began to cry all the more. Then she noticed his bare wrist. "His bracelet. Where is it?"

"At the bottom of Lochan Oran."

A pox on him! Did he think he could throw away his fatherhood so easily? Una turned toward him and leaped.

He gasped and drew back but she was too quick for him. She pulled his hair, then hammered against his breastbone with her fist. "The devil the stroll you've been taking! You'd have slain him!"

"Una, let me breathe!" Alasdair gently grabbed her wrists and pulled her hands away from him. "Aye, I would have drowned him but I didn't. He's the very image of his ancestor, a murderer and worse. Donald Ban Ard, he was called. And my God! You've given the child the same name as his monstrous kinsman. My own father bade me destroy the babe, lest he grow up like Donald the Corpse. But for all that, for your sake, I couldn't take the wean's life. Are you any happier knowing all this?"

"Devil! You'd kill your own wean because you don't like the looks of him!" She spat in his face. Donald howled. He was alive, he was well. And she had Alasdair to thank for it. What was she doing, spitting at the man she loved?

Alasdair wiped his face, then lowered his head until his cheek touched hers. He still held her fast. "I spared the child. I beg you, don't ask me to love him." He kissed her on the mouth, and it shamed her the way she devoured his lips and tongue. After a moment he broke away. "I'm returning home tonight," he said, "before I do anything I regret."

"My love, pray don't leave us." She leaned into him. He took a step backward, and she thought of the morning in the corrie when she had approached him and he had tried to elude her. Her Alasdair. He was as much a part of her as Donald was. How could she live without either of them? "The sins of his ancestor are not little Donald's."

"Indeed, you're right. The fault lies with me, for getting him at all. Forgive me, Una. I did wrong to come here, and now I'll do right by leaving. What do they say? 'Better a good retreat than a bad stand.'"

He kissed her again. When he turned and walked off, she followed him for a few steps, then remembered Donald and rushed back to him. As she gathered him into her arms, she scanned the blue darkness all about her, but Alasdair was gone. Again.

Chapter 8

That summer Seanag at last made a pact with Connach. He'd have to stop his drinking and his threatening ways, and if he did she'd wed him proper. But he must never strike her or Pol again nor bring any harm to Una, the daughter of Sorcha and Rory.

"That one," he'd muttered. "She deserves payment for what she did to me." But he had pledged her his word anyway. He loved Seanag, he said. She was weary of fighting him off. It was her resistance that roused his temper and his voice, she was sure. Once she was his, he would quiet down.

For a time Connach made a tolerable husband. Because he was the youngest of ten sons and had no land of his own, he never again went back to his home in Glengarry except to deal with cattlemen, and that he did rarely. In the summer he led a long drove to the south, but the rest of the year he stayed at home and in the fields. Some nights he spent drinking in the alehouse with the other drovers, but Seanag learned not to begrudge him that. Though he gave Pol an occasional skelp on the backside, more often than not he tried to woo his son. He picked thimbleberries for him and carved cunning little dolls out of pine deals. But while other weans crawled over their fathers like so many kittens, Seanag never saw Pol so much as take his father by the hand. When Connach carried his son, the child held himself stiff in his father's arms and fairly danced when his bare feet touched the ground again. At last she understood: Pol knew Connach wasn't made to be a da. When he tried to win the boy to him it was her love he was after, not Pol's. A man like that wasn't fit to have another chance at fatherhood.

Since she knew she could never kill a child in the womb, there was but one way to handle the matter. Seanag spent hours out on the hillsides plucking moss and gathering wild plants, and every other morning, before the others woke, she brewed together bits of holly leaves, butcher's broom, and dryas root. When the tea was cool, she drank to her own health.

Two years childless into the marriage Connach was complaining steadily. This time you'll take, he'd say, and he would be so tender with her that she would begin to feel sorry for him and ashamed of her deception. But always his tenderness would wear thin by the end of a month, and he would rail at her, threaten to slap Pol, or leave the house for days at a time and return home befuddled with drink. Then she would be thankful she'd remained strong.

But while her soul was firm, her body was crumbling. Her vision blurred, her hands shook. Her hair, once thick and golden, became as dull and brittle as straw and broke off in wisps in her hands as she tried to brush it. One night, as she lay abed with Connach, he found a bald patch on her scalp. "My love, you're ill."

" 'Tis nothing," she assured him, praying he believed

her. "I'm taking a medicine to cure it." She repeated herself so Connach could hear.

"Well, your medicines are not strong enough. I'll no sit by and let you lose your hair. If you're not well by summer, you'll come with me on the drove to Glaschu, and I'll find a doctor for you there. The streets are full of physicks everywhere you turn."

Seanag sat up and put her hand over her chest so Connach wouldn't feel the wild beating of her heart. "That's too far to travel and I'm not so ill." She knew that even the greatest of chiefs rarely saw a Glaschu physician, and from what she had heard it was just as well. Travelers who had been to the city and seen the surgeries said the doctors were more devils than men. They ripped babies from their mothers' bellies, painted lead on the tongues of sick folk, and bled those who were already bleeding.

Her dear Connach! He was a willing dupe to such butchers. Every year he spent good silver on lotions and elixirs to restore his hearing, and every year he heard no better than before. And now he was bitten with the thought of curing her. She would drink less medicine in the mornings, she would even risk having the child. "There's no need for physicks. I'll be better soon."

Connach stroked her belly, and she trembled at his touch, thinking of the doctors' touch of death. It was no fault of Connach's, though. He was only thinking of her. "When the doctors cure your sickness, I'm certain you'll take without trouble."

She knew there was nothing she could say to please him, short of a lie. "Connach, men and women have no say in these matters. Only the Almighty." And, she thought, the herbs.

He was silent a moment. She could feel him smouldering beside her. "What sort of woman are you that you cannot bear me more children?"

"You have no love for weans."

"A man should have a family."

"And you are less of a man if you and I can't make another child?" As soon as she said it she knew she had hit home. Connach squeezed her shoulder up to the point of hurting her, then began to ease her onto her back. She knew it was hopeless to resist him, yet she tried, pushing against his chest and turning her hips sideways under him. He merely continued coaxing her gently into position with his large, strong hands. "Not now," she said, "not now." If she could keep him from her for a few nights more, she would have no need to interfere with the course of nature.

He would not let her be, though she struggled in his grasp and struck at his face and arms with her fists. Years of handling cattle had given him the power to be patient and persistent. "Until you take again," he whispered.

She could feel his smalls, taut against her thigh and soft against her haunches. She ached for him and rallied herself against him until she thought she would split into halves of resisting and joining. At last she slid herself onto her back and felt Connach's weight settle down upon her like a sigh. His *slat* slipped into her and he began pulling the passion from her like a weaver working cloth on a loom. Thoughts of others that she loved—Pol, Una, and her poor friend Sorcha—flared for a moment, then vanished in a numbing bolt of desire for this man who was destroying her.

As she sat in front of the house, spinning wool on her wheel, Una watched a bank of dark clouds sweeping in toward the glen from the west. Lightning crackled in the mountains, unseen and distant. Soon it would rain, but then late summer always brought rain. In a short time it would be Samhainn, the harvest holiday, and by then, with luck, the corn would be in and all would be in readiness for the winter.

Soon her hands were covered with blisters and tufts of fleece. If the Morags had still been there, her work would have been easier, but Morag Bhan had married and lived far away on the banks of Loch Linnhe. Somehow she'd persuaded Little Morag to go with her, cutting a hole in the cloth of Una's life.

Pol and Donald trotted into the yard, chasing each other around her and the spinning wheel, swatting at one another until she paused at her work a moment to laugh with them. Pol raced up to her and wriggled his toes in the tufts of discarded wool that littered the ground. "I think my mother will come for me the day." One of his front teeth had fallen out only the day before, and now he whistled when he spoke.

"It may be," said Una carefully. Every day the boy said the same thing: today she'll come. But Seanag had set no time for her arrival. "You miss her, I know, but life isn't so bad here, is it? You have plenty to eat and Donald to play with."

Pol sighed and ran back to little Donald, who was throwing stones at a pair of magpies pecking about in the midden. Una thought of the evening two weeks ago that Seanag had come to the house with her son. "Let him stay with you a while," she'd pleaded with Una and her father. "Just for the shortest of times, until I come for him."

How she had shocked Una's father out of his mournful stupor. "Look at the face on you, Seanag!" he'd cried. "If you're being ill-used, stay with us. My poor Sorcha would be sore distressed if I turned you out."

"Thank you, I can't stay." A shawl hid part of the woman's face, but Una could see what her father had meant. Seanag's left eye was black and swollen, as purple as a neap, and one of her rabbity front teeth was cracked in half.

"Was it Connach who did this to you?" Una had asked her, though she knew full well it must have been. When Seanag said nothing, Una persisted. "Faith, why did you wed him? Anyone could have told you that he'd treat you thus." Wise Seanag was an utter dolt where Connach was concerned. "Are you afraid he'll do the same to Pol?"

Seanag had glared at her. "Connach is a good man, Una. He hasn't been here hounding you, has he, though he has reason to."

Una had shaken her head in amazement. "What can you mean?" said her father. "The man attacked her and she defended herself. Sorcha told me so."

"Well, I see you didn't know," Seanag said, gazing at the floor. "He's without hearing in that ear, my Connach." She raised her head.

"I deafened a man?" mumbled Una. It was a shameful thing but a little exciting, too.

"You're not safe from this fellow, Una," said her father.

"Aye, you are," Seanag assured her. "As I've said, he's a good man."

"Good men don't strike their wives," Una had mumbled, but Seanag didn't hear her, or else chose not to hear her. Poor Seanag! She'd had no easy life, but she took whatever the world gave her without complaint. Perhaps that was why she accepted Donald so readily, and perhaps that was why Una admired her so highly.

Una had not seen her boy for some time, and she looked up from her spinning to search for him. Donald was still standing at the midden, gazing at the great black cloud that now squatted low over the hilltop. He was lost to the world about him, but when Una called his name he ran to her, waving his arms in front of him. He never failed to come when she called.

"Let me look at you, *a'ghille*," said Una. She grabbed the child and pulled him onto her lap, laughing with him as he chattered away about some childish thing. The boy was big for three years, big like his father. Indeed, Donald had the look of a man about him. Because of his fairness— she would not call it whiteness—Donald wore trews and a shirt and a man's bonnet pulled low over his head while Pol wore nothing but a linen smock. As soon as she could trust him to keep from wetting himself, Una had paid a tailor to make the lad trews to protect his delicate skin from the wind and sun. "Where have you been, my heart?"

"Looking at the man."

"The man?"

"Aye," Pol said. Where had he come from? Una hadn't even heard him walk up, but there he stood, an arm's length in front of her. "A stranger. Look, you may see him for yourself." Pol put a strand of his long, sandy-red hair into his mouth and sucked it as he spoke. With his missing tooth and brooding eyes, he was the picture of his mother. He pointed to the crest of the hill where someone was making his way over the rocks toward the house. Una studied the man.

It could be only one.

She stood up. Donald hid his face in her skirts. She felt frightened and oddly satisfied. What a battle of senses was going on inside her! She hadn't seen Alasdair since he'd left her at the Field of the No Returning. "Why should he come to see me now?" she wondered aloud.

Pol looked up at her. His hair had fallen over his eyes, giving him a sly, wise look. "Donald's father?"

How much did Pol know about herself and Alasdair? There was no time for speculation. "That's no matter for you. Go now and take Donald into the byre, then fetch Rory from the fields. Donald, you mustn't leave until I or your grandda come for you. D'ye hear?"

The children stood transfixed, staring at the hillside. She coaxed and threatened them by turns, and somehow at last they started moving. When they were out of sight, she went back to her work at the wheel, her eyes stitched to the yarn to avoid looking at Alasdair as he drew nearer, though she could hear him whistling a pipe tune to himself. She stared down at her white-knuckled hands as if they belonged to someone else.

The whistling stopped. "Una?"

She'd told herself she would not flinch when he came up to her, but she flinched anyway at the sound of his voice. She looked full at him. A flintlock rifle lay across one shoulder, a dead roebuck across the other. "This is for you," he said, sliding the carcass off his back. *"Mo Dhia!* You are more beautiful than ever."

"What do you want of me?" He was her Alasdair and he was not. She knew him and she didn't know him. His legs were still lean, but he looked broader than she remembered. Red whiskers covered his cheeks, stopping just short of his mouth. His chiseled face was marred by the same look of pain she'd seen so often in her own mother's eyes. What had happened to her red man? "Why do you torment me?"

He laid the rifle on the ground and knelt beside her. "Una, there have been so many hardships in my life of late. It's your gentleness I need now, not your blame. Did you hear about Fiona and me?"

"What do you mean?"

"The marriage is forfeit. The MacLeod, the chief himself, has dissolved it, and I'm no longer a married man." His voice quavered. "Are you and I alone?"

"Forfeit?" She could not get past the word. She turned to face him. "But why?" A handfast marriage lasted only a year if no child resulted, but Alasdair and Fiona had been wed much longer than that. Were they no longer man and wife? He'd said it himself. "What has happened?"

"Una, my lovely Una." Gently he pulled the linen *tonnag* from her head and let her long, black curls tumble to her shoulders. It was wanton, she knew, to let her hair go free, but she did not stop him as he raked his hands through her glossy locks. She laid her chin on his shoulder and breathed in his musky scent.

"Won't you tell me?"

"My babies." Alasdair's voice broke into a sob, then steadied. "All gone. Beautiful children born still as stones. The last one . . . I dug a grave for it while it was still in the womb. Four in as many years, and a fifth that was never born at all."

"O, Alasdair!" There was no greater suffering, she was sure, than the loss of a child, and she wept inside for her red man. "I am so sorry to hear it!" She would have said more, but suddenly his mouth was on hers and she was kissing him with a fury she didn't know she possessed.

Water splashed on her forehead. Una looked up to behold the same black cloud Donald had been watching, only now it was directly overhead, lower and blacker than before. "There's rain in it," she mumbled, just as the cloud broke open with a splintering crash. Raindrops danced into her face and pearled on Alasdair's beard, but she was in no hurry to break his loving embrace.

"Come away now," he said, taking her hand. Then he stopped and stared at her arm.

She rose, and he rose with her, but neither made a movement to leave. Rain silvered Alasdair's eyebrows and drizzled down his face, but still he stood firm. "Your bracelets," he said. "I count seven."

"Let's in and I'll tell you!" gasped Una, for now the rain began to fall in earnest. Her *arasaid* hung on her like a dead animal.

"Tell me now."

"Two went to the tailor at Inverloch," she shouted over the rain. "For trews for Donald. Consider these two as payment for the one you threw into the loch." Oh, but she could be cruel to him, even when she didn't want to be.

"Come into the house."

It was peculiar, Alasdair inviting her into her own house, but she went with him, lugging the spinning wheel while he dragged the roebuck after him by its hind legs. Inside, she added a peat to the fire and brought him a cup of cream. If he had any notion of how her heart was breaking just to see him there, he'd have left her alone. "Do you recollect the last time you came to the house? It fairly killed me when we parted."

"Una." He touched her hair, and she drew away from him. "All I've ever wanted is a family. A loving wife, an . . . ordinary child, or several, if the Lord would see fit. But I could keep Fiona no longer. I couldn't stand the sight of her, though she was my wife and I loved her. I couldn't lie with her for fear of losing another wean." He paused to sip the cream.

Una looked at him but she could not think of anything to tell him that would make his lot easier. Four years of dead children—Alasdair indeed must have loved Fiona! Still, he loved the thought of beautiful, healthy children even more. Was that why he'd come, because she'd given him a living child? Una remembered Fiona standing by the byre, her face dripping with sowens. She was sorry for Alasdair's wife and happy for herself at the same time. "What of her, then?"

"I've tried to do right by her. I've returned her dowry to her and taken her back to her parents, but she's always in a hundred pieces over something, and her family is none too happy with her." He stopped and looked down at the floor. "They say she's touched."

He knelt before her and she took his hands in hers to steady herself. "Fiona? Mad? You don't believe it, do you?"

"Indeed not. Anyone would be addled by so much misfortune."

"Why did you come here, then?"

Alasdair leaned closer, gently forcing her backward, and cupped her breast with one hand. *"Arrah!* but you are bewitching, woman!"

She cried out in anger and brushed his hand aside. "Is that what brings you to Glenfinnan?"

She knew by the dark expression on his face that she'd hurt him. "I've never been able to put you from my mind. My love, I'd never harm you, but you tempt me so, and I'm nothing more than a man. Una, my heart. My love." He ran his fingers over her cheek. "Tell me to go, and you won't need to ask me a second time."

"Don't go," she pleaded, grasping the hand that stroked her face. If he were free to marry again, he must marry her. And if he would not marry her . . . well, she would leave her father for him, she'd leave Glenfinnan and the graves of her ancestors. But she could not leave her child. "What of Donald?"

"I promise you, I'll never lift my hand against him," Alasdair said. "I have a plan for the boy." He smiled, and she knew she could trust that smile. "In good time, I'll speak with you about it, but now's not the time."

When he bent his head toward her again, she moved her mouth to his lips, then drew back, aghast. Blood trickled from both nostrils, down his cheek, into his whiskers. "You bleed from the nose!" He stood upright and swiped his hand under his nostrils. Blood gushed onto his knuckles. It spattered her sleeves and his collar.

"A thousand murders!" someone shouted. "Heaven preserve us!"

Una struggled to put words together while holding Alasdair's plaid against his nose. Her father stood at the door, his head cocked in bewilderment. Pol and Donald huddled behind him. "Nosebleed," she said at last.

"They say that's the sign of true love," her father ventured. At that, Alasdair laughed, and Una knew he was not badly hurt, that the worst of the bleeding had stopped. She mopped his face with her stained sleeves.

Alasdair looked at her, then at her father. There was something very familiar and tender about his red-smudged face and the blood on his shirt. "I love your daughter," he told Una's father. "I'll have no other for a wife, should she meet my conditions."

Una was sure she'd not heard him clearly. "You wish to wed me?"

"If you'll have me."

She burst into sobs and grasped his hand to show him that she wept from joy and not despair. Alasdair and Donald were all she ever wanted. Suddenly she knew the terms of his proposal. He wanted another babe. Beforehand.

"What can you mean, wed her?" her father sputtered. "You'd talk of marriage? You, a husband already?"

"My childless marriage is dissolved," Alasdair whispered. "Fiona can bear me no children."

"I'm sorry to hear it, Alasdair Ruadh," said her father. He seated Alasdair in a chair by the fire. "This is madness," he said. "My family has had nothing but madness since I brought you down from the corrie into this house. Although," he quickly added, "it was an honor to help you."

Una could not hear Alasdair's reply and she could not quite make out her father's answer to what Alasdair had said. While the men continued talking, she set about the motions of preparing supper, her mind scarcely aware of what her hands were doing. So many years she'd waited for nothing but this one pinprick in time. Her head spun with happiness. Alasdair would never leave her again.

When Seanag returned from Una's house the dog was nowhere to be found. "Cu! Here, Cu!" She waited a bit and called again. "Cu!"

Connach was in the house. He'd built the fire up so hot that she could see its light as she approached the *tigh* and thought she could feel its warmth riding on the cold night air. When he met her at the door with a cup of warm milk and whisky, she let her hands linger on his for a moment, delighting in their warmth.

"Where's Pol?" he asked.

"Away, until I'm sure he's safe from you."

"What! The devil's plague on you, woman. I've done the lad no harm."

"Aye." Seanag sat down to drink her milk, and it was all she could do to keep from looking at him. "But you gave me your word you'd not strike me, either, and you see what that's come to."

"Didn't you give me cause?" He squatted beside her, and then she did look at him. He'd not had a drop; his voice was clear and his eyes were bright. He reminded her of the Connach who had told her stories and made her laugh so long ago. She'd lost her heart to that Connach. Was he still there, inside this one? "Seanag, I'm asking no more than any other man wants, a family and the love of my wife. These potions you've been drinking have addled your mind and made you lose flesh."

Aye, her potions. She remembered one morning some days ago. He had been watching her, although she was sure he and Pol were still asleep. She had thought it safe to sip a new medicine, mistletoe crushed in whisky—not nearly strong enough, she thought, to do real harm. But a few moments after the first sip a great pain seized her forehead and for an instant she could see nothing but white. It was all she could do to set the cup down on the table. When she could see again, Pol was at her side by the table, the cup in his hands.

"Pol. Stop." Was she shouting? Or whispering? She couldn't tell. The child's head snapped up. He stared at her. Suddenly he dropped the cup and bolted from the house.

"Seanag, what did you drink?"

It had taken her several moments to realize Connach was awake and even longer to understand that he was speaking to her. "Medicine," she'd told him.

He had come up to her so close she could feel his bare skin against her knee. "A strong medicine, that. Strong enough to kill a child in the womb, I warrant."

Her vision disappeared in a fresh bolt of pain. When she could see again, she tried to speak to him. "I'd never harm a child, husband. Surely you know that. My elixirs keep a child from forming."

She was not certain of what had happened next, whether Connach had thrown the cup down and struck her with his hand or flung the cup into her face. The force of the blow was so great she fell to the floor. She felt one of her teeth snap apart as a wave of pain engulfed her.

Connach jerked around and slammed his fist onto the table. "Why do you make me do this?" he roared. "Do you think I wish to hurt you? All I want is my due. I'll not tell you what they say about me at the alehouse. I thought they might be right. But all this time it was you who's been destroying my seed. Why?"

Because you're a bad father, she wanted to tell him, but she knew he didn't wish to hear her answer. He turned toward her and she closed her eyes, imagining another blow. None came, and she could hear him moving about as he dressed and finally left the house. When she could hear his footsteps in the yard she opened her eyes and called out his name. He'd broken his word again. She could forgive him that. It was the thought of being without him that she couldn't bear.

Seanag shook her head to dispel the memory. The smell of porridge and venison filled the room, and she heard her stomach growling. Connach finished his cooking and served her with great care. It was a strange sort of meal, eaten in silence, without Pol's chatter or Connach's roaring. "I've missed you sorely," he told her after they'd finished eating and Seanag had collected the wooden bowls and cups.

"Did you think I'd left you forever?"

He smiled. "No, I knew you'd be back, and I wager it won't be long until Pol is back as well. You can't live long without him." Sometimes he made her ill, the way he thought he knew everything about her. But it was true: she couldn't live without Pol, and she could not live with him and Connach together. She sat down before the fire, stroking her temples and trying to think.

"Are you cold, love?"

She nodded. Lately she was cold all the time, ever since Connach had made her stop drinking her medicines. She had promised to stop, but that hadn't been enough for him. He woke whenever she awoke and watched her from the bed. He trusted her as little now as she trusted him.

He sat down beside her and draped his plaid around her. "I have something for you, my love." He reached into his sporran and took out a tiny package wrapped in vellum. "This will make you well again."

Seanag opened the package and found a small box filled

with an evil-scented husk that looked like black driftwood. "What is this?"

"The poppy. It will cure you, *a'ghraidh.*"

Seanag shut the box and threw it onto his lap. "Nay, you may keep it! I've heard of the dreaming death. It swallows one's mind and gnaws a black hole in the heart." He gave her a lopsided grin. Might the man be foolish enough to believe it would help him? "Don't go taking it yourself, now," she cautioned him.

"Nay, love, it's for you. But if you'll not have it, I'll find another cure for you." He pulled her toward him and kissed her deeply. It would have been easy to give in to him then, his sweetness and love and the very warmth of him, but she excused herself to visit the midden.

The midden lay some twenty feet from the back of the house, a formless shadow-heap that stank from the waste of a thousand creatures living and dead. Seanag did not mind the smell. It was the scent of life, not death. She pulled a gray-green clump from the cuff of her sleeve, a ball of lichen and velvet moss so soft that Connach could not feel it, yet so thick that it would trap his seed in its thousand tiny arms. Her mother had told her of it, as she had told Seanag about all the other friendly plants. The moss was not much use without the medicines, but it was something sweet and wholesome that would not destroy what was left of her.

When she was finished, she breathed in the warm, welcome stench of the midden before she went back to the house.

Una was always awake before anyone else. Because of what she had done to her mother, she never slept deeply now. It was a penance she was glad to pay.

Outside it was still dark. Sleet fell in sheets against the

house, and she could almost hear it striking the corn that still lay in the field, waiting for the hand of the harvester. But none of that mattered now because every morning she woke up like a wife, on a warm feather mattress in a box bed next to Alasdair. Una nestled against his bare back, soaking up the strong male scent of him.

This was the same room he'd slept in when he'd come down off the corrie so many years ago, but it had been a room of sickness and sorrow then. Now it was a private nest for the two of them. She kissed his shoulder and found it chill on her lips. She'd build the fire and warm the house for her betrothed.

Out in the main room her father was sleeping soundly, the children clustered around him. For the week that Alasdair had been with them, poor Donald had suffered mightily. He was used to sleeping by his mother's side, but Alasdair would not allow it, so Una had not allowed it. The first few nights Donald had wakened her with his weeping and she had gone to him, reassuring him she was there and that she loved him and her love would always be with him.

Una laid fresh peats on both fires and soon a pocket of warmth began to form in the house. When she returned to Alasdair, she knelt down beside him and took him in with her gaze as best she might in the dim glow of dawn. She didn't want to wake him, even with kisses, but if she did, she knew she would have the joy of seeing his face light up with a foolish smile and feel the comfortable weight of his arms on her back. She remembered their first night together, two days after his arrival, and laughed to herself at her innocence.

"You know how this will hurt me," she'd told him. "Is there no other way to make weans?"

He had been lying atop her, kissing her neck, when he suddenly turned his head aside and began laughing until

142   *Megan Davidson*

tears glittered in his eyes. "*A'ghraidh,* you've borne a child. My poor old fellow at his finest is no size at all compared to a baby."

Because he was so logical, she'd not believed him at first and shied away from him and the memory of the pain he'd caused her at the corrie. But when she surrendered to him at last she discovered he'd been right. He fitted into her with the ease of an old friend paying a visit to the house. It was another piece of the lore of man and woman that her mother had failed to tell her.

Under the plaid, Alasdair began to move. First he rolled onto his left side, then onto his back. A playful thought entered Una's mind. She pulled aside the plaid which covered Alasdair's middle and gently laid her hand on his stones. They were cool and rippled, like real stones partly polished by the waters of the loch. Just then his arm shot up to his face and he kicked the plaid from his legs. "My love!" cried Una. She grabbed his arm, raised to ward off the blow of an invisible broadsword. The black dreams she'd hoped had vanished were back in force. "Alasdair!"

He sat up so suddenly that she fell onto his chest. His eyes were white circles with black centers, and she knew by the way he stared at her that he was looking at something deep within his mind and didn't see her at all. She crept forward and took his hand, certain she could allay his fear. "Back to sleep with you." She touched his cheek and he shuddered. If only he would cry out, as he had in the old days. A moment passed, and she could see by the warm glow in his eyes that he had returned to her. "Was it the corrie?" she asked. He shook his head. "Can you speak of it?"

Again he shook his head and slumped into her arms. Some new horror, greater than the one she had saved him from, had invaded his dreams to haunt him. All the love in her body went out to him. "Come, I'll show you something."

He lifted his head. What a relief to see him smiling! "I'll never forget the last time you came to my bed to show me something."

"This will be different." She took an unlit candle from its sconce and led him into the big room. Her father was stirring, but the boys were still asleep, huddled together by the fire under a pile of plaids. She lit the candle in the embers of the fire and shone its light over the sleeping children. "See? How beautiful they are!" Both boys looked golden in the candlelight.

Alasdair nodded, and she knew he was thinking of Donald. She hadn't wanted to ask him again, but with the lad lying in front of her so fair and serene she felt she had to. "What of my poor Donald? What will become of him?"

"Fosterage," he said, without a moment's hesitation. "I've given this matter some thought, and fosterage is the answer. Donald can live with a cousin of mine on Duneilean, in the Sound of Sleat, just north of the Isle of Skye. O, 'tis a lovely island, Una, with the waters lapping all around it and the *marchairean,* wide and white, perfect for playing. The children all learn to swim like otters. My cousin—Calum, like my father, so we call him Cali—he's a fine fellow."

Skye! So far away! She didn't like the sound of it. A tedious journey west through the mountains, then a long ferry ride. She'd not see her darling but once or twice a year. "Donald's too young to go so distant."

Alasdair smiled. "Don't fret. He needn't leave for a few years. O, Una! Cali has such a fine family! Six children, and one a boy about Donald's age. Donald will grow up free and good-hearted, away from the wickedness of the rest of the world."

"Unlike Donald Ban."

"Well, aye. Had Donald Ban been raised on Duneilean, away from the company of evil people, he might have been a better man, too."

"I will keep our Donald from bad company," she said, forcing herself to believe her words.

"Hah! When he's older, you'll not be able to keep him from leaping into Loch Shiel if he wishes to."

Una knew he was right, but she was resolved to do whatever she could for her uncommon child. "Alasdair, Donald must never hear about Donald Ban. It will cause him nothing but grief, for he'll see his fate sealed in the story."

Alasdair snorted and put his hand to his chin as he considered the matter. "As you wish. I will tell Mata and he will spread the word, you can be sure. In any affair, Donald Ban is scarcely mentioned anymore, even in his own birthplace, his memory is so black. There's nothing else troubling you, my love?"

There was nothing, save that she'd never see her poor child until he was grown. When she told Alasdair her fears, he was quick with an answer. "I'll arrange that you see him all summer long, more often if you wish. And Cali's boy will live with us, at least for part of the year. I've spoken to Cali about it, and he's keen on the thought of having another son."

Una sighed. That was the worst thought of all, that Donald would become a stranger to her, closer to distant relations than he was to his own mother. "If it must be, then it must be," she said. It would do no good to fight Alasdair, not when his mind was set. It might happen in the coming years that the man's heart would change toward the boy. It might also happen that Alasdair would leave her.

"There's a lass. Think on what I've said." She let Alasdair lead her back to the box bed in their little room and lowered herself onto his lap. "I love you, Una," he said, covering her neck with kisses. "Years ago, when I awoke and first saw you in this very room, says I to myself, if I'm dead I'm glad of it."

"Go on with you," she said, but laughed and ran her fingertips over his craggy cheekbones. She never tired of the hard, manly ridges of his face. He kissed her as his hands sought her breasts, and she pressed herself against him until she could feel the throb of his heart against her own. She loved the very life of him, the life she had preserved.

Did he love her? He'd walk away from her, as he'd walked away from Fiona, if there were no child or another child like Donald. She wouldn't think such things. She was loam, Fiona was clay. Alasdair's seed would not grow in Fiona, but in her it would thrive like the heather.

Chapter 9

Alasdair helped Una and her father bring in the harvest, going to the fields before dawn and returning to the house only when darkness came. But when the harvest was in, he told her he was leaving for Glenalt. "Stay a while yet," she begged him.

"I'll be back in a fortnight, love. There's Calum's corn to be brought in and the cattle to be taken down from the high pastures."

He left her with many a kiss and promise, but he left her all the same, only a few days before Samhainn, the harvest holiday. There was nothing for it but to spend the festival with her father and his brother in Inverloch and, while it wasn't what she wished, it was pleasant enough. Outside her uncle's house the air rang with the sound of sticks against leather and legs as the children played shinty on the frozen ground. Inside, the older folk sang and danced and made merry. Some of the women fashioned a doll out of the last sheaf of corn—"the maiden," they called it—and dressed it up in a shirt and blue ribbons, then took turns guiding it around the floor to the music of the pipes.

Una listened to two old men weave stories by the fire, each trying to best the other with a tale more gruesome than the one before it. Here was one about the water-horse, and another about the silkie—a man on land, a seal in the sea—and yet another about a young maid hope-lessly in love with a fairy-man. Una noticed that more than one listener glanced at Donald as the stories spun on, but Donald seemed not to care. The tales enthralled him.

A fortnight after the harvest holiday, Seanag came to Glenfinnan. The weather was bitter cold, and Una draped her shawl over Seanag as she led the midwife into the house. "Look how thin you are, woman!" cried Una. "Aren't you well?"

"Well enough, thank you. Where's my Pol?"

Donald wept and screamed at the thought of losing Pol, and even Una's father was so distressed he asked Seanag to stay until the weather turned softer. She thanked him but refused his kind offer, staying only the one night. Although she made polite conversation, never once did she mention her husband's name. Una knew it was useless to make her speak of the man. She'd go to her death defending him.

Hogmanay came and went, then Saint Brigid's Day. Still Alasdair did not return. Una was beside herself with fear and foreboding, though her father tried to assure her it was the cold and snow that kept her man in Glenalt, not a change of heart, nor some buxom enchantress. "He may have returned to Fiona," she worried aloud to him one evening around the fire, "or else his da may have per-suaded him to forsake me."

Her father would have none of it. " 'Tis an odd arrange-ment the two of you have, I'll grant you," he admitted, fishing for his pipe in his sporran, "and I'll not deny there have been times I felt like striking Alasdair for not taking you to a priest. Yet if ever man loved woman, this son of Clan MacLeod loves you, *a'ghraidh*. I can tell by the way he lifts his head whenever he sees you. I have no doubt but that he'll wed you proper, once his terms are met."

How fortunate that he'd raised the matter himself, Una thought. She'd had her suspicions for some time and was now nearly certain. "We may not have all that much longer to wait, Papa."

Her father's eyes lit up with the sort of cautious ecstasy she hadn't seen since her mother was alive and well. "You've taken, have you?" She nodded, and his face cracked open in a smile. "Well, that's grand!" To her great surprise, her father caught her by both hands and whirled her round and round, as he had when she was little. They fell to the floor in a heap, whooping and laughing. "Alasdair will be as pleased as a cat by the fire, once he returns."

"Sure enough," Una whispered, fighting back the dread that suddenly filled her heart. "Once he returns."

Lambing-time came, but not Alasdair. Snow fell afresh and the wind still blew raw into Una's face. She wondered if he loved her so little that he would not brave bad weather for her. It was at lambing-time she'd found him on the corrie, years ago. He should have been with her now as he was with her then. He owed her that much, at least. There was no question now that a child was growing inside her.

"What ails you, Mama?" Donald chided her one night as he tried to sit in her lap while she carded wool. "You're so fat."

"She's with child," her father said. "She's making you a brother or a sister. The baby is growing inside her and makes her big."

"Bring Pol back instead. I want no baby."

"Your mother does, and your father."

"I have no father," Donald announced in a soft, dull voice. "Pol said the shee gave me to you."

Una shivered. "Pol is mistaken, love. Alasdair is your father." She pulled the boy onto what was left of her lap and urged him to pat the babe inside her.

Donald put his hand on the bulge in his mother's middle and began pushing on it so hard she had to grab his hands to make him stop. He whined, and she released him, only to seize him by the arms again a moment later as he dug his fists into her belly. "I'm making it go away," he explained.

"You can't, *mo chreidh.*"

Donald twisted about in such a fury she was afraid she might hurt him if she did all she could to restrain him. At last her father seized the boy and struck him on his hurdies. Donald yelped, and Una winced. The child ran to the corner and curled up in a ball, his fingers in his mouth, whimpering to himself. The poor wean! She went over to him but he wouldn't look at her, and at last she walked back to her father.

"Don't strike him again, Papa."

"He'd have hurt the babe."

Una patted her father's arm. "You mean well, I trow," she reassured him, "and I know you care for Donald. Still, his life will be hard enough without the back of your hand on him."

"Ha!" Her da took his tobacco bag from his sporran and filled his pipe. "Life's not all honey and cream. There's the bitter part of it, too, hard things he must learn to accept." Her father stopped for a moment and stroked his chin. Una knew he was thinking of her mother, and at once felt sad herself.

"Donald is different," she said. "He'll need more affection than other weans to face the petty folk who cannot abide him as he is."

Her father shook his head and lit his pipe with a stick from the fire. "Folk such as Alasdair?"

That hadn't occurred to her, though she could see it was true. Alasdair still had no feelings for the boy. Una lifted her head high and looked full into her father's face. "Alasdair will warm to him in time."

Her father nodded. "A'nighean, do whatever you think best. You know the switch is the last thing I reach for." He puffed on his pipe, and a cloud of pungent smoke rose from his mouth.

Una sat down beside Donald, and this time he let her hold him against her breast and sing to him. It wasn't possible to love a child too much, she thought, especially a child like Donald. He would grow as strong and fine as his father, if only he had love enough to nurture him. And if it could not come from Alasdair, so be it.

He came back on the very first day of fair weather, with the smell of violets in the air. Mata walked at his side, and when Una saw them approaching the house, bantering and laughing, she thought it might not be so wretched to have Donald leave her, if only he could develop a friendship like that between his father and Mata. She left the cattle grazing in the pasture and hurried toward Alasdair, supporting her belly with one hand. Let him see her now and let him have a good explanation for his absence!

Alasdair and Mata carried their long German rifles on their shoulders as they walked. When they saw Una they both stopped short, the barrels of their guns clanging together like swords. Mata took a good look at her and gave a low whistle. "It's a good thing you left her when you did, Alasdair, or she never would have taken."

"When, love?" murmured Alasdair.

"Don't fret. It won't interfere with the harvest." She

wouldn't give him the satisfaction of saying how she'd missed him or needed him, and she hoped he hurt a bit, as she had.

"That's fine, that's grand," he said, striding up to her and laying his hand on her swollen midriff. She smiled in spite of herself; she'd missed his touch more than she'd thought. "We've nothing to do but wait, then. Forgive me, but I had no idea. If I had, I would have stayed."

"So I'm thinking," she said, unable to resist him any longer. She slipped her arms around his middle and clung to him a long time, ignoring the bite of his sporran as it dug into her big belly. How good it felt to hold her red man, to smell his sun-warm scent. "What kept you, Alasdair? I was sore worried."

The three of them began heading toward the house. "It was Calum Mor," Alasdair explained. "The *bodach* fell and hurt himself. He was too sick and dizzy to walk, and he was some time in the mending. I had to see to the calving of the heifers and the gelding of the young bulls—all he couldn't do that had to be done. I would have sent you word, but the snows were deep this year."

"And Calum? Is he still sick?"

Alasdair snorted. "That old rogue? Devil the bit! He's as spry as a hare. *Dia!* What a bother old people are!"

Una squeezed his arm, basking in the joy of being near him again. "I hope we shall have the fortune to grow very old together," she said, "and be a great bother to a great many."

Alasdair was afraid for his beloved. He watched her anxiously with each passing week as she became bigger and bigger, her feet so swollen that she could neither wear shoes nor go barefoot in the heather. She seemed well enough, but Fiona had, too. "What if something goes amiss?'' he asked Una one night in bed, but she only smiled and shook her head and told him he must have been shot by the shee to worry the way he did. All would be well, she insisted.

But all was not well between himself and Donald. Alasdair did his best with the boy, but it was not very good. Whenever he was with the child he wished he could be elsewhere, and though he played shinty with Donald and took him walking in the hills with Mata, he never thought of himself as the lad's father. If the creature threw a stone at a bird or pulled a dog's tail, Alasdair would ask himself, *Is this how Donald Ban behaved as a wean?*

Worst of all, his dreams had changed. Instead of struggling with outlaws in the corrie, now he was holding Donald underwater, smothering the child with his plaid or, most terrible of all, shooting the boy in the heart. But always Donald would rise from the loch or the heather, not a child any longer but a full-grown man. Alasdair woke from these dreams in a sweat, but he knew they must be false. He would never harm Una's boy.

The weather grew warmer and fairer as summer approached. Heather and gorse bloomed together, dappling the hills with amethyst and gold. By midsummer, Una was beautifully big and sweaty. Alasdair hunted often, not only for meat nor for the love of the mountains nor even to escape Donald, but to get away from Una and the hopefulness he felt whenever he looked at her. The life was fairly bursting from her, but nature had deceived him before.

One especially fine day he spent hours belly-down in the heather, stalking a red hind that was never quite within rifle range. She browsed before him, stepping away when he drew near, coming closer when he retreated. She was a wise old thing. He knew if he waited motionless for a minute more, an hour more, or half a day, eventually the beast would approach him and present herself. Thoughts of Una and her unborn, Calum and Mata and Fiona and his clan and house and books and all that mattered to him, left his mind as he concentrated on the wary animal. Finally the deer took a step in his direction, then another, then turned and presented a clear shot to the heart. Alasdair squinted and took aim.

He felt a hand touch his haunches.

Alasdair cried out. A great roaring sound filled the glen. The reek of sulfur smoke fouled the air. Alasdair's eyes streamed with tears. When his vision cleared, he saw the hind dashing from him, her cream-colored rump perfectly round in the distance. He rolled onto his back, his heart bursting with anger, aimed at what he didn't know. "What the devil . . . ?" he sputtered. Mata stood peering down at him, a bemused grin frozen on his face. "You! Alasdair cried. "Plague take you! What are you about, spoiling my shot?" He lay back in the heath, his head whirling, his face as hot as a bonfire. "You and your jests!"

" 'Twas no jest," Mata said. He looked humble enough, his bonnet in his hand. "As God is my master, I meant no harm." Mata stepped backward. "I stumbled and skelped you, and I'm sorry for it, but glad to have found you, all the same."

"Glad, is it?" Alasdair sat up and laid his gun across his knees. "Glad to be hungry tonight, are you?" Alasdair shivered as fear shot through his bones. *He touches me as I touch Una.* No, he wouldn't counsel such a thought! "You didn't come here to frighten away our supper, I'm thinking."

"Una's on her childbed." Alasdair felt his anger fall from his face as his heart filled with fear and longing. "Rory has gone to Craigorm for Seanag. They may be back already. Indeed, the child may be born."

Alasdair rose, found his musket, arranged his plaid

around his hips, and picked the bracken from his jacket. He was not ready for such tidings, nor for Mata's uncommon manner of delivery. "Brother, leave me here."

Mata draped his arm over Alasdair's neck. "Faith, you've held so many cold bundles in your arms you fear holding yet another. Still, you must go back. You belong with Una. What a great comfort you'll be to her."

"I doubt I'll be much comfort. If the baby is white, she'll fear I'll kill it."

"Will you?"

Alasdair ran his hand over the shining stock of his rifle, remembering the words engraved there: *Leben und leben lassen.* Live and let live. No doubt the German gunsmith who had made the piece regretted the violence of his craft. Live and let live. "Mayhap it's dead already."

Mata twisted his mouth into a sad smile. "Mayhap it's alive. Go to her."

There was nothing for it, sure enough. Mata was right, as he usually was. "Lead on, then. I'll follow." *Let this one be live and whole,* he prayed in silence as he trotted after Mata over the moor.

It was small, barely the length of her two hands. Its mouth was no bigger than a raspberry and its body had a wonderful milky smell that Una could not get enough of. The moment she'd felt the child slip from her belly she'd asked Seanag whether it was alive or no, and her second question never left her lips but Seanag had answered it for her. "She's lovely, Una. A little thing, but as red as her da and as full of the devil."

That much was wonderfully true. The baby had sparse red curls and eyelashes and wriggled about on Una's stomach as though it wanted to be up and walking already. It was so perfect Una almost forgot about the pain in her

still-contracting belly, but what gave her even greater pleasure than the babe itself was the pride beaming from the
face of its father.

"She's grand," murmured Alasdair, running his hands
over the child. "Look at her thrashing about like a
salmon." Una was so happy for the man. His face was
flushed. His entire body quaked with happiness. He was
drunk with fatherhood.

"As lovely a daughter as a man ever had, considering
she could not wait a little longer," Seanag said. Una saw
for the first time how weary the woman looked. It had
been a long labor, and Seanag was not the same cheerful
woman who had delivered Donald.

"Look, daughter, she has Sorcha's mouth," her father
observed. Una looked at the baby's trembling lips and saw
that indeed they did turn down at the edges. What a great
pity her mother couldn't see the wean.

She began to suckle the baby, who rooted desperately
at her breast and finally found her nipple. Suddenly she
heard a loud, piercing wail, but it was not the infant. This
cry was full of sorrow. Donald sat in the darkest corner
of the house with Pol's arms around him, howling. Poor
creature! She'd forgotten about him. "Come and see your
new sister," she said softly.

The boy crawled over to the bed and clung to her arm.
She could feel the wetness of his nose and mouth against
her skin. "Don't disturb your mother, Donald," warned
Alasdair. "She has had enough to worry her the day."

"Gentle, Alasdair. Donald needs his mother, too," said
Seanag.

Una patted the boy's silver head. His skin was warm, his
hair so moist it lay in stripes across his crown. "See? A
sister for you. Your father and I made her for you." Donald
glanced at his father, then at Una, and finally at the baby,
devouring her with his red eyes.

"Stroke her," suggested Seanag. "She'll not break."

Donald hesitantly ran his hand over the baby's rosy skin. His fingers left white dots where he touched her.

Alasdair leaned over Una and fussed with her wild hair, all his bluster falling away from him as he, too, admired the new life. "She'll need a name. What would you have her called, my heart?"

"Sorcha," said Una firmly. "Sorcha."

"Ach," sobbed her father. "How pleased your mother would have been."

"Only I would like to call her Cha until she's older," Una continued, "for Sorcha is too much name for her to carry just yet." She looked up at Alasdair, glad to find him smiling. Would the baby have those same granite-gray eyes?

Alasdair knelt down beside the bed and took Una's hands in his. "Heed this, Rory. And you, Mata and Seanag. Una, my dearest one, my only love. Will you have me as a husband?"

Una choked back laughter. What a question to ask her! "Indeed I will."

"Then let it be done now." Alasdair turned toward the others. Una could not see his face any longer, but she heard a trembling joy in his voice and imagined a wonderful radiance shimmering around his hands and upper body. "My dear friends," he said, "bear witness for us. I'd have us pledged here and now, if you've no objection, Rory."

"I'll be glad enough," replied her father, relief flooding his face. "It's five years I've been waiting for this day."

Alasdair faced her again, raised her hand to his lips and kissed it. She felt weary to the marrow, but her love for her red man stirred at his touch and warmed her like a fire. "Then we are joined," he said. "No one or nothing will tear us asunder." He pressed her hand against his heart, and she could feel it thudding like a watermill.

From the corner of her eye Una saw Donald reach out toward the baby. He'd been so quiet she had assumed he was asleep. What a good thing it was that he felt no anger toward Cha, she thought. Then, very deliberately, so deliberately she did not see it coming, Donald caught hold of the babe's fleshy cheek and pinched it hard.

Cha screamed. Donald screamed. Una screamed and clasped the babe against her. Alasdair lifted Donald up in his arms and held him tightly as the boy shrieked, flailing against his father's chest, his white head striking Alasdair's shoulders again and again. Alasdair glanced at Una, but before she could speak he had bolted from the house, trailing Donald's howls behind him.

Seanag picked up the bawling baby and crooned to her. "Is she hurt?" gasped Una, feeling angry at Donald and sorry for him, too.

The midwife smiled. "She'll be living," she shouted over the choking cries of the infant.

Even as she spoke, Una heard the sound of Alasdair's hand against bare skin and the frantic wailing of her boy-child. Una tried to rise but her father pinned her to the bed. "He'll hurt the lad!"

"He's your husband now," her father said, holding his forefinger up to her face in warning. "You're his wife. He'll do as he sees fit, and faith! I'd do the same. The wee devil, pinching his new sister! We've had this talk before, y'ken. He must be taught what's right, what's wrong."

Una felt hot tears slip over her face. "Aye, mayhap, but if only it were not his father who pained him."

In a few days, Una had nearly recovered from childbirth and had completely forgiven Alasdair for skelping Donald. After all, the man had been doing what he thought best for Cha. One night, while the children slept, she joined the others around the fire, nursing Cha and listening to her husband extol the wonders of his birthplace.

"Mata and I have built a little house for you, *mo chreidh,*" Alasdair said. "The Cuil, I call it, a nook for just the two of us and the weans. And wait until you see Calum's house, roomy enough for an army. And his hyacinths, as blue as Loch Shiel on a summer's day. Calum Mor himself bought the bulbs for my mother, and they still bloom about the door in the spring and smell like paradise."

He spoke of the acres and acres of good grazing, fields as level as a table and forests teeming with red deer. As he spun on and on, Una gazed at her father. The poor man had no heart in him since her mother's death; she hoped he might find a new home and perhaps a new wife in Glenalt. "You'll like the glen, Rory, and my father, once you're better acquainted with him," Alasdair said, as if he could see her thoughts.

"Calum Mor is a considerable man," said her father. "I'd like fine to see him and his house, but I won't stay more than a fortnight or two. My place is here. I'm a Clanranald man, and besides, I must keep the house as Sorcha would have wanted it kept. Can you imagine some frowsy *cailleach* in here, letting the chickens muck on the floor? Sorcha would never forgive me."

"Mama would understand," Una said thoughtfully. "If you were to stay, what would you have to show for it? A clean floor? Mama wouldn't wish for you to live and die alone here. And Donald would miss you sore."

"Do as you wish," said Alasdair. "You're welcome in Glenalt for a day, a week, a year. A lifetime." Una nodded her agreement.

Her father lit his pipe and disappeared for a moment behind a puff of white smoke. "A thousand thanks. I'll bide there long enough to see the two of you well ensconced, though faith, I think you'll not need my help for that. Won't you reconsider the matter of a dowry?" He smiled shyly. "You could take back a few of Calum's cattle."

"Here's my dowry!" Alasdair took the babe from Una and held the sleeping child out before him. They all laughed together, then fell silent.

Una was beginning to doze when a grand idea struck her. "Alasdair?" She glanced at him, then at Seanag. The midwife was still comely, but too thin, and her hair more gray than yellow. She deserved far better than life had given her thus far. "If Seanag is willing, I'd have her and Pol come live with us in Glenalt. What say you, husband?"

"Whatever you desire, wife, if Seanag would have it so," he said.

Then Seanag did something Una had not expected: she began to weep—great wracking sobs that shook her frail body like a sapling in a storm. "O, dear Seanag, have I offended you?" Una clutched her friend's hand.

Seanag struggled to speak. "Indeed not," she said, still sniffling, "but no one has ever extended me such kindness before. If you'll have me, I'll go. For how long I can't say."

"And Connach?" Una continued, forcing herself to mention the beast aloud. "He'll give you leave to go with us?"

Seanag glanced nervously from Una to Alasdair. "He's gone south with his cattle and won't be back for some time. Doubtless I'll be back before he returns."

"What!" Una cried in disbelief. "You'd return to that creature?"

Seanag fumbled with her hands, and for a moment the woman who was never at a loss for words was as tongue-tied as a child. "O, Una! I don't know what has befallen him. The shee bewitched him, perhaps. At times he rages about the house like a madman. I'd stay but for Pol. The other day Connach beat the boy's back until the blood ran. They could hear his screams in Inverloch, I'm thinking."

Una was about to make an angry reply when Alasdair spoke. "Pol and you have a home in Glenalt if you wish

Take advantage of this offer to enjoy
Zebra's newest line of historical romance
novels....Splendor Romances (formerly
Lovegrams Historical Romances)- Take our
introductory shipment of 4 romance novels
-Absolutely Free! (a $19.96 value)

Now you'll be able to savor today's best romance
novels without even leaving your home with our
convenient and inexpensive home subscription
service. Here's what you get for joining:

- 4 BRAND NEW bestselling Splendor Romances
  delivered to your doorstep every month
- 20% off every title (or almost $4.00 off) with your
  home subscription
- Shipping and handling is just $1.50.
- A FREE monthly newsletter, *Zebra/Pinnacle
  Romance News* filled with author interviews,
  member benefits, book previews and more!
- No risks or obligations...you're free to cancel
  whenever you wish...no questions asked

To get started with your own home subscription,
simply complete and return the card provided.
You'll receive your FREE introductory shipment of
4 Splendor Romances and then you'll begin to
receive monthly shipments of new Zebra Splendor
titles. Each shipment will be yours to examine for 10
days and then if you decide to keep the books, you'll
pay the preferred home subscriber's price of just
$4.00 per title. That's $16 for all 4 books with
$1.50 added for shipping and handling. And if you
want us to stop sending books, just say the word...it
that simple.

4 Free BOOKS are waiting for you!
Just mail in the certificate below!

If the certificate is missing below, write to: Splendor Romances, Zebra Home Subscription Service, Inc., P.O. Box 5214, Clifton, New Jersey 07015-5214

FREE BOOK CERTIFICATE

Yes! Please send me 4 Splendor Romances (formerly Zebra Lovegram Historical Romances), ABSOLUTELY FREE! After my introductory shipment, I will be able to preview 4 new Splendor Romances each month FREE for 10 days. Then if I decide to keep them, I will pay the money-saving preferred publisher's price of just $4.00 each... a total of $16.00. That's 20% off the regular publisher's price and I pay just $1.50 for shipping and handling. I may return any shipment within 10 days and owe nothing, and I may cancel my subscription at any time. The 4 FREE books will be mine to keep in any case.

Name _____

Address _____ Apt. _____

City _____ State _____ Zip _____

Telephone ( ) _____

Signature _____ SP0198
(If under 18, parent or guardian must sign.)

AFFIX
STAMP
HERE

SPLENDOR ROMANCES
ZEBRA HOME SUBSCRIPTION SERVICE, INC.
120 BRIGHTON ROAD
P.O. BOX 5214
CLIFTON, NEW JERSEY 07015-5214

||...|..||||...||.|.|.|..||.|.|..|.||..|..||.|..|||..|

it." How stupid her rage seemed in the face of such generosity, Una thought.

"I'm beholden to you both," Seanag whispered.

"Dear Seanag! Have no fear anymore." Una ran her hand over her friend's brittle hair. "Soon we'll be on our way north," though tomorrow would scarcely be too soon, she added to herself. It would be a good start on a new life for all of them, as far away from that devil of a man as they might go.

What Connach wanted most was a bath. His mouth was full of dust and the reek of the cattle still clung to him, but when he reached Craigorm he found the house abandoned. Even the dog was gone. The crockery was clean and neatly stacked, the fire was built and ready to be lit, the floor was swept and strewn with reeds. It was a house for ghosts.

Connach picked up a dish, turning it in his hands, then threw it to the floor with a crash. He kicked the fire apart and beat his hands aginst the stone walls until his palms turned red. "To hell with you, *a'ghraidh!*" he cried.

There was no doubt but that she'd gone off to be with the slattern Una, and Connach set out at once to prove himself right. He didn't need to know the way precisely; something pulled him in the right direction. His path led to Loch Shiel, and when he came to the far shore of the great loch he felt compelled to throw a stone into its waters to break the stillness of its surface. The calm disturbed him.

To everyone he met he put the same question: "Where will I find the house of Gentle Rory and his daughter Una?" Some people seemed fearful of him and would say nothing, but after he offered a penny to one old woman, he had no trouble finding the house. It was quiet and tidy, a dead house, just like the one he'd left. Inside, he almost choked on the emptiness of it, the cold fire and the stale smells of smoke and urine.

Connach sat down heavily on a chair and fumbled in his sporran for his pipe and tobacco. They slipped from his grasp. Seanag had slipped away from him, too. Where was Seanag now? Una had magicked her into going north, or else Seanag would never have left him. When he found her again, he would never let her leave.

That Una! He'd known she would be trouble for him the first time he'd seen her, staring at him with her wide blue eyes, boring holes into his heart. *Dia!* She could stare straight through a man! Connach shivered. He was so cold and his fingers so stiff. Where was Seanag? He needed her. If he could find her, he'd never raise his hand against her again. Damn her! She brought out the hottest rages in him.

He was not hot now, but frozen, as cold and empty as this burial-ground of a house. He searched his sporran once more, and his tinderbox fell into his hand. That was what he needed. A fire to warm him. Connach gathered a handful of kindling from the fireside, lit a piece with his tinderbox, and watched patiently as the stick ignited and burned lower and lower. When his fingers began to smart he dropped it and lit another, watching as it burned down to a black nubbin.

A voice came to him, the voice that was constantly inside him, giving him direction. *The thatch. Connach, look at the thatch. Dry as tinder, aye? What a great loss to Rory if his house should catch alight.*

He lit another stick, and when it was burning brightly, walked outside and held the brand up to the roof. The thatch came to his forehead, weighted down by a neat row of stones tied across the eaves. He lit a few straws. They sputtered and burned out. He lit another, thicker stick and placed it on the thatch as high as he could reach. It glowed and flared, burning a black hole in the roof. The straw and heather, still damp from a thousand rainstorms, fought back against the flame. Connach watched as the fire died down, spurted up, died down and burst into life again, marking a red line of slow progress across the dark thatch. He blew on the blaze to enrage it, then added another burning stick and another and another, until half the roof was orange with flames that bowed down in the wind and crackled sweetly as they ate their way around the house.

How fine it looked! Black smoke billowed from the roof. He could hear the rafters hissing and cracking, and eventually one gave way and crashed into the house amid a red fountain of sparks. His face was hot from the flames. Ashes showered his clothing and prickled his eyes. He had never felt happier. "I hope you're hurting!" he shouted at the house. "I hope you can feel the fire in your bones."

The entire roof was aflame now. The fire and smoke stretched a length of yellow, red, and black tartan across the sky. The smell of it was overwhelming, the death-smell of the thatch and rafters. The smoke stung his eyes, and he sat down at a safe distance from the fire to clean his face with his plaid. He should leave. Soon the whole district would descend on Una's house to salvage what was left. It was a good fire, fierce and brave. Like the fire of his hatred for the woman Una, it would not be easily extinguished.

Chapter 10

Una arrived at Alasdair's home in Glenalt in the blue of the evening, the baby in her arms and Donald half-asleep before her on the saddle. The house wasn't much different than her father's black house in Glenfinnan, taller and longer, but still nothing more than unmortared stones and thatch. She felt her heart sink inside her; she had expected something grander.

Two gillies ran up to help her dismount, only to be pushed aside by Alasdair's father. Calum appeared hale enough, if a little thinner and grayer. "Welcome, Una!" he called to her. "How lovely you look, and after such a long ride, too." He glanced at Donald and quickly turned his gaze toward the baby. "Is this my granddaughter?" Calum stroked the child's red curls.

Una nodded, unable to speak. Alasdair had warned her Calum would have no use for Donald, that the old man would be thinking of nothing but Donald Ban. She hadn't believed him, but now she saw with dismay that Alasdair had been right all along.

"Come, let's away inside!" Calum helped her from the horse, chatting to her and her father about the house, mumbling something to Alasdair and introducing himself to Seanag. Una marveled at his ability to keep so many words going at once among so many people.

"Come, *a'nighean,* and take a look at your new home," said Calum as he led her to the door. Her father and Alasdair trailed behind her, with Seanag and the children bringing up the rear. Una wondered where the haughty man she'd met before was hiding. This Calum was a gentleman.

It wasn't until she set foot over the threshold that Una saw what a fine life she could have in Glenalt. A flock of serving maids fairly ran to her, one taking her wet shawl and another handing her a cup of claret. "What do you think of this, *a'nighean?*" Calum swept his hand around the room.

"An ugly, drafty, ill-conceived dwelling, to be sure." Alasdair slipped up beside Una and rested his hand on the small of her back. "Now, I have a far better house than this for you, mistress, almost finished and just right for the *mios nam pog.*"

"Any house is just right for the month of kisses," Calum grumbled. He turned to face Una. "Alasdair tells me you've pledged yourselves to each other, and that's all well and good, but I have planned a great wedding here for the two of you, and there's no stopping it. Guests are coming from Skye and Harris and Lewis and beyond to make merry. There will be cakes and wine and whisky galore. Even a priest if you like."

Una smiled, enjoying the idea of a fine, big feast. Let the whole world know of her love for her husband!

Alasdair stuck his head between Una and his father.

"A needless expense, a wedding like that. Except for the whisky, of course."

The two began to argue. Una turned away, loath to stick her neb where it didn't belong, and distracted herself by taking a good look about the room. It was big, three times the breadth and length of both rooms in her father's house and almost twice the height of Alasdair. There were lofts on two sides of the house, sleeping areas for the servants, perhaps. Noticing her interest, Calum showed her a great fire built up in a proper hearth with a proper chimney, chairs with padded seats and rows of copper pots and kettles. Her father and Seanag, each holding a child, came up to her and tapped her on the arm. "Look at this floor!" said her father, stamping on the stone flags. "Little did I think my daughter would ever set foot on a fine floor such as this."

"There are four maidservants, two men, and three boys," whispered Seanag. "And there are more *gillies* who sleep in the byre. You can have a girl to help you with the children."

"I'd hoped you would," said Una, but she did not have time to elaborate, as Calum Mor was tugging her forward again. He stopped at a wall made of logs that hid part of a tiny room. "How pretty!" said Una as she peeked behind the partition. In the faint light she could see a narrow box bed covered with some plush, exotic fabric and a laquered table littered with pistols and dirks.

"I sleep here," explained Calum. "It's aye small, but it was far worse when Alasdair had his damnable books here."

Una looked up at Alasdair. If he could read, then he must have had the English, too. She'd known nothing of these talents. What else didn't she know about her red man?

Alasdair snorted and laughed. "The devil of a time I had convincing him to add this wall," he said, leaning against the logs, "and then the old man goes and uses it for himself."

"It was built for you?"

"Aye." Alasdair paused. "For myself and Fiona. Before I built a house for her, we slept here."

Una turned from the little room as if something had pushed her out. If she lived to be as old as Loch Shiel, she would never get used to thinking of Alasdair and Fiona together.

Suddenly she heard a great thud and a crash and a wailing scream. "Donald!" cried Una. She ran to a set of shelves against a wall where a gaggle of servants had gathered, wringing their hands and shaking their heads. There before them sat Donald, surrounded by half a dozen small boxes and scores of black and white figures.

"My chessmen!" cried Calum.

"He meant no harm, Calum Mor." Una scooped up the figures and began tossing them into the first box she seized. "Look you, nothing is broken." She patted Donald on the knee, but he rolled himself into a ball and refused to look at her. She inspected the box and sighed: nothing seemed to be fitting quite right.

Calum was scarcely appeased. "Look what the creature has done," he growled to no one in particular. Una tried another box, but the pieces still refused to lie flat.

Alasdair came to her rescue. "Una, my dear," he laughed, "it's clear you're no gameswoman. You've got all the blacks in one box by themselves, and the whites mixed in with the backgammon counters. Come, leave that to the servants." Then—O, most excellent man!—he turned to Calum Mor and said, without a pause in his speech, "Da, take Una to the byre. How she'd love to see your English milk cows."

Calum's face brightened. "My cows! Come see them. The finest in the district. Their milk tastes like cream."

Una rose and straightened her *arasaid*. She thought to take Donald by the hand, but looking at him, still huddled against the wall, she decided to let him be. It would be better if he kept his distance from his new grandsire for a while.

That night Una made her bed with her children on one side of her and Alasdair on the other. When she heard snickering coming from the servants' beds, Alasdair assured her she had nothing to be ashamed of. "We're man and wife, Una. Let those gowks laugh till their teeth fall out. It means nothing to us." He pulled his plaid over the two of them, covering their heads, creating a warm pocket as intimate as the womb.

Una woke early, as she always did. Alasdair was gone. She rose to find him, but walls appeared where they shouldn't have been and even the floor was cold and unfamiliar. After she used the midden, she woke Seanag. "See to Donald," she told her. "I'm off for Alasdair." And taking the baby in her arms, she walked into the mists of morning.

At the top of a rise not far from the house Una could see the roof of a small black house some distance down the glen. It had to be The Cuil, the house Alasdair had told her about. The damp heather pulled at her skirts as she walked through it, and by the time she reached the house her *arasaid* was soaked through from the hem to her knee. She imagined Alasdair removing her wet clothing and wrapping her in his plaid, as he had during the night.

A gray movement caught her eye. Her mind held its breath. The shee, but no—nothing but a tiny cat with a leveret in its mouth, emerging from a basket by the side of the house. When Una went to get a better look at it, what she saw made her gasp. There was not one basket, nor two nor three nor four but twenty, fifty, a hundred, more than she could count—great creels three feet high made of oiser, smaller round baskets of wooden strips, straw, rushes, even one made of rags. They lay in rows against the back of the house and in a pile to the left, where the cat had appeared. Hugging Cha to her, Una inspected the closest heap of baskets. Some were quite new and hard to the touch; others were tattered and rotted through, but they were all lovingly made in a dozen different weaves, by far the loveliest Una had ever seen. Some even had designs and pictures woven into the warp: hounds, stags, and bluebells. Not even decay could hide the careful workmanship.

It was all very odd, and certainly nothing Alasdair would do.

She picked up one of the smallest rush baskets and was examining it when she heard someone singing inside the house. With the basket still in her hand, Una approached the doorway. The voice was high and sweet.

> To grasp the salmon by the tail
> Were just as easy a thing to do
> As to grasp the hand of a deceitful love.

No man's voice, that. The hair on Una's arms bristled. "Who's there?"

The singing stopped and a woman came to the door. Una had the feeling she had seen the woman's pale brown eyes once before, long ago or in a dream. She was tall and neat, well-dressed in a white *arasaid* with blue and russet stripes at the hem, but her hair was a rat's-nest of red spikes and long, uncombed curls. "Una? Welcome."

There was no mistaking her speaking voice, the voice of the woman Una wanted least to see in this world. Una sputtered and snarled as she tried to find words to match her fury. "What are you doing here in Glenalt? Go home to your parents or whoever will have you."

Fiona smiled wanly. "Good morning to you, mistress. You seem distressed to find me here, and for that I'm sorry. Admiring my basketry, I see."

Una threw the basket to the ground. "The work of an idle mind. Or a deranged one."

"Both, perhaps, or neither. They're round and beautiful and could hold a great deal, but I have naught to put in them, so they rot." Fiona reached out to pat Cha's head, but Una stepped backward, pulling the baby out of reach. "A son or daughter?"

"A girl-child."

"Alasdair's? Of course she is, little firetop. He's quite a sire, isn't he? Such a pretty thing, not at all like the first. Surely you're not afraid I'll hurt her? She looks every bit as beautiful as ours."

As yours would have looked, Una thought, had you not been barren. But she held her tongue. Something about the woman's wild hair made her stop short of being cruel. "You cannot stay, Fiona. Alasdair and I are wed, and it's not decent nor proper for you to be here. Alasdair will be sore grieved to find that you've confronted me so."

"I confronted you, now?" said Fiona, plucking at her sleeve. "O, forgive me, but I do not fathom you. Here's me singing, and along comes a bit of a thing with a baby, telling me I must leave my own house."

"I have a right to do so," insisted Una. "You have no claim to Alasdair any longer, and you'll not live where I can see you."

Fiona sat down before the doorway, hugging her knees to her chin and biting at her knuckles. After a few moments she picked up a peat and crumbled a bit off in her hand. "Don't be too harsh on me, little Una. You have children and a man who loves you, and I have a dead womb and no husband and a house hard by the cairns of my babies." She broke the peat in half and carefully set one section down beside her. "Where would I go? Who would have me? The wild beasts, maybe, or the wild rushes? Don't the priests speak of a baby among the rushes? In a basket?" She looked up at Una with her burning eyes, and Una stepped back still further.

"Alasdair alone was kind to me," Fiona continued. " 'This house is yours,' he said, 'for aye.' It was the house he built for me when we were wed. The house you seek is further down the strath." The woman paused, smiling. Then she laughed softly to herself, crushed the peat between her hands and threw the pieces up in the air. "Such a ninny I am! You think he'll stray from you, leave your hot belly, and come to my cold bed?"

Una gave a tiny cry. The thought had been with her since early spring, when Alasdair had left Glenfinnan. It hurt to hear Fiona speak of something so ugly and private. "Alasdair would never serve me so basely."

"Perhaps not. Yet you've imagined him with another, and that's why you'd prefer me well out of his reach. The only stone in your road, Una, is that I have no place to go. No place in this life. Do you think I want to stay here, in the house where we lay together, where my babies died?" The woman's eyes flickered as she glanced sideways at Una. "Give me my child back now. You've held her long enough."

Una fought to keep her stomach from leaping out of her body. "This is madness. I'll hear no more of it." She lifted the baby to her shoulder and ran with her through the yard. She could not tell whether Fiona followed her or not, but just as she reached the edge of the bracken something hard struck her between the shoulder blades and squeezed a moan out of her. Una turned and saw Fiona with a peat in one hand. "Would you hurt Alasdair's baby?" she cried.

"No, I wouldn't do that," said Fiona, and she tossed the peat to the ground. "You'll take good care of her?"

Una ran toward The Cuil, her shivering legs scarcely able to support her. Cha began to wail, and a noise like the keening of a hundred women rose up behind them and seemed to swallow the entire glen.

She found him asleep, wrapped from nose to foot in his plaid and surrounded by candle-ends, woodchips, and a dozen tools. The bothy was filled with the smell of freshplaned wood, and she was touched by the work he had done to get the little house ready for her. But it wasn't the first time he'd built a house for a woman. As she stood, trying to decide whether to kiss the man or dig her toe into him, Cha cried out and woke her father. Alasdair sat up, squinting into the dim light. "Ah, my treasure, is it you? I'm so glad you found me. I came here early to finish the window-frames, and now you can help me."

Una took in each feature of his face, alight with the pleasure of seeing her. His plaid lay tangled at his feet, and he was naked save for his shirt. He looked warm and golden, and she longed to creep up beside him. "Creature," she said, without conviction, testing the word to see how it sounded used against him. She tried to imagine Fiona's haughty face.

Alasdair cocked his head. "Have I offended thee, love?"

The baby had fallen asleep in her arms, and Una did not know what to do with her. It didn't seem right to be holding her in the midst of so much confusion and anger, and at last she laid the child down tenderly on a pallet of reeds in a corner of the room. She turned to face Alasdair again. "I saw Fiona in the house close by here. She lives there, she says."

Alasdair yawned, scratched his chin, and smiled. "Well,

aye, she does. Had I the chance, I'd have told you about her myself.''

"Seeing her there at the doorway was a dirk in my heart,'' Una growled. "Why did you not tell me she lived here?''

Alasdair shrugged. "I would have, as I said.''

Ah, he'd been afraid that she would not have gone with him to Glenalt. Well, perhaps she would have, and perhaps she should not have. "She's taken leave of her senses.''

"Distraught, perhaps," Alasdair sighed. "Her mind is addled from the deaths of our poor children. I told you she wasn't well. Her own parents drove her from the house, afraid she might harm the little children in the family during one of her rants, though I doubt she would. When she came to Glenalt last spring with only the clothing on her back, I let her stay and provided for her. What could I do? She was my wife and she is my cousin. Surely helping her any less would be indecent." Alasdair stretched out his hand toward her. "Come, you have no reason to be jealous, *m'chreidh*. It's you I love.''

The man was so calm! How could one argue with him if he didn't argue back? "The baskets . . .''

"A harmless business. Una, you've saved the life of a stranger lying broken on the heath, and you've taken Donald into your heart. Please, don't hate Fiona. Don't fear her. She'll never lay a hand on you or the children.''

She has already struck me with a clod of turf, she wanted to tell him, but she kept the thought to herself. Suddenly it seemed like a childish thing to say. As a little girl, she had thrown many a peat at the two Morags. Without understanding why, she began to feel a twinge of pity for that wild-haired woman. Alasdair grasped her hands and began to pull her forward so lovingly that she found it hard to resist him.

"Come, love, let me show you this," he said, taking her into a small adjoining room, dimly lit with sunlight leaking through two shuttered windows. The room smelled old and damp, and Una soon saw why: rows of leather-bound books stood neatly arranged in shelves across the wall. "*Dia!* What is this?" she cried. She had never seen more than two books together at a time, and it hurt her eyes to behold so many all at once, drawn into ranks like an army.

"My library." Alasdair's voice was edged with pride. He took a volume from the wall of books and showed her a page, a drawing of a strange man dressed in fur with a musket in his hand and a large bird on his shoulder. "This is from Sterling. The man that sold it to me said all the finest people in London have read this book."

"What use would a Gael have for such a book?" she countered, at once in awe of the book and afraid of it.

Alasdair smiled, then opened the book to a page full of black markings. It looked as if someone had dribbled black sand in straight lines across the paper. "Books contain all the knowledge of the world, Una. You may learn the ideas of great men who have been dead many years."

Una shook her head. "This looks like difficult magic indeed."

"Not magic, but learning," Alasdair said. "And not difficult, though first one must learn the English, as there are no books in our tongue." Alasdair paused and stroked her hair. "Nothing would give me greater pleasure, love, than to teach you to read."

Una snorted. What a great waste of time that would be. Reading was fine for priests and chieftains and scholars and all those who had no work on their hands, but if it could not be done in the Gaelic then what was the use of it? Then a fine thought struck her. "Teach Donald to read, Alasdair. He's clever and quick."

"Una, don't make light of this."

Una looked away from him so he could not see the confusion she knew was sketched upon her face. He had very nearly succeeded in putting her mind at ease about Fiona, only to give her something new to puzzle on. "What I said was not in jest."

Instead of answering her, he held another book under her nose, black-bound and very worn. "This is the word of God, Una. It was my mother's. She taught me to read from it, not long before she died."

His voice was strained, and Una touched the faded cover gently. She could imagine Alasdair's mother, holding her little boy on her lap and showing him pages from the black book. "The only Bible I wish to see is the priest's."

"Here, my heart, look at this." He opened the book and began to read from it, though his words sounded like gibberish to her.

"Could Fiona read?" she asked suddenly.

"What does it matter? Aye, she could, though she didn't care for it. But you—you'll learn to like learning. These letters mean nothing to you now, but they're the only difference between a man and a gentleman, a woman and a lady."

Una stared at the book. It said nothing to her, though somehow it had spoken to Alasdair and moved him greatly. On an impulse she snatched the Bible from Alasdair's hands and held it behind her back.

Alasdair glared at her. "Give it over!"

"I'll not! Not if you speak to me thus."

He lunged at her and caught her by one elbow. The book fluttered to the floor like a clumsy bird. "Och! Och!" he cried, his hands in the air, horrified. How stupid she'd been! Nothing could mean more to him than the book his mother had given him.

Una stooped down, retrieved the Bible, and dusted the cover with her sleeve. "I'm sorry," she whispered. "O, Alasdair! I am sorry."

"Una." He took the book from her and set it back

tenderly on a shelf. "What am I to do with you?" He buried his face in her hair.

He's scarcely thinking about reading now, she thought, pushing herself into his caress. Somehow she found herself on her back with Alasdair atop her, his hands searching for her breasts. It was an easy matter to slip her own hand under his plaid and take him firmly in her fingers. Now she had him by the tiller. He gasped, then snorted, then sighed deep in his throat like wind in a sail.

"Here is Ri, upright and upstanding," she whispered. It was a great jest between them. From the very first she had called his *slat* Ri, the king, certain it was the chief of all such manly things.

"You'd best find proper lodging for him," Alasdair panted.

Inch by inch she raised her skirt and petticoats. Alasdair stripped off his plaid and shirt, then reared himself over her. In a moment he was in her, filling her with the sweet pressure that alone could sear her mind and purge the thought of Fiona from her. Alasdair groaned. "You make me crazy-mad." Back and forth he rocked atop her, and in the midst of this tide of loving she pushed him suddenly onto his back, still coupled to her. "How now?" he muttered. "Who is the king here, woman?"

"Why me, for the moment," she chuckled. "Nay, you, if you wish. Can you not give me a ride while on your back, your majesty?"

Alasdair pulled her face down onto his lips and kissed her mightily. How grand it felt lying atop him, at once his conqueror and his protector. She met him thrust for thrust until at last she blazed with the fire only love could kindle. Beneath her, Alasdair's body clenched. She could feel Ri convulse inside her and in her mind saw the very essence of the man hurtling into her most secret reaches. Alasdair collapsed under her and lay as still as his own discarded plaid.

"My love?" She ran her fingers across his great freckled neck. *Dia!* Had she killed him with loving? No, his heart still thudded within him. He was wondrously warm and alive. What a fine piece of work! She had exhausted him back into sleep.

Perhaps, when he woke, he would be so filled with kindness that he would offer to teach Donald to read. It was lovely to think so, and she fell asleep atop her husband, with thoughts of her wedding warming her mind.

Days melted one into the other at Glenalt as Una acquainted herself with the people and the land, all the while avoiding the black house where Fiona lived. Alasdair and Una took long walks in the hills, which were steeper than the gentle slopes of Glenfinnan and harder to climb. Once Alasdair led her up onto a high hill called Cadha Ceo, the Misty Pass. From it she could see wide pastures full of cattle, more than she had seen anywhere except at the droves in Craigorm. The beasts dappled the green glen with red, gold, and black—all theirs to come, he assured her.

At last The Cuil was completed and she began spending her nights there with Alasdair and the children. Sleeping at The Cuil was better than sleeping at the big house, where Calum Mor stayed awake half the night, smoking his pipe and staring at Donald. She knew from the first that the old man would never be close to her son, and it hurt deep in her bones whenever she saw the boy sidle up to his grandfather and watched the man gently push Donald aside. But Donald was not one to give up. For some reason she couldn't fathom, he had claimed Calum as his own and looked up at him with eyes full of love and trust.

As the time of the wedding crept closer, guests began arriving from afar. Una's sisters came from Loch Linnhe. Morag Bhan was a girl no longer but a woman with two daughters of her own, and even Little Morag was getting broad about the hips and narrow through the waist. Her sisters spoke easily about children and cooking and spinning, and Una was delighted with them. She would never have guessed in the old days in Glenfinnan that she would be glad to listen to the chatter of the Morags.

Una met Calum Og of Duneilean—Cali, Alasdair called him—and his wife Ros, Donald's future foster parents. They were as peculiar a couple as Una had ever seen. Cali was as tall and thin as a basket-needle, while Ros was short and stout. Cali was quiet and soft-spoken, but Ros talked on until she wearied everyone around her. Ailments were her favorite subject, and she was forever suggesting cures: anise, milk baths, doses of fish oil, and sometimes, for stubborn children, merely the back of the hand. Una thought the woman had a great store of knowledge, but she wondered why she didn't measure it out when needed, as Seanag did.

"It must be good to have a child that can be so easily cured of what ails him," sighed Una one golden afternoon. She and Ros were sitting with the little children just outside the house, amusing them with songs and stories while the older ones played shinty. She watched Donald as he and Anghas, one of Ros's six children, sat together drawing tartan patterns on each other's arms and legs with charcoal. He was one of the very few youngsters besides Pol who ventured to play with Donald, yet it was a pity Anghas was so handsome, with soft brown curls and rosy skin. Next to him, Donald looked like a corpse.

"Are you speaking of your lad?" asked Ros. "He could be cured if a body were willing to take the trouble."

"Is it so?" Una blurted out. Since Donald had been

born, not a soul had suggested that he could be helped, let alone cured, not even Seanag. "What must I do?"

"You might feed him clay from your kaleyard," Ros said, "or the grease of a seal, or have him drink seawater or his own water. All these cures have worked for different people."

That evening, Una told Seanag of Ros's cures, but the midwife merely told her to cease being foolish. She tried to feed Donald a morsel of clay, but he would have none of it. Seawater and seal's grease were not at hand and the thought of drinking urine turned her stomach. Perhaps it was just as well, she sighed to herself. Life was hard enough without complicating it further.

Chapter 11

He was sweeping northward. Slowly, leisurely. Enjoying his journey. The summer was nearing its end and the weather was not so wet or cold that a body couldn't spend a night outdoors. Soon, when he found his Seanag, he would never sleep cold again. She would go with him or he would make her go with him. The simplicity of his mission pleased him.

All about him the heather was dying, a patch of blazing purple set here and there amid an expanse of lifeless brown. The red deer were in rut, and the air was alive with the hoarse barking of the stags and the whistling of the hinds. He was not above culling the herds now and then when a good shot presented itself, though he'd known men who had been hung for doing just that. It was no matter. He was a careful and deadly poacher, and like the deer, driven by passion.

He spent three days in a bothy on the easternmost tip of Loch Morar, taking a dram when he felt like it and

enjoying the comforts of the widow who owned the house.
During the day he fished the loch, admiring the wild swans
feeding on the clear waters. How was the travel up north?
he asked the widow one morning. It was only four miles
to Loch Hourn, she said, but four miles of hard walking,
and when he came to the loch he'd be obliged to take a
ferry across. Couldn't he stay longer? Surely there was no
need for him to hurry away.

That's fine, he told her. He could tarry with her a few
days longer.

That evening he watched the swans on the loch and,
when one flew over his head, he shot it and lugged it back
to the bothy for supper.

Connach left in the morning, before the widow awakened. When he arrived at Loch Hourn the weather was
wet and drear, and the wind blew in fierce from the Sound
of Sleat. He had to speak with several fishermen before
finding one to take him across the ferry at Kinloch. The
waters were rough, and by the end of the crossing both
Connach and the boatman were dripping wet. A fitting
start for the devil's journey, Connach thought.

Once safely ashore, Connach waved to the boatman and
headed northwest up Glen Beag, following the seamews
that drifted over the barren valley. On the morning of his
second day in the land of the MacLeod he came to a
jumble of rocks and just beyond them the gray-green sea.
But where was Glenalt? Ever since the harlot Una had
deafened him he could not get a good bearing on directions, and more than once he had found himself walking
away from his destination.

He came across a tall woman stalking along the beach,
a big creel on her back, searching for seaweed and shellfish
in the froth of the ocean. At first he thought he had stumbled on Seanag, but as he neared the seaweed-gatherer he
saw she had red hair and carried considerably more flesh

in the right places than his wife. "Good day, mistress!" he called to her. "Am I near Glenalt?"

The woman examined him with bright brown eyes. She didn't look altogether decent. Her hair blew wild in the wind and the hem of her *arasaid* was covered with sand. "You are in Glenalt, my pretty man, the arse-end of it." She pointed to a steep cliff above them. "Here's the Woman's Rock, and beyond it the Paps of Glenalt, and farther south the crags called the Watching Cliffs. And to the west . . ." She nodded toward the ocean. "The land's not so good to the west." The wild-haired woman burst into laughter.

Connach liked her at once. It was good hearing a woman laugh again, just as good as knowing he hadn't lost his way after all. He offered to take the basket, and the woman immediately slid it off onto the sand. "I'm called Fiona, daughter of Alan Mor. And you, pretty man?"

Connach hefted the creel onto his shoulders. "The son of the devil," he muttered.

To his surprise the woman laughed again, harder than before. "Are you now? But what shall I call you? Old Blackie, as the children say? The thief that steals men's souls?"

"My name is Connach." He walked along the beach beside the woman, talking to her easily as she padded by the water's edge, intent on her prey. When she found a clump of sea-fodder to her liking, she seized it and tossed it into the creel, ignoring the brown tendrils that flapped about her wrists.

"This will be my wedding feast," she said, pouncing on a big tangle of dulce.

"What do you mean, woman?"

She smiled again, and this time she seemed sweeter than he had thought at first. "My husband—my once husband—is marrying soon," she explained, "and I'll not be going to the wedding. He had been mine, but he'd had the handfast bonds dissolved between us, not because I was barren, mind you, but because he wished to marry some *drabhag* named Una."

"Una? Una, the daughter of Gentle Rory?"

She thought that was his name, Gentle Something.

"Tell me more of this Una. Does she have a friend? A woman named Seanag?"

She did—a frail, close-mouthed creature, a widow, Fiona thought, who liked to walk the moors.

"Well, she's no widow," growled Connach. Hell roast her if she had posed as such. "She's my wife, but she's gone and left me, so I've come here to bring her back to Glenfinnan."

Fiona eyed him shrewdly. "You and I are alike, then."

"Aye? Think you?"

She cocked her head and gazed at him through half-open eyes, as though she were gazing deep inside herself. "Aye, for you have a wife, but you don't, and I have a husband, though he's not my husband. We are and we aren't. We have and we haven't. We've been abandoned, the both of us, by those who are supposed to cherish us."

Now it was Connach's turn to stare at her. He wasn't certain he trusted her but he did admire her wits. "You've the right of it. Tell me, if I carry this sea-slop home for you, will you cook me some of it? I haven't eaten hot food for nigh two days."

Fiona patted his shoulder. "My mother told me I was the sort who'd sup with the devil and drink his soup, and now I will do so in earnest."

That night Connach ate boiled kelp, dried dulce, and kale fried in muttonfat. He drank cup after cup of dark heather beer that Fiona had brewed herself. She spoke all the while he ate, and though he watched her intently, he heard but little of what she had to say. She was rounder in the face than his Seanag, and her eyes shone in a comely way whenever she asked him a question.

"Will you have a pipe?" she said. "I have tobacco."

Connach drew his pipe from his sporran and smiled as Fiona filled the bowl, handed him the pipe, and proceeded to prepare another pipe for herself. He'd never seen a woman smoke before, yet he was not surprised that she did so. In a way, it was just what might be expected of her. They smoked together for some time in silence, adding the pungent odor of tobacco to the fierce scent of the peat fire. "Why do you call yourself the devil?" she asked at last. "You've no horns, have you, save the horn all men bear?"

Connach grinned and blew a ring of smoke toward her. "I've had a vision," he said. "In Sterling some years back, when I was taking the drove through there."

"A vision? A dream, you mean."

"Nay, I was awake. In any case, I believe I was awake." He laughed when he saw the puzzlement in her face and hurried to explain. "Here we sit, smoking tobacco, but there are those that smoke summat else. In Sterling I met a sea captain, kinsman to a droving friend of mine. The captain had voyaged to Cathay and lands beyond. He knew a bit, the captain did, and he bade me join him in a different sort of smoke than this."

Fiona crept closer to him, blowing smoke out her nostrils. "And was it this strange pipe you smoked that gave you your vision?"

Connach nodded. "It was. I've never felt the same, before or since. There was nothing in front of me or behind me, only blackness, but the blackness had a comfort to it, and a soft voice called to me there in the midst of it. 'Connach MacColl,' said the voice, 'you are my child.' "

"And was that the devil himself?" whispered Fiona.

"Whisht, now. Wait a bit. 'You are my child, you are

mine,' it said. 'You must do as Old Fogaidh tells you. Do
as I bid, and you shall have this.' And suddenly I was
rushing up through the blackness, gasping for breath, and
surging through me was a power I'd never felt before, not
even during the bloodiest brawl.'' Connach held out his
hands, and the smoke from his pipe danced around his
long arms. ''My fists were the size of two heads of kale, it
seemed to me. And then I unclenched them.''

Connach stopped, enjoying the look of frustration on
Fiona's comely face. Her eyes flared wide open and her
lips parted. ''What was in them, Blackie? What?''

''Why, guineas in the one and Seanag in the other.'' He
blew a thin stream of smoke into her face, but she merely
blinked against it. ''Can you not take me to her?''

''I can,'' she said, ''if you can take me to a wedding.
Neither you nor I can stop it, but we may yet put some
fear in this woman Una's heart.''

Connach laughed. In a far corner of his mind he could
see Gentle Rory's house wrapped in flames. The need for
vengeance burned inside him like a torch. ''Mayhap,'' he
said.

With so many people, every night was festive now at the
big house in Glenalt. After supper—a rollicking, noisy
affair, to be sure—a guest or two would play the fiddle or
pipes, and any young man who wished to would dance or
show his mettle by posturing with his sword. They would
tell stories, too, but made no mention of Donald Ban Ard.
Una saw to that, and enlisted Mata's help in spreading the
word.

After an hour or so of such fare, the true entertainment
began. Mata would sit near the fire with his lap-harp before
him and sing until Una thought he would collapse with
weariness. He had a high, clear tenor voice, surprising for

a man of his broad build, and such talent with the harp that he could move folk to tears with one song and then swing them into laughter with the next.

During one such evening of music and gaiety, Una had some difficulty finding Donald. At last she discovered him in an unlikely spot: in Calum's lap, his head on Calum's knee, dead asleep. It was the first time she could remember the man holding his grandchild. Seeing them together made her think of the night at Lochan Oran when Alasdair had first held his son. She stooped down and, without a word from Alasdair's da, gathered the sleeping child into her arms.

"This fairy wean's the weight of a calf!" Calum said. "Are you certain you have him, woman? My arms are cramped beyond telling."

Una cringed at his cruel description of her son. The whisky had been flowing like snowmelt that night, and much of it had flowed down Calum's gullet. "He's not too heavy for me yet," she said, though in truth her arms shook as she clasped Donald tightly to her chest.

After Calum trudged off to his sleeping chamber, Una bedded down the children by the fire and fell asleep beside them at once, only to be roused from a dream sometime later by a rough, wet kiss on the neck. Alasdair lay on top of her, and he wore not a stitch. "'I would give love for love . . .' Won't you sing with me, Una?" he coaxed her in a throaty voice.

"It's not singing you're after," she chided him gently, running her hand down his broad neck and back, finally clasping his muscled haunches. In some way she didn't quite understand, she gained power from the very feel of his skin beneath her fingers. The hardness of him nudged her through the plaid, and she knew the man was eager to be at her. "You must be aye weary. Come lie down and sleep beside me," she said slyly.

Alasdair snorted. "Sleep? Faith, the evening's entertainment has just begun!" he whispered in her ear.

"Get along with you," said Una, but she smiled to herself at the thought of Ri inside her. "You've had a dram too many."

"Ri has not. See you? How straight he stands!"

"And does he wish to be standing all night," she countered, enjoying his banter, "or would he rather lie down in a velvet bed?"

"His only thought is to know you better," Alasdair murmured. She breathed in his words as he slowly slid the length of him along her thigh, prodding her belly before easing into her, humming one of Mata's songs to himself all the while. Pleasure rippled through her. She caught her breath. He washed against her, the tide on the shore. She surged against him, seafoam following the waves back into the ocean. They were part and parcel of each other, sand and shoreline, surf and water. She could not tell where they separated into man and woman. Where she began and the other left off. Where her soul lived, and his.

Una was the first to give over, her heart fairly leaping from her in senseless delight. Alasdair was not long in following her, but stayed staunch within her for some time. "How I love you, wife," he mumbled into her neck.

"Husband," she said, gripping his shoulders, and she knew that was all she need say.

Again she slept, and again she was awakened, this time by the screaming of a frightened child. Donald. Poor thing, the long, loud evening had been too much for him. Una went to him and hugged him, and soon lulled him back into quiet dreams. She was returning to bed when she heard another, softer sound coming from Calum's chamber. There she found Alasdair kneeling beside his father.

"He thinks he heard the *ban-sith,*" Alasdair explained.

Calum nodded. "I did hear her, keening for the dead. Someone will die this night."

Una smiled and patted his hand. "Little father, it was no fairy wife you heard but only our Donald, crying out in his sleep."

"Even if it is the *ban-sith*, I'm not afraid of her," said Calum. Before Una could think of a reply, the old man turned over and fell into a sound sleep.

Alasdair shrugged. "Too much whisky."

Una said nothing. How unfair it was that her lively Donald was always being compared to death.

In the morning she was again awakened by wailing, not Donald's this time, but a chorus of adult voices, male and female, and among them Alasdair's. She looked about for Donald and Cha, but they were gone. Una sat up, shaking with fright. Had the shee crept by in the night and stolen her children? It was all she could imagine.

She called out for them, frantic with fear, and Seanag came. The midwife squatted down beside her. "What is it, Seanag? Where are the children?"

"With Rory and a serving-maid at The Cuil. I sent them there to keep them calm. Una, be strong. Calum is dead."

Una felt her insides turn to ice. "Calum Mor? Dead? But he can't be, Seanag! He was well just last night."

"Come."

With Seanag's help Una staggered up to the partition that separated Calum's sleeping-chamber from the rest of the household. The little room was crowded with people, all weeping and singing their doleful *coronachs*. Above the dirges rose Alasdair's wail of misery, starting as low as thunder and ending in a shriek of heartbreak, only to start all over again.

Una still could not believe that the old man was dead. She pressed against the throng of bodies and finally worked her way to Calum's bedside. Alasdair lay on his father's back, the horrible sounds of mourning spilling from his lips. The man's neck was twisted back at an odd angle, as if he had been trying to get a final glimpse of his son before leaving the world. His eyes were open in mild surprise, and Una half expected him to ask why people were making such a great commotion.

"Alasdair . . ." She touched her red man's arm, but he neither heard nor saw her. She slipped back through the crowd and found Seanag by the fire. "Is there nothing that can be done, Seanag Bhan?" A tear slipped down her face.

"Nothing, my jewel," whispered Seanag. "Ros is for tasting his blood, to see if that will restore him, but I know he has crossed over."

Una gave a strangled cry, remembering her foolishness at the corrie. "Surely that's naught but folly." She paused, suddenly unsure of herself. At least Ros's notion offered hope. "Do you agree?"

Seanag nodded, the weary nod of a woman who had seen death too often to be afraid of it. "If it weren't, I'd not be sitting here idle, now would I? Go back to your man, my treasure, and bring him what comfort you may. Why waste one's toil on the dead when the living are in pain?"

Once again Una struggled through the throng of keening mourners and crouched low by Calum's bedside. Alasdair was still weeping over his father, but someone had at least seen to Calum Mor. He had been rolled onto his back; his eyes were closed and his hands crossed lightly over his chest. He seemed to be smiling. Perhaps she should fetch Ros. She touched his hand. It was as cold as clay.

Una stood up. Suddenly the voices of the mourners receded far into the distance and their faces began spinning round and round the room. She toppled backward into the arms of an astonished wedding guest and sank into blackness as deep as the grave.

She awoke in the morning in The Cuil, with Cha asleep on one side of her and Donald on the other. A small fire crackled merrily inside its stone ring. Had Mata done this for her, or Seanag? Neither was about, and Alasdair was likewise missing—with his father, she guessed. Her mind spun like an eddy. If only Calum's death had come after the wedding, she thought, if it had to come at all. But no, as they said, man waits for Death, and Death waits for none.

Chapter 12

A round, white sun floated in and out of the clouds, invisible one moment and boldly there the next. The wedding feast was in its second day, and Una thought it might go a third. She stood in the crowded field next to the big house, with Cha in her arms and Donald at her side, half-listening to a guest recite the virtues of his two deerhounds. Such beautiful animals, slate gray and lean, but Una didn't trust them. They gazed at the baby with hungry amber eyes, and Donald was so frightened of them he'd hidden behind her skirts and refused to budge. Their master must have sensed Una's distrust. "Pat Mol here, mistress," he said. "More lamb than hound, that's my Mol."

Una leaned forward and ran her hand over the bitch's rough head. Mistress. She truly deserved the title now. The ceremony yestermorn that had confirmed her wifehood had lasted no time at all, a spate of Latin intoned by a drunken priest. Calum would have had something to say about the man, Una was sure. She sighed, thinking how proud the old man would have been to have seen his son. Alasdair had looked like a great chief in a belted plaid of black and red cross-striped tartan, with a gray jacket and new blue bonnet. Only his red-rimmed eyes had borne witness to his mourning.

Una began to look around the field for a glimpse of her bridegroom, but a low growl brought her mind back to the hound. She looked down at it just as its master jerked the animal round by the nape of the neck and slapped it on the muzzle. "I don't let them growl at the ladies," he explained. The hound sank to its belly and glared up at Una with hatred in its eyes.

"Will you be coursing them the day, Iain Beag?" She had no interest in the dogs, but she could feign interest for her guest's sake.

The man's face brightened. "Aye, I will, after a bit. I've a stout-hearted roebuck tied nearby in a thicket, and I thought I'd let Mol and Cath have a go at him. He'll make a nice taste for the company, roasted on the open flames."

Loosing dogs on a frightened, captive animal wasn't Una's idea of sport, but the weary guests would welcome such a diversion. Iain left to see to his beast, and Una scanned the crowd again. Donald raised his head from her skirts. "There's Da," he said, pointing to a flash of red floating on a sea of fair-colored heads.

"You clever lad!" Una cried, and bent down to hug him. Since they had arrived at Glenalt, Donald had warmed to his father. Now he called him "Da" and didn't back away whenever Alasdair approached him.

With Donald jogging at her side, Una made her way through the field, past tables piled thick with sticky cakes filled with nuts and black currants. At last she worked her way over to where Alasdair stood, his back toward her, speaking quietly with two drovers. Una silently glided up behind him and slipped her arm over his, laughing at the

look of surprise on his face. Then he frowned at her, and
her laughter caught in her throat. "Ah, mistress, Calum's
kin now for certain," said one of the drovers in a sad voice,
and Una suddenly knew they had all been talking about
Alasdair's father.

"I'm sorry to disturb you," she said, backing away from
the sorrowful trio. "I'll just be going." How could she be
so stupid! For one happy moment, she had forgotten his
misery of the past few days.

As the day rushed on, Una clung to Alasdair like a barna-
cle amid the sea of guests. Late that afternoon they shared
a meal of cold fowl, bannock bread, and port while Morag
Bhan played with Donald and the baby. Una was lifting
her third cup of wine to her lips when the sound of a shot
startled her. It seemed to startle the wine, too, for it leaped
up and dashed over her breast.

"*Dia!*" barked Alasdair. "Is a row a'brewing?"

Before she could reply, Una heard another shot, then
a piercing cry. "The Almighty preserve us!" she gasped.
"My da!"

She ran toward the sound of the commotion and found
her father sitting cross-legged on the ground, weeping into
his hands. Seanag and several others crowded about him,
trying in vain to console him. Next to her father stood
Fiona, her hair so neatly kerched that Una didn't recognize
her at once. Beside Fiona was a tall, thick-set man, holding
a smoking pistol in each hand. When she saw Seanag glance
up at him with love in her eyes, Una remembered him.
She took a step backward.

"Who the devil are you?" Alasdair demanded. "What
have you done to my wife's father?"

"My name is Connach MacColl, and I have done nothing
to anyone." The man raised his head high and burned
his gaze into Una's face so hard she stepped back yet again.
"I shot my pistols only to gain these folks' attention, for

I had news for Rory here. His house has burned to the ground. I saw it myself."

Una wrung her hands in dismay. "It cannot be," she muttered.

"Aye, it can and is," Connach crowed. "Nothing left but charred rock and ashes. *Dia!* You should have seen the red flames lapping at the roof." The man fairly licked his lips as he spoke and there was no mistaking the rapture in his voice. A whisker of fear flicked through Una's body as she listened to him.

"Och, och mar tha mi!" groaned her father. "Alas, my lot! Where will I live now?" He jerked his head up to examine the people before him, and Una knew he was wondering what would it be like, spending the rest of his days among strangers.

"Is this true, man?" snarled Alasdair. "I'll play shinty with your stones if you're telling me false."

"May my tongue cleave to my palate if I'm lying," Connach replied. "Send any man to Glenfinnan and he'll bring you back a handful of the ashes."

"How could such a thing happen?" wailed Una's father.

"Lightning, they think," Connach offered.

Una's head spun like a leaf in an eddy as she knelt beside her sorrowing father. She wrapped her arms around him, but she hurt too much inside to speak a word. Una had been born in that house, had given birth to Donald and Cha in the same little room where she'd so carefully tended their sire. Now it was gone.

When Una heard Seanag's soft voice she strained to hear it. "Why were you chosen to carry such a message, Connach?"

"Why, the hand of convenience singled me out," said he. "I was heading north anyway to fetch you back."

Una glared at the creature. Her hatred of him helped her find her tongue. "She'll not go with you," she said.

"She'll not be dragged from her home like Iain Beag's deer and torn to pieces by hounds." She was on the verge of cursing Connach when a great volley of barking rang out across the glen, and Una dimly realized that Iain Beag must have let loose the very dogs she had just mentioned. But all was not well. The barking suddenly ceased and a strange silence filled the field, broken here and there by shrieks and shouts. The crowd crumbled and faded away, slowly at first, then faster and faster until men, women, and children were running all around her.

"Donald!"

He was gone.

She had forgotten about him entirely, but in an instant she was on her feet, battling the throng of wedding guests. She gathered her skirts and joined a stream of men flowing toward the far end of the field where she saw Iain's two hounds, their hackles raised, their jaws dripping with foam. At their feet lay Iain Beag, dazed and groaning, blood trickling down his cheek. And before the hounds, not five arm-lengths away from their murderous amber eyes, crouched Donald. What in the name of the Virgin had happened?

"Donald!"

The boy obediently stood up and took one step backward. The dogs stepped forward. Donald froze.

"Donald!" Her whole body began to shiver. It looked as if the dogs were protecting Iain from Donald, but how could that be? What harm could little Donald do to a full-grown man?

The male dog bared its teeth at the boy. She'd lose her beloved son! Una tensed, ready to spring forward between the child and the hounds. She could not move, could not even open her mouth to cry out. Alasdair had pressed himself hard against her, pinning her arms to her sides.

"Take care, Una," he whispered. "Move but a muscle and the dogs may attack."

"Shoot them!" The words burned like whisky in her throat.

"And risk hitting Iain Beag or Donald? Nay, we can't."

The dogs advanced toward the motionless boy one pace at a time, so slow it hurt to watch them. Una could only look on in terror, her heart numb.

A rush of wind swept around her. A swirl of tartan blurred past. Una glimpsed a glint of silver. An explosion ripped across her ears. She heard a dog yelp and saw it fall to the ground, blood pouring from its mouth. The other beast sprang straight at her. Like Donald, she froze. The hound brushed past her. She could smell its doggy stench. There was a cracking sound, a whine, and a thump. Her mind swam with fear and confusion, but she could see that Donald was unharmed.

"Dia!" Alasdair turned away from her and knelt down by the body of the great hound. A throng of guests and servants lifted the creature from the ground, and as they did so Una could see a man sprawled underneath the carcass, drenched in blood.

Connach.

She ran to Donald and threw her arms around him. Although she was likely to crush him, she could not stop herself.

"Mama, the dogs . . . the big man . . ."

The dogs were dead, one felled by Connach's masterful shot, the other very nearly beheaded by the force of Connach's pistolbutt against its skull. He'd had time to reload only one pistol, Una thought. Did the brave man kill himself for her son's sake? She watched, holding her breath, as he sat up, opened his eyes, and rubbed a white swatch across his smoke-stained forehead with one swipe of his hand. "Brandy, for the love of God," he murmured.

Una sat down with Donald on her lap and stroked his hair. She searched the crowd for Seanag, but the midwife had disappeared. What should she say? What should she do? Connach was a terror to her dear friend, yet he'd saved her heart's joy. Shouldn't she thank the man? Perhaps, as Seanag insisted, some part of him was as kind as other parts were cruel.

"Mistress?"

Una looked up and beheld Iain Beag. His face was fully as white as her own son's and a red lump as big as a turnip jutted out over one ear. "Iain! You're well! Mairi be praised!"

Iain shook his head. He pointed a trembling forefinger at Donald, and the boy burrowed down deep in Una's breast. "This one," whispered Iain, "he killed my dogs, that fairy calf, and he very nearly killed me."

"What's that you say?" whispered Una. "Connach killed your dogs. Donald would never hurt anyone."

Iain laughed without mirth. "I saw him throwing stones at Cath and Mol and said, 'Stop, creature!' Then I was down on the ground with my head broken open and the dogs standing above me barking to wake the dead. And then ..." He stopped speaking. Tears brimmed in the corners of his eyes.

"I'm sorry, Iain Beag," Una said, "but Donald meant no harm. The stone that struck you was pure mischance, I'm sure."

Iain stretched his neck for a better look at the boy. "The work of the old Cheater himself." Iain reached out to touch Donald's shoulder, but Una pulled the child away. She stared straight and hard into the wounded man's eyes, but he returned her gaze with ease. "A short life to him," he said, then turned and trudged away.

Such a common curse! She'd said it herself a hundred times, but never had it sounded so deadly to her before.

Donald squeezed her hand and she squeezed it back. "There, there, my heart," she crooned to him. "It's all past. Shall we find the big man and thank him?"

A handful of gillies washed the blood from the grass and the wedding went on, louder and rowdier than before, the visitors excited by the sight and scent of death. Una could find Connach nowhere among the horde of guests. Finally she came upon Alasdair, seated on the tongue of a cart, sharing a pipe with Mata. "Where is Connach?" she asked.

Alasdair nodded, and the smoke from his pipe danced about his head. "Gone. I offered him ten pounds for what he did, and he thanked me for the silver but refused to accept it. Then he took his leave." Alasdair smiled and shrugged. "He's a puzzlement, that one."

"I wish him well," said Una, which wasn't quite what she meant, "and I'm grateful to him. But the man frightens me, *a'ghraidh.*" Should she tell him about the incident at Craigorm? she wondered. No, leave old wounds unopened, Seanag always said. "I'm so happy he's gone and left Seanag in peace."

Alasdair sighed and turned his face from her. He picked at a splinter of wood on the tongue of the cart. "Seanag's gone with him. I couldn't persuade her otherwise."

"Seanag has gone," she repeated, but the words were as unbelievable on her own lips as they had been on Alasdair's. "You are mistaken. Seanag wouldn't leave without telling me."

"She left without telling you to spare you the pain of parting," said Mata. "Pol went with her."

"The man beats her! He'll slay her!"

"I hardly think so." Alasdair set about retying his garters, though they were perfectly tight. "If you must know, I think he loves her very much, and she him."

How could such clever men be so dull-witted? she thought. "I'll go and fetch her back myself."

"Indeed you'll not. Who'll look after Cha and Donald? Who'll keep me warm during the *mios nam pog*?" Alasdair stood up and went to her, encircling her with one arm. She was smothered in his warmth, the scent of his tobacco, and the strength of his opinions. "I know you don't care for the man, but Seanag seems to have him in hand. Have patience. You'll see her soon enough."

She looked out over the darkening sky and fastened her gaze on the Paps. Seanag would be looking at them now, too, gauging the distance of her long walk to Glenfinnan and her journey back to Glenalt. Una leaned her cheek against Alasdair's hard arm and kissed his sleeve. "I pray you're right, love."

Chapter 13

Una had dreaded the day Donald would leave her, but at last it came. The weather glowered at Una and her family when they began their sea voyage to Cali's island, but in the late afternoon, the sun came out to gild the ocean and brighten the prow of their little vessel. Duncan the Boat sang as he rowed. Alasdair's long red hair rippled in a rising wind. So peaceful, Una thought. The inside of the womb might be as peaceful. If only her heart weren't so heavy.

"Look, Mama! A silkie!"

Una barely heard the boy's excited voice over the slurring of the waves. She looked where Donald was pointing just in time to see a bewhiskered black face dip beneath a swell. "A seal, *m'sholus.*" The boy continued to peer into the home of the silkies, alert for more signs of monsters. When he leaned forward for a closer look, the boat lurched and water splashed onto the gunwale.

"Sit down!" Alasdair barked. The boy crouched beside

Una as if he had been struck. "Would you tip us all into
the sea, wheybrain?" He scowled, then drew back his hand.
Una felt Donald all but push himself into her as he tried
to escape his father's displeasure.

"You're over-rough with him," she chided Alasdair, and
wrapped both arms around her child.

"He's too old to be hiding behind his mother's skirts,"
Alasdair grumbled, then abruptly turned his gaze on the
swelling ocean. When he looked back at her, his face was
soft with concern, but it was not for Donald. "Are the
waves sickening you, love?" he asked her.

"Perhaps a little," she said. It was a good thing that
she'd left Cha at Glenalt. The ocean was calm for that time
of year, Duncan had said, but even that calm was enough
to turn Una's digestion. Or perhaps, she thought, it might
have been the new life stirring inside her and not the fault
of the sea at all.

"Not long now, mistress," shouted the boatman. Surely
he wasn't talking about the baby? "Duneilean draws near."

She didn't want to think of her journey's end: a warm
welcome from Ros and Cali, a few nights' pleasant stay
with them, and then a hard farewell, harder than leaving
her old home in Glenfinnan. She breathed in deeply, letting her mind fill with the salt smell of the sea, the slap
of the waves against each other, and the shimmer of the
sun on the water. Donald would be happy in his new home,
happier than he was at Glenalt. At first it had been pleasant
enough. There was so much to learn about Glenalt, and
Cha had distracted her. But then the winter had set in,
and Alasdair began speaking of his books again. He'd
shown them to her, but it was Donald who'd wanted to
read. He'd never said a word about it but stared at his
parents as they hunched over books by the fire. Then one
evening, when Alasdair had been reading to Una, Donald
astonished his father by repeating a long passage in

English. One glance at Alasdair's blank face had assured Una the boy had not made a single error.

"Teach him, Alasdair," Una had said. "Here's a willing pupil for you and a bright one."

Alasdair had shut the book. "What need has the boy of reading?" he replied. "There are no books on Duneilean. Teach him what you learn, if you like." And she'd wished, for the first time in her life, that she had the patience for such work.

"There's the island now," cried Duncan. Una turned and saw a black spit of land jutting out of the water to her left. All about it stood tall skerries, sea-rocks white with the droppings from hundreds of black cormorants, seamews, and puffins so fat they seemed likely to roll from their nests into the ocean at any moment. The birds took to the air in a cloud as the boat sped toward the rocks and settled again when it had passed. Una shivered to look at them.

The boatman used all his skill and strength to wrench the boat around the skerries, and soon they were in soft waters again, riding into a cove edged with beach grass. In the distance a man, a woman, and a flock of children were heading toward the boat.

Donald took her hand. "Am I going to live here forever?" he asked.

"Nay, my jewel," said Una, "only for a little while. You'll be Cali's and Ros's foster son, and Anghas will be ours, just as Mata and your da were fostered long ago. You'll learn to hunt and swim and ride a horse." She bit her lip. *You'll learn all the things your father should be teaching you.*

Donald had ceased listening. Instead he was pointing to a tiny figure that jumped up and down on the hillside, flapping its arms and screaming like one of the frenzied island birds. "Look! There's Anghas! Anghas! Hallo! Hallo!"

He hung so far over the side of the boat that Una was afraid the waves might pitch him overboard. She grabbed his shirt with one hand and clung to him fiercely. "Wait a bit," she told him. "Wait. Wait."

That evening there was great merriment at Cali's house, as well as a river of whisky and singing and storytelling, but even in the midst of such celebration Una felt empty. She tried to tell herself, as she had for several years, that fosterage would be good for Donald, and she truly believed it; however, the separation from her darling would be torture for her. The only things that brought her comfort were thoughts of Alasdair, Cha, and the unborn child within her.

She was one of the first to fall asleep that night, not long after the youngest weans, heedless of the loud voices and Mata's harp, but she could not stay asleep. Dreams of Donald walking away from her, not heeding her pleas to return, haunted her mind and would not let her rest. After hours of sleeping and waking, she was roused from a dream by a hideous shriek and wild movement beside her.

"O, my poor husband!" Una cried, flinging her arms around the haggard man. His entire body glistened with sweat. "Whisky! Hurry!" she called to no one in particular, and in a matter of moments found herself holding a horn cup full of spirits, though she wasn't sure who had brought it to her. But when she put the cup to Alasdair's lips, he refused to drink.

"Donald?" he said, gazing around the room with eyes still turned toward some other world.

Una looked at the child, who was sitting up in his bed-clothes, his hair in spikes about his head like a cap of icicles. "Donald is well enough," she told Alasdair, and patted his disheveled hair into place around his shoulders. "Calm yourself, husband. It's naught but phantoms of the night." She continued to soothe him, but all the while puzzled over what he had meant by asking for Donald. It was the first time she could remember him mentioning the boy after waking from one of his nightmares.

When all save the two of them had returned to sleep, Una could not bridle her curiosity. "What was it you dreamed of?" she asked Alasdair, raising herself on one elbow to stare down into his wide-open eyes. "The outlaws again?"

"Aye, the corrie."

"But you spoke of Donald . . ."

Alasdair regarded her with a thoughtful look. "As you say, it's but a phantom, and nothing to fear. In any affair, I don't wish to speak of it. On the morrow we leave Duneilean, no matter what Ros and Cali say. Whenever that wean is with me, he haunts my sleep."

"O, Alasdair," Una whispered, "you speak of him as a ghost, but he's your own precious son." Una nestled into him and held him close, but the man was already asleep.

Just before Hogmanay Una gave birth to a dark, howling imp of a lad, a true child of the winter storms. He was named after his grandfathers, Calum Rory, but Una called him Rory Og, and soon that was all the babe was called. Though Seanag wasn't in Glenalt to help with the lying-in, Pol held Una's hand throughout the entire birthing and two serving-women made perfectly respectable midwives in her place.

As soon as the child was dried off Alasdair took him into his arms. Later he carried the wean about with him in his plaid wherever he went. Alasdair spent so many nights at the fire with Cha in his lap and Rory Og on his shoulder that Mata called him *duine cearc*, the hen-man, but Alasdair didn't seem to mind.

Even with Cha and the baby to distract her, Una pined

for Donald all through the dark days of winter. Had Ros found a way to bring some color to the lad's skin? Did he miss Glenalt? Did he miss his real family? She nursed these questions and a hundred others as she minded the weans and sat for long hours, spinning wool into thread. Sometimes she thought of voicing her fears to Alasdair, but kept silent, afraid of waking his dark dreams again. As the winter wore on, Una grew accustomed to bearing her sorrows in silence.

The snows stayed very late that year, and when Beltane came, the feast of spring gaiety, the streams around Glenalt were still running high with snowmelt. The old gray stonehorse that Alasdair himself had raised from a foal chased his mares about the fresh pastures until he shuddered with exhaustion.

Una sent three serving-girls into the fields to pick violets, arbutus, and harebells to freshen the house for Donald's return. She arranged the blooms in clusters throughout the big room so that the stark walls gleamed with color. When the house was cleaned and full of flowers, Una took all the chesspieces out of their boxes and placed them in small groups on shelves and tabletops. She loved handling them, although she hadn't the patience to learn the game. Sometimes she carried a gamepiece around in her *arasaid*, just for the pleasure of running her hand over the smooth wood.

With the house decorated and ready, Una had time to watch the people of the glen enjoy the holiday. Calves and lambs were roasted whole, and hillsides were covered with revelers eating and drinking and starting fights among each other. It saddened Una a little to think of the celebration her own people must be having back in Glenfinnan, a celebration she and her father would not be part of. She had at last persuaded him to stay with her in Glenalt, but his old heart was nearly always heavy with memories of

Sorcha. Una was determined to make Beltane a merry time, for his sake.

In the late afternoon, into the thick of the feasting and drinking walked Donald, a head taller than when she had last seen him and just as white, with Cali like an extra shadow beside him and Anghas, handsomer than ever, tagging along behind. She almost fell over Donald to welcome him, covering him with kisses and caresses. He didn't slink away, she was glad to see, though she knew some day he would.

Later in the evening, when she went to give him some honey-cake, he was nowhere to be found. She searched out Alasdair and made him hunt the boy with her, high and low inside amid a din of cheers and laughter, and outside in the blue of the gloaming. Una was crossing the byre-yard when Alasdair caught her by the waist and jerked her hard toward him. There was a rumble of hooves. The gray stone-horse flew past so close she could see the red centers of its flaring nostrils. On its back sat Donald, entangled in the animal's flowing mane, his own hair streaming out silver behind him.

"God's curse on him! He'll break my horse's legs and his own fool neck!" Alasdair shouted.

"Let him go," she said. She wondered what it must be like to race so fast and free on the back of a great beast. "He'll do the animal no harm."

"That wean begs a whipping," mumbled Alasdair. She took a good look at the man's face and knew he wouldn't punish the boy. The honest shock of admiration shone in her husband's gray eyes.

Years rolled past like so many drops of rain sliding down a window-skin. Una bore a stillborn son and gave birth to another son named for his father, but it was Donald who filled her mind. He was gone for great stretches of time, and whenever he returned he had grown taller or fleshed out or changed some way in his face and bearing. Each time she saw him anew he was a different child, inside as well as out. He kept to himself, with Anghas his sole companion. "It's just the path to manhood," Alasdair assured her. "He's learning to be his own man."

Still, Una wasn't sure. None of the men she admired—her father, Mata, Calum Mor, Alasdair—were lone dogs. They craved company. Indeed, she knew only one man who preferred to avoid his kin and clan.

During his summers Donald helped his father prepare the herds for the long droves south. Alasdair rarely went himself now, since his legs ached if he walked more than a few miles. Instead he busied himself hiring drovers and choosing breeding stock. Una had only to look at him to see his heart wasn't in his work. As soon as he could he excused himself from the company of the drovers and slipped off to The Cuil.

Donald was exactly like his da. He had no skill in droving, but what he lacked in cattle-sense he more than made up for with pen and paper. Alasdair had relented a bit where Donald's reading was concerned and taught Donald English. The boy taught himself to read, ploughing through every one of Alasdair's precious books. Una loved nothing better than to watch him reading or scribbling away in his "daybooks." What great things he must be writing, she thought.

June 3

How may one track the passing of time? There are the seasons, of course, "the cold, wet three and the warm, wet one," as Mata calls them, and the holidays, Samhrainn and Hogmanay and

Beltane. There are other cycles, too—ploughing, sowing, and reaping; breeding, calving, and slaughtering. Though I've now lived 15 summers, time has lost some of its meaning for me. Once it was a simple matter, dictated by where I was living, either in Duneilean or Glenalt. But now my mother has succeeded in persuading Alasdair to break my fosterage, and it is harder to keep pace with the year. Anghas has worked some magic on his parents and still spends his summers in Glenalt. He vows he'll buy me ink and books and paper galore once he is a grown man with silver of his own, though he himself can neither read nor write.

Then there is Seanag. Not many years ago her presence was a good marker of the seasons. She lived in Glenalt from just after Beltane to a day or so before Samhrainn, while Connach was cattle-dealing or driving his herds south. But now she lives in Glenalt year-round. Even Connach can see that Seanag is no longer well enough to make the yearly journey from Glenalt to Craigorm and back.

At first my mother was delighted. Seanag is with her all the time now, as is Pol, a big lump of a lad taller than me. But Seanag has changed. She walks with difficulty and looks very like a hag. Only when she laughs and shows her broken rabbit-teeth does she look like the strong Seanag of old.

Now it is I who walk the heath, looking for whatever plants Seanag needs to brew teas to treat her ailments. Seanag has her own little bothy in the hills where the herbs grow thickest. Mammy asked it of Alasdair. "I don't deserve such a gift," says Seanag, but the house is as dear to her as Pol. There she has found a measure of peace and freedom from her husband.

June 10

Today Connach returned to Glenalt. It was a rare, warm afternoon, the sort of day when the cattle stand in the loch to keep cool. The big drover met with Alasdair at The Cuil and the two sat for hours talking and drinking. Connach downed pint after pint of whatever brew Alasdair set before him while my mother huddled in the room of the books, keeping the little weans close to her, as though her husband were entertaining Lucifer himself.

Connach stayed long and left just as the sun was touching the horizon. "Never suffer that man to sit in the house again," Mammy commanded Alasdair.

"Well, I can't promise you that," Alasdair mumbled, speaking around the pipe in his mouth. "He's my head drover now. I just asked him would he live here in Glenalt with us and lead the droves south. Connach knows cattle. He has a way with the beasts."

"Connach is a terrible man," she said. "He hasn't given up the drink. Mayhap Connach had charmed you, as he has charmed Seanag."

"Well, any man needs a dram now and then. You're too hard on the fellow."

Thus they squabbled back and forth for some time, with me listening, wondering why Alasdair allowed my mother to have such a free say in matters. Connach seems like a fine, manly fellow to me, and if Alasdair wished to hire him, that should be reason enough. My mother fears him because he is harsh with Seanag, I reckon, though he loves her and she him. I am beholden to him, that's certain.

Una could judge whatever weather was coming from looking at the sky, but the summer storm caught her by surprise. She was walking with Donald and Anghas down the strath, carrying a creelful of cotton grass and moss and juniper berries for Seanag. Her mind was on the midwife, not on the weather. When she at last glanced upward, the heavens were black. Rain began to fall like a river and lightning shredded the sky.

"A house!" cried Anghas, pointing toward a faint light,

and both boys raced toward Fiona's cottage. Una could do nothing but stumble after them, pulling strands of hair away from her eyes as she ran, abandoning the creel. She'd scarcely spoken a word to Fiona since the wedding, for most times the madwoman kept to herself.

When Una reached the bothy she flung herself inside. There was no need to ask for entrance, not out on the moor in the middle of a storm. Even her worst enemies—and she counted Fiona among them—wouldn't have refused her shelter.

Baskets. Baskets everywhere. She had very nearly forgotten them, but there they were to remind her of the clutter of Fiona's mind. The boys had cleverly overturned two wicker creels to use as chairs and sat warming themselves by the fire, wringing out their plaids and chattering away at each other as if they were the only two creatures in the house. Una blinked as her eyes adjusted to the semidarkness of the room. Somewhere, behind some basket, Fiona was watching her.

"Mistress?"

Una jumped, as if the house itself had spoken to her. Fiona lay against a far wall, covered only to the waist. The boys, who doubtless had noticed her earlier, paid her no mind.

"Ah . . . forgive me, Fiona, bursting into your house this way," stammered Una. "The storm . . . the boys. You can hear the thunder drumming."

Fiona prodded the plaid beside her and her voice faded to a whisper. "Love, wake and see this."

The plaid heaved, wriggled, and groaned. A great shaggy head appeared next to Fiona and a pair of hooded eyes looked Una over carefully. *"Mo Dhia!* See what the fairies have brought into the house. Good day, mistress. Or bad day, rather. What a downpour! Look at these big lads!

What's the one of them doing in a fop's breeches? Come,
what has happened to your tongue, woman?''

"You devil of a man!" cried Una. Still, she wasn't surprised to see him with the wench. She'd suspected just
such a thing when she'd first seen the two of them together.
"How can you deceive Seanag so?"

Connach raised one eyebrow. "Deceive, mistress? Nay,
I'm deceiving no one."

"This is indecent!" It was a weak word indeed to describe
the way Connach and Fiona made her feel. "It's wicked.
It's wrong."

Connach smiled. "Mayhap, but it's all of Seanag's doing,
none of mine. She's too ill to . . . accommodate me."

"I see Fiona is accommodating enough," growled Una.
Surely the lynx-man was lying. Seanag wouldn't arrange a
lover for her husband. "Seanag is ill. She can't be blamed
for that."

Connach sighed, laid his hand on his cheek, and nodded. He was the very picture of regret. "It's true, she's not
herself. My poor darling." For a moment Una felt sorry
for the big brute of a man. Her pity vanished in an instant
when Connach rose full naked in the firelight, bolted over
to her, and caught her by the wrist. She whimpered in
spite of herself but stood fast.

"Harlot!" spat Connach. His fingers dug into her flesh.
"If not for you, she'd never have changed. It was you who
turned her against me."

"I swear it wasn't!" She felt the strength of the man's
hand course through her and fought the urge to tug her
arm free. Connach had broken the arms of many a man,
it was said. She glanced at the boys, who gazed up at her
in concern but wisely said nothing.

The drover thrust a tiny glass vial under her nose. "On
every drove I visit the chemists in every city, seeking out
medicines. And why? Because of you, devil take you! O, I

trow they're worthless, the lot of them, but I'll search until I find the one that brings back my hearing, and the other that will restore my Seanag.''

Connach smiled broadly, and Una saw why: she had aroused him. She covered her heart with her hand and looked away.

"You should be getting out of those wet clothes, mistress.''

Fiona leaned forward, stretching her arms toward Connach. "Love, set her free. Come lie down here with me and let the woman wait out the weather. You gave your word to your wife.''

Connach grunted, then broke his grip on her. Una kilted up her sodden skirts and went back to the fire where Donald and Anghas sat, staring at her with frightened eyes. "Are you hurt?'' asked Anghas.

"Not at all.'' Her wrist ached. It was striped white where Connach had held it. "We'd best leave.''

"Go if you like,'' said Donald.

"Let's bide a bit yet,'' mumbled Anghas. "It's aye wet.''

A short while later the rain was as strong as ever. Little murmurs, snorts, and sighs came from the pile of plaids where Connach and Fiona lay huddled together. Una shivered, imagining goblins and nameless, shameful creatures coupling in darkness. "Come with me,'' she told the boys, eager to quit the sinful house, but the lads were stubborn. They were more afeared of the storm than of Connach.

Donald blinked. "I should be wearing a plaid.'' She pleaded with him, but he pulled away from her and wouldn't look at her. "I'm staying where I am. I'm soaked through to the arse in these hellish breeks!''

She stared at him aghast. He'd never spoken so coarsely to her before. "So be it, then. Anghas?'' The boy shook his head. Well, they'd probably come to no harm. Connach hated her, not them.

Una pulled her shawl over her head and plunged into the rain. After a few steps she was drenched. She tugged the shawl onto her shoulders and let the rain strike her in the face. It was warmer than she expected, like tears, or like Alasdair's kisses late at night, washing Fiona and Connach from her mind.

It was warm in Seanag's bothy, and Una grew drowsy. When Cha handed her a cup, she sniffed it: chamomile, woundwort, sowthistle. To smell it was bad enough, but to drink it! Well, she'd have to, to keep Seanag happy. And perhaps it would do her some good.

"What in Mary's name convinced you to stand out in the rain?" Seanag asked. "Would you catch your death of cold?"

"I was walking," Una corrected her, between sips and sneezes. "Quickly, too."

"Teach me how to make that, Seanag Bhan," demanded Cha.

"All in good time," said Seanag, pouring herself a cup of the coal black tea. "You have a head for healing," she told the child. "Someday you'll be as clever as I used to be."

Now what girl would not have turned as pink as a rose at such a compliment? thought Una. But not Cha. The hoyden held her head up high, shaking out her red curls. She *was* clever, and handsome, too, with much of her father and even more of her grandmother in her downturned lips and wise blue eyes.

Enough of this dallying. Cha had to leave. "Be a good lass and run outside now and fetch some globeflowers for Auntie Seanag," Una instructed her daughter. After protests from Cha and threats from Una, the girl finally dragged herself out of the house.

"You have something to tell me," Seanag said. "Why else be rid of Cha?"

Una fished a black knight from her *arasaid*. She set it down on Seanag's table and slowly turned it round and round. "Connach." Seanag's eyes opened a little wider. "Connach and Fiona. I saw them coupling. And Seanag, the man says he and that woman have your blessing."

Seanag gazed at her over the rim of the wooden cup. "They do, my dear."

"My poor Seanag! Why do you let that creature treat you this way? First the beatings, now this humiliation."

"Connach hasn't struck me in years. He's been too loving, if anything. It's a child he wants, not a dead wife. And . . . well, I'll tell you it all. I can't have a child."

"Seanag, I'm sure you're mistaken. You had Pol."

The midwife shook her head. She fetched a whisky-skin from the wall, poured some of the water of life into her tea and Una's, then took a big gulp of the mixture. Briefly she told Una about her plan to thwart Connach's fatherhood and deny him more children, and how her cures were wearing away her health. "Those herbs you gather for me these days are more than a tonic. They're my life."

"You poisoned yourself? O, Seanag!" Una twisted her hands together in front of her face.

"Wait, now. I'm living, aren't I? All these years Connach had been trying to put a baby in my dead belly, and at last I told him, enough! He was murdering me with loving, asking no more than his due, mind you, but I couldn't even give him that. So I told him, find yourself a woman that has no reputation to lose, a woman who can bear your child and make you feel like a man again. And faith, he wasn't long in the searching."

"Fiona is barren. She and Alasdair had four dead children."

Seanag nodded and smiled. "So I've heard. But Fiona

and Alasdair are cousins, and sometimes cousins are too close. You see that Alasdair had no trouble getting children with you, and so it will be for Fiona, I predict.''

A great lump rose up in Una's chest and moved to her throat, then to her eyes, and suddenly she was kneeling beside Seanag, leaning against her knees and sobbing into the midwife's *arasaid*. ''Seanag, I'm so afeared you'll die and leave me.''

''I won't—not soon, at least,'' Seanag whispered. ''You need me too much for me to leave you.''

Una hugged Seanag's legs to keep them from shaking. ''How do you mean?''

''Connach won't hurt you, not while I'm living. It's the one pledge he's kept for me, all these years.''

''Pledge?'' squeaked Una. The room began to tilt and sway. She eased herself back into her chair. ''What pledge is this?''

''He would have taken his vengeance on you for his deafening, only I made him give it over. I wouldn't have married him otherwise,'' she said softly.

Una drained her whisky in one gulp. She'd never let the man within arm's length of her again. ''Perhaps he's not yet found a fate horrible enough for me.'' Suddenly Connach's face, full of terrible joy, appeared to her, and the answer to a question she'd gnawed on for years burst upon her. ''Connach burned my father's house,'' she said simply. ''To grieve me.''

''Aye,'' Seanag said, ''I've always thought so, since the day of your wedding. There's no proving it, of course, and he'd never confess such a thing. But now you can see how wise it is for you to avoid Connach at all costs, to keep the children from him and Alasdair, too.''

''Alasdair?''

''Aye, him especially. What if Alasdair thought Connach put one paw on you? Were the two of them to go sword to sword or even fist to fist, there'd be nothing to take home afterward."

Una closed her eyes and shuddered at a sudden image of Alasdair and Connach, lying still and silent on a patch of red heather. No, Alasdair would never know what happened to her that day at Craigorm. *God look after all of us,* she prayed in silent desperation, *and after my Donald most of all.* She couldn't say why, but it was him she feared for more than Alasdair, Seanag, or even herself.

Chapter 14

October 12

The harvest is finally in and Samhrainn is over. Rory Og thieved the last honey-cake from me this morning. I took the last apple from him this evening.

It is over two years in the waiting, but at last I shall have a plaid like any ordinary man, and a bonny new jacket, too. The tailor has offered to make them for me, in return for ten pine-martin skins, which he'll stitch into fine sporrans for the chief.

> *Calfskin soft as butter.*
> *Red stitching on the cuffs,*
> *Horn buttons carved to look like targes.*
> *A jacket any gentleman would be proud to wear.*

My mother is less than pleased about my new clothes. The sun will scorch your legs into cinders, says she. And the waste of silver! You'll need all you can get when you go to university. What is

*the point in going, says I, unless I can go looking like a man
and not a milksop?*

*When I told Pol my plans for schooling, he was aye amused,
but he has his own ideas. A new regiment is being formed in Fort
William, says he, a regiment of Gaels, to keep peace in Glenfinnan
and throughout the west. I told him soldiering would be a miserable
life, marching all day and eating bad food at night, but he says
it would be no worse than the life he's living now, walking softly
around his da, who has a temper on him.*

October 13

*Today I rode my black garron into the hills on what must surely
be the last fair day of the year. From the foot of the East Pap down
the drove road to Abhaircuil to Lugach we galloped, and went
through the village at a walk. The children there stopped playing
to stare at us, a white man on a black horse. One very young
child ran inside its house crying "Fogaidh! Fogaidh!"*

*"You think I'm the Fiend?" said I to the other creatures, who
stood about gawking.*

*"No, you are one of the silver ones," murmured a golden-
haired boy with eyes the color of the sky. The others nodded among
themselves.*

*"No more than you," I told them. "No horse will let the shee
ride him." And as the little goblins pondered this I set off at a
gallop again. I shall be happy to leave this ignorant place a year
hence.*

October 15

*It's a wonder I can write. My hand is shaking, and whoever
reads this will know that's true by the spots of ink littering the*

paper. The devil take Alasdair and his lies and promises. The devil take my mother, too, for betraying me. I am undone.

After supper he comes up to me and takes me aside and walks out the door with me. He puts his arm around my shoulder and I know there is some bad work afoot. Then he hems and haws and speaks of marriage and children and the honor of a man and his land. "Is it me you're speaking of?" I ask. "You know full well no woman will have me. They are all afraid of bearing little white calves with red eyes. If you have some news for me, please speak it outright."

"Donald," says Alasdair, "I know you'd like to study in Glasgow, and I know you are nigh seventeen and nearing the age for it, but I cannot spare you here. I need your help with the cattle and the corn, and the next summer you can join Connach and Pol on the drove."

"What!" says I. "I'm no cowherd. I have a head for books, anyone may see that. Surely my mother won't let you do this to me."

Then he gazed at me very sadly, and I hated the look of pity in his face." Your mother knows," he said. "She is sore disappointed for your sake, but she understands that this will be better for you. You'll be happier here, Donald, I promise you. Glasgow is no place for a lad with your . . ."

"Deformity," I told him.

"Appearance," said he. "You'd soon find that the most educated of people are also the cruelest."

"Lies," I said, "all lies, meant to keep me in my place. Why aren't you leaping into the air at the chance to be rid of me, if only for a few years? Is it because you're ashamed to loose me on the city and let the world see this blot on your fine lineage? You're afraid lest someone say, 'This is the son of Alasdair Ruadh? I would not let such a monstrosity walk the streets.'"

When I looked in his eyes, they told me I'd hit on a truth. I have never struck my father. He rarely lifted his hand against me. But just then I slapped him, full on the cheek with the back

*of my hand. It was a sorry decision, but some part of me is glad
I made it. Before I could make another move I was on my back
with him atop me, clamping my wrists to the ground, fair crushing
me into it. It shames me to say that I wept to find myself so helpless.*

*My mother came wailing out of the house and didn't stop until
Alasdair let me stand. "Is it true you'd keep me here, I asked her,
away from university?"*

*"It's best for you, love," said she. I could scarcely believe the
words that were coming from her mouth. "It's here you belong,
not in some foreign place among strangers who don't know you
or love you."*

*"I belong in university!" said I. My eyes were so bleary I could
barely see her. I ran inside to pen these lines so that the world
might know my sorrows, but the writing of them has brought me
less comfort than I'd hoped. Somewhere, in all this great glen,
there's one open heart that will list to my words.*

> *High in the night sky the eagle is soaring,*
> *Quiet and cooling the wind on his wings,*
> *Lonely the rage that about him is pouring,*
> *Known but to him is the song that he sings.*

*I sought out Pol, for, though he is dull-witted, he never speaks
false. "You'll find Pol and his da at Ewan's house," Seanag said.
"That's where my man's silver goes now, to keep him full. Send
them home straight away, for it's not proper that they stay there
the night."*

*Ewan Mor is a huge fat man who can hold more water of life
than any other creature in the district. He so loves a dram that
he keeps his still inside his house, in its own large stall, like a
milk cow. It bubbles and hisses away on its own fire, distilling
Ewan's livelihood by turning grain into liquid silver.*

*Pol and Connach were at Ewan's, as Seanag had said. "D-D-
D-Donald!" sputtered Pol when he saw me enter. "Welcome, and
take a chair, only there are no more chairs, so you'll have to sit*

*on the floor!" This sent all four of them—Pol, Connach, Ewan,
and a man I didn't recognize—into whoops of laughter.*

"What brings you out so late the night, Donald?" asked Connach. "Does your mother know you're here?" His companions
shrieked with laughter.

I smiled readily. Taunting is Connach's way of speaking, and
he means no harm by it. Being with Connach is like playing at
the troigh is dorn gulbann, the stunt that young men do to
frighten each other and the womenfolk, standing bent double over
the edge of a cliff. Have nothing to do with Connach, my mother
has warned me a hundred times, but I fancy the man. It was
rumored he had killed several men and even beaten his wife. "I
left the house to give my parents a little privacy," said I, and was
rewarded with a volley of snorts and snickers. "As I was leaving
the house, Gentle Rory of Glenfinnan, the old man with the sad
eyes, takes me aside and says, 'You wouldn't be taking yourself
to Ewan Mor's house, would you? It's no good company you'll
find there.' "

"Why, the brainless old fart!" cried Connach. "We're the finest
company on the face of the earth!"

I sampled some of Ewan's whisky, and, after several cupfuls I
was on the edge of sleep when I heard Pol give a soft yelp, like a
coney in the claws of a hawk. Something was happening, but it
was happening much slower than it should have. Pol and his
father rose to their feet, the man behind the boy, and I saw that
Connach's hands were clamped under his son's armpits. Pol's feet
rose off the ground.

Fain would I speak but couldn't. Ewan and the stranger and
I gazed at Connach as he began turning in a circle where he
stood, slowly at first and then a little faster, until Pol's legs were
jutting out nearly straight before him. Pol clung to Connach's
plaid with the terror of a small child who didn't know whether
its father meant to play with it or kill it. Finally Connach heaved
Pol upward and sent him spinning into Ewan's still.

A great crash followed by a hundred little smashes, clatters, *and bangs rocked the house.* "*A thousand murders!*" *shouted Ewan's wife over the frightened shrieking of her children and the wordless bellowing of her husband.*

Since Connach and the others made no attempt to move, I rose with great effort and stumbled over to Pol, who lay sprawled amid the remains of the still. Half-burned peats lay everywhere and whisky ran in rivulets over the floor. Connach looked at us both but said nothing. "*Are you living?*" *says I.*

Pol's knees were burned, and he was bleeding from a cut on his face and another on his hand, but the rest of him seemed to be well enough. His eyes sparkled with surprise, as though he'd expected to find himself in as many pieces as the still. "*So I think.*"

"*My still!*" *moaned Ewan, shaking his fist in Connach's face.* "*See what you've done to my lovely still, you pig's turd!*"

Connach produced two silver coins from his sporran, then tossed them at Ewan. He made as if to leave, seemed to think better of it, and caught me by the elbow. In three strides both of us were out of the house and into the cold before I had my wits about me. Connach propelled me through the heath by the force of his right arm, the same considerable arm that had flung Pol halfway across the room and smashed a pistolbutt through the skull of a great hound. It was an arm to be reckoned with.

At length Connach paused to rest under a jumble of rocks, and I sat down heavily next to him in the frozen bracken. "*You'd wonder why I threw Pol into the pot.*" *I told him I had wondered that.* "*He spoke disrespectful of me,*" *Connach said.* "*Uncommon disrespectful. A bastard, he called me, for taking Fiona to bed. He does not understand that his mother is too sick to be a proper wife, if you take my meaning, but someday I'll see her well again.*"

"*I'm sure you will,*" *says I, though I had no idea what Connach was talking about.* "*Why did you haul me from the house?*"

"*I wanted some company, and you seemed a likely choice. You're a good lad, Donald. Better than some give you credit for.*" *Connach gathered some wood and lit it with his tinderbox.*

"Is that why you saved me from the dog?" says I, warming my
hands before the flames.

"Perhaps," he replies. *"Perhaps I just don't like dogs. Well, off
you go home now, a'mhic. I'm staying here the night."* Connach
made water against a boulder, shook the drops from himself, then
wrapped his plaid around his shoulders and sank down near the
fire.

I did not leave, however. I had no wish to return to that house
of lying. *"I'm not going home the night,"* says I.

*"Ah, is that how it is? And why not, pray? Have you done a
mischief? Or has someone done a mischief to you? No matter. It
all comes to the same."* Connach laughed and patted my knee.
*"Come and stay the night beside me, just as my brothers and I
used to do. We'll keep each other warm."*

I hesitated, then undid my belt, covered myself with my plaid,
and lay down next to the big man. When I woke in the morning,
the drover was still asleep, even though frost gleamed on his plaid.
One of his huge hands lay like a rock on my shoulder. What a
fine, warm feeling it was, having that hand there to protect me.

As autumn wore into winter and the first snow came
and went, Una saw less and less of her beloved Donald in
the young man who shared the house with her and Alasdair. He reminded her less of his da and grandsires and
more of a moody, dangerous stranger. Not even his own
brothers and sisters were safe from his black moods. Donald ignored them when they pestered him for affection
and teased them whenever they were troubled. He pinched
them until they cried out in pain and even her father
threatened to strike him. Why couldn't he treat the children like a Christian? Una asked him once.

Because they made him sick, he'd snapped back. They
were so damned bonny he couldn't bear to look at them.

One morning Una woke to find rime-ice covering the

eaves. A sign of death or the rage of God, the old folk were fond of saying, and she crossed herself. She had not even finished pinning up her hair when Cha ran to her in a panic. "Come to the byre, Mama! Make haste! Donald has slain Rory Og!"

"It's not so!" cried Una. She hurried to the byre with Cha behind her, and there she saw Donald, standing with his legs widespread, an astonished look on his face. Before him lay Rory Og in a crumpled heap, his left arm twisted under him. "The creature tore a page of my daybook," Donald fumed.

"Fetch your father!" Una cried, pushing Cha in the direction of the house. She knelt down beside Rory, her heart slamming against her ribs in fear. She was joined at once by a gillie and a maidservant, who hovered over the boy, afraid to touch him. Una felt his pulse; he was living. As she moved his arm, his eyes flew open and he squealed in pain. "O, my poor wean!" Una wailed.

"He's shamming," Donald said.

Una shook her head, worried for Donald as much as for Rory Og. "Nay, his wrist is broken." Tears blurred her vision and she turned away from her older son. Under Una's direction, the gillie gathered Rory into his arms and was heading toward the house when Cha returned, leading her father by the hand. Without waiting for an explanation, Alasdair took Rory from the gillie and ran home. Una followed, leading Cha and the servants. It troubled her that Donald stayed where he was.

Alasdair set Rory's bone and splinted his wrist, and Una put the boy to bed with a full cup of whisky and a dose of comfrey and the softest words she could give him. When she went to look for Donald, she found him where she had left him, his arms crossed, his face as grim as death. She hurried toward him, still unwilling to believe her best-beloved had done the devil's work. "What possessed you, *a'mhic?*" she asked him.

Donald said nothing, but silently awaited his punishment, a look of defiance distorting his face. Una was about to repeat her question when Alasdair darted up behind her and stepped in front of her. For an instant Una was certain that the man would strike the boy, but Alasdair merely stretched out his hand. "Give me your book," he said.

Donald clutched at the journal he always carried with him under his plaid. Una thought she saw a breath of fear cross the boy's face, then his features hardened and he jammed the book into Alasdair's hands. It was the fourth of its kind he'd written in as many years.

Alasdair returned to the house, the book under his arm. In his shadow went Una, wondering where he intended to hide the papers so that Donald could not find them. To her shock, he shooed the serving-women from the fire and thrust the journal into the red coals. The pages burst into flame, withered and curled in on themselves, a nosegay of brittle black rose petals.

Una sucked in her breath as she picked up one of the ash-flowers and poked it to bits in her hand. "Poor Donald! But who can say he did not deserve it?"

"He deserves far worse," Alasdair said. "Your love will ruin him yet."

Donald vanished for the rest of the day, and when he returned in the evening, Alasdair had worse waiting for him. Una gritted her teeth as Alasdair slashed his belt across Donald's bare back five, ten, fifteen times. She winced at every blow, though Donald was silent. It was the first time he had been whipped since he was little, but she did not try to stop Alasdair. Donald's pain would balance the suffering he had caused his young brother, she thought.

But Donald's pain was short lived. That very night he gathered papers for a new journal, and by the next evening he had fashioned one. Every night of the next fortnight, Una would awake in the dark hours of the morning to see him scribbling away by candlelight. She was curious to know what he wrote, and even more curious to know what words had perished in the fire.

Chapter 15

When starting a diary afresh it is important to begin with the correct date according to the calendar of the Romans, and MacShimi, the tutor of Dunvegan's children, assures me that this is the first of December. Dates must be entered correctly. I wouldn't wish a man reading this after my death and coming across some brainless error. Everything here is as accurate as I can make it.

Yesterday my father burned my old journal. He did it in a fit of anger, after I had teased Rory Og. There's nothing he'd not do for the creature. That much I understand full well, but I wish he'd not have done that.

> *Burn, flames, and glow, peats,*
> *Eat up my words and swallow my memories.*
> *Long may the pen search in vain for those leaves,*
> *And long may my mind search the embers.*

December 6

    The winter is here in earnest. There was snow this morning and the eaves look like the mouth of a wolf, hung with great fangs of ice.

    Today I discovered that Pol has gone to the garrison and enlisted in the regiment there. When I brought this news to Seanag, she was not to be consoled. "Now he'll die in some foreign war," she said, "and not even be buried in his own soil among his own people."

    "Soldiering will do that one some good," Connach said. "Cure him of his idleness." It didn't seem to bother Connach at all that he was likely the cause of Pol's leaving.

December 20

    This morning a storm blew in and pitched an arm's depth of snow on the glen, but the tailor came by this evening anyway, braving the cold to take a last measurement of my shoulders. He promises he shall have my new jacket ready for me in a matter of days, and he'd best not be deceiving me.

    If I were in London now, or Glasgow, there would be great merry-making and feasting on goose and puddings and cakes. So I have read, and so Connach tells me. But here we have no Yule. It is a sin, says my mother, to treat the birth of the Criosd *lightly. Instead, Alasdair reads aloud each night from his Bible but, as it is not in the Gaelic, only he and I can understand it. I can't see what use it is.*

    Tomorrow, if the weather's not too cold, I shall visit Connach and Fiona and bring them a fine mess of salted herring. The man is uncommon fond of his shoal-fish. He never thanks me when I bring them, just sits by the fire with his whisky, looking at me and smiling in that wry way he has. He understands more with all his silences than most people with all their empty talk.

* * *

Connach was comfortably drunk. It was a good evening for drinking, gloomy and full of mist, with a freezing wind out of the north. He sat before the blue coals of the fire, alone. Fiona had taken to bed just after supper. She'd been aye weary of late. Thinking of her made him think of Seanag, who was never very far from his mind these bitter cold days. He'd left her with a good fire and plenty to eat, but he worried for her all the same.

Connach took a small glass vial from his sporran, fingered it lovingly, and sniffed at the cork. It gave off a faint memory of a powerful funk. The vial had once held a healing liquor, but now it was quite empty. Seanag had drunk the full of it, but the devil the bit of good the dose had done her. He would have to go back to the physick for another, stronger philtre, and where would the silver come for that?

That strumpet Una! he thought. Seanag's sickness was all that slattern's doing. He could see her in his mind's eye, as wet and trembling as she'd been that night at Fiona's bothy, with her breasts firm under her shirt. He imagined her on her belly, her face to the ground, and him bending over her, stripping her *arasaid* from her just as he'd skin a deer.

He heard a shout at the doorway and pocketed the vial.

"Connach? Halloo!" Someone parted the plaids, eased himself inside, and stepped into the circle of firelight. It was the *gealtach*. Snowflakes sparkled in his long hair, the color of snow itself. Connach stared at him with the same pleasant terror he'd felt when he'd led the creature away from Ewan's house.

"Welcome, Donni." The creature came closer into the light and set a dripping basket by the fire, then undraped his soaking plaid from his shoulders. Connach laughed softly. "Well, here's half the village!"

"Do you like it? The tailor was done with it just this morning." Donald wore a jacket the likes of which Connach had never seen before and hoped never to see again, a jacket so ridiculously ornate that even the vainest chief would be embarrassed to wear it. The leather could hardly be seen through the clutter of red piping, silver buttons, and brocade trim.

"It's something to see, Donald," Connach chuckled without taking his eyes from the *gealtach's* jacket. "Like you, it makes its presence known, doesn't it?"

Donald sat down by the fire and Connach offered him a dram from the same wooden cup he'd been using. "Drink up! Take the chill off." He winked at the *gealtach* and smiled. The boy's eyes glowed in the firelight, as red and round as two big currants. What a curiosity that would be, if the eyes could be preserved, to take them in hand and show them about down south at fairs. Would people believe that such eyes came from a human being? How could the woman Una cherish such a monster?

Dia! Why hadn't it come to mind before? Connach recalled his promise to Seanag never to lay a hand on Una, the daughter of Gentle Rory. All these years he had spent yearning to repay the drab, and here the answer was sitting in front of him. "What's in the basket? Ah, shoal-fish. *Gle mhath!* Here, take some for yourself." Donald refused. Connach nodded, waiting for just the right moment. "Is it true you got a thrashing?"

Donald gave a start. "Aye, for no reason whatever. But it's well known my da has no love for me."

"Just so," Connach drawled, "nor you for him. I heard you struck him."

Donald's jaw very nearly dropped into his lap, and Connach had to use might and main to keep from smiling. "Who told you this?"

Connach cut a herring into chunks and popped one into his mouth. "Fiona. She hears all. It's true, isn't it? You can't keep news like that to yourself, you know."

"It's true," said Donald. "I'm sorry for it, but he brought it on himself. He forbade me from going to university."

Connach nodded as he chewed away at another piece of fish. "Seanag tells me you had your heart set on studying in Glaschu, that you're quite the scholar." The *gealtach* sputtered some nonsense about his parents forcing him to stay in Glenalt lest the city folk think ill of his father. "Ah, I see how it is. He'd try to prevent you from becoming another Donald Ban Ard."

"Who is that?"

Connach smiled to himself. This was too easy! Donald's parents must have kept the story from him. "Why, your ancestor, several generations past. A man just like you in appearance and temperament."

"He was another *gealtach*?"

"Aye, indeed." Connach drew a deep breath. "A great hero of a man, who did much for the honor of his clan and his chief. He was educated abroad, as you wish to be. I'm surprised your family hasn't told you of him."

"It's no surprise to me," said Donald bitterly. "It's just as you thought. They wish to keep me a child and a cowherd all my life." He paused a moment, entranced by his own thoughts. "This will speak my mind better than I." The *gealtach* pulled from his plaid a well-thumbed sheaf of papers bound in leather. "My daybook. Pol says you have a little English." Connach nodded. "Fine, then. I needn't translate it." Donald thumbed through the pages, found one that suited him, and began reading.

Adders in the heart are not so poisonous,
Nor a dirk in the back not so deadly
As the cruelty of a mother and father.

"Strong words," mumbled Connach. "A man should
show his parents more respect." This time he couldn't
suppress a smile, but the creature was staring into his book
and didn't see him. "You could get to Glaschu yet, Donni,
without their help, if you had a mind to."

"Not without silver," said the creature, "and I have
none. I was born with nothing and I will die with nothing,
just as Alasdair desires."

"And if I were to help you?" Connach licked grease
from his hand and stretched it out toward the *gealtach*. "I
need but your pledge of obedience." He cocked his head
in what he thought might look like a trustworthy gesture.
"Come, give me your hand on it. I'll have you at university
come harvesttime." The lad hesitated. Connach assessed
him quickly. He began to draw his hand away. "Perhaps
you would rather herd cattle."

Donald caught him by the wrist. Connach's heart
warmed in his breast. "If you're giving something, you're
expecting something in return. You'd not have me harm
my parents, would you?"

Connach smiled. Did he look fatherly enough? "Faith,
did I speak of harming anyone? I need your assistance."

"To what purpose?"

"Ah, you'll have to trust me there. I'm planning a wee
task for you, to see whether you're the lad for me or no."

Donald frowned. His white lashes fluttered, and for a
moment he had the gentle look of a pony about him. "Pol
says you've killed a man before."

Connach rocked back on his heels, stunned, but only
for an instant. "Pol's mouth is too big for him, but he spoke
the truth. Man and woman both. A beggar in Sterling. A

doxie in Doune. A peddler in Tayside. A cheat of a chemist in Perth. No one of consequence.'' Connach reached for another piece of herring, thinking of those he'd killed over the years. It vexed him a little that he could not recall their faces.

Donald twisted a button on his too-grand jacket. "You want me to kill someone. With you. As a proof of my allegiance.''

"Clever lad.'' Now that the *gealtach* mentioned it, it seemed like a good idea. Connach had been wondering exactly what he was going to do with the boy, and now he had an inkling. There was no faster road to a bit of silver than taking it off a corpse. He stretched out his hand again, and this time Donald took it. "You'll not regret your choice.'' A strange tenderness welled up inside Connach, as if he possessed the creature somehow, and that was a great comfort.

Anghas came to Glenalt just as the heather was beginning to bloom. Though she loved the boy like one of her own children, Una suspected he'd brought something frightful and evil along with him into the glen that year. It started with the weather, the first snowy Beltane that Una could remember. The snow and ice killed every flower, and many lambs froze to death.

The weather was not the only murderer in Glenalt. The old tinker who had made Una's bracelets was found on the heath, his head ripped apart by two musketballs. His ancient gennet had been butchered and his cart ransacked of everything of value. The rest had been broken to bits. Una wept when she heard the news, for the tinker had been kind to her.

Connach and Mata, an unlikely pair of man-hunters, set out to find the murderer and returned with a poor broken man who screeched his innocence even as he was strung up on a tree. He'd had the tinker's earring in his sporran and had been using the handcart for firewood. "Base creature," said Donald after the hanging, but his smug voice troubled Una. Though she said nothing, in her heart she felt the broken man was telling the truth.

Donald was trouble on foot that spring. He was hard to live with, when indeed he was with his family. Once, Donald struck Anghas in the face and bloodied his lip. "You're becoming bad goods just like that creature Connach," Una scolded her son, and instantly regretted it: he was five days gone from the house.

But all this evil was not part of Anghas himself. He was as sweet-natured as he had ever been, with a sort of silly dreaminess about him that Una had never noticed before. One morning she learned the cause of it. She was walking to the midden when she saw that Cha was there ahead of her. Una slipped behind the corner of the house to give the girl some privacy, but something was wrong; hadn't she seen two people? Una craned her neck and stole another peek. Cha and Anghas were squatting on the midden together, their clothes draped modestly over their laps. They were not a foot apart, and even this small gap was bridged by their hands.

What was more intimate than sharing a midden? Una had never even suspected Cha and Anghas of such familiarity. How familiar were they with one another? She sank back against the wall, letting the stones support her. Anghas and Cha. Anghas was eighteen, barely a man, the whiskers just beginning to show on his cheeks, and Cha was but a wean of fourteen, one year younger than Una had been when she'd lain with Alasdair. But that was different, wasn't it? She prayed to the Virgin that these children weren't in love.

She sought out Mata's opinion on the matter, since he

knew all the secrets of the household. "Are Anghas and Cha sweethearts?" she asked him one morning as he was finishing his breakfast.

"I suspect so," he said. The young couple's courtship was a favorite topic of private speculation among the servants, Mata told her, and some had even laid wagers on a wedding date.

That was proof for Una. Alasdair had been too preoccupied with his cattle and books to notice anything unusual in the behavior of his daughter or foster son, but when Una told him Cha was in love, he listened to her very carefully.

That evening Una and Alasdair sat down with the young couple and confronted them with what Una had witnessed and Mata conjectured. "Anghas, do you love her?" asked Una. Her knees trembled under her skirts.

"Indeed I do," gulped Anghas, and he took the girl's hand and gripped it so hard his nails became white. "Cha is my heart of hearts." Cha's face turned as red as her hair.

"*Arrah,*" sighed Alasdair. He leaned back in his chair and lit his pipe, but forgot to draw on it. "Then you must have my consent if you wish to wed her."

"Another day and I would have been asking you for her hand," Anghas sputtered. "I have a little bothy for her on the island, and my father will give us some cattle and housewares. You'll never have to worry for her."

"Can you not keep her here?" Alasdair asked. "I'll provide a house and dowry and . . . "

"Whisht!" cried Una. She glared at her husband and could all but see the visions of grandchildren in his eyes. "Cha is much too young to wed. She knows nothing of men."

"I know a little," Cha said softly as she clung to Anghas's arm.

"How much is that?" Una demanded.

Both lad and lass fell silent and stared at their feet. Una knew at once what must have happened between them. "A wean," she said simply.

Cha and Anghas looked at each other, she with love in her eyes and he with horror and pride and shock all in one expression. "Is it so, my calf?"

Una noticed that Alasdair did not even wait for Cha's nod. "You have my permission to marry," he said, "as quickly as possible, I'm thinking. Do you wish to pledge, or do you favor a priest, or both?"

"Cha is still a wean herself!" cried Una. She didn't really want to prevent the marriage. Cha was in love with a fine young man whom Una herself admired. What better husband could she want for the girl? It was the love match her parents had, that she and Alasdair had. But if only she could have a year or two more of Cha as a child, a little girl at home with her parents. She wasn't ready for Cha to be a woman, a wife, a mother.

"Not a wean any longer," laughed Alasdair, "not with one of her own in her belly. Faith, but you Glenfinnan women know how to trap a mate. Throw him on his back you do and fairly suck the seed from him, like the fairy-maids the old wives warn the boys about."

Una slipped her hand under his sporran, putting an end to his taunting. "You weren't complaining at the time, as I remember," she said softly.

June 10

Anghas and Cha are to be wed this summer's end. Isn't that a pretty piece of news? Had anyone bothered to ask me, I could have told him that the two were turtledoves from the very day Anghas set foot in the glen this year. Anyone with eyes to see could

*tell so from the way they gawked at each other, their mouths as
wide as cooking-pots.*

*They are so sickeningly in love, forever nuzzling and pawing
each other, even with other people about. And my mother and
Alasdair are just as bad, making preparations for the wedding,
speaking of nigh nothing else, and at night rolling about in bed
like a bride and groom. It's a hard thing to bear for a man who'll
never have a wife of his own.*

July 2

"Have you any ken of women?" Connach asked me today, and
when I told him I hadn't, he cursed aloud and said it was time
to remedy that, that too much talk of marriage wasn't good for a
man. He took me to a house full of women, at least half a score
of them, and he chose one of them for me, a young one, very fair
of face. She didn't turn away from me, and she lay stock-still as
I rammed away at her and emptied myself into her. "Aren't you
afraid I'll put a little white child in you?" I asked her afterward.
"What would you do with it?"

She made a motion with her hands, as if she were wringing
the neck of a bird. She wounded me to the quick, that woman,
and I gave her a smart slap for her impudence. "You'd slay my
child?" said I. "Have a care what you say. I've killed before."
She was much afeared of me then, and pulled a sgian from her
girdle. It was an easy matter to take it from her, but I was a little
sorry I'd hit her, so I put the knife in a safe place and tupped her
again, and this time it was far better than before.

They say Cha is with child by Anghas. What sort of devil has
decreed that my babe will not be suffered to live and theirs will?

July 8

Now I am well and truly a thief of the most disreputable kind. I have stolen my own father's cattle, twenty head. Repayment, Connach calls it. Just yesterday we drove the cattle to Glengarry to Connach's brother Duncan and received sixty pounds for the lot. In Carlisle they would fetch far more, but we daren't take them so far.

Connach killed the young herdboy, who was so afraid of Connach that he wet himself. "You said no harm would come to anyone," I scolded Connach. "I never told you anything of the sort," said he. "The lad would have roused half the district against us." If Mammy and Alasdair hear tell of what I've been doing, they'll not let me into the house.

Fiona tells me not to bother my head about my parents. Connach is your father now, she says. She has been in a terrible way since Connach left for the low country this morning. He would not take me with him, would not even give a reason for his leaving. I shall not even speculate on his intentions, though I hope he returns soon. Life with him is wild and uncertain, but there is never any doubt that one is living.

Chapter 16

What love is deeper than mine for my man?
His smile in the morning, his sigh in the evening
Are truly all I breathe for.

Seanag sang to herself as she gathered a handful of the
white yarn into her hands. How soft it felt! It was kind of
Una to give her some decent wool so she could weave cloth
for a pretty *arasaid* for Cha. Una's little spitfire should have
something good to wear at her wedding and on her journey
to her new home over the water. She'd miss Cha.

She had just begun threading on her loom when her
old dog scrambled to its feet and gave a rusty woof. The fur
along its back stood on end. Seanag gathered the trembling
dog onto her lap. Connach. He'd been gone almost three
weeks. She was used to his strange comings and goings,
but O! how she'd hoped that this absence would be the
final one. No, she would never be rid of him, and in a
way, that was all right. "Come in and welcome to you,

a'ghraidh," she said. Connach appeared from nowhere and entered the house. He had lost considerable flesh since she'd last seen him. His eyes were sunk in hollows in his face and his clothes hung loose on his great frame. "You don't look yourself, beloved. Fiona said you were in Glaschu, but it's too early for the droves."

"I wasn't droving," said Connach. "I went to Glaschu for you."

"Spare me your taunting."

"I'm speaking the truth." He gave her a tremendous smile and sat down at her feet. The dog struggled and whined in her arms. "Still not my friend, Cu?"

She led the dog outside and tied it fast. When she returned, Connach was standing by the loom, admiring the fine wool of Cha's *arasaid*. "Beautiful, my love. Is it for you?"

"For Una's eldest daughter. She and Anghas mac Calum Og are soon to be wed. I'm seeking to be of use, you see, while I still can."

"Don't speak that way, my darling." Connach reached out and took her hand in his great paw. "It fair breaks my heart to see you wasting your strength on the spawn of that strumpet. Once you're well again, I want you to leave this middenheap and come to Glengarry with me, where we both belong."

"Once I'm well," repeated Seanag. Sometimes Connach could be deaf in both ears. "I shan't ever be well," she sighed, and laid her free hand on top of his. "Promise me again you'll do no harm to Una or her people." Connach drew his hand away. He didn't appear to hear her, for he smiled broadly and pulled something out of his sporran: a small brown bottle. "Yet another cure?" she sighed.

Connach gave her a pitiful look, as if she had hurt him to the quick. "The chemist swore it would restore you, but you needn't try it if you're set against it. I have the poppy as well. Perhaps you'd prefer that."

Seanag shook her head wildly. "No dreaming death for me. I've heard what it does to folks' wits. Give me the chemist's potion," she said, hoping to appease him.

Connach reached out toward her and drew her into his arms. "O, my love! Imagine yourself well again, with your hair grown back thick and yellow and the luster in your eyes as of old." He bent down to kiss her, and for a moment Seanag remembered how it felt to be young and pretty and in love with a passionate man. With all her heart she wanted to believe him, but her head would not let her be so foolish. When a sudden dizziness overcame her, Connach helped her into a chair by the fire and shoved the amber-colored vial into her hands.

Gentian water, probably, or peppermint in glycerin or some other such harmless concoction, like the ones he'd urged on her before. She would no doubt go on downing Connach's "cures" until the day she died. Or he did. Well, she'd brought it on herself, hadn't she?

He gave her a cup of water and poured the medicine into it. The mixture sparkled pale gold in the sunlight. She'd not the slightest doubt that it would be worthless. She sniffed at the shimmering liquid. It gave off a pleasant scent. "All?" she asked.

Connach nodded. She drained the cup. A bitter taste stung her palate. She had heard of such things before. She touched the side of Connach's head and drew him close to her. "Was this the dose the chemist told you?" she asked.

"Faith, no," Connach replied with a grin. "He wanted me to give you but a drop from a goose quill every day until you were better. How long might that have been? I want you well today, tonight, nay, this moment. Do you feel better now, *m'chreidh?*"

She tried to bring her hand down but it stayed where it was, her fingers twisted in Connach's hair, refusing to obey her. "Connach, this is poison." The calmness of her voice astounded her.

Connach blinked like a frightened child. "Nay, love, it will cure you. If it has a foul taste, pay it no mind. Tonight you'll lie in my arms, just as we first did."

He hadn't meant to. Thank God for that much! He hadn't meant to kill her. "I love you, Connach MacColl," she whispered, "as foolish and as vengeful as you are. O, my love! Remember your promise to me." While there was no pain in her body nor fear in her heart, tears began gathering in her eyes at the thought of leaving Connach behind without a hand to rein him in.

Only a day earlier, the big house had been cheerful and pleasant, warmed by the expectation of the wedding. Now the wake had destroyed all that for Una. The cold spring had killed so many flowers that there were precious few for the midwife. Una draped the bier with branches of heather and sprigs of silverweed, sedge, and every other bit of green or flowering plant that could be found, certain that Seanag would be happy in the company of her dear herbs.

Una sat for hours keening by Seanag's bier, her children gathered around her. Only Donald was gone, hunting in the hills. She clapped her hands in doleful rhythm and swayed back and forth as other mourners howled about her, but in the deepest places of her heart she could not believe that Seanag had left her. Her one comfort came from knowing that Donald had nothing to do with Seanag's death. The murderer had made himself plain.

It was late in the afternoon when Alasdair led her outside. A light mist hung in the air. "Let me stay with Seanag," she said, but the feel of her red man's arm around her gave her strength to leave. The numbness she'd felt all day long slipped away from her, and peace took its place. She squeezed his hand. "Where are we going, love?"

"Not far," said Alasdair, and took her to a lonely field of corn. The plants were still small and green and made a rustling music as they shook in the wind. A woman was walking past the field, but when she saw Una and Alasdair she gathered her skirts and trotted away like a deer.

"Fiona," whispered Una. Was the woman on her way to meet her lover? Or had she just come from him? Una clutched Alasdair's arm. "Let's leave this place, *mo luran.*"

"There's no need. We're alone now." Alasdair knelt by the edge of the field and folded her unprotesting body in his plaid. "Life from death," he whispered to her. "O, Una, give me life from death."

She pressed herself against him as they slumped together to the ground. Her nostrils filled with the smell of black earth and whisky. When he entered her, she gasped with pleasure and clung to him, biting his neck gently, forcing herself so close against him that she fancied the two of them were one creature with one purpose: to grip fast to life. Alasdair flinched at the height of his passion. A moment later she herself was arching under him as fire ripped through her body and her breath stumbled from her mouth in long, stuttering moans. What this man's love did to her never ceased to awe her. As she lay still, trying to recover her senses, she thought about how pleased Seanag would be to know that another life might be in the making so soon after her passing.

They lay together, heedless of time. Now and then the wind carried the sound of mournful wailing up to them from the house. Una was watching the sun dance on the western mountains when Alasdair roused himself to leave. He shifted his weight and she felt Ri slip from her, wet

and warm. She looked down, then gently touched the tip
of the glistening creature. "Wait," she whispered. Alasdair
settled himself on her again. "I'll show you something."
She would not let her dear Seanag go unavenged. Reaching
into her bodice, she pulled out a glass vial. "I found this
on the floor next to Seanag. She was poisoned."

Alasdair examined the vial. "Perhaps. Perhaps she just
gave over. She was very ill. I'm glad she lived as long as
she did." He held the bottle to his nose. "Some kind of
medicine, I ween."

"Connach poisoned her!" Why couldn't the man see
things as clearly as she did? "I found strands of his hair
between her fingers. She was fighting him off even as she
lay dying."

"I can't believe such a thing. Connach would never . . ."

"Indeed he would," said Una firmly. "He'd rid himself
of her so he might marry Fiona." *And take vengeance on me,*
she thought. Perhaps now was the time to tell Alasdair
everything. "If the man's innocent, why hasn't he come
here to mourn his wife?"

Alasdair shook his head. "He must have his reasons.
Una, I've seen him embrace her with great tenderness. He
might strike her, aye, but he'd never slay her."

"Seanag was my dearest friend, and my mother's
friend." Una took a breath. "That beast took her from
me, and he owes me his life for it. Alasdair . . . "

"My love?"

Her voice dropped to a whisper. "I dread the man so!
Now more than ever, with Seanag gone. I fear for my life!"

Alasdair looked down at her, his mouth frozen open in
a silent "O." Now she'd started, she must needs finish.
"His lack of hearing? I'm the cause of it." She told him
about the day that Connach sought her out in Craigorm,
how she had struck him after he made bold with her. "I
never meant to harm him, I swear it, but Connach will

never believe me. Seanag said she kept him from me, that she was the only reason I was still living."

"A thousand devils!" murmured Alasdair. "The man attacked you! Why did you not tell me this before?"

Una felt the water welling up in her eyes and spilling over her cheeks. "O, my treasure! Because ... because I was afeared for Seanag, afeared for you, and aye, for Connach, too! But now ... " Now she was afeared for herself and her children. What if Donald were with Connach? What unspeakable thing might the drover do to the boy to make her suffer?

"Son of the devil! And I thought myself lucky to have him!" He was looking at her no more, but at some far point on the horizon. "I'll hunt him down. Fiona will know where he is."

"She'll not tell you." Una grabbed his arm and wept into his sleeve, not knowing whether her tears sprang from relief at the telling of her secret or from a small, black foreboding that had risen inside her. "Your gillies will seek him out."

Had the man heard her? "There's no corner of these mountains that will hide him," he said. "All of Glenalt is an old friend to me." Alasdair sighed and kissed her forehead. "Dry your tears, my love." He wiped her face with the hem of his plaid. "I'll bring you this creature, and you may ask him about Seanag yourself. If he's guilty, then I myself will have the pleasure of dealing with him."

Una shuddered. "And Donald?"

"Don't worry for him. I'll fetch him home alive and well for you." He kissed her deeply on the mouth, and for a moment she forgot her hatred of Connach. All she felt was fear and peace: fear for Alasdair, peace at the thought of justice.

"Mind how you go!" She stroked her red man's hair,

red no longer but tawny-gold streaked with silver. He was still beautiful and still hers. "You'll take no risks?"

But Alasdair was already on his feet, taking big strides toward the keening house.

In the morning Una woke alone in her bed. She didn't have to search the house to know that Alasdair was gone. But as she walked about the byre and the fields, she began to chew at her fingers and turn a chesspiece end over end in her hands. All Alasdair's gillies and clansmen were at work in the pastures, on the hills, or on the loch. Una ran her nails up and down her arms. With Seanag gone, there was only one person to turn to.

She found Mata in the byre, bandaging the leg of a lame mare. "Alasdair has gone after Connach," she told him.

"Why might he do that?" Mata said, rising from the horse's feet.

Una's hands twitched helplessly in front of her. Mata didn't know! Alasdair hadn't trusted even him. "Mata, I asked him to bring me Connach. The man killed his wife. But I never meant for Alasdair to hunt down Connach alone." Devil take her red man! So arrogant and sure of himself!

Mata must have seen fear on her face, for he put his arms around her and hugged her to him. "Don't fear, *a'nighean*. I'll take a few lads with me and we'll have a look for that man of yours. He'll not have gone too far."

Mata lost no time assembling a "tail" of stout, honest men, and Una soon found herself following them into the hills. It was not long before they left her far behind, however, and she cursed herself for not having the wits to ride a pony. Winded and footsore, she had just persuaded herself that she should return to Glenalt when Mata came running pell-mell toward her through the heather like a man on fire.

She knew at once. "Alasdair!"

Mata nodded and pointed to a rocky hillside. Four gillies were picking their way down the steep slope, carrying a litter made of two saplings and several plaids tied together with leather garters. "My love! Not dead, surely? O, my ruination!"

Mata placed his whisky-skin in her trembling hands. "Courage, Una. He's not dead, but sorely hurt." She took a good pull of the fiery liquor before following Mata to the litter.

"*A'ghraidh!*" she cried when she saw her beloved. His eyes were half open, his plaid smeared with blood. "My soul! My love! My light!" She stroked his face, remembering the day she'd found him in the corrie.

Alasdair blinked, then smiled, and for a moment Una believed that there had been some terrible error, that he was only bone weary, not injured. "Beautiful," he whispered, reaching out toward her. She had just touched his fingers when his eyes rolled back into his head and he collapsed into a black sleep.

"Set him down, set him down!" she commanded the gillies, and the startled men obeyed her at once. Alasdair's right knee was swathed in a linen bandage, dark red and brittle to the touch. She forced herself to examine it. "This is Connach's work, I'll wager."

"Aye, Connach, doubtless," Mata grumbled. "That's a pistol shot, sure enough. There were the marks of hooves all about, Alasdair's cattle that Connach had lifted. But Una, Donald was with the fiend."

"Donald's no reiver!" Una glowered at Mata, but she knew that he'd told the truth. Somehow her Donald had become part of the evil that had settled in the glen that year.

Mata stretched out his hand in front of her. In his palm lay a button in the shape of a targe. "This was in Alasdair's fist."

Una threw herself across Alasdair's chest and let the tears pour out over his plaid. "O, my poor wean! My poor husband! What's to become of us all?"

The gillies who bore the litter were strong and fresh, and made short work of carrying the big man back to Glenalt. When Alasdair was safe at last in the house, Una cared for him herself. She let the servants bring water and herbs and clean rags but wouldn't trust them to touch her husband. When she'd made him as comfortable as she could, she cut the bandage away from his leg and washed the blood from his skin. What she saw made her bite her lip. Alasdair's kneecap was cracked in half. A shard of bone protruded through the flesh. "Mother Mairi help me," Una prayed. "Take care of my dear man."

A fever set in and Alasdair burned like a torch. Una spent all night and the next day and night tending him, determined not to lose him. All the time she worked over him, trying to stop his bleeding and cool his raging fire, she thought *I brought him back from the dead once before. I saved him once before.* For two days the whole house seemed to hold its breath, unsure of the fate of its master. Sometimes he would wake screaming in pain, and Una, Cha, and Mata would spoon whisky down his throat and soothe him back to sleep.

Mata sat beside him the entire time, leaving the house only to visit the midden or to attend to some emergency among the drovers. Now and then he'd pluck a tune on the harp, but more often he would just sit and frown, his hand on Alasdair's thigh or shoulder, as still as a part of the man's own body. Once he shaved Alasdair's face completely smooth with his own dirk, leaving not a nick on him. Mata's touch was so loving, so tender, that Una had to turn her head away from him to drive a raging envy from her heart. *He loves Alasdair as I love him,* she thought, but it was such a monstrous thought that she could not believe it, not of Mata.

The first morning Alasdair opened his eyes and asked for whisky she knew he was going to live. The fever had broken and his pain had subsided. Walking was another matter. The bone was badly broken, the nerves damaged. Una didn't have to mention it. Alasdair knew. "I'm halt," he said, after she'd brought him the dram he'd asked for. "You're wed to a cripple now."

"It will heal, my love," she whispered, stroking his cheek. "You'll walk again, I swear it." The hopelessness in his voice disturbed her far worse than his wound. "Who did this to you? Not Donald?"

Alasdair shook his head. "Connach. He would have finished me had Donald not pulled him off. But that doesn't help my leg, does it? What good is a man who can't walk? A hundred thousand curses on them both! O, Una! Forgive me for not doing better by you."

"Whisht now." Una held his head as he sobbed into her breast. Seanag had been right. How much better to have kept silent than to risk the life of her man! And poor Donald! What would Alasdair do to him? He might tell Dunvegan about the attack and the stolen cattle, then have the boy captured and dragged back to Glenalt. If he did, what would become of her poor wean?

Una did all she could for her red man. She kissed him and sang to distract him, but she could not touch the despair within him. Mata sat down at the bedside, his face desperate with love and suffering. He stared at her a moment, then opened the front of his shirt and held an imaginary infant to his breast. Immediately Una pulled down the front of her *arasaid* and took her own breast in her hand. She rolled her nipple between her fingers until it grew firm, then slipped it into Alasdair's slack mouth. He gave a start, but when at last he began to suck, he worked his lips so gently she could scarcely feel them. Una nursed him as if he were her child, stroking his head with the same joy and fascination she had felt for all her babies. After a few minutes of quiet suckling, her red man sank into a peaceful sleep.

Una looked up at Mata, who still sat by Alasdair's side, gripping the sleeping man's hand. What she did not wish to accept earlier was written plain on Mata's face, the utter and undying adoration that Anghas had shown Cha, that her father had shown her mother, that Alasdair had shown her. Una touched Mata's wrist and looked him straight in the face, silently pleading with him to answer her unspoken question. He returned her gaze, and after an eternity or more had passed, he nodded. "Alasdair has no ken of this," he said.

As if even that barest of admissions was too much for him, Mata rose hastily and strode from the house, leaving Una to wonder if he had taken her heart with him.

July 14

There is no going back now, not since yesterday on Cadach Ceo. We were droving the last of the cattle north to Innisaid, where Connach planned to sell them to his brother Lachlann. Alasdair took us completely unawares, all alone, his sword drawn and his face as furious as a storm at sea. "You breathing lump of shite!" he shouted to Connach. " 'Twas you who killed the tinker and sacrificed an innocent man. You think you may take whatever you please, you son of the devil! My wife, my cattle, my son . . . even Seanag's life."

Connach let out a great roar and drew his blade. Alasdair didn't stand a minute before he was on the ground panting, and quick as a cat Connach was on him and planted his foot on Alasdair's neck so hard the man daren't move.

"Not much of a sworder," says Connach. He raised his claymore.

"Put up," says I. "Let him go."

"Too scairt to quit your beloved da?" Connach sheathed his blade, then cocked his head, as he always does when he's taunting a body.

"Come away now," I told him. I just wanted my silver, the silver that was rightfully mine. I didn't want Alasdair's blood on it.

"You have too much love in you," Connach muttered, and then, before I even knew what he was about, he seized hold of his pistol and fired at Alasdair. Shot him in the knee. Alasdair cried out like the ban-sith, *and there was blood everywhere.*

"Hold!" said I. Alasdair's face was as white as my own. He sat in a red puddle of his own making, twisting in pain. I caught Connach by the elbow and pulled at him mightily until he broke free of me. "Enough!"

Connach laughed. "Let's finish him." Then he smiled and drew his dirk. "Or shall we make a gearran *out of him?" He slashed the air in front of his belly. "How your mama would fret!"*

He looked so bold that I feared he might do as he said, so I cursed him roundly and slapped his cheek. His whole face turned black. "It were best you hadn't done that," he growled, and started to pick his way up the hillside.

"Donald! Stay!" called my father as I began to follow Connach. I stopped. "Stay, or you'll rue it."

"I'm sorry, Da," said I. "I'm sorry it had to come to this." And I ran off after Connach. What else might I do?

I have no love for Alasdair. Did he get off the moor alive, I wonder? It's no great matter either way. He's no da of mine. A true father values all his children. If I were Alasdair's son, he'd not have denied me my schooling. So says Connach. "I am your father now," says he.

* * *

Connach crouched in the miserable shieling, downing a bowlful of drammach. When it was gone, he cooked more and ate that. Too much wasn't enough. He had a hole in his stomach that couldn't be filled. As he added more meal and water to the pot, he looked up and saw the *gealtach*, staring out the doorway into the rain. He was always restless, that one. It was true—the tiny hovel that they shared was poor shelter for two big men, but they couldn't do better for the time being.

When Donald finally fell asleep against a far wall, he groaned and struggled in his dreams. He'd not been well of late, not since he'd lost his head and took a skelp at the devil himself. "Come, Donni, wake up. Eat a bit." Connach kicked Donald's outstretched foot. "You can sleep later."

The creature cried out suddenly and sat upright. He turned toward Connach, his face a deathly shade of blue in the light of the peat fire. "What did my father mean, that you had tried to take his wife?"

Connach chuckled to disguise his sudden fear. "Why, he'd accuse me of shagging the blessed Virgin if he'd thought of it. I never raised my hand against your mother. Faith, the man even accused me of killing my Seanag. Put no store in any of it. You know how far you can trust that one." Donald said nothing, but dragged his damned book onto his lap, found his pen and inkpot, and began to scribble with a passion.

Connach had been none too pleased with the *gealtach* of late, and the creature had been none too pleased with him. The slap in the face had much to do with it, and the shooting of Alasdair. Part of it was living together in close quarters without whisky or women. One day Donni would be of no use to him anymore and he could desert the boy.

Even looking at him was not as entertaining as it once had been. "You've lost another button. That's what comes from twisting them about so."

The *gealtach* looked down at the loose bits of thread hanging from the front of his jacket. "Ach! Now I must needs have all the buttons replaced."

Connach smiled. "When you and I are finished, you'll have enough silver to buy a dozen jackets such as that."

Donald set his book aside and scowled at Connach. "Aye, let's speak of this," he said. "I'd just as lief finish this business now and get what schooling I can on whatever silver I have."

The boy had him! Well, he might as well be hanged for a cock as a hen. Connach turned his sporran inside out. Nine silver coins—three pounds for each of three cattle they had just so hastily sold—slid from the pouch and clinked onto the clay floor. "You'll be a lean scholar then, I'm thinking."

For a moment the creature stared at the coins, then swooped upon Connach and caught him by the collar. His white hair flew out wildly all around his head as he shouted in rage. "Devil take you! What have you done? That's my silver you've stolen, you whoreson!"

"Not stolen, not stolen," Connach insisted. "Borrowed." He rose to his feet, pulling the *gealtach* up with him. He looked down at the frantic boy and grinned. "I spent it on medicine for Seanag. You'll get back every penny in a few days."

The creature stopped his raving to gaze up at Connach. "Why then and not now?"

Connach snorted to keep from laughing; the monster's impatience was that amusing. "Fiona tells me that Alasdair is planning a nice dowry for your sister—the best cattle he can spare."

The *gealtach* was silent for a moment as the words sank

into his skull. "Yes, Alasdair would do that, give to Anghas what rightfully belongs to me."

Connach placed his hands on the boy's shoulders and smiled. "Soon you'll be quit of them both."

The *gealtach* squinted and his jaw sagged. "Connach, I'm quit of you. Tonight. I'm finished reiving cattle. I'm finished watching you use Fiona any way you please. I'm going back to my mother and Alasdair, if they'll have me. Faith, they've good reason not to." Donald seemed to think of something, then picked up his journal again and scrawled a few lines in it.

"Donald." The boy looked up at him. "Donald, please don't leave me." He searched the creature's glowing eyes. Steady, steady, he thought. When the moment was right, Connach slammed his fist into Donald's shoulder and sent him flying sideways into the wall of the shieling. His papers soared about the room. The entire hut shuddered, and for a moment Connach thought it might fall down on top of them.

"You'll go nowhere save where I tell you." Connach walked over to the boy, who lay in a heap, gasping and blubbering like a child. Connach reached down and sank his hand in the *gealtach's* snowy hair, then a thought came to him. His fingers uncurled. Gently he stroked the monster's head. "Donni, it's true I have but little silver for you. Still, I do have this." He reached into his sporran and pulled out the small, vellum-wrapped parcel.

The *gealtach* wiped his bloody nose with his sleeve and nodded at the package. "What's this?" He sniffed the air like a frightened coney. "It smells like smoke. Is it tobacco?"

Connach laughed and shook his head. He unwrapped the parcel and showed Donald the dry, woody substance inside the vellum. "Nay, nothing so commonplace. Only the best for you, Donni. Only the black poppy for you."

The *gealtach*'s eyes opened wide. He pushed himself against the wall, intent, it seemed, on pushing himself straight through it. "The dreaming death. Where did you get it?"

"Why, from the chemist in Glaschu, of course. Come, have a pipe with me."

"I want none of it," he sputtered. "I've read about the way it eats men's brains."

"God in heaven, lad, that's but stories for the weans," purred Connach. "You'll think straighter than ever before, and write better, too," he said with a wink. "You'll see your thoughts take shape, like tartan on the weaver's loom." He held out the package again, and again the *gealtach* retreated, but not quite as far as before. He was aye stubborn, that one. "Come, lad. Take but one pipe with poor Connach for the sake of the long ago. Then you can go back to your family." But better you go to hell, he added to himself.

The creature gave him a hard look, then bent low and breathed in the scent of the husk. "You swear you'll not interfere with my leaving after the one pipe?"

"Aye, you've my word." Connach carefully set the parcel down on the dirt floor and unrolled a lambskin that lay by his side. Inside were two long wooden straws the chemist had given him. Connach lit the poppy with his tinderbox and watched, satisfied, as tongues of blue smoke curled around the brown pod. Putting a straw to his lips he sucked up the smoke and held it in his lungs. His mind welled up with the familiar feel of the poppy, filling him with a contentment so deep that he couldn't find space for it within his body.

He handed the other stick to Donald, and the lad fingered it in suspicion. Connach sucked up another lungful of enchanted smoke, then spooned half the contents of the porridge pot into a bowl. The gruel was scalding hot but he fairly drank it down. The pain felt good to him. At last he raised his hollow stick in salute to Donald, who was already taking a tentative puff.

"*Slainte mhath,*" murmured Connach. "To your health."

Chapter 17

A fortnight passed, then two. Alasdair's leg healed, but he refused to try walking. Mata suggested a stick, and Una herself selected one from among the many that Mata brought her. It was blackthorn, waist-high, strong and smooth, with a grip thick and long enough for her love's big hand. But Alasdair would not use it. Una worried that the shee had shot him with their magic arrows, taking away his will to be up and walking.

Since the day he had suckled her she'd not spoken about his injury, and whenever she mentioned Donald or Connach, Alasdair would screw his face up into a knot and say nothing for hours. Still, no one was dispatched to hunt down the thieves. *Heavenly Father, watch over my boy and my husband,* Una prayed every night. She prayed that Alasdair's rage would soon give o'er, and that he would forgive his erring son. Certainly, the man had a right to be angry, and Donald deserved punishment. Perhaps he should have been forced to spend a winter by himself on the fen. Without that devil Connach to deceive him, he'd soon be her sweet wean again.

While Alasdair spoke little, there was one subject he never tired of: Cha's dowry. Una saw his eyes glow with his old look of determination whenever he mentioned his daughter and the cattle he intended to give Anghas. "And who can be trusted to choose these fine cattle?" Una asked him one evening, after he had spent some time describing them. Alasdair stared at her, stupefied. "Perhaps Mata can carry you out to the field to make the selection," she suggested.

"And break his back in the process," Alasdair said. He looked up at her, and at once she recognized the old strength in the set of his face. "You've always been a good judge of a man's health, Una. Can I walk, do you think?"

She sat down on the bed beside him, leaning her head against his chest. "Wasn't it I who chose a stick for you?"

The next day he took a few steps, supported by Mata's strong arm and the blackthorn cane. Willful man that he was, he was soon using only the cane. He walked slowly, his eyes focused straight ahead and one arm stretched out to the side. Una knew he must be suffering, but it did her heart good to see him on his feet at last.

One lovely evening, while the sky was still full of light from the dying sun, Una took his hand and guided him toward the walled field hard by the house. There Mata had brought together the best cattle so Alasdair would have no trouble choosing a dozen likely beasts. A small throng of men began to cast lots as to which cattle would be chosen. Children perched on the wall and pretended to throw stones at the cattle, while their mothers gathered to exchange the freshest gossip.

Cha and Anghas walked sedately beside Una, nickering to themselves as Alasdair talked. How he talked, proud man! He did his best to distract them all from his unsteady gait. When he reached the field, he braced himself against the stone wall, standing without help. "Do you like that brindle bull, Anghas? Faith, he fairly plows the ground as he walks, does he no? You shall have him, and the red cow with the short horns. They'll give you a dozen fine calves. May you have as many weans yourselves. What is the reason for the love of a man and a woman—or a bull and a cow, for that matter—if it's not for the sake of children, eh? Children to build the strength of the clan. Children to support you in your gray years. Children . . ." His words faded. His hand flew to his eyes.

Una ran up to him but he brushed her aside. The walk was too taxing for him, she thought, his pain too great. "Alasdair's not well," she told Anghas. "Come, husband, Mata will help you back to the house."

Mata ran up to the wall and vaulted over it. "Is Alasdair ailing?"

Alasdair waved Mata away with one hand while he raked the other across his face. His cheeks were flushed. Water dripped from his eyes. "I'm well enough, and I'd like to be done here. Anghas must soon be on his way south with his cattle or he'll not get a good price for them."

"As you wish," whispered Una. The man needed to rest, but to gainsay him now while he was testing his courage would only make matters worse. "Hurry now and choose. Save your speech-making for a wedding toast."

Una watched him carefully as he selected several fat steers and heifers. "What will you do with all the silver you get from the sale of these creatures, Anghas?" asked Una. She said it only for the sake of conversation and to drive her thoughts away from her husband's strange behavior. Alasdair had made it plain a fortnight ago that Anghas must use his dowry to set Cha up in a household that would do justice to her lineage. "But perhaps you've been too busy with Cha to think about silver."

Anghas was ecstatic. He hugged Cha close to him and laughed, eager to tell the world how he was going to provide for his new bride. "I shall hire some serving-girls, as many as Cha wishes and the house can hold. I'll buy hens and a rooster and copper pots that shine like the sun." Anghas had gifts in mind for others, too, including Una. "You shall have wine and lace, little mother. And there'll scarce be a shop in Glaschu that has paper in it when I'm done spending for Donald."

Instantly Anghas stopped. Una held her breath. Little the good it did, since Alasdair had clearly heard the name. His back stiffened and the walking stick fell from his hand. "Who is this Donald?"

Anghas looked at Una for help. "Do not taunt me so," she said quietly. "You know well enough. Donald, our eldest son."

Alasdair pivoted on his good leg, one hand on the wall, and retrieved the stick. "Rory Og is our eldest son. I have no son named Donald. I know of no Donald who is related to me, save Donald Ban Ard."

Una felt her heart quiver in fear. "Donald is our son, no matter what he has done. I beg you, don't abandon him." If she but had that little bracelet, lying tarnished on the bottom of Lochan Oran, the man wouldn't be speaking thus!

Alasdair stood, quiet and tense, poised for battle like an unbroken stone-horse wrestled to a momentary standstill. "Una, I know you'll grieve to hear this, but Donald is dead to me. If he's brought before me, I'll deny that he's mine."

"Deny him?" Una ran up to Alasdair and gripped his arms. "Pray reconsider. Flog him if you must but don't drive him from the house."

"If you do, he'll not find shelter anywhere in the clan," Anghas said, clearly worried for his friend. "Not when people discover that you won't have him. They'll despise him. Is that what you wish?"

Alasdair sighed. Una knew his decision troubled him sore. "It is. And Connach shall have worse if I find him. Each bird flies with its own kind, and I am clipping the wings of these two crows."

Dia! A broken man! A man without a home, thought Una. "My love, you can't do this to the lad," she cried, shaking him. "You yourself said the boy saved you from Connach."

"He did." Alasdair's voice was steady again. "But my mind's decided. And think on this: I could have Donald hunted like a blackcock and shown as much mercy, but instead I shall be kind."

Without another breath Alasdair seized Anghas by the arm and hobbled back toward the house, dragging the young man along with him. Cha and Mata followed. Una stared at Alasdair's retreating back, trying to hate him but able to muster no feeling blacker than distrust. She'd trusted him to be forgiving, and he'd failed her, but she'd not been lamed by a servant and betrayed by a son. So wasn't Alasdair in the right?

She stared at the cattle. Her head ached and her legs couldn't move. It was a wonder she could breathe. She threw a stone at the beasts and watched, weeping, as they wheeled and galloped about in chaos. What would her Donald do, now that he was indeed fatherless? He had her, it was true, but what might she do for him?

The berries on the rowan trees turned scarlet, and the hazelnuts grew brown and fat. Still there was no sign of Donald. In the company of her father, Una undertook a pilgrimage of sorts to the graves of her kinfolk, hopeful the dead would have answers that the living did not. They

stopped first at the Field of Cairns where Calum Ruadh
and Seanag lay sleeping the long sleep, but she found she
couldn't ask anything of her dead father-in-law, and seeing
Seanag's grave only made the tears well up inside her. She
braved the hard march to Glenfinnan, over twenty miles
distant, to the cairns of her mother and three brothers,
and there she begged the dear soul of her mother to tell
her whether Donald was alive or no. Would she see him
again? But the stones of the cairns were mute. Why had
her dead friends, even her own mother, forsaken her?
She'd counted on their wisdom, and they'd seen fit not
to give it.

When she arrived back in Glenalt, Anghas had already
left on the long drove south, taking Mata with him for
advice and protection. Only Cha, the little weans, and a
few servants met Una in the yard. Alasdair was in The Cuil,
sulking, said Cha.

That night, as she wrapped the children in their bedclothes, Una found a small stack of books, three of Donald's old journals, hidden under a pile of plaids. An even
more surprising find was the piece of blue rag lying with
them—Alasdair's old bonnet, missing these many years.
She ran her hands over the leather covers and the stiff
pages crammed full of the strange marks that her darling
had written. She made out one letter, then another, but
that was as much as she could do. Perhaps these were more
secrets, meant never to be revealed.

As Una gazed at the faded ink, then at the worn cap,
an idea slowly took shape in her head. These were Donald's
letters, Donald's thoughts. Perhaps that was why the shades
had been silent, to let her Donald speak for himself, not
through them but through the father, who for so long had
both denied his son and suffered from him. She held a
page up to her nose and breathed in deeply to catch the
scent of her lost boy.

In the morning she went to The Cuil, the notebooks tucked under her *arasaid* to keep them safe from the mist. When she entered the bothy she began to unwrap the books, then stopped. Alasdair might not be pleased to see them at first, not before she explained her intentions.

"*M'lurag?*" Alasdair was awake, his hair bright red once more in the light of the fire. When he saw her he pulled himself to his feet and limped over to meet her. For a few minutes she let herself become lost in the sweet hunger of his touch as he stroked her face. "I've missed you sore," Alasdair said at last. "You should have come to me earlier."

"You should have been waiting for me," she countered. There was no point in giving the man the upper hand.

"Are you weary after your long journey? You'll not leave me again for so long, I hope." He sat down and gently drew her onto his lap. Before she knew what was happening his hands had discovered the journals.

Una eagerly pulled the notebooks from her *arasaid* and handed them to Alasdair. As he sat motionless, she paged through the books for him and pointed out the few letters she knew. "Donald's," she whispered. "Read them aloud to me. Somewhere in this kaleyard of words is a clue to finding him, I'm sure of it."

Suddenly he jerked himself upright and she slid from his lap. Her bottom struck the hard planks of the floor with a thwack and the journals fluttered about her like enormous moths. Alasdair, his bad leg jutting awkwardly behind him, thundered in anger. "Find Donald? Let him stay lost, say I. I'd sooner find the devil in my bed than ever see Donald again. For once and for aye, woman, Donald is gone. Grieve for him and be done with him. Don't read his writing. Burn it."

Una gathered the journals into her arms. "I promise you, I'll not mention him again. To know he's living and well is all I ask."

Alasdair's eyes narrowed and the muscles in his great long face began to twitch. He snorted, then jabbed at the books with one finger. "List to me, Una. These books are the ramblings of an unfortunate creature whose life should have been taken away the moment it drew breath. I regret I wasn't man enough to do it."

"The pox take you!" The notebooks flew from Una's arms as she leaped at Alasdair and—Mother of God!—fell to the floor on top of him. " 'Tis Connach you should kill! Not Donald! He did nothing all his life but beg you to love him."

She flailed at him with her fists, then her open hands, covering his arms with scratches as he shielded his face. "No, Connach's not to blame! 'Tis you! You did this to him. Never a kindness for him. Never a kiss but I won it for him, never a word of praise but I must needs put it in your mouth. O, Alasdair!" He was all the husband she had ever wished. How could he have failed her so? She fell across his chest, sobbing, and by and by she could feel his hand caressing her hair. "I'm so sorry, *m'ghraidh,*" she murmured.

"I did whatever I could," said Alasdair softly. "It's true, I wasn't the best of fathers, nor was my father before me. I did my best with Donald, but he and I weren't meant to love one another."

"That I don't believe." Una sat up. Carefully she wiped her tears from her face and tucked her ravaged hair under her headscarf. If she were to believe it, she'd have to stop loving one or the other of them. She couldn't do that. "When you're ready, come down to the house. I'll see that you have something to eat." Turning so that he would not see the tears gathering again in her eyes, she walked out of The Cuil.

* * *

He'd never seen her more wrathful, but there was nothing he could do to appease her.

Alasdair picked up one of Donald's journals with a mind to lay it on the fire. Instead he held it, fingered it, and at last cracked it open. The smell of mildewed leather struck him in the face. He read a line, turned the page, and read another. A dreary day full of rain. A gathering and the people who had been there. Una's listless attempts at reading. Hunting seals with Anghas, gathering whins with Seanag. And all of it better written than Alasdair could have managed himself. He looked through the second notebook. Here was a difference: the death of Laocoon and his sons, strangled by a kelpie.

Alasdair stretched out on his bed but sleep didn't come to him. It was you who did this to him, he thought. No, by God! He hadn't made Donald into a rogue. Indeed, he had tried to do right by the boy, teaching him to read, holding him in his arms, giving him every possible helpful gesture. If there had been a natural restraint on his own part, surely he had concealed it well.

From out on the pastures came the whinny of a horse. Alasdair thought of the night he had seen Donald, sitting like a cavalier on the back of the gray stone-horse as if he'd been born to ride the wind. For one thrilling, frightening moment, he'd been proud to have such a son.

Alasdair sighed and curled himself into a ball. He was weary. Dead weary.

He was at the corrie. A dank wind blew into his face and the wind roared around his head. A man stood with his back to Alasdair, but there was no mistaking the creature. His long hair fell over his shoulders like a frozen waterfall. "Donald."

The figure turned to face him. "Father?" Alasdair looked into the face and saw, not his son's bloodless features, but the same face that stared back at him from clear mountain pools. Then the face changed, and it was Una in every shape and detail, from the black curls to the upturned lips. Then it changed again, and became the face that had glared at a little boy for trying to tear down his mother's cairn.

Alasdair cried out, and Donald's face took on its familiar ghoulish whiteness. He grinned, and his face changed yet again. It was a man's face, the mouth full of fangs, like a cat's mouth. "Father," said the apparition.

Alasdair reached out toward the creature but his hand passed through it. "You're not my Donald. Who the devil are you?"

Donald held out one of his journal-books. Blood dripped from the binding onto Alasdair's hand. "Read this and discover the depth of the waters of Lochan Oran."

Alasdair woke in a sweat. Frantically he looked about the room, but Donald wasn't there. To be sure, the boy was in his head. It was the first black dream he'd had in months.

Alasdair rose and searched for the third journal. He touched it reverently, relieved to find it free of gore. The little book opened to the first page.

> *In vain the infant in his cradle*
> *Weeps for the coming of the day*
> *When the loving hand shall touch him,*
> *Scattering his fears away.*
>
> *Through some fault not of his making*
> *He is rejected and despised,*
> *Smothered on one hand by loving,*
> *On the other choked with lies.*

Alasdair could bear to read no more. He shut the book but the verses were etched for aye in his mind. Una had smothered the child with love; a boy might resent that. And lies? When had he lied to Donald? Faith, every word he'd spoken to his son, every glance he'd shot in the boy's direction belied the word "father."

O, my Donald! What a wretch I am! It was I who gave you such heavy secrets.

summer winter both neither

> *dark the day*
> *black my mind*
> *my father death*
> *at a serpent i suckled*
> *to death am i born*
> *i do as old blackie does*

"Is anything in her?" asked Mata. He tapped the rifle that swung back and forth across Anghas's back with every step the young man took along the drove road.

"Aye, any more and she'll burst," said Anghas. "Why? Do you see a deer?"

"It's two-legged brutes I'm thinking of, *mo luran,* murderous wildcats and badgers wearing plaids." Mata scanned the purple hillside.

"Thieves?" Anghas stopped for a moment, gazing at Mata with his blue woman's-eyes. "Donald and Connach?"

Mata shifted the weight of his harp from one shoulder to another. He'd been a fool to bring it, but how else was he to pass the lonely evenings on the drove? "Mayhap. It wouldn't be the first time they had their sights on Alasdair's cattle."

Anghas had no reply, and Mata took advantage of the young man's silence—temporary, to be sure—to take in the splendid scene before them. To the right lay Glen Beag, and to the left were the sea-cliffs and the great, sprawling water below. One steer paused to snuff the salt-spray and toss its head in the direction of the cliff. Mata drove it away with a shout.

"Alasdair would cut Donald off, but Una feels differently," said Anghas.

Mata looked up and dragged his sleeve across his forehead. It would be a long, slow walk south if this fellow spoke of nothing but Donald. "If there are faults in her child, a mother will find a way to forgive them, and Una is determined to make Alasdair forgive those faults."

Anghas picked up a stone and tossed it at a cow that had stopped to make water. "Is that a vain hope?"

Mata held his hand up to the boy's mouth to block the flow of words. "Enough, my friend! If you wish to help Donald, then keep your neb out of this business."

They walked on in silence. The path was broad, but on both sides the cliffs grew steeper and steeper, one hillside plunging into the glen, the other into the sea. *Creag Faire*, they were called, the Watching Cliffs. The story was that a woman who had lost her man in a storm continued to wait every evening for him, still hopeful of his return. If he squinted, Mata could almost see her, a black shadow on the edge of the rocks.

Mata began singing to fill in the emptiness of the evening. He should have been satisfied with talk of Donald, for now there was nothing. Anghas walked with his eyes downcast, glancing now and then at the ocean, as if he didn't trust it to stay put. Perhaps he'd been too hard on the lad, Mata thought. Suddenly Anghas darted past him. "Watch this! Watch, now! *Troigh is dorn gulbann*. A foot and a fist from the toe!"

Anghas ran to the sea cliff and drew up abruptly at the very edge, sending a spray of pebbles into the air. Before Mata could lift a hand to stop him, he had leaned far out over the cliff, one foot thrust before him in the air. Mata held his breath, entranced, as the youth placed one fist before his toe, then the other, until it seemed that only the will of God kept Anghas from pitching head foremost down the steep slope and onto the rocks below. Even the cattle stopped to watch him.

"Do you see, Mata? A foot and two fists."

The words shook Mata from his trance. "Come away now, half-wit, or it's my fist you'll be seeing. What would you have me tell your bride should you fall into the sea?"

Anghas carefully hauled his lean body back onto the rocky edge. His grin gleamed white through the red of his face. Mata caught him by the arm and led him from the cliff. He thumped the lad on the shoulder, partly to reward him for his brave feat, partly to keep him from repeating it. "Brainless boy," he muttered. Then he could contain his relief no longer and clutched the young man in his arms.

"Ah, how tender! Give him a kiss!"

"It's one of the cattle speaking," whispered Anghas. Indeed the voice seemed to come from the animals, which stood in a clump on the path, bawling and snorting.

Mata raised his head and backed away from Anghas. "Who addresses us so rudely?"

Connach stepped forward. There was no mistaking him, raw-boned and well-muscled, his skin as brown as a polecat. Donald appeared at his elbow. God in heaven, but the lad was lean! He didn't look to have eaten in days. Both men fairly bristled with weapons: a rifle, broadsword, and a brace of pistols. "A good evening for droving," said Connach, "and for loving."

"For raiding, you mean," said Mata, afeared that Con-

nach had somehow sensed his secret. Mata snatched the
rifle from Anghas's back and took aim at Connach. His
hands trembled as badly as poor Seanag's. "Go on now,
the both of you, or you'll sore regret it."

"Mata," Anghas whispered, "spare Donald."

Mata nodded. "Donald, step aside." Mata noticed something different about the boy. His jacket was dirty and his
hair hung in white strings about his head.

Donald laughed and stalked in front of Connach, into
the aim of the rifle. "I'll step where I please. Perhaps I'll
step off the cliff, as Anghas almost did. I'm fair at such
tricks myself, y'ken." He nodded at Mata. "Drop the gun,
old man, and surrender my cattle."

"My dear friend," Anghas murmured, "in the name of
Heaven, stay back. The cattle are your sister's. I'd give
them to you if I could."

"Of course you would, dear friend," Donald said, his
face distorted in a sneer. "And if your bride presents you
with a wean as white as its uncle, you'll be in a thousand
pieces with joy, I'm sure. Friend, indeed! Why, you sidle
up to Alasdair and lick his arse so he'll treat you like the
son he wished he had. But Donald has nothing. Even the
whores are loath to shag that monster—one of the silver
ones, *urusig*, fairy calf!"

He let out a hideous sound, part laugh, part screech, as
fearful as the keening of the women on a field of slaughter.
For what or whom was that lad mourning? wondered Mata.

He had no time to hazard a guess. Something exploded.
Fire ripped across his chest. Donald pushed him backward.
He fell on his shoulders, the lap harp cracking into kindling under his weight. The wires dug into his back, pinged
and snapped. His beautiful, beautiful singer! No more
music from her. Connach came up to him and stood over
him, a smoking pistol in his hand. "A short life to you,"
said Mata. "You've slain me and broken my harp."

"I'm sorry for the harp," Connach answered.

It might have been the shot. It might have been the hasty movements of so many bodies. It might have been the will of God. Whatever the cause, Mata suddenly felt the earth shake as the panicked cattle roared past him, sending bits of mud and heather into his face. "O, woe betide us! The cliff!" He sat up. The pain in his chest stung like a hundred nettles.

Connach came to life. The pistol clattered to the ground as he sprang after the cattle. "Ho-ro! Ho-ro! Stop, you shite-headed collops! *Obh obh obh!*"

Donald stood where he was, watching, too terrified to take one step. The cattle streamed by in a yellow tide, but nowhere in all that frenzy was Anghas to be seen. One after the other the cattle galloped up to the edge of the precipice, paused for an instant as if to reconsider, then leaped out toward some ledge of safety only they could see. For a breathless moment each seemed to float on the air, just as Anghas had dangled between rock and sky during the *troigh is dorn gulbann.*

Then each beast fell.

Mata lay back in the heather. For a long time the world was very quiet, with only the cries of the terns breaking the stillness. He couldn't see his wound but he could feel his life leaking slowly from it. Where was Anghas? Was he dying, too? Or poised somewhere in a delicate balance between the living and the dead?

Someday

   by now the tide has carried the cattle out out out to sea. anghas has disappeared trampled into dust says connach. all will be well yet all will be well. i long for home. i long to hear my mother sing to me.

child see the stars shine down on thee
how much more wretched canst thou be?

connach sleeps. he sleeps on and on and on, like the dead. my only friend.

not glasgow he tells me but the colonies. no one will even notice your color there he says. but it will take silver to pay for the boatfare. i must ask him about this when he wakes. ask for the poppy too. it pushes down the pain inside and i forget what is lost forever.

my heart is breaking for home
for the taste of cream and honey
and the smell of linen
there is naught but filth all around me
i was made to be unloved of man and woman
never to sip the honey of life
or to know peace in my heart

throw your heart on the dungheap says connach. along with mata that whoreson. mata. i'd not meant for him to pass over. i shall miss his stories. and anghas. where is anghas now and why should i care about him the deceiver.

see where trust has led me
into the pen with the brutes
such was i to put my heart in your hand
with the grace of an eel you came then
slipping into the heart of the father
poisoning the love of man for son
taking the place that was rightfully mine

my head throbs my mind is full of brambles where is the poppy i wish my mother were here to sing

* * *

"Alasdair?" She eased herself past the doorway and into The Cuil. It was her house, the house Alasdair had built for her, but just then she felt like an an intruder. "Alasdair?"

He sat alone beside Mata, who lay stretched out like a corpse on the box bed Alasdair and Una had so often shared. A plaid covered Mata from the belly down. His chest was one great wound, as clean as Alasdair's care could make it. Alasdair raised his head to look at her, his face strained with worry. "He's sleeping," said Alasdair. "Where is the priest?"

"He comes." She knelt beside him, and all the herbs and ointments she'd brought with her stayed inside her *arasaid*. There'd be no need for them now.

"And Anghas?"

Una stroked Mata's thinning hair. "He'll be living. The lad's nose and one arm are broken. He can barely speak, and Cha is beside herself with worry and relief."

"He's fortunate," Alasdair said. "Few men have survived a fall from the Watching Cliffs, and fewer still have run five miles with the blood pouring from their faces."

Una pressed on. She had to speak her mind, she knew, or she'd lose her courage altogether. "It was Donald. Connach fired the shot, but Donald pushed Mata down and left him for dead. Anghas told me. You were right, I think. Donald has become another Donald Ban Ard."

Alasdair put his arm around her and laid his head on her shoulder. She felt the warmth of his breath against her neck and quivered under his touch. "Whatever Donald is, he is himself," Alasdair said, "and it was I who helped destroy him. I was a fool to ever think otherwise."

Una did not believe him. She took him in her arms as she had taken all her weans when they were little. Her red man's sorrow was so great she could feel it throbbing through his body. "Alasdair, you are not to blame. List to me! Dunvegan must be told. How many other folk might Donald harm?" There it was, now. The worst was out, and it hadn't been so difficult. She'd spent hours torturing herself, thinking how she might ask to have her poor boy rendered up to justice, and now it was done, in the blink of an eye. She didn't even feel the need to weep.

He held her close and patted her hair. "Would you have me cause the death of our own child?"

She shook her head, unable to speak. Donald was no longer her child. She'd lost her hold on him. Her Donald wouldn't have done what this Donald had done.

"Give me a good wake," said a weary voice. It was Mata. "A wake with three nights' singing and drinking."

"Mata, there'll be no wake yet," Una said, caressing his bristly chin.

"You've sent for the priest. I heard."

"He is coming to pray for you, dear Mata." Alasdair whispered.

"Your eyes are red from weeping. You wouldn't weep for the living. You never could keep secrets from me."

No, but you have kept secrets from Alasdair, thought Una. Suddenly it struck her as senseless that here was Mata dying, and the man he loved most was not even aware of the heart full of hidden love and grief that was dying as well. "Kiss him, Alasdair. Kiss Mata. He would do well with a kiss."

Mata shot her a look of pure puzzlement, then his pale cheeks flushed bright pink and his eyes lit up. In their glow, Una could see the kind friend she had trusted so deeply. Now she would repay that friendship.

"Very well," Alasdair said, and he carefully bent over Mata and kissed his cheek. Mata whimpered.

Una clenched her fists. Her heart burned with jealousy.

Whisht, woman! She must not let Mata die like this. Regardless of his weaknesses, he was still her dear friend. Yet if she weren't cautious she would drive her husband away from his beloved foster brother. She took a deep breath. "Is that how you'd thank the man who's been closer to you than your own shadow? Your heart hasn't served you as well as he."

Alasdair looked up suddenly. "I've done what I can."

"You can do more," Una insisted. "When you and I take our final parting, I hope you'll give me no such lean kiss." *Give him a kiss that burns through to the soul and releases it, the kiss he'd fain give you.* "Kiss him again, my jewel."

Alasdair hesitated, began to speak, then stopped. Slowly a look that might have been resignation or even understanding spread over his face and he drew close to Mata once again. This time he pushed his lips hard against Mata's, kissing him with such force that he might have been sucking the life out of the man.

"A thousand thanks," gasped Mata. "A honey-kiss that was. Thus the hero Naois and beautiful Deirdre kissed when . . ."

Una shook her head. "No story now, *seanachaidh.* Sleep, sleep." Mata turned his head to one side. His breath came light and easy, and soon he dozed off.

Una and Alasdair sat by the sleeping man, taking turns bathing his wound and feeding the fire to keep him warm. "You've suspicioned this before," said Una.

"I have."

"Yet you kept silent."

"What else might I do? Risk losing Mata? I'd sooner risk losing . . . you."

He drew her close and kissed her, not with the passion he had kissed Mata, but with a sweet tenderness that she held dearer than any other touch, the suckling of her babies, or the furious thrusts that had produced them. After a few moments she broke free. "I've taken."

He nuzzled her cheek. "Ah, that's grand! If it's a son, I have a name for him."

Chapter 18

Mata was buried on a miserable day full of sleet and rain. As custom dictated, Una and the other women were not allowed in the burial field but gathered in a little flock on the hillside beneath it, listening to the keening of the menfolk. While Una waited, the sun broke through the clouds and the rain held off until the men rejoined the women. "It's the Lord, showing respect for Mata of the Golden Voice," one old man told her.

When Una returned home after the burial, she found the chesspieces she so loved to handle scattered hither and thither about the house. Some lay half-burnt in the hearth, some had rolled under tables and chairs, and some were strewn about the midden. "Who could have done this?" Una wailed as she crouched on the floor, gathering stray chessmen into her skirt. "Did no one see who did this mischief?"

But of course no one had. Every creature who could

walk had been at Mata's funeral. " 'Tis the prank of a child," one of the servants ventured.

Una turned to the woman to tell her that no child of her house would ever do anything so mean-spirited when she caught sight of Alasdair standing just inside the doorway. In his hands he held the scorched remnants of a book. She rushed over to him, two sooty pawns and a splintered queen in her hands, and saw at once that the blackened pages he held were all that was left of his mother's Bible. "My love! What has happened?"

"My books," murmured Alasdair. His eyes were bright with tears. "Someone has burned my books."

"All?"

"Nay, not all. Many. Piled outside The Cuil, doused with brandy and set ablaze." He stopped, looked into the house, then into her hands. "What happened here?"

"While we were at the Field of the Cairns, someone went into the house and played the devil with the chesspieces. Some are ruined. Many are lost." She paused and gently touched the blackened book. A page crumpled under her hand. "The books . . . the chessmen . . ." she wondered aloud.

"Who knew which books to burn to cause me the greatest grief? Who knew your love of the chesspieces?"

Una fell onto his chest, weeping. "Donald! O, Alasdair! Why?"

Alasdair caressed her face as he held her close. "I don't know, love. Donald wreaks destruction all about him. It's his mark. Some men wear certain colors in their tartans. Others grow a beard. Donald destroys." Una felt him take a deep breath. "Donald Ban Ard murdered his parents."

Una pushed herself away from him. "You yourself said that our Donald was different."

"True enough," sighed Alasdair, "but what if I'm mistaken? What then, my heart?"

Una threw herself back into his arms, craving the protection of his embrace. She was preparing a bold answer for him, then it slipped away from her, along with everything she ever imagined she knew about Donald. "I know not," she whispered into his plaid.

The evening after Mata's burial, as she was returning from the midden, she saw a man leaning against the wall of the house. She realized she'd never seen him before, yet there was something about the fellow and the easy way he held himself that caused a little bubble of fear to rise inside her stomach. He might have been one of Mata's relatives come to pay his respects. As she walked stiffly toward him he stood up straighter and smiled kindly at her. "Good even, mistress. My name is Lachlann Mor, from Innisaid in Glengarry. Would you be Una, wife of Alasdair? A word with you, pray."

Whatever the fellow had to say, she'd not speak with him. She couldn't. Her head spun like a child's whirligig. "Not just now."

"You're ill?"

"Nothing that won't be resolved come spring." She put her hand on her belly and sighed. The stranger smiled with his mouth open, as if he were about to bite her. A wad of saliva rose in her throat and she swallowed it. What made her fear this man she didn't even know?

"I understand, mistress. I'll tell the lady to be patient and keep her wits about her."

"What lady is this?"

"Why, Fiona is her name, mistress," the stranger said. "I know her not, but as I was driving my cattle past her bothy she comes up to me and bids me seek you out. She gave me no reason, but said she'd see no one save you. I'll just tell her she must tend to herself."

"Stay, I beg you. If she needs me, I must go to her. Inside with you now and have some supper." Fiona. If anyone knew where Connach and Donald were it would have to be Fiona. Perhaps she had grown weary of keeping secrets and decided to tell Una where her son might be found. Or perhaps she was ill.

Una hadn't seen the woman since the day she and Alasdair had lain in the green field. All that summer long Fiona had kept to herself, though now and then a hunter would tell of seeing her on the shore, gathering seaweed and shellfish. The gillies said betimes they'd seen a tall man leaving her bothy at the peep of dawn—Old Blackie, they speculated. One way or another, Una was sure, they were right.

Una was halfway to Fiona's house when she realized she should have taken a companion. Fate, it seemed, wanted her to seek Fiona out alone, which was just as well: she had privy matters to discuss with the woman. When she reached the little bothy the last light of the sun was fading and the moon had already cast a silver glow on the heather. "Fiona?" she called softly at the doorway. She heard a shuffling sound, a tiny cry, then Fiona's voice.

"Una? Is it you? Enter and be welcome." Una hesitated, and the woman guessed the reason. "I'm here alone. You've naught to fear."

Una slipped into the bothy. A small fire smoked in the center of the floor, filling the air with the smells of burning peat and boiled raspberry leaves. Una gazed about. What a change there'd been! Not a basket anywhere. "Fiona?" Where was the woman?

"Here. Abed."

Fiona lay in her box bed by the wall, the very bed where Una had surprised Connach and Fiona only three summers past. Even in the dim light Fiona looked pale and weary, and Una felt ashamed to think she had nearly decided to ignore Fiona's summons. "Come close," Fiona said.

Una knelt down beside her and found the one basket in the room, a small wicker affair lined with a sheepskin that wiggled to and fro. She peered inside. There lay a pretty baby, sound asleep, its wet, pink mouth working an imaginary nipple. It could scarcely have been a month old. "A babe!" gasped Una. "No one told me you were with child."

Fiona reached down and ran her hand through the red-gold fuzz on the child's head. "No one knew, I suppose. I did my best to keep folk from knowing lest someone be tempted to take the wean from me. There are those who fear me, you know." She looked up at Una, and Una forced herself to stare straight into the woman's eyes. "How I wept and worried over this wean. But look at him! As healthy as his da."

"A beautiful child. Has Connach seen it?"

Fiona frowned. "He has." Fiona's face went suddenly blank as she drew the lambskin away from the child's shoulder. A round, black burn the size of a guinea disfigured the babe's pink skin. Una knew only one man so monstrous he would burn his own child. "Son of a fiend!" she muttered, clutching the bed for support.

"His hot pipe fell on the poor thing," Fiona whispered.

"Was pressed to his skin, you mean," growled Una. She patted the child's silken arm, careful lest she wake him. "How could you let such a thing happen? Small wonder God took the others from you."

Fiona picked up her sleeping son and held him close against her. "More pity and less blame, I beg you. The boy wet him. No one could have stopped what happened. Please, can you help the child? You have Seanag's touch for healing."

Una bent closer, laying one finger carefully on the skin

at the edge of the burn. The pus would have to be drawn out and the whole thing kept clean and dry, but the child would heal. Until the next time it angered its father. "The boy will do fine."

"Thank the Virgin for that." Fiona lay back on the bed. "I smell death everywhere, you see. So many goblins have been lying in wait for my babies."

"And fathering them."

Fiona turned to face her. "And who was it fathered your fairy calf?" she asked.

Una glared back at her. A lifetime ago, Mata had told her the story of Maccus and Murdo, no doubt hoping it might inspire Una and Fiona to sheathe their swords. It wasn't to be. "I saw whins growing by the door. They'll make a fine poultice." She rushed from the house, sending a big gray cat scuttling from her path. When Una returned, she plastered the crushed plants on the child's burn. He cooed at her, twisting his face into what could have been a smile. When he rooted at Fiona's breast, Una longed to nurse him herself, no matter he did have the look of his father about him. "The babe is healthier than you."

"I've been sleeping but poorly on account of his wound. Faith, you should hear the poor thing wailing in the night! But now we'll both be able to sleep."

A chill draught of wind struck Una from behind and she glanced nervously around the room. The very cleanliness and order of it were just as threatening as the old confusion of baskets and the shadows of baskets. If she closed her eyes, she could almost hear Connach snoring under the plaid that covered Fiona. The sooner she asked her question the sooner she'd be quit of the place. "Fiona, where is Donald? I'd fain like to see him, just the once, to tell him I wish him no ill. He must never come back to Glenalt, now that Mata's death hangs over him."

Fiona raised an eyebrow. "Mata's death?"

"You're not aware of it?"

"I fear there's much I'm not aware of. But Una, I can't be of help to you, for I've no idea where Donald is, nor Connach neither."

"You'd have the cheek to say that to me?"

"It's true," Fiona answered. "Blackie has been here, and when he left he returned to Donald, but little I know where either is now."

What a great fool she'd been! Fiona would betray her man no more than she'd blame him for burning her child. Una rose and straightened her skirts about her. "Then I must be leaving. I'll send a lass to you tomorrow, to make sure the child is better."

"Stay a little yet." Fiona caught her arm and held her fast. With a great clatter a dozen bracelets hurtled out from under Fiona's sleeve and crashed onto her wrist. "Here, you must take one of these, as payment."

Una drew away from the woman and gently pulled her arm free. She wanted nothing of Fiona except her knowledge of Donald. "A thousand thanks, but I need no . . ."

Her eye caught one of the bracelets, made from twisted strands of silver and gold. It was the twin of the bracelet Alasdair had thrown into Lochan Oran, only larger. "Where did you get such a one?" She placed a fingertip on the bright circlet.

"Take it if you like." Fiona wrenched the bracelet from her wrist and held it out before her. "Donald gave it to me, and all these besides, but where he found the silver for them I can't say."

Una took the bracelet in her hand and turned it over and over. She had longed so deeply for its return; now here it was. Only one man in the whole of Scotland could have fashioned such a treasure. "I know how he came by them," she murmured, and she blinked back tears at the thought of the murdered tinker.

For how long had Donald deceived her? No longer! She wanted to hate him, just a little, if such a thing were possible, but no matter how wicked he'd become, he was still her child. Surely love was the greatest of illnesses!

Una sat by the fire and wept. Some time later she jerked upright, suddenly awake. How long had she been dozing? Fiona and the baby were asleep and the fire was nothing but embers. The bracelet she'd been holding had fallen to the ground. She seized it and slid it onto her wrist; her skin felt like ice. Perhaps now that the bracelet, or its twin at least, was back in the family, her good fortune would return.

Demonic hissing came from outside: a catfight. The sooner she was quit of the accursed house the better. She felt her way to the doorway, then out into the warm, starless night. Una hadn't gone but a few steps when she saw a white ghost rising from the mist, a torch glowing in its hand. She gave a little cry, then a whoop of joy. "Donald!" She ran up to him and threw her arms about his neck. It shocked her how tall he'd grown and how mannish he smelled. "Calf of my heart, I've missed you so. But by the blessed Mother of God! You're as thin as a stag in winter."

"Mammy," Donald whispered. He lowered his head as if to kiss her cheek, but suddenly drew back. Una drew back, too, then reached into the breast of her *arasaid* and pulled out the caul she always kept there. "Take this, my darling. It will protect you, and I fear you need protecting."

Donald snatched the caul from her and crumbled it into dust. Una cried out, but Donald cut her short. "Whisht! It's you who need protection. Inside with you now. Connach will be here soon." He caught her by the elbow and none too gently thrust her back inside the bothy.

"Donald?" Fiona, sitting up in bed, rubbed her eyes, as if she too had been seeing ghosts. "Where's my Blackie?"

"On his way," Donald mumbled. He ordered Una to

sit by the bed, then began building up the fire with fresh peats and kindling. "Do you have whisky, Fiona?"

Una watched as the woman pointed into the darkness and Donald followed the gesture. She mustn't let Connach see her. If she were clever, she could creep past Donald and Fiona, then out the door without anyone being the wiser. She rose silently. Two strides and she was halfway to the door. "I don't see it, Fiona." Donald was pushing aside plaids and bits of furniture in his search. Another stride, then another, and she was at the door.

Suddenly she heard a shout and the tramp of feet and hooves. Una felt a strong pair of hands clasp her arms from behind and hurry her back to the bed. "No more of that, woman," Donald warned her.

Una collapsed on the floor, holding her hands to her face to try to keep back her tears. *Woman. Woman?* She was his *mother* still, apart from all else. How could he call her *woman?*

She heard a clatter outside and looked up just in time to see a man stumble into the house, doubtless pushed from behind. In the darkness it took her a few moments to recognize him. "Alasdair! What has happened to you?" Alasdair tried to speak but his mouth was gagged with a strip of linen and his hands were bound behind him. As he knelt beside her, she took his head in her lap and used her *tonnag* to wipe away the blood that trickled from his nose. She tugged at the linen strip, but Donald pulled her hand away, bent over his father, and loosened the gag without removing it.

This strange young man—her son, their son! She searched his face for some time, convinced that his old look of affection shone from his eyes.

Una was reaching out toward him when Connach lunged into the room. Her heart froze at the very sight of him. "You fiend from hell! What have you done to my family?"

Connach gazed at her in surprise, then his face burst
into a wide and pleasant smile. "Mistress! How good of
you to visit! I see you've been speaking with my brother
Lachlann. Many thanks to you, Donald, and you, Fiona,
for your assistance." The lynx-man made straight for the
whisky-skin and drank deeply from it.

· "Fiona!" Una couldn't bear to look at the woman. A
strategem! She'd suspected as much at the very first, but
she'd listened to her heart instead of her head. The deceiving serpent would do anything for Connach, even let him
harm her own baby and abuse the man who had been her
husband. "May the plague take you!"

"He said he'd kill the child," whispered Fiona.

"Ach, aye," Connach added. "I'm always true to my
word. Didn't I vow to repay you for your kindness toward
me, little harlot?"

Una swallowed hard and looked up at him. He was so
tall, so broad—an imposing figure except for the oddly
peaceful set of his features. Una spoke to that sensible
drover's face, to keep the fright at bay within her. "Connach MacColl, I'm truly sorry for the harm I've done you.
You shall have silver or cattle to repay you for your lost
hearing. Name what you wish." Alasdair shivered against
her chest in silent protest.

Connach laughed and took another pull of whisky. He
swayed where he stood. "Dear Una, my hearing is nothing
compared to the other, deeper hurt you've caused me.
What is the loss of an ear compared to the loss of a wife?"

"I don't understand," Una said. "What had I to do with
you and Seanag?"

"Don't play me for the innocent!" The simple hand-
someness of his features disappeared in a sudden snarl.
"It was you who baited her until she left me, you who took
my own child from me. You who—*Dia!*—you who gave
the woman *her own house,* without a by-your-leave from her

wedded man.'' Connach fell to one knee, then slowly rose again. Una shuddered. Her poor red man, with the blood running down his shirtfront, leaned forward to shield her from the raging drover. ''That's not to forget the matter of my hearing,'' Connach continued, in a softer voice.

What horrible revenge was Connach plotting? Una wondered. If she accepted all the blame he threw at her, he might forgive her. But as she was trying to shape an apology, something in her rebelled. ''Devil take you!'' she growled. ''I tried to save the woman's life, while you struck her and abused her and finally killed her. Who was it then who was badly treated?''

Connach fixed his cat's-eyes on her. ''What did you say?'' he asked. He took a step forward. She caught her breath. Alasdair struggled to free himself from his bonds. Connach took another step forward, then lurched sideways and toppled onto the box bed beside Fiona.

The baby cried out and Fiona clutched it to her breast. ''The whisky,'' she said. ''It's put my Blackie to sleep.''

''Thanks be to Heaven!'' cried Una, fumbling with the leather thongs that bound Alasdair's hands. ''Donald, dear Donald! Come free your da. Let's away from here, all of us.''

Donald knelt beside her and, after only a moment's hesitation, forced her hands away again. ''I'm afraid that can't be, Mother. I must keep you here until Connach awakens.'' He pulled a steel pistol from his belt and wedged it between his thigh and belly. At the sight of the pistol, Alasdair flung back his head and tried to stand, but Donald pushed him back onto his haunches. ''Now then, rest easy, the two of you. You'll come to no harm.''

''Connach will kill us,'' Una said, struck by how calm she felt in the face of such a terrible realization.

Donald smiled and stood up, pistol in hand. ''Nay, I

won't let him do that, though he does have his plans. One of them is to get me my silver.''

"Your silver? But I offered him silver galore!'' Una cried.

"He puts no faith in your promises.'' Donald's voice sounded hollow and indifferent. "What's more, he means to make you pay in different coin as well.''

He backed away and sat next to the fire. Una let him go. What could she possibly say to this stranger with a pistol in his hand and poison on his lips? For a moment she'd thought she'd seen him as he had been as a child, so sweet and trusting, but it was only her fancy. Alasdair had been right: she should have grieved for him as dead, for dead he was, inside, thanks to Connach.

Alasdair trembled. She stroked his face to calm him and keep him from doing something rash. She prayed for Donald to fall asleep. From overhead came the sounds of Connach snoring and Fiona softly singing to her baby.

> Here's a lock and here's a key.
> Here's a warning to the shee:
> Keep . . . thy . . . distance!

Chapter 19

Long claws shredded her skin and dragged her from her bed in her parents' house. "Papa!" she shouted. "Mama!"

She forced herself awake. Connach stood over her, a sleepy, thoughtful expression on his face. "Good morning, *a'nighean*. It's time for your reckoning."

Una sat up and ran her fingers through her ragged hair. As she gazed about the house, trying to set her mind to rights, a strange odor, like that of a burned honey-cake, filled her nostrils. She watched as Connach began pacing the floor, a piece of bannock in one hand and a pistol in the other. Now and then he paused to peer out the doorway into the darkness. Had morning not come yet, or had they slept through an entire day?

Alasdair lay beside her, twitching in his sleep. When she looked up, she saw that Connach was watching both of them. He turned to face Donald and Fiona, who were talking quietly in a corner. "Donni, fetch the horse. It's too far for the cripple to go on foot."

The three of them exchanged a few words and Donald left. "Where are we headed?" Una asked, fighting to keep her voice steady.

"To hell and back." Connach shoved the bannock into his mouth. "You'll discover soon enough." He knelt down beside her and brushed his rough fingers against her cheek. As she reached up to pull his hand from her face, he caught her by the wrist. "What's this?"

The tinker's bracelet glittered in the darkness. Fiona spoke from her bed. "I gave it to her, Blackie, for saving the child."

"Slattern! It's worth something, you know."

Una clasped the bracelet with her free hand to protect it. He couldn't have that! Now that the caul was gone, the bracelet was even more important. Having it might set everything to rights again. "Let me keep it! It's not yours to take!"

"It's mine now, mistress, and I'll caution you to keep nothing but a civil tongue." Connach tore the bracelet from her hands and forced it onto his own broad wrist.

"Return it!"

It was Alasdair. Somehow he had rid himself of the gag. His voice was hoarse and rusty, his face still daubed with blood, his back bent and his hair as tattered as rags. How she loved him!

"I'll thank you to show some respect," said Connach quietly.

"Respect? Respect for you? I have more respect for the worms that ply the midden." Alasdair spat at Connach, missing him. "You'll get even less respect from my gillies when they find you."

Connach smiled, then laughed. "You think they're searching for you the now? Nay, I'd stake my three smalls that my brother Lachlann has persuaded the lot of them that you two have been out a-courting the night or some such nonsense. When your people do raise a doubt or two, we'll be done with it.''

"Done with it," repeated Una. She shuddered deep inside, wondering what this "it" might be. She would not put the question to him, though; she would not give him the satisfaction of knowing her fear.

It was a long, lonely trek over the moors. They arrived at Seanag's bothy just as the sky in the east turned from black to gray and a fine mist began to rise from the glen. The only sound was the exultant song of a lark. Una could see at once why Connach had chosen to take them to this silent place of death.

Connach untied Alasdair's hands and feet and pulled him from the back of the lathered pony. At once Una set about chafing his wrists and ankles. The poor man could barely stand, his legs had been so tightly bound. "What would you have of us, Connach MacColl?" Alasdair demanded. "Whatever you'd do, spare my wife. She's never meant you any harm."

Connach laughed. "Don't play the hero with me! It's her I mean to punish. I'll have a bit of sport with you, Gimpy, and in the end you'll be of service to me."

"I beg you, speak plainly," Una said. She remembered what Donald had told her about the silver, and a thought occurred to her. "Isn't it silver you want? You may have what you wish."

"O, I'll have it, I promise you," said Connach. "Afterwards." He pointed at Alasdair. "This creature will hie himself home and bring back all the silver he has. Should he fail, he'll lose a wife."

"Whoreson!" spat Alasdair.

Connach backhanded the air an inch from Alasdair's nose. "Mind your manners, Haltshank." Connach lost interest in them and called to Donald. "Halloo! My little white one! Where is Fiona? She'd best take the child into the bothy."

"She was late in the leaving," answered Donald, "and she told me not to concern myself with her. She travels slowly because of the wean."

"Would that she were here to see this. No matter. We can wait no longer. Watch me. I may need your help in this." Connach turned toward Una, then Alasdair, his lips tilted in a strange half-smile. After a moment he drew his broadsword and drove it deep into the heather at his feet. "Come, Hobbler. Take the blade. Defend your lady."

Connach walked briskly toward Una. She backed away, then paused. Shouldn't she stand her ground? Connach pursued those who ran. Wasn't it wiser to resist?

Alasdair limped forward, shouting, confusing her even more. "Flee, flee!" he called to her, and "Stay, stay!" to Connach. Just as the drover was about to lay his hand on her, she ducked under his arm and spun away from him.

"Donald! Help us!" she cried, but Donald was standing by the pony, holding its reins and rubbing its neck, as transfixed by the horror in front of him as he'd been by the sight of Ian Beag's hounds ages ago.

Alasdair collided with Connach and both men crashed to the earth. As Connach pounded away at Alasdair's face and ribs, Una saw a flash of silver at the drover's waist: the pommel of his pistol. Slowly she crept around behind him, but when she was only an arm's length away from him, Connach lumbered upright and turned to face her. He was on her at once, his hand tearing through her *arasaid*, his fingers sinking into her breast. They dug deep, and she knew their intent. Connach's prize was to be her shame.

Something struck her face, and the next moment she was lying sprawled in the bracken. As she struggled to sit up she could hear the growls of Connach and her red man as they wrestled with each other yet again. Brave Alasdair was no match for Connach. When he went down a second time, she saw that fresh blood smeared his chin.

Una tried to stand, but Connach was too quick for her. He pushed her to the ground, plunging against her, his rigid *slat* nudging her swollen belly. "God protect my babe!" she cried.

Una saw Alasdair stumbling toward her, the broadsword in his hand, but too slow, too slow! Connach saw him, too; he rose and drew his dirk. "Donald!" he called. Una looked at her son, still standing by the horse, a goodly distance away now. Donald pulled off his swordbelt and let it fall to his feet.

"He'll not help you!" she crowed. It was a witless thing to say, since Donald had already been a great help to Connach, but her words meant something to the man. He stared aghast at the boy and the useless weapon. He stared just long enough for Alasdair to stagger up beside him and aim a blow at him. Una dragged herself to her knees and held her breath. Connach parried the sword with his dirk, then ran the blade across Alasdair's forearm. Una flinched at the sound of Alasdair screaming. The sword fell from his hand just as Connach tripped him up and sent him toppling backward. Then the drover leaped on the hapless man, wound his dirk in Alasdair's long hair and plunged the blade into the earth.

Alasdair was helpless. Connach would kill them both. Who could prevent it? Una searched hastily about her clothing for a weapon, but all she found were two knights, a queen, and a pawn. As she fingered them, a thought came to her. She could not fight the lynx, but she could match wits with him. "Connach!" He gazed at her, grinning. "At last, my love." She extended her hand to him, surprising herself and Connach. He dropped his dirk and his smile. "How I burn for you!"

For some time he simply gaped at her, as if she were speaking in a foreign tongue, then he went to her and lifted her to her feet. He held her so close she could smell the bannock he had eaten. As she threw her arms around his waist, one hand brushed against the barrel of his pistol and her mind soared with hope.

Connach clung to her false embrace. Una knew what he waited for; she mustn't disappoint him. She ran her hand over his flank and slowly edged her fingers under his plaid until she touched the hardness of him.

"*Drabhag!*" spat Connach, but he pressed himself even closer against her and stroked her throat. "I could break your neck, strumpet," he murmured, "but *Dia!* Such a neck!"

Una felt her gorge rise as Connach pressed his mouth against hers and gave her a hard kiss, full of water. With great care Connach undid her belt. Una inched her right hand down his back, over his shoulder blade. He lifted her skirts. She could hear his rough breathing and see the white mist that he spewed into the air. She prayed that neither Alasdair nor Donald was watching.

"Una, so beautiful," murmured Connach. "I knew all along it was me you loved, not that cripple." Her right hand strayed to his side. "I forgive you, Una." He eased away from her a little, raising his sporran and the front of his plaid. She couldn't look at him. Now her hand was at his ribcage, now at his belt, now at the hammer of one of the two pistols clipped to his belt. But when her fingertips at last touched the scrolled steel butt of one pistol, she froze.

His hands had been traveling, too. They were at her naked waist, her belly, her entry. Before she could take another breath she was being lifted so high her toes were nearly off the ground. Connach thrust himself into her and surged against her. She couldn't move, she couldn't breathe. But she could pray. *Mary, Mother of God! Preserve the wean!*

The pistol lay cold against her hand, and to her joy, her fingers began to move again. As she pulled the pistol from the belt, the clasp that secured the weapon shut with a snap. Surely he must have heard.

Connach nickered in her ear. *"A'ghraidh!"*

Una smiled to herself.

As Connach worked himself back and forth inside her, she worked her fingers around the heavy pistol. Now she was holding the grip firmly in her hand, the muzzle aimed at his gut. She was a mother and a healer, not a hunter. She had never fired a gun before, but Heaven left her no choice. Una pulled back the hammer, then wound her finger around the ball trigger. *Mary forgive me!*

A thunderclap shattered the heavens. Una shrieked as the gun tore a strip of skin from her thumb and flew from her hand. Connach grunted and slid away from her. The sickening pressure of him disappeared. The air reeked of sulfur. Crimson blotches stained her shirt.

"Hateful man." Tears blurred her vision. Where was her tormentor? The creature that stood doubled-up before her was pale and blood-stained. Una fought an urge to run to him and try to stanch his bleeding. "Hateful, unloved . . ."

"Ach! Ach!" It was Donald. She saw him drop the pony's reins and totter forward. "Mammy! Connach!"

Connach stood as still as death, his hands pressed hard against his stomach. Blood streamed black over his fingers and scarlet from his mouth. "My Seanag loves me." He grimaced and somehow pulled himself up a little straighter. Una felt her heart fill up with pity for him: the man she thought of as the devil was weeping.

"Killed by a . . . woman," Connach whispered. "My God!"

She heard the sound of running footsteps. In an instant Donald was beside the dying man, gripping him by the shoulders. The boy turned toward her with horror in his eyes. Connach whimpered once, shook all over, and fell face forward into the heather, where he lay like a stone. *"Obh! Obh! Obh!"* Donald threw himself down beside the body and tried to shake the life back into it. "Connach, awake! Awake!"

"My love. He's gone." Una stretched her hands out toward Donald. "Come to me, my darling."

The boy sat back on his haunches, poised to flee.

"Donald, go to your mother."

Una jumped. The words came from just behind her, over her head. It was Alasdair. "Comfort her, son. She's been brave beyond telling." Alasdair rested one hand on her arm and beckoned to Donald with the other. Donald backed away.

Una turned toward Alasdair, half-afraid to look into his eyes. His hair stood up short and straight on one side of his head where he had cut himself free from Connach's dirk. "Did you see?" she asked. He stroked her cheek with one hand. Of course he had seen.

Donald stood up and frowned at Una. "He's dead."

"Donald, I'm sorry," she said. What a thing to be saying! But it was true.

"M'mhic, m'mhic," Alasdair murmured. "My son, my son!"

"I'm not your son! I'm no one's son!" Donald lifted his bloody fists in the air, as though he would strike himself or were asking God to. She could scarcely bear to look at him. "Even the most careful mother can lose a child to the shee," he said. "You must have turned your back for a moment, Mammy. They're aye clever at stealing weans."

Una shook her head. "This is madness."

"Madmen speak the truth!" Donald shouted. "Connach is dead! I let him die."

"So much the better!" she cried. "It's meet to cause the death of one who used you so badly."

Donald ignored her and turned to his father. "You did right to distrust me, Da. I might have killed you."

"M'mhic," said Alasdair. Una heard the heartache in his voice and wished to her soul that she could rid him of his pain. "O, Donald! When you were born . . . I almost drowned you. How could a father even think of doing such a thing? Will you forgive me?"

"Nay, I wish you'd succeeded." Donald clutched his forehead with both hands. *"Arrah!* There's something running and jumping about in my head!"

Again Alasdair reached out toward Donald, and again the boy stepped back. *The more we beg him to come, the more he retreats,* Una thought. It struck her that, for the first time she could remember, Alasdair was seeking his son and his son was drawing away.

"My son! O, my son!" Alasdair cried. "Give me your hand." It was a plea that came from the caves of his heart.

Donald smiled, and Una swallowed hard. The smile was Connach's. The boy rolled the body onto its side, probed its midriff, and came away with Connach's second pistol. Dumbfounded, Una watched as Donald flung himself on his knees before Alasdair. "Da, Da! Bring it to a finish this time, Da!" He gripped the pistol by its barrel and thrust it out before him. "I'll meet Connach on the other side!"

Alasdair hobbled backward in terror. After him scrambled Donald, still on his knees. "Finish me! Finish me!" he cried. "Put an end to what you started!"

Donald was at his father's feet once more when Una regained her wits, stepped forward, and gently lifted the pistol from his hands, just as she'd remove a weapon from a curious wean. "No, Donald," she said softly. "Torment yourself and your da no longer. He'd never hurt you."

"I'd have let Connach kill him!"

"Where is your swordbelt, Donald?" The wild-eyed lad looked up at her as if she had slapped his cheek. "You didn't go to Connach's aid, did you, my jewel?"

"Devil take you!" Donald shrieked. Suddenly he bolted upright and began racing up the hillside.

"Donald! Donald! Come back, my calf!" She took all the shame, the hurt and weariness in her body, and hurled them into her voice. It echoed among the hills as her son disappeared amid the sunlight and shadows checkering the flank of the mountain. Una stared after him in disbelief. Her red man came up to her and wrapped his plaid about her shoulders. "Let's away after him, Alasdair!"

"A pregnant woman and a cripple? At least let me catch my breath. Perhaps he'll return. Are you hurt?"

"Nay, but I fear for the babe." In a mist of color and motion she recalled the day she'd first encountered Connach; she could still see his drunken grin and smell the stench of whisky. How she'd feared for Donald then, still in the womb. How she feared for him now.

"All will be well, I'm sure," Alasdair said. He stared at her intently, as if he could see what she was thinking. Then, without a word he knelt by Connach's corpse and pulled something from it. His hand glittered in the morning sun. "Look, my love. It's not the same as Donald's, I know, but very like it. Will it do, do you think?"

It was the tinker's gold and silver bracelet. "O, my beloved!" She clasped Alasdair to her and wept in relief. Wherever Donald was, whatever blackness swarmed over his mind, he had a father at last. "Alasdair, we shouldn't abide in this wretched place."

"Indeed not," agreed Alasdair, but he hadn't the strength to rise. Instead he dropped the bracelet into his sporran and stretched out on his back in the heath. In the space of a few breaths he fell asleep. While he lay beside her, as silent as a second corpse, she wiped the blood from his face and rested, waiting.

The sun was high and bright overhead and Alasdair was just waking when Una heard the stamp of a horse's feet. As if in a dream she looked up to behold her father riding toward her on Alasdair's new stone-horse. "Connach is dead," she shouted.

Her father dismounted, but as he went to fling his arms around her he stopped abruptly. "God in heaven! Look at the blood on you, lass!"

"But not mine." Una kissed her father's cheek and prayed he'd ask her no more questions. "Who sent you here?" As she spoke, she knew. "Fiona?"

"Herself indeed," her father said. "That drover Lachlann . . . a pox on him! He scattered the cattle and horses last night and fled. This lickerish brute was tethered in the byre, so it's him I'm riding."

"Poor Fiona," Una sighed. She began to regret having cursed the woman that morning. "She has her baby, but she's lost her man."

"So much the better for her, considering the man." Alasdair stepped up and grabbed the black stallion's halter rope. "By your leave, Rory, I'll take your mount. Connach's nag is too small for me, and I must be after Donald."

The old man stared at him, his mouth agape. "As you will."

Alasdair pulled himself up onto the horse's back. "I implore you, let me go with you," Una begged him.

Alasdair shook his head. "No, this is my lot. It will be an easy matter to track him through the heath. Make your way home and wait for me there." He bent down to kiss her, then rode off across the strath at a canter.

She watched him disappear. "Papa, will you help me find the other pony?"

"You're too ill to walk?"

"If I'm to follow Alasdair, I'll need to ride."

"But he bade you go home!"

"I must seek my poor boy." The words plucked a string in her memory. "My own mother did no less."

"But see what became of her," said the old man, his voice catching on a sob.

She hugged him around the middle as she did when she was small. "Aye, Papa, but she was at peace."

Una dismounted and held her hand out to the black stallion that stood, head down, one ear cocked back, only a few paces from the mouth of the Creag Faire, the Watching Cliffs. The horse lifted its muzzle and sniffed her outstretched fingers. She felt its prickly whiskers and the velvet of its nostrils. It was Alasdair's mount. But where was Alasdair?

A scream of despair rose from the strand. The horse rolled its eyes and snorted into her hand. *Jesu deliver me from the shades!* She crossed herself. Una peeped over the edge of the cliff, half expecting to see the ghostly fisherwife. Below her lay a white strip of beach and beyond, the foaming gray madness of the sea. Wading in the surf was her red man, who looked up at her and waved solemnly. "Alas, my love!" he called. She could hear him above the breakers, above the keening of the wind and the shrieking of her own terrified mind.

Over the side of the cliff she went, heedless of the jagged rocks and the briars ripping at her clothes. By the time she reached the shore her toes and fingertips were bleeding stubs. Alasdair stood knee-high in spindrift, with Donald in his arms. Water streamed from the boy's hair. The sleeves of his treasured jacket were spattered with blood and sea-foam.

"My son!" cried Una. She ran into the tide, grimacing at the sting of the salt on her raw feet. As she stroked Donald's stiff hair, his neck twisted in her hand like a length of chain. "My poor wean! It can't be so!" Tears ran down her cheeks and into the water. Half the sea was made by woman's sorrows, her mother had once told her.

"I saw him fall from the cliff," Alasdair moaned. "The waves dashed him back on the rocks. O, my son!"

"How could he have fallen? How?"

Alasdair began to speak, then stopped, then began again. *"Troigh is dorn gulbann.* He leaned out over the cliff, as lads do when they are testing their mettle."

"It was a mishap, then?" she cried, seizing the front of Alasdair's shirt.

Again Alasdair hesitated. "I will go to my death saying that it was."

"Heaven save us!" Una held her hand to her mouth and bit her white knuckles. She felt as if she had been torn in half, and each half tossed aside. "Did he leap? Tell me! Did he leap?" She could not bear the thought of her child's soul damned to eternal suffering.

"Nay, love." Alasdair shook his head. His voice was soft and his face relentlessly sad. "Mischance." She knew he was imploring her to believe what he himself did not. "Fate's work."

"Or the devil's." Una closed her eyes. Her mind was numb. She was sure her life was seeping from her, but it was easier to believe what her husband was saying than to contemplate the truth.

She followed Alasdair to the beach and helped him lay Donald in a patch of dry sand. She tried to kiss his cheek, but she could feel the chill of death rising from him, and she could not touch her lips to his skin. As she brushed away the grit that clung to his jacket, a leather notebook slid from his bosom onto the ground. If she hadn't known better, she would have thought it fell straight out of his heart. "Alasdair! His writings!"

"Leave them be. No good comes from disturbing privy letters."

Una caressed Donald's head with one hand and spread the journal out over her skirts with the other. The binding was ruined, and some of the pages were blurred, but many, nay, most of them were unharmed. She thrust the papers under Alasdair's nose. "What do these say?"

Alasdair took the journal from her, handling it warily, as if it had thorns. "Why must you know?"

"To discover the truth," she said simply. "To discover how I failed him."

Alasdair leafed through a few sheets. "There is nothing here you need to know," he said, tucking the pages back into Donald's jacket. He held Una's face between his hands. "No one failed him, Una, not even himself. It was the way of God, a mystery none can fathom."

Una rested her head against his warm, wet shoulder. Her love for Alasdair almost made it possible to bear the horrible heartbreak of the death of her firstborn. If only she had reached him sooner! Surely she could have saved him.

Una clung to Alasdair as he gathered his son onto his lap, ignoring the pools of salt water that formed in his plaid. Donald's eyes were still open and staring, pink no longer, but pale gray. As Una watched, Alasdair drew the lad's transparent eyelids closed. "Look at the cheekbones on you, *m'mhic.*" Alasdair smiled. "The very image of your grandsire's." Alasdair patted the boy's limp hand, then pulled the bracelet from his sporran and held it up to sparkle in the sunlight.

Una gasped. "Don't, my love!" The sea was a hundred

times deeper than Lochan Oran. Carefully Alasdair raised Donald's arm and slid the bright bracelet onto his son's wrist. God bless her red man! Una felt her shoulder tingle, as if a hand lay on it. Had Donald touched her as he'd left on his long walk into the heavens? She looked about but saw nothing.

"Come. No reason to linger here." Alasdair rose with Donald in his arms, and slowly they made their way along the strand to a gentle path up the hillside. When Una reached the top, she looked up in the direction of Seanag's bothy. A cloud of black dots hung in the gray sky. "Do you see them?" She pointed toward the hovering specks.

"Aye, birds."

"Such birds led me to you at the corrie."

"Did they?"

Una nodded. "Now they will lead us three home."

Epilogue

Una tried to quiet the tiny wean who fussed and struggled in her grasp as she toiled uphill toward the Field of Cairns. "We're almost there, Seanag Bheag. Look, can you see the stones?" Before them on the hilltop stood a score of cairns, gilded by the light of the noontide sun. Behind her, Cha called out, and Una waited for her daughter. The lass made but slow progress, what with her little Mata clinging to her arms.

Donald's cairn was high and wide, though it hadn't always been so. Every few days, whenever the weather allowed her, Una had gone to the Field of Cairns to lay a stone on Donald's grave. And while she'd been there, she'd not forgotten Seanag or her father-in-law. Their cairns were bigger, too. But today was a time for remembering Donald alone. It was a year to the day since she'd found him at the Watching Cliffs, and she'd finally gathered the strength to return what rightfully belonged to him. Perhaps he'd sleep the better for it.

"See yonder?" whispered Cha. She pointed to a large, single stone on a mound of earth. Una saw a woman, her back toward her, singing softly to herself. A child sat in the heath nearby, picking handfuls of grass and throwing them into a wicker creel. "What brings her here?"

"It's only fitting that she's with her man, Sorcha, today of all days." Una took a stone from the field and laid it at the base of Donald's cairn. Again she looked at the singing woman, remembering something Alasdair had told her long ago. "Keep a keen eye on Seanag and Mata, if you please. I must talk with Fiona."

Cha reached out and took the baby. "As you think best. Only take care. They say the silver folk visit her at night."

"And you believe them. Fiona has suffered enough." Una looked sharply at her daughter, remembering another brash young woman, then turned and walked across the field to Connach's grave. She cleared her throat as she came up behind Fiona, so as not to startle her. "A good day to you, mistress," she said softly.

Fiona turned around and smiled. "And to you, Una Nic Rory. My, we haven't seen much of each other this long time past, have we now? Isn't it fine to have good weather today?" Fiona nodded at the sun, but it was already half-shrouded in clouds. "Where is Alasdair?"

"He'll . . . he's just on his way," Una replied, though she knew the man was lost in his memories, too hurt and confused to visit the cairn that day. Una hunkered down beside Fiona and pulled at a little clump of heather that had affixed itself to the grave. "Once I told Connach that no one loved him. I was wrong, I see."

"I loved him. I love him still," said Fiona. "When the aching grows too deep, I come up here and speak to him. He was wicked to you, mistress, and death was no more than he deserved. Faith, he deserves damnation for all he did, but ah! if the truth be told, I sorely miss my Blackie!"

Una gave another tug at the heather, and finally pulled it out by the roots. "Fiona, I'd ask a favor of you."

"A favor! Of me?"

Una drew a sheaf of musty papers from her *arasaid*. "Donald was forever at the writing of his journals. When he was buried, I put his papers in his hands, all but these, the very last things he wrote. I took them from his poor drowned body. Even Alasdair knows nothing of it. Last night I thought I could hear them speaking to me under my pillow. 'Return us,' they said. 'We belong to Donald.' So I've brought them back to lay under a stone in his cairn."

"That's wise, I'm thinking."

"Likely so. And I'd be happy to be rid of them, Fiona, if I but knew what they said. Alas, I've no gift of the reading."

"Alasdair won't read them to you?"

"Alasdair says I've no business knowing what's in them," Una continued, "but I do. How else might I find out what happened to him? Perhaps I wronged him."

"Surely not. You've always been a good mother." Fiona took the papers from Una's hand. "These are much-loved papers, Una, well-thumbed and bent and smudged with tears. Keep an eye on the wean, will you?" She glanced at her son, who was carefully rolling the creel backward and forward, and began reading.

As she read, her face grew paler and tighter, and Una feared she'd made a horrible error. "What does he write?"

Fiona took a deep breath. Her eyes were full of sorrow, and her voice was soft. "He says he loves you and his father dearly and is sorely confused. He writes that he ... he wishes he could have you sing to him again, as when he was little. The rest is simply verse and description— weather, the sea and such. If you thought there were grave secrets hidden here, you were mistaken."

"O, how glad I am to hear it! I knew it was so!"

"I think you may bury these now with a heart as light as love can make it." She handed the papers back to Una and sighed, as if she were shoving a great stone off her chest.

"A thousand thanks." Una dabbed at her eyes with her sleeve. Suddenly she leaned forward and kissed Fiona on the forehead. "Not only for reading these pages, but for fetching my da when we were sore beset."

Fiona smiled and clasped Una tightly by the shoulders. "No need of thanks," she said. "It does me good just to sit beside you and look into your blue eyes with so much living in them."

Suddenly Una noticed Fiona's son, who sat behind his mother, blinking and grinning as he stuffed a wad of grass up his nose. Una nodded toward him, and Fiona caught him by the hand. "Here, *m'hic!* Come to me now, Donald! What an imp!"

Una stared at the little boy. With his ginger-colored hair and big, square face, he was all his father's son. "What did you call the lad?"

"Why, Donald. Doesn't it suit him? Did you think I'd name him for Connach?"

"I did."

Fiona patted Una's hand. "Connach took so much from your son, it seems only right he should give the lad something in return, and that's why the child bears Donald's name. I thought whenever you see my Donald, you might think of your own boy and see a little of him in the child. Did I do wrong?"

"Nay, you did right. Thank you, Fiona." Although she was beholden to Fiona, Una was glad when the woman set her child in the creel, eased it onto her back, and walked off silently from the Field of Cairns. When Una went back to Donald's grave, Cha was having quite the struggle with the two weans, both of whom were screeching like the *ban-*

sith. Cha looked up grim-faced as Una approached. "I swear I'll never have but the one wean!"

"Don't say that, *a'nighean,*" Una said. "Children are a woman's harvest. Besides, Anghas would be aye vexed with you." She caught Mata up in her arms and tickled him under the oxters until he howled with glee. "Will you take them home with you now, dear? I'd like some time alone with Donald."

Cha sighed, but she kissed a stone on the cairn by way of parting and gathered a child in each arm. "You'll not stay long?" She glanced at the sky, and Una looked up, too. Granite gray clouds had covered the sun and the crests of the mountains. "The weather's changing. You can smell the rain in it."

Una watched Cha trudge down the hillside, the head of a child just visible over each shoulder. Now, alone. But not completely. She shoved the papers under some of the larger stones near the base of the cairn. The pages were still visible, though, and she was obliged to fold them into small squares and stuff them inside chinks in the cairn. *Donald, Donald, Donald. Now your papers are all around you.* She stood up and leaned against the cairn, resting her head on the rough stones, embracing them. Her mind raced round and round. *My Donald! The rain is coming, the rain that brings the Holland-flowers back to life in the spring, but you will sleep on through the rain.*

He might be gone from the earth, but she felt him still living inside her. Although she would always love him, he had needed something she could not give him. And what was that? She would never know. Even Donald didn't know. Had Fiona been telling her the truth? It no longer mattered. In her heart of hearts, Una knew that Donald was free at last, and if she had harmed him, he had forgiven her.

A drop of rain hit her nose, then another, and in the

space of a heartbeat the sky tore open and all of Loch
Shiel seemed to wash over her, thrumming in her ears,
scrubbing the tears from her eyes. She clung to the stones,
and in a short time the wind began to gust fiercely and
the rain grew sparser and sparser until it stopped altogether. When she could no longer hear it, she lifted her
head from the cairn and looked about. Except for a bank
of black clouds rolling southward, the sky burned blue and
cheerful.

She was drenched, a silkie with black seaweed in place
of hair. For a few moments she stood by the cairn, taking
in the feel of her drowned garments and her living body.
Then she set about stripping. Off came the steaming *arasaid,* the blouse, the *tonnag,* the linen *curraichd* that covered
her head. When she reached her shift she hesitated, but
in an instant that was gone, too, and she stood naked and
trembling in the sunlight.

What would folk think if they came upon her in such a
state? That she was wanton? That she was mad or shot by
the shee? Whatever they might think, they would never
truly know the deep ocean of peace that encompassed her
just then.

Taking her time, she spread her gown and underclothe-
ing out over the sunlit rocks, and when she was pleased
with her work she sat down at the base of the cairn, hugging
herself to keep warm. The sky grew darker and darker,
like a blue cloth that became deeper and richer with each
dip in the dying vat. After a time the *reull feasgair,* the
evening star, came out, then the lesser sisters of the heavens, one by one. The stars had never seemed quite so
comforting before. She felt like singing to them. "Child,
see the stars shine down on . . ."

Heather crackled, a horse snorted. Her voice died in
her throat.

"Una?"

She could barely see him in the twilight, a dark figure on horseback. He dismounted and limped to her, and then he was sitting beside her, draping his plaid around her. "What is amiss? Your clothes . . . Are you all right, my calf?"

She nestled against his chest. "I am. O, Alasdair! I can't describe the feeling, but I know that Donald is well. He's content now. He's forgiven us. And himself. *Arrah!* I know I don't explain myself well."

Una could say nothing more, and he said nothing in return. Did he understand her, or did he think she'd lost her senses? She was about to ask him when he started to sing. She'd not even known he had the song in his head, yet he sang it perfectly, without pause. She laid her head on his shoulder and breathed as softly as she might so as not to disturb him.

> Child, see the stars shine down on thee.
> They guard thy sleeping and thy waking
> From nightfall until morn's first breaking.
> Child, see the stars shine down on thee.
>
> Child, where go the stars by day?
> Into the arms of their fathers and mothers,
> Safe in the arms of their fathers and mothers,
> Asleep in the arms of their fathers and mothers,
> At peace are they.

She ran her hands over his face, handsome still. A thousand stars danced in his tear-filled eyes. " 'Twas on a night like this I saved your life," she said.

He smiled down at her and kissed the top of her head. "How fortunate for you. Come, dress yourself. Would you have me lose my wife to cold weather?"

"You will warm me. You and Ri." Una tugged his plaid

away from her shoulders until she was lying naked in his arms. His strong hands traveled down her back, and a beautiful smile alive with admiration and desire ebbed across his face. "Give me life from death, Alasdair!" she gasped, staring into eyes the twins of Donald's, despite their charcoal color. "O, best beloved, give me life."

ROMANCE FROM JO BEVERLY

ROMANCE FROM JANELLE TAYLOR

ANYTHING FOR LOVE   (0-8217-4992-7, $5.99)

DESTINY MINE   (0-8217-5185-9, $5.99)

CHASE THE WIND   (0-8217-4740-1, $5.99)

MIDNIGHT SECRETS   (0-8217-5280-4, $5.99)

MOONBEAMS AND MAGIC   (0-8217-0184-4, $5.99)

SWEET SAVAGE HEART   (0-8217-5276-6, $5.99)

ROMANCE FROM FERN MICHAELS

DEAR EMILY   (0-8217-4952-8, $5.99)

WISH LIST   (0-8217-5228-6, $6.99)

AND IN HARDCOVER:

VEGAS RICH   (1-57566-057-1, $25.00)